PENGUI

So Close

By the same author

So Close

A Blacklist Novel

SYLVIA DAY

PENGUIN BOOKS

PENGUIN BOOKS

UK | USA | Canada | Ireland | Australia
India | New Zealand | South Africa

Penguin Books is part of the Penguin Random House group of companies
whose addresses can be found at global.penguinrandomhouse.com

First published by Penguin Michael Joseph 2023
Published in Penguin Books 2023

001

Copyright © Sylvia Day LLC, 2023

The moral right of the author has been asserted

Set in 12.15/14.40 pt Garamond MT Std
Typeset by Penguin Books
Printed and bound in Great Britain by Clays Ltd, Elcograf S.p.A.

The authorized representative in the EEA is Penguin Random House Ireland,
Morrison Chambers, 32 Nassau Street, Dublin D02 YH68

A CIP catalogue record for this book is available from the British Library

ISBN: 978–1–405–91837–4

www.greenpenguin.co.uk

For Shanna

'There are no facts, only interpretations.'

– Friedrich Nietzsche

Witte

The party is a lively crush, yet I'm keenly aware of one singularly significant presence – my employer's wife, a woman who has been dead for many years. Manhattan glitters in the vast night enfolding the penthouse tower. Clouds froth against the floor-to-ceiling windows, at turns obscuring then revealing the stygian spread of Central Park and its reservoir far below. The tower creaks as it sways ever so slightly in gusts of evening wind, the plaintive sound hidden beneath the music and sea of conversation.

Within the glass walls, tension seethes. Dangerous electricity charges the air, the inevitable result of confining rivals in a neutral space. Restrained by decorum and the fear of losing face, adversaries bristle, claws and fangs only briefly and resentfully sheathed.

The event is a black-tie reception in honour of a new cosmeceutical line. The attendees are the best known of Manhattan's young elite, a collective pool of the too-beautiful and too-rich. Among them are celebrated friendships and infamous feuds. It's a testament to Mr Black that he could bring such a diverse – and divisive – group together in his home.

Like chess players, the guests have chosen their positions for the best advantage. Mr Black's longest-known friend, Ryan Landon, stands opposite the spacious living room from Mr Black's business partner, Gideon Cross, the two men perpetuating an enmity passed down from their fathers. As regretful as their discord is, I can still admire the purity of their open dislike of one another.

In contrast, Mr Black's main adversaries – his half-brothers Ramin and Darius – undermine him whenever it benefits them. And then there is Amy, Darius's wife, the only woman in the room who won't look at Mr Black. Not even a surreptitious peek.

The spaces between these key players are filled with reality television personalities and influencers, models and musicians. Bursts of light bounce off the glittering dresses and wide windows as mobiles capture a seemingly endless number of selfies that will be shared with millions of followers. Most companies pay exorbitant fees for such photographic endorsements, but that is not the case tonight. An invitation to the penthouse is a social coup, as is proximity to Cross and his wife, Eva, seemingly the world's most popular couple, if measured by media coverage.

I glance around the living room, assuring myself that the waiting staff are present but unobtrusive, supplying canapés and beverages while clearing away the discarded Baccarat glasses and Limoges plates.

Extravagant bouquets of Blacklist lilies decorate the sterling-silver tops of African blackwood tables, adding texture and glamour without colour or fragrance. Music weaves through the room, effervescent and of the moment. The singer is present, slouched against a wall with his arm around a woman's waist and his lips to her jaw. His eyes are on Mr Black, but they shift to me just as the smartwatch on my wrist gives a haptic signal announcing the arrival of new guests.

I move to the foyer.

The moment the sleek brunette glides through the front door on limousine heels, I know my employer will seduce her.

She's arrived on the arm of an attractive gentleman, but that's irrelevant. She'll succumb; they all do.

The lady resembles the late Mrs Black: inky hair, sultry green eyes, crimson lips. A beauty, yes, but a pale imitation of the woman immortalized in the portrait Mr Black treasures. They all are.

I greet them both with a nod and offer to take her wrap, standing by as her attentive escort assists her instead.

'Thank you,' she says as her companion hands me her shimmery wrap. She's speaking to me, but Mr Black has already captured her attention and her gaze is on him. Despite his deliberate withdrawal to the fringes of the room, his towering height makes him impossible to ignore. His energy is a lashing inferno checked only by a tremendous force of will. He is a man who composes himself with a stark economy of movement yet somehow gives the impression of furore. I can see the effort it takes for our new guest to look away from him and take stock of the festivity.

Mr Black's sister, Rosana, holds the command position in front of the windows. She is a tall, dark beauty in a beaded turquoise dress. Gleaming hair the colour of mahogany drapes her shoulders, a striking contrast to the silvery blond of Eva Cross, who stands beside her, petite and curvaceous and dressed in elegant blush-hued silk. Eva is Rosana's co-ambassador in the new venture; the two women so very different, yet both are tabloid and social media darlings.

I look at Mr Black, searching for his reaction to the latest arrival. I see what I expected: a focused gaze. As he scrutinizes her, his jaw tightens. The signs are subtle, but I sense his terrible disappointment and the resulting surge of self-recrimination.

For a moment, he'd hoped it was her. *Lily.* A woman whose exquisite beauty is immortalized in a single image that hangs in his private rooms but whose profound significance haunts this home and the man who is its master. That he continues to search for her in every woman is heartbreaking.

Lily was absent from Mr Black's life before he acquired my services, so I know her only posthumously, but I'm in the position of overhearing a great deal. That she was incredibly lovely is universally acknowledged; many say she remains the greatest beauty they've ever seen. Though her given name suggests delicacy and fragility, acquaintances describe her as independent, sharp-witted and bold. She's remembered as being kind and encouraging, entertaining and deeply interested in others, a quality which I would argue is far better than being interesting.

For some time, I had only those scant impressions and opinions until a tormented night, when Mr Black was wild with drink and half-mad, no longer able to suppress the furious grief inside him. I understood then the extraordinary hold she continues to have on him; I can sense her power when I look at the massive portrait of her that dominates the wall opposite his bed.

In his room, her image is the only spot of colour, but that isn't what makes the photograph so striking. It is the look in her eyes, feverish and incisive.

Whoever Lily was, her love for Kane Black consumed them both. That obsession remains the most perilous element of his life to this day.

I watch as our newest guest wades through the others, separating from her escort as she moves towards Mr Black. She is fire-bright in a crimson dress, but she is the moth, and he is the flame.

A popular periodical recently declared him one of the sexiest men alive. Mr Black is nearing thirty-three and wealthy enough to afford me, a seventh-generation majordomo of

British lineage, impeccably trained to handle any situation from mundanity to extreme crises. He is remote and unreadable, yet women are drawn to him without any thought of self-preservation. Despite their best efforts, he remains staunchly unavailable. He is a widower who remains deeply, thoroughly married.

His most frequent escort, the slender blonde who hovers nearby, gleams in ivory and pearls. She's his mother, although no one would suspect the relationship if it weren't widely known. Age isn't the only thing Aliyah hides well. The lone clue to her nature is her manicure, the long nails filed into a modish almond shape resembling talons.

As I turn away from the coat cupboard, I hear the pop of a champagne cork. Crystal flutes clink merrily, and conversation hums. A small fortune in designer shoes clicks and taps across obsidian floor tiles so liquid-like in their pristine reflectiveness one is reminded of the calmest of nocturnal waters. Mr Black's residence is a study in maximalism: dark woods, natural stone, rich leathers and hides . . . all in the darkest of shades, creating a space as elegant and masculine as its owner.

My daughter assures me he is blessed with uncommonly good looks and cursed with something she claims is even more compelling: a brooding, edgy torridity. The fact that he once loved so deeply and remains so shrouded in private grief has potent allure. His air of unattainability is irresistible, she says.

It's not artifice. His many sexual liaisons aside, Mr Black is taken in the most profound sense of the word. Lily's memory hollows him. He is a husk of a man, yet I've come to love him as a father would his son.

A woman laughs too loudly. Too much to drink, clearly. And she's not alone in over-indulging. A flute falls from someone's careless grip and shatters, with the unmistakable discordant music of tinkling shards of glass.

Witte

'Did you show her out, Witte?'

Mr Black enters the kitchen the next morning dressed for the day in a Savile Row business suit and perfectly knotted tie, neither being part of his attire prior to my employ. I schooled him in the fine points of bespoke clothing for gentlemen, and he was an avid learner.

On the exterior, I can scarcely see the unpolished young man who hired me six years ago, so recently widowed and paralysed with grief that my first task was managing anyone who approached with queries or condolences. In time, he harnessed his pain into fiery ambition. That – and his singular intelligence – revived the pharmaceutical company his father had made insolvent through embezzlement.

Against all odds, he succeeded – brilliantly.

I turn and set his breakfast on the black marble-topped island, positioning it perfectly between the silverware already set out. Eggs, bacon, fresh fruit – his staples. 'Yes, Ms Ferrari left while you were in the shower.'

One dark brow lifts. 'Ferrari? Really?'

I'm not surprised that he never asked for her name, only saddened. Who the women are means nothing; only that they bring Lily to his mind.

I have never seen him show genuine affection to any woman but his sister, Rosana. He is polite to paramours, always. Attentive when in pursuit. But liaisons are limited to a single evening. He has never sent flowers to a lover, never indulged in a flirtatious phone call, nor invited or escorted a woman to dinner. I've no knowledge of how he treats a lady with whom he is intimately entangled. It is a gap in my understanding of him that may never be filled.

He reaches for the coffee I set in front of him, his mind clearly running through his agenda for the day, his latest lover dismissed from his thoughts for ever. He rarely sleeps and works far too much. Deep grooves on either side of his mouth shouldn't be there on one so young. I've seen him smile and have even heard him laugh, but the amusement never reaches his eyes. He suffers life; he does not live it.

I have urged him to take a moment to enjoy his accomplishments. He tells me he'll enjoy life better when he's dead. Reuniting with Lily is his only true aspiration. Everything else is simply killing time.

'You did an excellent job with the party last night, Witte,' he says, rather absent-mindedly. 'You always do, but still. Never hurts to say I appreciate you, does it?'

'No. Thank you.'

I leave him to eat and read the day's paper, heading down a long hallway with its mirrored walls to the private side of the residence he shares with no one. The lovely Ms Ferrari spent the night in a bedroom on the opposite end of the penthouse, in a starkly white and sterile suite methodically designed to be nothing like the rest of the home. It's a space Lily would not favour, as if that alone would be enough to prevent her spectre from watching and knowing.

Shortly after hiring me, Mr Black purchased the penthouse while the tower was still under construction. He oversaw the design of the raw interior minutely, from the positioning of the walls and doors to the selection of materials. Yet, I can't say the space reflects his personal style. He chose every piece

7

of furniture and accessory with his beloved Lily's tastes in mind. He didn't want a fresh start, free of her memory; he simply wanted a residence in the city, and he made certain to include his late wife. There are reminders of her everywhere, on nearly everything. In that respect, I feel I know her.

Elegant. Dramatic. Sensual. Dark, always dark.

I pause on the threshold of Mr Black's bedroom, sensing the lingering humidity of his recent shower. The his-and-her suites occupy one entire side of the residence, with walk-through wardrobes, matching marble-slab bathrooms and a shared sitting room.

The lady's suite has a view of Billionaires' Row and the Hudson from the foot of the wide, deep bed and of Lower Manhattan to the right. Sunsets spread fire through the sumptuously appointed and lavishly furnished room, warming the subaqueous decor that I refresh with exuberant bouquets every few days at my employer's request. Her room is ever in readiness, waiting for a woman who was gone before it became hers. Her *LRB* monogram is embossed or embroidered on nearly everything as if to assure Lily that the space belongs only to her. Her garments fill the wardrobe and drawers. Her private bathroom is fully stocked.

By rights, the empty echo of abandonment should mar the beautiful suite, yet there is a strange energy here, a precursor to life itself.

Lily lingers, unseen but felt.

The master suite is spare in comparison. Mr Black sleeps atop a slender platform chosen to diminish any possible distractions from the immense image commanding the wall directly across from where he rests his head at night. Fleurs-de-lis decorate his drawer pulls and are embroidered on his sheets. New York is laid out like a gift at his feet beyond the windows, but he's positioned his bed with the view behind him and Lily's picture in front of him. It's emblematic of how he lives his life: indifferent to the world and possessed by a woman long departed.

Mr Black ends his days with Lily. Her portrait is the last thing he sees, and he wakes to the sight of her. Unlike her room, his is tomblike, cool and eerily quiet, devoid of animation.

Turning away from the north-eastern views over Central Park, the woman whose immortal perfection dominates one's attention draws my gaze. It's an intimate, earthy picture. A life-size Lily reclines across a dishevelled bed; her torso draped in a white sheet and her slender limbs tangled in her long black hair. Her lips are swollen from kisses, her cheeks flushed, her eyes heavy-lidded with desire and possessiveness. Against the ashen wall colour, she beckons with a siren's song of beauty, obsession and destruction.

I've caught myself staring more than once, arrested by her flawless face and potent sensuality. Some women entrap men in webs by the simple act of existing.

She was so young, barely in her twenties, yet she left a profound impression on everyone who met her. And she left her husband in torment, destroyed by doubt, guilt and heartbreaking questions . . . the answers to which she took to her watery grave.

3

Witte

As I merge the Range Rover into the traffic, Mr Black relays clipped orders into his mobile. It's barely eight in the morning, and he's already deep into managing the various aspects of his growing dynasty.

Manhattan overflows around us, brimming with streams of cars and people rushing in every direction. In places, bags of rubbish are piled several feet high on the pavements, waiting to be hauled away. The sight put me off when I first came to New York, but now it's just part of the tableau.

I've come to enjoy this city, which is so different from the rolling green dales of my homeland. There's nothing one can't find. The energy, diversity and complexity of the people here are unrivalled.

My gaze darts back and forth from the traffic to the pedestrians. Ahead of us, a delivery lorry blocks the one-way street. On the left pavement, a bearded man takes a group of excited canines on their morning walk, deftly handling a half-dozen leashes. On the right, a mother dressed for a run pushes a jogging pram ahead of her towards the park. The sun is shining, but the towering buildings and thickly leafed trees choke out the light.

The traffic delay stretches.

Mr Black continues his business dealings with self-assured ease, his voice calm and assertive. The cars begin to creep forward, then pick up speed. We head downtown. For a short time, we're blessed with green lights in succession. Then our luck runs out just before we reach our destination and a red light stops me.

A flood of people rushes by in front of us, most with heads down and a few with earbuds that I suppose offer some respite from the cacophony of the busy city. I glance at the time, making sure we're on schedule.

A sudden pained noise sends ice through my veins. It's a half-strangled moan that is vaguely inhuman. Turning my head swiftly, I glance at the back seat, alarmed.

Mr Black sits still and silent, his eyes dark as coal, his face drained of colour. His gaze is sliding along the pedestrian crossing, following. I look that way, seeking.

A statuesque brunette hurries away from us. Her hair is short and sleek, cut into a bob that skims her sculpted jaw. It's not Lily's luxuriant mane, not at all. But when she turns to walk down the pavement, I think it might be her incomparable face.

The back door swings open violently. The cab driver behind us yells obscenities out of his lowered window.

'*Lily!*'

That my employer should go so far as to shout out his wife's name staggers me like the crack of gunfire. My lungs seize with shock.

The woman's gaze darts towards us. She stumbles. Freezes in place.

The resemblance is uncanny. Eerie. Impossible to comprehend.

Mr Black leaps out just as the light turns green. His response is instinctual; mine is arrested by confusion. I know only that my employer is beside himself, and I am trapped behind the wheel of the Range Rover while the madness of New York City's morning commute rages on all sides.

Her face, already pale as porcelain, turns bloodless. I read the movement of her lushly red lips. *Kane.*

Her astonished recognition is intimate and unmistakable. So is the fear.

Mr Black glances towards traffic, then lunges between moving cars in an explosion of powerful physicality. The barrage of honking becomes deafening.

The harsh sounds visibly jolt her. She surges into a run, pushing her way through the throng on the pavement, her emerald-hued dress a beacon in the crowd.

My employer, a man who attains without pursuit, gives chase. A black town car reaches her first, driving too fast.

One moment Lily is a streak of green in the urban jungle's unrelenting grey. The next, she is a jewel-bright puddle on the dirty New York street.

4

Amy

I smile at the server, a slow, easy curving of my lips. 'I'll take another manhattan.'

'Oh God,' Suzanne moans dramatically, rubbing at her temples. Her tightly coiled glossy black curls dance with the movement. 'I don't know how you do it. If I drank alcohol at this time of day, I'd have to take a nap.'

I cast a longing glance at her cocktail fork and imagine stabbing her in the eye with it. I use words to the same effect. 'How's the book coming?'

She winces, and I hide my smile. She's going to start blathering about organic creativeness and refilling the well, and I'm going to picture her pretty face with a gaping hole where her eyeball once was and the dark void behind it where a brain should be.

'I'm such a huge fan,' Erika Ferrari gushes.

Is she fucking *kidding*? I had to work quickly to connect with Erika and invite her to lunch before Kane dragged her away from last night's party to shove his cock into her. To realize Erika accepted my invitation solely to gain access to Suzanne makes me livid. The stupid cunt *used* me!

Erika leans forward as she kisses Suzanne's ass for greater emphasis.

And just like that, Suzanne's anxiety is gone, replaced with a bright smile. She has the most beautiful lips – plush and naturally darker around the edges and softly pink within, like natural lip liner. 'Oh, thank you! I'm so happy you enjoy my work.'

My gaze skips across crowded tables to find the bar, hoping to spot the bartender making my drink. Another gulp, and I'll be staring at the bottom of an empty glass. I cannot sit through a single minute of the Suzanne and Erika Mutual Appreciation Show without alcohol. Thank God I have a gift for deleting inanity from my memory banks. With any luck, I'll consign this lunch to oblivion by dinnertime.

You know what you need, Amy? my mother-in-law once told me with her signature backhanded sweetness. *Culture. Try finding some friends who can elevate you. Writers, artists, musicians . . . People who can teach you something.*

As if I don't know anything. Yeah, I went to public school and did a two-year stint at a junior college before finishing my marketing degree at a university. True, I hadn't known my water glass was to my right or that you set forks on the left. None of that makes me worthless.

Aliyah thinks I'm not good enough for her precious Darius. If only she knew – I've fucked all three of her sons.

So, Suzanne – who was born just plain Susan – is my dash of literary sophistication. She writes trashy romance novels about billionaires who fuck like champs and the women who tame them. She's the perfect middle-finger response to my bitch of a mother-in-law.

Because of Aliyah – and Kane – I'm wasting two hours of my life with two women I can't stand. Erika and Suzanne are presently discussing the sexual exploits of fictional people with the kind of excitement I reserve for reality. It's obvious Ms. Ferrari is secretly recalling being fucked senseless by Kane and imagining she'd lived a scene out of a book. She tries to be discreet about checking her phone, no doubt having left her number behind before Witte showed her out the door with his oh-so-British aplomb.

How that scene would've played out is etched in my mind. The polite rap on the door. The perfectly polished silver tray resplendent with an elegant coffee service and a single white rose. A white silk robe waiting in a bathroom stocked with anything a woman might need to disguise the inevitable walk of shame. And when Erika returned to the bedroom after her shower, she would've found the clothes Kane had peeled off her body neatly laid out on the white velvet bench and her hastily kicked-off shoes next to the foot of the already stripped and remade bed.

Witte is nothing if not faultlessly efficient.

And Kane. So predictable. I'd known the minute Erika showed up that he'd nail her. She looks like his dead wife and me. She doesn't know it, but she's the latest subject in the exhaustive study I affectionately call *Women Kane Black Screwed and Screwed Over*.

So far, superficial resemblance seems to be all Kane requires to nail a woman six ways to Sunday. He's a total headcase. Suzanne needs to write a book about him. In fact, I'd give her the title of my study for her next novel. I can be generous when I'm not sitting next to a lookalike who's glowing, puffy-lipped and sleepy-eyed.

God, I'm in a foul mood.

Erika Ferrari. That stupid name must be fake.

She sneaks a peek down into her Chanel tote, where her phone lies face up. Suzanne gives me a sidelong, knowing glance.

I look desperately around the packed restaurant, searching for my drink. Most of the men are dapper. The women have great hair and designer ensembles – but those wearing makeup are a rarity. Why they think that's acceptable is beyond me.

Why go to the trouble of doing your hair if you can't be bothered to put cosmetics on your face? Nothing is worse than half-assing it.

'How did you meet Darius?' Erika asks me, reaching for another roll from the breadbasket.

'Kane introduced us.'

She perks right up at the mention of his name. 'And how did you meet Kane?'

I give it a second for effect, then, 'I was leaving a restaurant, and he stopped me on the street. I look like his wife. That's his kink. Dark hair and green eyes. Red lipstick really works for him, too.'

Erika's smile wavers a bit. 'Well, some men have a distinct type.'

Her hand lifts self-consciously to her hair, which falls in dark waves that would touch her bra band if she wore a bra. She isn't and doesn't need to; she's small-breasted, like me. And like Kane's wife, who had him by the balls and never let go.

Kane doesn't care about anyone. If you're not standing directly in front of him, he's already forgotten you. If there is anyone who could be said to live in the moment, it's Kane. He's already discarded yesterday, doesn't give a flying fuck about tomorrow, and has just enough interest to stroll through today. But he's psychotically hanging on to Lily's memory.

Which makes zero sense to me.

He's not the type of guy who suffers willingly, so I have to believe that reminding himself she's dead gives him pleasure somehow. Or it's a gimmick to attract women, like a hot guy with an adorable puppy. How sick is that?

'We hit it off,' I go on, keeping my tone light. *More like we hit it, period. All night long.* 'Then, we ran into each other a couple of times.' *I stalked him.* 'On one occasion, Darius happened to be with him.'

16

And my now-husband had stepped right up as a replacement body in my bed. It should've ended there, but Aliyah ensured her middle son got what he wanted – his ring on my finger. And that she got what she wanted – my social media management company, Social Creamery. She regrets me now. That's my sole comfort.

'What was she like?' Erika asks. 'His wife.'

'In the writing world, we'd call her a Mary Sue,' Suzanne says with a giggle. 'Amy prefers calling her Mary Poppins.'

Confusion crosses Erika's face.

A humorless laugh escapes me. 'Practically perfect in every way.'

'Oh.'

'At least that's what the people who knew her would have you believe. None of the family ever met her because they'd had an estrangement from Kane for years. Her friends will tell you she was gorgeous, smart, glamorous, the perfect hostess, great at everything, so on and so forth, yada yada . . .' I tell her caustically. 'Everyone loved her.'

'No one likes to speak ill of the dead,' she says primly, her gaze full of judgment.

'Waxing poetic doesn't make them any less dead. And, weirdly, Kane won't talk about her at all. As in don't even mention her name within earshot because he turns glacial.'

'Yes, well . . . Maybe he's ready to move on,' she says, with a smug smile that makes me want to yank her out of the chair by her hair and punch her in the mouth. I fight the urge to show her the selfies I've taken with all the women who could be our lookalikes, only because I don't want her to think I'm insane.

I mirror her stuck-up smile. 'I'm sure that's why he still wears his wedding ring. Didn't you notice the pattern on the china? The flower arrangements? Her name was Lily, and everything he owns has lilies on it.'

She gives a microscopic shrug. Right. Those critical details had escaped her. I don't know why no one else sees what I do. Just mindlessly ignorant people fucking up the world. When I mentioned the explosion of lilies all over Kane's shit, Darius told me I was reaching. *He's got girly taste, so what?*

Erika's smugness evaporates. By the time we finish lunch, she won't be glowing anymore. She'll feel used and a lot less special. Her self-confidence will carry a dent in it for a long time, maybe forever. I hate that she slept with Kane, but it's nice to know I'm not the only one self-destructive enough to fall for his charm.

The server, handsome but overwhelmed, gets a genuine smile from me when he brings my drink. I swallow deeply, closing my eyes a minute to savor the cool bite of bourbon stirred with sweet vermouth. The resultant warm buzz from the alcohol takes the edge off my bitchiness, and suddenly, my eyes are stinging from the salt of tears.

Jesus. I shove the sadness back with anger.

It's pathetic how I've let one night with Kane Black define my life. My shrink says I've got daddy abandonment issues that skew my decision-making. That pisses me off even more. What kind of woman lets men twist her up this way?

Kane will never understand or acknowledge what it felt like to be plucked off the street and whisked up to the penthouse by a man who looks and carries himself the way he does. In that one night, I began to feel like I might be worth something to someone extraordinary, that every wish I'd ever had might come true. I would be Mrs. Kane Black. I would live within the penthouse's dramatic beauty, welcoming into my home as guests the very people who once made me grovel to win their business. Surely, he felt the same spark I did. That's why he chose me, then charmed me so completely I was under his thrusting body within hours.

It was over a year later when Aliyah showed Darius the picture she'd secretly taken of Lily's portrait tucked away in Kane's bedroom, which none of us had seen because Witte somehow always materializes if anyone strays into that end of the penthouse. I'd peeked over Darius's shoulder as he looked at Lily, and in a distant part of my mind, the screaming started and hasn't ever stopped.

Erika touches my arm, trying to lure my attention back to her. 'Do you work with Kane in the Crossfire Building?'

It rubs me the wrong way that she doesn't call him Mr. Black. Who cares if she fucked him? He's forgotten her already. They're not friends and never will be.

'Social Creamery is headquartered in the Crossfire,' I answer, sliding my tongue along my bottom lip to catch every drop of my last sip, feeling the familiar surge of rage as I name my business. 'But I don't have to go in every day. I built it to run like a machine.'

Yet another cog in the growing Baharan Pharmaceuticals empire.

I can't talk about the company I built from the ground up without resentment clogging my throat. Social Creamery had been my independence, my proof I could make something of myself. I studied social media trends comprehensively, finessed ways to exploit platforms' strengths and weaknesses, built a stable of influencers who could market and sell damn near anything, hired copywriters who were witty and knew how to fucking spell – the world really is full of uneducated idiots – and I took my natural charm door-to-door to convince accounts to trust me with their brands.

Then Aliyah slithered in and suggested we pull Social Creamery under Baharan's umbrella so that it would be a combined family business, and I would have access to more resources. Darius thought it would be wonderful to work side by side, and I didn't know Aliyah well enough at the time to be wary.

Once we signed the paperwork, it wasn't long before she began undermining me and my ideas and questioning my business ethics. She stole the loyalty of my staff with gifts and bonuses, most of which were my idea, but she took credit for them. Would-be allies distanced themselves to avoid repercussions from her until the whole company was against me.

Suzanne and Erika lean into each other, speaking in raptures about a woman's dress as she passes our table on the way to the restroom. A bodycon style with an abstract print, it's an interesting garment that would look a hell of a lot better with shapewear taming the bulges underneath.

I take another slow, deep drink and hum with pleasure. And anticipation.

One day soon, my entire life will change. I'll claw Social Creamery back and everything else my 'family' took from me, plus interest. In the meantime, more so than the vows I share and the ring I wear, my company binds me to Darius, his brothers and Aliyah. Damned if I'll walk away without it.

The ring of a cellphone has Erika darting for her bag with idiotic eagerness. Her disappointment when we all realize it's my phone that's ringing has me laughing inwardly.

The humor flees when I see Aliyah's name on the screen.

'Hello, Mom,' I greet her, knowing how much she hates me calling her that.

'Amy,' she replies in the surprisingly deep and husky voice that takes me off guard more often than not. 'I was trying to track down your husband, but I just remembered what day it is.'

The not-so-subtle reminder that Darius is keeping his Friday afternoon fuck-date with his assistant kills my buzz. Bitterness coats my tongue.

It hurts. For better or worse, Darius is *mine*. I even think he loves me and would be a better man to me if I could ever stop thinking about how Kane fucked me like he'd die if he stopped. But I can't, and my husband is screwing his highly efficient assistant right now. The pretty blonde always brings me coffee precisely how I like it and is so nice I want to beat her bloody with my purse.

'Maybe I can help you?' I ask sweetly.

'Don't worry about it. I'll send him a text.' Her voice is honey-smooth when she rocks my world. 'Kane's wife has returned from the dead.'

5

Aliyah

I study my reflection as I carefully wipe the bright pink 'Rosana' shade off my lips and switch to a nude gloss. Stepping back, I eye the result and nod – much more fitting for the circumstances. I smile, imagining the look on Amy's face when I hung up on her. If there is anything reliable about my daughter-in-law, it's that she's always wasted drunk by five o'clock. If I handled the call right, she'll be blacked out by three instead.

The girl is beautiful but useless. She had one skill, and we've exhausted it. And her fixation on one of my sons is hurting another. For that alone, I want her out of our lives. It won't be long now. What started as a glass of wine with dinner became two. Then the entire bottle. Why not add a splash of whiskey in the morning to kick off the day? Followed by a cocktail with lunch. All too easy, really. She wanted to tumble face-first into the bottom of a glass. I just gave her a little push to help her along.

'Are you ready?' Darius asks, stepping into view behind me. He's put on his jacket, and a frown mars his brow. His cologne is subtle and soothing, a woodsy scent I custom-designed for him. It suits him. He is as firmly anchored as a sequoia, strong and steadfast. He really is a credit to me. Too many mothers raise sons with no respect for women.

I face him. 'Did you lock up those blueprints?'

'Yes, of course. Where do you think I've been?'

His dark hair falls artfully across his brow. His lean face resembles mine, but the pale blue of his eyes comes from his father: such a strong trait, those eyes. Ramin and Rosana have them, too.

He scowls. 'We're almost done. We could get our comments back to the architect today.'

'And he won't get to them until Monday.' I smooth his lapels.

If only Amy knew that her husband spends his Friday afternoons working with me on the design of our proposed Seattle research facility. Instead, she thinks the worst of her husband. A little suggestion is all it takes to trigger her paranoia.

Darius isn't faithless like Paul, my first husband. I'd suspected Kane's father was having an affair but couldn't prove it. I chose to believe I was too essential for him ever to end our marriage, not just as the mother of his child but to the company I'd helped him build. Baharan Pharmaceuticals was everything to him, our shared life's work, and he adored Kane – or so I'd thought, right up to the moment I learned he'd pulled every cent he could out of the company and run off to South America.

I straighten Darius's tie. 'I'm disappointed in you.'

'Why?'

'Because you're being so irritable about supporting your brother in a time of personal crisis.'

His brow arches. 'I can't, and I won't because he'd never show me the same courtesy.'

'Darius.' My tone clears the barest hint of sulkiness from his face. 'You don't know that. And if you won't do it for him, do it for me. This is distressing for me, too.'

The look he shoots me is caustic, but I don't care if he thinks I'm a hypocrite. I did what I had to do to survive. Because of how I changed after Paul's betrayal, I did better with my second marriage and outlasted the terms of the prenup, so I got what I was due. And it's not like I didn't support Kane to adulthood.

In any case, it's futile pointing out that Darius has never had a crisis of any kind because Kane has insulated him since re-entering our lives. Darius owes so much to his older brother – his freedom from student debt, his livelihood and even his wife.

When Kane approached me about resuscitating Baharan Pharmaceuticals six years ago, I thought we might finally become a family. My second husband – who hadn't been remotely interested in raising another man's son – was finally out of the picture. Kane took my advice about seeing his brothers educated for key positions within the company. I'd thought perhaps my children would all be together at last, but only Rosana was happy about reuniting with her eldest brother. Darius and Ramin bristled against Kane from the first, resenting being viewed as obligations.

I doubt even dethroning Kane as head of the company would soothe the resentment gnawing at Darius. He can't stop feeling that his responsibility for his younger siblings has been usurped. And really, it's probably best that the brothers aren't close. It could be problematic if they ever formed a united front.

'I just don't understand why we have to rush over there,' he argues. 'He'll need time to get his new story straight, and his wife is being treated for whatever is wrong with her. We're putting off something important for nothing.'

'Oh? Do you truly think it's nothing that Kane's been telling everyone he's widowed when he's evidently not?'

Though Lily apparently seemed near death on the street and might yet die. The driver who hit her didn't brake and fled the scene, according to Witte, when he called while she was being loaded into the ambulance. I don't tell Darius that something about Witte's voice gave me chills like someone was walking over my grave.

'Are you surprised Kane lies?' my son scoffs. 'Come on. And I'm not saying his wife isn't a concern. I'm just saying she isn't a concern at *this very moment*. Kane's been getting along just fine without us in his life for years. He can deal with his own bullshit. It's not my problem.'

He says that because he doesn't know much about the past. He was a high school senior and at school when the Greenwich police came by our home in Saddle River asking about my eldest son, whom I hadn't seen or conversed with in years.

The detectives said their questions regarding Kane's character and temperament were just 'routine.' Maybe they were. When it quickly became apparent that I had very little knowledge of my son's adult life – I hadn't even known he had legally changed his surname – they asked me why we were out of touch, and I told them the truth: he didn't get along with my husband, his stepfather. They'd glanced at each other, thanked me for my time and left.

I still don't know if their visit had anything to do with his wife. I didn't even know he was married at the time of the interview. And I've never discussed it with anyone, not even Kane, who appeared on my doorstep just days later to discuss rebuilding Baharan.

Our relationship is tenuous at best, and I won't risk a rift that might jeopardize my position at Baharan until I can take over the company.

'Of course it's your problem,' I press. 'It's a problem for all of us. What brought her back *now*? What has she been doing all these years?'

'I can tell you why she's back. That stupid Sexiest Man Alive issue is everywhere. Kane's damn near getting more out of it than Dwayne Johnson! So she sees the coverage, thinks he's a better bet now that he's rich, and she comes home. I'm not an idiot, Mother. I'm just not seeing her being a threat until and unless she survives *and* causes trouble.'

I made sure Social Creamery viralized Kane's inclusion in the magazine's feature of sexy men because celebrity equals wealth. It irritated me that I hadn't anticipated former friends and lovers – not to mention supposedly dead spouses – scuttling out of the shadows to revel in his glow. But how could I have foreseen something like this?

I don't even know her maiden name. There was never any memorial service after she died – *supposedly* died, that is. Or at least nothing I was invited to or could find an announcement for. And Kane refuses to discuss her. It infuriated him anytime I even remotely broached the subject of his marriage, so I stopped. And when all was said and done, a college sweetheart I had never met had nothing at all to do with me.

'I figure she left him,' he continues, 'and he's been lying to everyone this whole time to save face.'

'That would be a little extreme, don't you think?'

'So is the penthouse! And hiring Witte, for fuck's sake. Kane's ridiculous about a lot of things. You're getting yourself worked up over nothing.'

Fury ices my blood. I will not be talked down to or allow my thoughts and feelings to be marginalized. I ignored my instincts with Paul and learned a hard lesson, and it's one I will never forget. 'Watch your tone, Darius. I'm being cautious, not hysterical. Protecting Baharan and this family is important to me, and I won't apologize for it.'

'In that order,' he mutters.

'Don't forget the morals clause in our ECRA+ agreement with Cross Industries. If we're embroiled in a scandal – and a faked death in the family is obviously scandalous – it'll be ruinous. We can't afford to lose what we've invested, let alone whatever restitution Gideon Cross might demand.'

Paul's embezzlement resonates with Cross, even though he avoids mentioning it directly. His father, Geoffrey Cross, is infamous for heading a Ponzi scheme with investor losses in the billions. When someone thinks of the Cross name now, it's Gideon they think of first and foremost, and he won't allow anything – or anyone – to tarnish the successful image he's worked so diligently to craft.

Darius frowns, and I can see in his eyes that he's processing the possible ramifications. 'Let's not get ahead of ourselves. Everything is going according to plan. Rosana is the face of the new cosmetics line, and Eva Cross is out to prove to her husband that she can spearhead a successful collaboration the size of ECRA+ Cosmeceuticals. If Rosie stays golden, Eva will make sure everything moves ahead. We just need a semi-plausible story to cover Kane's marital situation, so we'll figure one out.'

'Well, aren't you confident, considering you don't know anything about Lily or what happened between her and Kane in the past.'

'You act like she's the problem, but for all we know, it's Kane we need to worry about.'

I shoot him a look.

'In any case, we're going to the hospital, aren't we?' He grins. 'We'll know soon enough.'

He doesn't apologize for initially arguing against going, and I don't press the point. I also won't forget.

None of my children will ever know what I went through to reclaim Paul's chemical patents from the partner he bankrupted, and because of that ignorance, they'll never comprehend what Baharan means to me. One day, I may tell Rosana. She'll need to prepare for what it means to be a woman in this world, how vulnerable we are and how easily we fall prey to predatory men.

I don't know what my eldest child may or may not have done. Kane is a man, after all: nothing is beneath him. But I won't make the same mistake I made with Paul. I'm not going to be left destitute. Baharan will go on, and I've more than earned the right to run it myself.

'There is a possible bright side,' he says. 'The accident sounds serious, right? Kane's already taking the week off, something he's never done before. Maybe he'll step back longer and give us the opportunity to convince the board that a new facility in Seattle is a great idea.'

Then we'll ensure the contractor who wins the bid is the one we've heavily invested in. We've padded enough unnecessary flourishes into the design that can be removed, that we can safely bid lower than anyone. With the profit from the build, I can acquire more shares, and when everyone sees what the facility brings to the table, they'll remember that Kane was too cautious.

I skirt Darius and head to where my clutch rests on a mid-century console – my favorite piece of furniture in my office, which pairs so well with the Jasper Johns hung above it. I fluff my hair and check the backs of my earrings, trying for an appearance of nonchalance. The walk is long since I have the largest office at Baharan. I have an impressive view of Midtown from both glass walls caging my corner office.

'If it's *really* serious, maybe she'll die,' Darius suggests. 'And you'll have worried over nothing.'

I tuck my bag under my arm, catching the reflection of my white cigarette pants and gold silk top in the glass. An essential oil diffuser perfumes the air with the scent of azaleas.

'Seriously, Mom. Don't stress about this. No one keeps Kane's interest long.' Darius stands by the closed door – a tall, dark figure against the lustrous walnut panel. 'He enjoys the hunt. If she sticks around long enough this time, he'll get bored and pay her off.'

Love and beauty fade. Vows are worthless. Blood is life. My children are young yet, but they'll learn those lessons eventually.

Darius opens the door as I approach.

I pause on the threshold and touch his forearm. 'Text Ramin again. Make sure he's meeting us there.'

'I'll call him.' Darius pulls out his phone.

My hand falls back to my side, and I stride through the door with my head high.

6

Lily

I wake to the sound of my heartbeat. It's slow and steady, accompanied by a relentless computerized *beep beep beep*. Surfacing from a deep, heavy blackness, I hear far-off voices, but distance muffles the words, and there's a vicious pounding in my head.

The medicinal smell betrays where I've ended up. I force my eyes open, blinking away a gritty film that clouds my vision. Something clogs my throat, and I fight the weights holding down my arms to claw at my neck, then my jaw. The steady beating of my heart picks up, and I cough, my nails tearing at the tape securing the tube snaking oxygen into my lungs.

'*Setareh*, don't!'

Your voice . . . that endearment . . .

My gaze darts around the darkened room, skipping across the pale blue walls. I find your tall, dark form untangling from the shadows in the corner and gliding swiftly to the door.

'Nurse. Get in here. She's awake.'

The tape pulls away from my lips, and the tube shifts, scratching far down in my airway. Pain blankets my body. A scream of agony writhes in my mind and chest.

'Stop,' you order, your voice so torturously dear to me. You step into the light, and tears flush my eyes clear.

My love. What dream is this?

Lines bracket your firm, full mouth. Your eyes, as darkly

intense as ever, look bruised. The lankiness of youth has left you. You've filled out, your shoulders and chest now broadened, your hair shorter. Like the finest whiskeys, you have aged into something more robust and potent.

You catch my wrists and restrain me, your touch an electric shock that seizes my muscles. Your skin is warm, rough satin, and your strength is achingly gentle. Suffocating, I suck air in through my nose and smell you, that intoxicating scent I could never forget. Sultry, earthy and utterly masculine.

My heart spasms, and the beeping from the monitors become a wailing siren of alarm.

'Sir, step back,' a man says briskly.

You release me and open space for the nurse. It's enough for him, but not for the doctor who quickly joins us.

'Mr. Black.' She steps into view, pulling on latex gloves. 'Please give us some space. Your wife is in good hands.'

Your gaze never leaves my face as you withdraw and disperse into the darkness. I feel it on me, fiery hot and piercing when I tumble into coveted oblivion.

7

Witte

Mr Black exits the hospital room but looks back over his shoulder through the glass inset in the door. He scrubs his hand over his face, and then his arm drops to his side and his hands fist as if braced for an assault. His foot taps an impatient, unrelenting staccato against the floor.

When we met, he was a man constantly in motion – pacing, sitting and standing in endless repetition, lobbing rubbish into the many miniature basketball hoops he had a fondness for affixing over dustbins. Over the years, he's become more sub-dued. He is a once fiery mortal man slowly tempering into hardencd, unbendable steel.

The only time I've seen him regress is the night he told me about Lily. He walked ceaselessly up and down the library. Up and down. Up and down. It was an anniversary of some sort, either of her death or a milestone in their relationship, and he couldn't stop himself from talking about her.

I was startled when he presented his wife's driving licence to the intake nurse, establishing his right as next of kin to manage her care. I hadn't been aware he carried her identification in his wallet, although in hindsight, I'm not surprised; he wants her with him everywhere. It's even still valid for another two years, having been updated to her married name in the days immediately following their wedding. As fate would have it, his sentimentality was advantageous.

His head swivels towards me now as if only just recognizing that I'm close. 'Witte.'

'Sir.'

'She's conscious.' His gaze returns to the viewing window, and he stares – unblinking – for too long.

I remember Lily's gaze when she spotted him on the street, the sheer, abject terror so vicious it spurred her to run directly into the path of oncoming traffic. I can't reconcile her reaction with the man I know.

I lost her where I found her. I will never forget those words or how he paced like a beast in a cage when he finally told me about her demise. The depth of his anguish was so profound I understood how tempted he was to follow her into death, his will to live sinking deeper by the day into suffocating darkness. Now doubts creep into me, an insidious black fog slipping through hairline cracks.

I'm reminded that he never tasked me with arranging a funeral or memorial service. Sensitive to his unfathomable mourning, I waited for him to initiate such a public farewell, but he never broached the topic in the ensuing years. And while any grave for her would be empty, she wasn't even memorialized with a cenotaph.

We endure the wait together, standing side by side. The dismal, scuffed corridor bustles with foot traffic. The smell of chemical disinfectant is pervasive, but it fails to hide the underlying scent of malaise and decay. Somewhere nearby, a man in agony shouts profanities.

There's no other family to worry over Lily. No parents or siblings, no extended relatives. No one. At least she told my employer that was the case while they were together. Indeed, in the intervening years, no one claiming to be family has enquired after her. Only the police are asking questions, focusing primarily on gathering descriptions of the driver who fled the scene. It's through witness interviews and traffic camera footage that they'll learn the rest: a wife lost all awareness of surrounding danger because the greater fear was her husband's pursuit. Then Mr Black will face a different tenor of questioning altogether.

It's fortuitous that I spied Mrs Black's slender handbag beneath the undercarriage of a saloon parked at the kerb and could tuck it inside my jacket unseen. It's best if the authorities aren't aware of the Nevada driving licence I found inside that bears a photograph of Mrs Black with the alias Ivy York. The handbag itself would raise further questions, as it's a less than impressive counterfeit of a luxury brand. The detectives would undoubtedly find it curious that the wife of a notably wealthy man accessorizes with cheap knockoffs rather than the best money can buy.

If Mrs Black recovers from her ordeal, the detectives will pose their questions to her. How she answers could decide the fate of a man for whom I've committed to taking a bullet.

Mr Black crosses his arms. 'We need to make arrangements for the necessary medical equipment and staff at the penthouse, with round-the-clock care.'

This statement sparks a million questions; I ask only one. 'How quickly?'

'As soon as I convince the doctors it's best, and we get through the paperwork. I want her under the same roof, every minute.'

Body language is a powerful thing; his is raising the hair on my nape. It doesn't seem likely that Mrs Black will be in any condition to leave hospital soon. Is it a risk to her health to move her? The question must be asked. My extensive training includes managing medical emergencies and patient protocols. Still, is it my capabilities that make my employer's request possible or a less than pressing concern for his wife's welfare?

It frightens me that a single look from Lily has shaken the foundation of my deeply personal, intrinsic knowledge of the man my heart has adopted as a son. I have lived with the belief that no man has ever loved a woman as deeply as Mr Black loved – *loves* – his wife. Is it possible that his love is what she fears?

'I'll see to it.' I begin sending messages to those of my contacts who can assist me in realizing Mr Black's request.

'And put two guards in the elevator vestibule of the penthouse. No one leaves – or arrives – without my knowing about it first.'

I glance at him, disconcerted. Lily is not just to be a patient but also a prisoner.

Another doctor rushes towards Mrs Black's room. Most of the medical staff wear theatre blues and athletic or orthopaedic footwear. This man wears expensive loafers and decently tailored trousers. The grey hair at his temples wars with the unlined youthfulness of his features.

My employer bars his way, looming ominously with a height advantage of at least a foot.

Introducing himself as Dr Sean Ing, the neurologist begins to speak to Mr Black. I move a short distance away to afford them privacy. The conversation is brief, then the doctor enters Lily's room, shutting the door with a hushed click behind him.

'She's disoriented and exhibiting paranoia,' Mr Black shares, his gaze locked on the view through the glass. 'The CAT scan showed no brain trauma, but her symptoms are concerning.'

A nurse hurries down the corridor in our direction and joins the others in Lily's room.

It's an age before the two doctors step out and join us.

'Mr Black.' Dr Hamid manages a smile weighted with weariness. 'Let's go to Dr Ing's office.'

'How is she?'

'She's stable. We've given her something to calm her, and she's resting now.'

'Don't let her out of your sight,' Mr Black tells me, his gaze darting briefly to the door separating him from his wife. A muscle tics in his jaw, but he follows the doctors down the corridor to the lifts.

I am still looking in that direction when his mother and brothers emerge from the lift beside the one Mr Black departed in. Mrs Armand strides into view with her blond hair swaying around her shoulders and her voluptuous figure clad in a fitted white trouser suit.

She pivots neatly when she sees me, her youngest sons falling into rear flanking positions with near-military precision. The resemblance between them is evident, but she is a lustrous pearl in contrast to her sons' dark colouring and black suits.

Subtly, Aliyah changes her mien, slowing her stride and softening the determined set of her features. With less effort than is required by a flick of the wrist, she appears strained with concern. The performance is for the staff and visitors who mill around the nurses' station, and her audience is captivated. Gazes follow. Heads turn.

She ignores me when she reaches the door to Lily's room, peering through the window. Before the hospital staff can intervene, she steps away without entering after noting the absence of the man she seeks. 'Where is he, Witte?'

The exasperation in her tone chastises me for failing to volunteer information before she enquired.

I slide my mobile into my pocket, my preliminary tasks complete. 'He is discussing Mrs Black's prognosis with the physicians overseeing her care.'

Her head whips towards me. 'What do we know?'

'Hopefully more when Mr Black finishes his conversation.'

Ramin huffs a humourless laugh. 'Could you be more evasive?'

'Absolutely,' I say smoothly.

'So, we're just going to sit around and wait?' Darius sets his hands on his hips, spreading his jacket open to reveal a lean, powerful torso beneath a fitted shirt. 'I'd rather be spending time with *my* wife.'

'Me, too,' Ramin concurs with a wicked gleam in his blue eyes. Since he's unmarried, the intimation is clear.

'Fuck you,' Darius snaps.

'What? Amy makes great martinis.'

'You're a piece of shit.'

Aliyah snaps her fingers, marginally breaking the tension between the brothers. 'Enough. Ramin, get us some decent coffee. Darius, get the names of the doctors.'

As the brothers walk away in different directions, Aliyah turns her dark gaze towards me. 'You and I are the only ones who really worry about Kane. We need to keep an eye on things, make sure he's protected.'

'As you say.' But my thoughts are with the woman beyond the door who has only a man she evidently fears to manage her care.

8

Amy

'A lovely gesture, Mrs. Armand.'

Witte takes the huge bouquet of yellow roses I've brought to the penthouse with me. They'll clash with everything else in Lily's bedroom, making my pricey gift impossible for Kane to ignore – if he bothers to go into her suite at all. I've been stopping by a couple of days a week for the past three weeks she's been home, and I have no idea if Kane even knows of my efforts.

Gesturing toward the living room, Witte shuts the front door behind me. 'Please, make yourself comfortable while I put these in water.'

I step deeper into Kane's domain, my heels tapping quietly. The urge to hurry is hard to resist, but I manage it. I'm irritated by my jitteriness.

Fucking Witte. I don't know how the tight-ass does it, but he's an even better bullshitter than Aliyah. If I had half a brain, I might fall for the warmth of welcome in his voice, but I'm not an idiot. I know he can't stand me.

'How is she?' I ask over my shoulder, midstride, adjusting the strap of my tote bag. Took me forever to find the damn thing earlier. It's becoming a serious pain in the ass to pull together outfits casual enough to hang out with a comatose woman yet still sophisticated and flattering enough to make me look good if I run into Kane. At least I made it here before it started raining. A summer storm is rolling in. It's humid as hell outside, the pressure lowering.

'Mrs. Black's condition is unchanged.'

'I'm sorry to hear that.' It pisses me off that I can't decide whether I really mean that or not. She's just lying there like a corpse. Either die or wake up already. 'We'll just keep our thoughts positive.'

Entering the living room, I shake my head at how fucking clean everything is. Not a speck of dust anywhere. The floor shines like a spotless mirror.

Kicking off one of my high-heeled mules, I press the sweaty ball of my foot against the polished black. I expect the tile to be cool to the touch, but it's the perfect temperature.

A shiver of desire runs through me. The extravagance of penthouse-wide heated floors reminds me of how sensual Kane is.

Jesus, I'm a fucking joke.

The condensation that outlines the shape of my toes swiftly evaporates, leaving behind only the faintest smudge. It's quiet enough to hear my breathing. The penthouse seems sepulchral, filled with secrets I *will* expose. One way or another.

So many questions. And the one person who can answer them is locked away in her own mind.

I'm sliding my shoe back on when the man I can't stop craving appears as if I conjured him in a fever dream. I force myself to look away as Kane approaches. How does a man that big move so silently?

And God is he tall. Everything in the world must feel too small to him.

'Amy.'

I shiver. His voice is a weapon, deliciously low, and it cuts through me like a well-honed blade. I turn my head, my gaze starting at the oxfords that are as highly polished as the floor, then rising to settle on the intersection of his legs. His tailors have some trick for disguising the club between his thighs. I'm guessing he got that big dick from his father because neither Darius nor Ramin is as spectacularly endowed.

Maybe that's why Aliyah is such a bitch. She used to get plowed by a mighty cock until Kane's dad got sick of her shit and fucked off.

Lifting my gaze, I try to find the right smile. Sincere sympathy is what I'm going for, but my mind blanks when I lock eyes with him. He's goddamn immaculate, as Witte would say. He's ridiculous and totally unfair perfection from head to toe. His three-piece suit looks freshly pressed but somehow still drapes possessively over muscles I know are hard and defined. Sapphires set into a fleur-de-lis pattern twinkle from his cufflinks and tie clip. His Windsor knot is so perfect it looks photoshopped, and I want to loosen it with my teeth.

His glossy dark hair would sport waves if he grew it long enough, but it always looks fresh from the barbershop because Witte handles trimming and shaving and God knows what else. I remember how those black strands felt in my hands, thick and silky. He's got a powerfully square jaw and a firm chin, with sculpted cheekbones that direct attention to cruel, sensual lips.

Some men would be too screwed up emotionally and mentally by a miraculously returned-from-death wife to care about how they look. Not Kane. No, he's hotter than ever. And he looks this good working from home, which he's been doing the past three weeks since he arranged for *her* to be discharged from the hospital. Aliyah is furious about that. She can't stand the existence of another woman in Kane's life whom he considers more important. It's almost enough to make me enjoy having Lily around.

'Hi.' I mean to say more but can't. I spend hours planning the interactions I'll have when I'm alone with Kane, but whenever the opportunity arises, my goddamn mouth stops working.

There's no way around it: Kane Black is terrifying. He's gorgeous in the way of an uncontrolled fire, so destructively mesmerizing that you've burned to ashes before you realize you're in danger. He has a way of being eerily still while making you feel as if he's whirling around you like a tornado. I'm no psychoanalyst, but I'd bet that women – myself included – are aroused as much by the fear he evokes as by his physical attractiveness. It's not pleasure alone that his type of sex appeal promises; it's devastation.

His gaze licks over me. Kane's eyes have always reminded me of coal. Flat, hard and unfathomably black.

Does he notice my hair? It's *her* exact shade, matched to the swatch of her hair I cut the first time I visited. The difference is slight enough that no one I've crossed has noticed anything, but Kane is more observant than most. I didn't cut it short, as her hair is now, choosing to stick with the style Kane's been looking at for years in that old photo.

I'm more like the Lily he's crazy about than *she* is at this point, and I'm hoping that's working in my favor.

Abruptly, his face softens, and my breathing constricts. I don't think he's really looked at me since I married Darius, but he's definitely looking now. My pulse quickens, and I shift on my feet. There's a flask of vodka in my bag, and my mouth waters at the thought of it. I don't care what anyone says; there's nothing wrong with liquid courage.

He slides a hand into his pocket, casual as you please, and he's instantly both sexier and more accessible. 'Witte tells me you've been coming to sit with Lily a few times a week.'

I start to shrug that off – I'm just a good person doing a good thing – but then I think that's too blasé for the circumstances. 'I wish there was more I could do.'

'You've been reading to her.' It's a statement, not a question.

Reaching into my bag, I pull out an e-reader and some gossip mags I picked up at the newsstand on the corner. 'I don't know what she likes, so I try for a little bit of everything.'

The corner of his mouth lifts in a half-smile, but his gaze is cool. 'Romance novels.'

'Oh . . .' It would be my luck if Lily were another one of Suzanne's fans. I fight the urge to roll my eyes. 'Good to know. Well, there's been a few in the rotation. I'll add more.'

I've also told Lily dozens of stories about the many look-alikes Kane has fucked, running through the participants in my study with meticulous detail. If it's true that the subconscious is always aware and recording info, I've given plenty of juicy particulars for Lily to use in divorce court.

Then again, she left him for some reason. Maybe she already knows exactly what kind of man she married. If so, perhaps she returned because she can't stay away either.

Damn it. Not knowing her story is driving me crazy.

Kane steps closer, and I suck in a quick, surprised breath. I catch his scent, that unique blend of cedar and the beach. *It's bespoke*, Witte told me when I asked. And addictive. I keep breathing in to smell him, trying not to look like I'm gulping air.

I've avoided being near him or even looking at him for so long, living off memories instead of the flesh-and-blood man. It's the only way to prevent making a fool of myself.

There is nothing safe about being this close to him now. Adrenaline floods my bloodstream. Fight or flight. Or better yet, fuck. My nipples harden into painful points, and my clit swells and begins to throb.

'I appreciate it,' he says, his voice low, the words unhurried. He reaches out and gently surrounds my arm within the circle of his hand, sliding down the silk sleeve of my blouse to grip my wrist with the barest of pressures.

It's intimate. Sensual. Dominating. And I'm here for it. Totally. I've dreamed of this moment for nearly two years. I sway toward him in open invitation. I want to tear into him, gouge that dusky skin until bright red drops glisten. He'd like it. He likes sex rough and animalistic – rutting like a beast who enjoys the kill as much as an orgasm.

His gaze drops to my chest, and he bares his teeth in a lightning-quick smile. It's boyish, mischievous and utterly disarming.

'Sometimes it's good to have family,' he murmurs absently. And just like that, Kane's arm drops back to his side, and he withdraws. I'm dismissed in an instant.

Family?!

My horrified stare brings a spark of derisive amusement to his eyes. A split second there, then gone.

'Mr. Black.' Witte stands at the top of the two stairs that lead down into the sunken living room. 'Dr. Hamid has arrived.'

Arousal turns to rage and boils up from my gut to burn my throat. I want to scream but swallow it back. Everything that's gone wrong in my life results from crossing paths with him.

'I'll see her in my office,' Kane instructs Witte, turning away from me.

It's all a damn game to him, the sadistic bastard. The world is filled with people who are just tools or toys, things to be used when it suits him. Physically, he's a big man, but his body isn't his weapon. He doesn't raise his voice or swing his fists. No, his chosen implement of destruction is more insidious – he prefers to mindfuck.

Fine. I like games. I built my business off gaming algorithms and perceptions to my clients' advantage. If I can't fuck Kane in bed, I'll fuck up his life. I was going to do the latter anyway; I just got distracted remembering how good the former was.

If only I understood what Lily is to him, what she means to him. Is she a vulnerability? If not, can I turn her into one? His obsession with her is his weakness, but in what way? I don't care if she can break his heart or just drag his public image through the mud. I don't care if his personal life falls apart or Baharan takes a hit. One way or the other, he's going to suffer. It'll be a bonus if I can make Lily suffer. And I fucking deserve one.

My mouth curves at the thought of Kane pushed off his pedestal and broken.

I head toward the hallway leading to the room where Lily lies, oblivious.

'Amy,' he calls after me, halting my exit.

Glancing over my shoulder, I catch his eye. Anticipation bubbles up as if I hadn't just corked it and swore it'd be the last time I did so. My brow wings up, questioning.

'Thank you.' He looks and sounds sincere.

I don't buy it. Not at all.

9

Amy

Lily Black lies in a luxurious bed big enough to make her tall frame seem childlike. The room is so spacious that even the bulky medical equipment can't make the space feel cramped. The walls and headboard share the same cobalt velvet damask, leaving the bed and the pale woman unconscious in it as the only bright spots in the hushed gloom.

Against ice-blue silk pillows, Lily's coiffed hair is inky black. A clear, thin oxygen tube bisects her face, but her lips are painted a lush red, as are her perfectly manicured nails.

It's creepy, the beautician said to me when I'd arrived in time to catch her working. *Like working on a cadaver.*

Yeah, creepy. And crazy. The whole room looks like a mausoleum for her carcass. The sky has darkened outside, giving the impression that it's dusk instead of noon. The floor and table lamps are all on, the slender silver bases topped with indigo drum shades and chandelier crystals that throw prisms of light against the dark walls.

I've wondered if Kane fucks her while she's unconscious, but when I mentioned it to Darius, he told me I'm insane even to think that. Whatever. The entire family is delusional, and I refuse to be gaslighted.

Sheer curtains hang from brushed nickel rods. Heavy velvet drapes the same hue as the walls flank the windows and pool on the polished sodalite floor. In a navy armchair with silver tacks, Frank – the nurse – sits quietly with a tablet. He glances

45

up with a smile when I step deeper into the room, then stands, knowing the drill. When I show up, he gets to take a break.

The moment he leaves the room, I dig out my flask and unscrew the cap with shaky fingers. I'm still so pissed at Kane; I want to break something. I study Lily as I lift the cool aluminum to my lips, but my eyes close when I toss my head back, and the welcome warmth spreads through my stomach. My tote slides off my shoulder and hits the royal blue rug with a thud. The other flask is still full. Thank God.

Kicking off the towering heels I wore to approximate Lily's height, I walk toward the bed as I take another drink, my fingers gliding over the various pieces of furniture as I pass them. While the depth of color aligns with the rest of the penthouse, there are textures in this room and patterns within the textures. It almost feels like swimming deep underwater, at the point where sunlight is a faraway shimmer. Bouquets of stargazer and black lilies fragrance the air, clearly defining the space from the rest of the condo, which smells of Kane.

The decor could easily be termed masculine, yet the result is sensual bohemian femininity. The room is opulent. Expensive. Faux animal hides draped on chairs and crystal obelisks on marbled tabletops. On the vanity in front of one of the windows, a set comprised of a silver hand mirror and two brushes with *LRB* etched into the backs waits for its owner to wake the fuck up and use them. The pen and notepad on the nightstand bear the same initials.

Someone put thought into this room. It doesn't seem possible that it was created overnight or even within a week, filling me with questions. Was it Kane who styled this for her or Witte? Maybe the decorating was hired out to a professional. I hope that's the case, and Kane didn't care enough to design it himself.

Distantly, the darkening sky rumbles a warning.

Looking toward the lifeless figure in the bed, I eye the jewelry she wears on her left hand, safely below the intravenous line providing her with liquid and nutrients. At first, I'd scoffed at the wedding ring Kane had given his precious Lily.

A ruby. Really?

I don't care how big a gemstone is; a wife should get a diamond, for fuck's sake. And not a halo of small ones but a big fat 'love of my life' statement stone. Even Darius had known that.

It wasn't until I'd tried the ring on myself that I realized the stone changed color with the light.

An alexandrite, I'd discovered after research. Far rarer than diamonds, especially in the size Kane had given her. And far more expensive per carat than pretty much every other stone on the planet.

'You're an asshole, Kane,' I mutter, licking vodka off my lips. 'And you're a bitch,' I tell *her*.

I return to my bag, shove the flask away and pull out a magazine. I take the chance of checking the nightstand drawer and grin when I find a bottle of the polish used on her nails. I laugh when I recognize it as one of Rosana's new ECRA+ shades. 'Blood Lily.'

Of course.

I sit on the edge of the bed, reach out and run my fingers through Lily's hair. The strands are glossy and vibrant with life. They slip and slide, settling neatly onto the pillow when I let them go. Her skin is like white satin. Flawless and smooth, soft as down feathers and free from the sun damage every other woman her age fights, including me.

Somewhere, there's a bag collecting urine from her catheter. And she wears a diaper for shitting. So . . . maybe not so fucking perfect after all, huh?

'I've decided I want you to wake up,' I tell her conversationally. 'I need to know how you fucked him up so badly.'

Because I really want to fuck him up, too.

The thin straps of her red negligee bare her shoulders and arms. Her nails are crimson spots on the ruched ice-blue silk of the duvet. The taped IV needle draws my gaze to her vein, which pulses visibly, a direct line to her heart and brain. I touch it, feeling how cool the liquid is that's dripping into her, how it's chilled her skin.

'You feel like a corpse,' I tell her.

But she doesn't smell like one. I lean closer and sniff, catching the faintest trace of perfume, something floral with undertones of deep musk and tropical breezes. I like it. My face is inches from hers, taking in every detail. Her lashes lie like black lace fans against her cheeks.

Thunder cracks the sky and the penthouse quakes. Her eyes slit open, luminous green, staring with serpentine ferocity.

I tumble to the floor, screaming.

10

Aliyah

'Virtual makeovers are ubiquitous, and we've maximized that feature with filters.'

Ryan Landon clicks a button on the remote in his hand, and the photo of Rosana on the screen instantly transitions from brightly lit to dark and moody. 'By offering the option to see how their selections appear in daylight, candlelight, multihued nightclub lighting, fluorescent or LED, overcast or sunny, and many more, we increase the opportunity for the customer to expand their selections.'

Eva Cross smiles. 'And since we offer customizable palettes, they could put together a work and after-hours kit or a wedding and reception kit.'

'The possibilities are endless!' Rosana exclaims with delight.

Ryan smiles, and we are all charmed. Kane's closest friend is a handsome man with wavy brown hair and hazel eyes. They've known each other since college. And while Ryan's LanCorp is best known for video games, the company was the only choice Kane considered to build a mobile app supporting our new cosmeceutical line.

Eva had objected to Ryan. So, too, had Rosana. Eva's company, Cross Industries – built by her husband, Gideon – is considered an industry leader, more significant and with far more resources at its disposal than LanCorp. Other voices within Baharan concurred.

Insisting on Ryan – and getting him – was retaliatory, our counter to the Crosses' strict morality clause. While such clauses in co-ventures are standard, the wording read like preemptive censure. A judgment of my family, of the way I raised my children, and of Paul's untrustworthiness. Valid or not, it rubbed me the wrong way, so I tied Ryan in to rub the Crosses the wrong way. His participation also ensures we have someone at the wheel who is motivated to minimize the Crosses' contributions and maximize ours.

The ECRA+ name already puts Eva's initials first: EvaCrossRosanaArmand. The plus stands for the power of Baharan, the potent ingredients that elevate everyday cosmetics to the level of serums and elixirs. Eva is the media darling of the moment, and she came to the table with plenty of capital, but that doesn't outweigh what Baharan's research brings to the partnership. And while it was Kane's idea to expand into the beauty space and approach Eva as a partner, I directly oversee every facet of the collaboration. And Ryan is a Baharan investor, even if he is too busy with his company to serve on our board.

As my thoughts turn to Amy and Lily, I try to ignore the sick foreboding that sits in my belly like an icy rock. Both of my daughters-in-law are liabilities. Either could be the force that knocks down the house of cards we've assembled so carefully.

Ryan catches my eye, and I nod my approval. The half dozen employees with him are the head architects behind the curtain that made the app what it is. In usual circumstances, they would be leading the presentation, not Ryan himself.

'An excellent idea,' I praise, 'beautifully implemented.'

'Thank you. Now, for many of your customers, how the colors look on Rosana and Eva will inspire them to purchase.' He clicks the remote, and the side-by-side images of the two girls change again. 'The app users will be able to see a variety of combinations with a quick tap on their screens.'

'Allowing users to make us over could be really fun,' Eva says with a huffed laugh, 'or go really unflatteringly wrong.'

'We thought of that,' he assures her. 'If a user tries to deliberately create an unflattering combination on either of you' – he demonstrates – 'the app will default to barefaced photos. Once the ECRA+ skincare line is ready to launch, we'll also rotate in those products as defaults.'

'Whoa.' Rosana laughs with delight. 'That's awesome.'

'And it's individualized for each of you. While some combinations aren't flattering on Eva, they can look pretty dynamite on Rosana and vice versa. See?'

Eva nods as his presentation switches between the example of her face to an instance of Rosana's. 'Impressive.'

'Keep in mind we also have thematic photos of you both throughout and the fifty models of various skin tones, ethnicities and ages you selected. The latter has turned out to be very popular in-house. I hadn't realized that consumers with gray hair are largely ignored in the beauty space. There's a void, and you're going to fill it.'

'That's the plan.' Eva smiles, but her gaze is shrewd. 'Who decided what was flattering or not for each of us?'

'We ran every possible combination through the same in-house aesthetic team that helps shape our avatars' appearances.'

'That's a great place to start,' she says smoothly. 'I'd like to run through all those possibilities myself, though. If you don't mind.'

'Of course not. Your image is your brand, and we understand that. You'll both be granted access during testing and can utilize all the features without restrictions. You'll be able to see those flagged for removal and add or subtract from that list.' Ryan's smile doesn't waver, but his gaze on her is noticeably more intense. 'Our software is proprietary, so we ask you to test the app onsite.'

'That's quite an inconvenience. And likely to be incredibly time-consuming, given the number of possible combinations.'

'It's a precautionary step and protects us both.'

The focus with which he studies her might lead someone who didn't know better to think he's attracted to Eva. After all, she's a lovely woman, with blond hair and deep gray eyes. Petite and slender, she's got the figure of the moment: full breasts, nipped waist, overly curved derriere. I'm unsure whether those curves are as natural as the shade of her hair. Eva also has an overt sensuality about her that's evident in the way she moves, the lustiness of her laugh and the throaty tone of her voice. It's all too much, really.

But Ryan is devoted to his wife. What simmers between him and Eva Cross is enmity.

It's *so* much fun watching them work together.

'But we don't want users to get hung up playing with your photos,' he goes on. 'We want them to buy, so after every three combinations, the app prompts them to upload their photo to play with. You can see what that looks like here.' He watches them as they stare at the monitor, then he glances at me. He's smart enough to know that while the girls are the faces of ECRA+, I'm the driving force behind Rosana. She always takes my advice.

'Once they follow the prompt,' he continues, 'we lay out detailed instructions for the selfies they upload, and then the software takes them through how the colors work on them. They can choose whatever combinations they like for their photos. No limits.'

'You've thought of everything!' Rosana exclaims, bouncing excitedly on one of my aqua leather club chairs.

While the color palette of my office is beachy, with shades

of taupe, teal and cream, the design is mid-century. Wood-paneled walls and vintage furniture warm up what would otherwise be a starkly modern office space. The overall feel is masculine, which disconcerts visitors just enough to give me an advantage. It also serves to exaggerate my femininity, which is always a plus.

There is no sofa. The designer had argued for two, saying a cluster of individual chairs would look cluttered. She knew design, but she didn't know me. Just the thought of having an inviting horizontal surface to lie on in my office makes my skin crawl.

The sky darkens to a deep gray, and raindrops begin to splash against the windows.

'We think so,' Ryan concurs. 'But we can never be too careful. We've been beta testing for months, but it's time for you both to give it a spin. Once you've determined you're ready, we'll do a soft launch with the models and influencers who contributed during the development stage. We'll integrate their feedback and then take it live.'

'Will we hit our timeline target?' I ask. Launching a cosmetic line is a celebrity trend, making the beauty space more crowded and competitive by the day.

'That depends on how long it takes to receive your feedback and how extensive any requested changes may be.'

'I love it already.' My daughter reaches for and squeezes Eva's hand, her beautiful face alight with joy.

I sigh inwardly. She hasn't yet experienced enough adversity in life to be wary. She can't picture future falling-outs, lingering disagreements or opposing visions. I should've given her more roadblocks to stumble over as she matured, as I did with her brothers, but then Kane's resurrection of Baharan started making waves – and money. I'd had to circle back to my eldest to begin rebuilding the company as a family.

There was no way I was going to lose Baharan a second time.

And so Rosana is naively optimistic. Eva looks just as hopeful, but that wolf she married ensures she's protected.

I'll just have to work harder on Rosana. So far, the seeds of distrust I've stealthily planted have failed to take root, but I won't give up. A good mother doesn't shelter her children from harm; she throws them into its jaws so that the scars toughen their skin.

A flash of brightness distracts me, drawing my attention to the storm outside. The sunlight has been blocked by roiling gray clouds, blanketing the city in dusk-like gloom. It's the middle of the day but feels much later.

As I look back at the presentation, I see a text notification lighting the screen of my muted phone. I pick it up with my thumb on the fingerprint scanner, and the message displays.

She's awake.

I I

Witte

With a soft rap on the open door to Mr Black's office, I announce the arrival of the tea service I prepared in advance of Dr Vanya Hamid's arrival. At my employer's nod, I wheel the trolley in and set to work, measuring the appropriate amount of Nilgiri tea for the pot of freshly boiled water.

Mr Black sits behind his elegant yakisugi desk, the charred wood a deep, lustrous black. It's bespoke to accommodate his long legs and torso. The chair, too, is custom-made, with arms that pair with the desk and cognac leather upholstery. He's settled in with an avid gaze, his intense focus on every word that falls from the doctor's lips.

The knot of his tie is loose, the clip askew. His hair needs a trim, and the shadow of a beard darkens his jaw. I usually address his barbering with fixed regularity, but he is too restless of late to sit for proper grooming. That he looks so dishevelled during video conferences worries me, but I also grasp the unintended benefit of planting at least a seed of doubt in the minds of the detectives. They drop by every few days to see if they can question Mrs Black. Instead, they see a man who looks as if he's hanging on to sanity by his fingertips, a husband consumed by fear and worry for his wife.

Undoubtedly familiar with facing anxious family members, Dr Hamid's posture is relaxed and at ease, although concern threads her melodic voice. Her dark hair is elaborately upswept, and her trim figure resplendent in a pale blue shalwar

55

kameez, a traditional South Asian trousers and tunic ensemble embroidered with glittering gold thread.

Mr Black stands when she finishes speaking, turning to face the panoramic view of the city lost in a grey haze of rain. Large banana leaf plants frame the unadorned wall of windows, bringing a bit of the green from Central Park below into the clouds where he resides. He rubs the back of his neck; a blatant tell that fully betrays his frustration and anxiety. There are no answers to the question he has asked repeatedly: *Why won't she wake?*

Since her momentary spell of consciousness on the day of the accident, Lily has slept without ceasing. And with every day that passes Mr Black grows more agitated.

Thunder splits the sky with a roar as if heaven itself resents the hubristic height of the tower in which we reside. The clamour is so enveloping that it very nearly drowns out the sound of a woman's terrified scream.

Mr Black skirts me at a dead run, agile and quick as a gazelle, displaying the athleticism and speed that once hallmarked his game as a point guard in basketball. I wait, allowing Dr Hamid to precede me, then following her quick, steady pace while sorting through a mental checklist of possible scenarios and the resulting required actions. Through open doorways, I see the windows dripping with tears from the sky.

We enter Mrs Black's bedroom and come to an abrupt halt.

Amy Armand hugs herself as she leans against the wall. My employer already sits on the side of the bed, both hands fisting the duvet on either side of his wife's slender hips. Lily sits upright, her pale arms wrapped around his shoulders, her cheek pressed to his as tears sparkle on inky lashes. The bright red of her nails glistens like drops of blood amid the dark strands of Mr Black's hair.

In her present surroundings, Lily Black embodies the brightest of full moons on the darkest of nights.

Bending, I collect the junior Mrs Armand's handbag and shoes from the floor and approach her, lightly encircling her upper arm in a respectful grip.

'Mrs Armand,' I murmur, 'allow me to escort you to the door.'

'What?' Her gaze is riveted to the tableau on the bed.

I smell the alcohol on her breath and sigh inwardly. Such a lovely girl, with so much potential, but she fights demons of which I'm unaware.

'The doctor will need to examine Mrs Black,' I murmur as I lead her gently out of Lily's bedroom, 'and we must afford her privacy.'

She resists when I exert slight pressure, her eyes wide and staring. I want to stare, too. It is so rare and strange to see Mr Black in an embrace, with his head bowed and knuckles white with strain. An unwilling supplicant.

He is not a demonstrative man. He avoids physical contact in public aside from what is necessary for proper etiquette and politeness. I've often thought of him surrounded by an invisible wall that keeps others a safe distance away.

But there are evidently no barriers capable of protecting him from Lily.

The sky opens, and a torrent descends.

Lily

With my cheek pressed to yours, I exhale. A shudder moves through you as my breath caresses your ear. The restless flexing of your fingers in the duvet makes me shiver, and I can't stop once I start. The need to crawl inside you, to be united with my heart, is overwhelming. Holding you in my arms is everything I've ever wanted or needed.

You nestle your nose against my throat and inhale a hard, ragged breath, pulling the scent of my skin into your lungs. You nuzzle me as you exhale. You aren't returning my embrace, but it's not necessary. You mark me like an animal and take my mark on you in return. I feel you breathe me in again, then again, as if you've been submerged and without air for too long. Suffocating.

I know the feeling, my love. All too well.

Your body against mine is both hard and feverishly hot, like a column of stone that's spent hours beneath the glare of the sun. You're vibrating, every muscle reacting to the press of my body to yours. My indrawn breath fills my senses with the smell of you, a scent that takes me back to the night we met. Bonfire and salty air, the sharp bite of a storm carried on the evening breeze.

Ah, lilies, too. My chest aches with suppressed sobs.

You haven't forgotten Lily.

Witte

I wait with the younger Mrs Armand until she enters the lift with a blank, dazed expression. She is digging frantically into her handbag as the doors slide shut, not looking at me and offering no farewell.

I nod at the two guards flanking the penthouse entrance as I pass them, shutting the door soundlessly. Alone, I can admit that the scene I've just witnessed has shaken me to the core.

I cannot reconcile the woman who ran from Mr Black in the heart of Midtown with the wife clinging lovingly to him in the bedroom. The reactions are so outrageously different as to defy logic.

Thrusting aside my disquiet, I traverse the long, mirrored hallway to Mrs Black's bedroom. My employer now stands in the farthest, darkest corner. He stares at the two women, who speak in hushed tones, and doesn't acknowledge my return, his attention riveted, his stance wide and arms crossed. Commanding. Aggressive. The nurse, Frank, stands behind and near the doctor, at the ready. I call upon years of experience to disappear into my surroundings.

Dr Hamid holds one finger up, moving it from side to side as Lily's gaze follows. It is disconcerting to see Mrs Black looking so artfully groomed as if she's just indulged in a short midday nap instead of spending weeks unconscious.

She is, without question, the most ravishing creature I have ever seen. The photo Mr Black treasures is a shadow of the dynamism present in the living, breathing woman.

Beyond that staggering beauty, Lily is fearfully composed while facing a situation that would frighten the wits out of damn near anyone. She is in an unfamiliar place with unfamiliar people. Even her husband must seem a stranger; their separation has been lengthy and his evolution dramatic. And yet it was the younger Mrs Armand who screamed in shock.

'How many fingers am I holding up?' the doctor asks.

'Two.'

'And now?'

'Still two. Where am I?'

'You're at home. Can you tell me your name?'

'Lily Rebecca Yates. Whose home?' She looks at Mr Black. 'Kane . . . ?'

'Ours,' he answers gruffly.

A look of wonder sweeps over her face, her eyes luminous with tears. 'Ours,' she repeats in a whisper.

As I have, Dr Hamid has paused at hearing Lily's maiden name. I am also taken aback by her voice. From the looks of her, I expected her to speak in husky flavours of smoke and Scotch. Instead, her tone is high and girlish, with the faintest hint of an underlying throatiness. I've never heard anything like it, yet I respond with surprising fervour. I want to listen to her speak at length, to have the time to catalogue the nuances of a voice that by rights should irritate but delights instead.

'Do you always give your maiden name?' the doctor asks.

Lily blinks slowly, then lifts her left hand and studies the ring there. She swallows visibly before she answers, 'I'm not married.'

A low growl rumbles from my employer's chest.

'It's okay,' Dr Hamid says firmly. 'There are no wrong answers. How old are you, Lily?'

60

'Twenty-seven.'

Mr Black stiffens beside me. The doctor glances at Frank for confirmation, whose head shakes in denial.

The doctor settles deeper into her perch on the edge of the bed. 'Do you remember the accident?'

'Accident?'

'You were hit by a car about a month ago.'

Lily is too still for a long moment, then asks, 'What's the date today?'

I catch the doctor's gaze as she glances at Frank after answering. Her full lips are pursed, her brow furrowed. All of us turn our heads to look at Mr Black. He is ashen and tense, so much so that I could almost swear the air vibrates around him.

Lily studies him, too. Then her hand – laden with a price-less stone that is deeply purple indoors and the same verdant hue as her eyes in sunlight – reaches out to her husband, trembling. 'Kane . . .'

He stands unmoving for a long, fraught minute. Then his arms drop to his sides, and he takes a jerky step towards the bed as if resisting a lure and failing.

I'm at a loss for what to do when he pivots abruptly and exits the room with long, fast strides.

14

Witte

'Well.' Lily's delicate hand floats softly as a butterfly back down to the bed. My gaze is briefly arrested by the scorpion tattoo on her inner wrist that's the size of a pound coin. With a deeply indrawn breath, she gathers her composure. 'It seems our marriage needs work.'

'Do you remember being married now?' Dr Hamid asks.

'No. Did I wear white or black?'

'When?'

'At the wedding.'

'I don't know. You've been in my care nearly a month, but really, we've just met.'

Mrs Black looks at me, and I find myself arrested by those striking emerald eyes. 'Were you there? At the wedding, I mean.'

'No, madam. The pleasure was not afforded to me, as that was before my time.'

Her gaze narrows slightly, and she looks towards the windows. 'Are we in London?'

'Manhattan,' I tell her. 'I'm English, however, as you surmised.'

She takes stock of the room as if cataloguing every surface. She is near in age to my daughter, but there's a hardness in her jewelled gaze thankfully absent in my child.

'Mrs Black —'

Lily suddenly shakes with laughter that soon verges on

hysteria. Tears well, then trickle down like trails of liquid diamonds. Despair is weakening her, casting a troubling shadow over her vivid beauty. She squeezes her eyes shut and slides down into the bedclothes. 'I want to wake up now.'

The doctor doesn't take her eyes off her patient when she asks, 'Frank, what's the status of the ambulance?'

He looks up from his mobile, his mouth thinned into a tight line. 'It's here. They've got the gurney in the elevator and are on the way up.'

'We're going to take you to the hospital, Lily,' Dr Hamid says soothingly. 'Now that you're awake, we need to run some additional tests. I'm going to be with you every step of the way.'

'Please excuse me,' I tell Mrs Black, fiercely reluctant to leave her. She is as fragile as spun sugar, delicate threads of sanity hardening to breaking point. 'I'll direct them back here.'

I leave the room, coming to an abrupt halt in the hallway to avoid colliding with Mr Black.

He ceases pacing. His dark eyes are as wet as Lily's and look equally wild.

'You should be with your wife,' I tell him. 'She needs you.'

'That's not my wife.'

Something cold and slippery slithers around my vitals. 'Mr Black –'

'She looks like Lily. Has her voice. Her skin. Her scent.' He rakes both hands through his hair and grips his scalp. 'But there's something about her eyes . . . Don't you see it?'

I stare at him, roiled by confusion. His wife's exquisite face is unparalleled. More than that, she looks at him as she always has in her portrait, with a feverish love, a possessive hunger. He's slept beneath that gaze for all the years I've known him. How can he not recognize it?

His hands drop heavily to his sides. 'Arrange for private

security at the hospital,' he orders, his words raw as if cut glass lines his throat. 'No visitors. Anyone who asks for her should be followed until they've been identified and vetted.'

I nod my acquiescence. 'I'll see to the emergency personnel now, then address the security. Do you want to keep guards on rotation here as well?'

'Yes.'

'Will you be travelling to hospital with her?'

'Of course.' He scowls. 'What do you take me for? You think I'd let her go alone?'

The storm wind shoves against the building, which creaks and moans like a ship on a heaving sea. I look back before I turn into the entry hall.

My employer hovers in the space outside his wife's room, notably more haunted by her revenant than he ever was by her memory.

15

Amy

'Baby, we have to go.'

Darius's voice startles me. When his arms circle my waist from behind, I have to fight the urge to spin around with my fist swinging toward his handsome face.

Heart hammering, I struggle with my anger. 'God! Don't sneak up on me like that!'

His body is warm against mine, his signature scent infusing the air in my walk-in closet. It's my favorite room in our condo, a former guest bedroom I closed off from the main hallway and opened to the master bedroom. All white and mirrored throughout, the open shelves display my purses and shoes, while the racks are precisely arranged as specified by a professional organizer. It is the closet of my dreams, but I can't find anything to wear.

I swear the maid is stealing and randomly rearranging my things so it's harder to notice what she's taken, but Darius says I'm imagining things. I am *So. Fucking. Sick.* of no one believing a word I say. Except for Suzanne. How twisted is it that the one person on my side is someone I can't stand? At least I can trust her.

'You're jumpy today,' my husband murmurs, his firm lips grazing my shoulder.

'What the hell am I supposed to wear?' It's so important I get it right. Aliyah will be there with her judging gaze. And Kane. Most importantly, Lily is back from the hospital after a few weeks in physical therapy, and she may make an appearance. I've rifled through her closet at least a dozen times, and I know her style is dark, sultry and dramatic, which is the total opposite of Aliyah's predilection for light, sexy and classic.

So . . . how do I overshadow Lily without hearing passive-aggressive backhanded compliments from my bitch of a mother-in-law? I picture duct tape wrapped around Aliyah's head, sealing her vicious mouth shut, and I almost laugh out loud. The cool gray of the tape would clash so perfectly with her warm neutrals. And how *fabulous* would the strands of her bottle-blond hair look stuck to the adhesive when she rips it off with her clawed nails?

'It doesn't matter what you pick,' Darius breathes, his voice low and rough as his hands push into the cups of my bra. 'You'll always be the most beautiful woman in the room.'

I study our reflection in the full-length mirror that covers the entire wall at the deepest point of my closet. I'm wearing a new lingerie set, a deep emerald green with black stripes and black lace. I've recently purged most of my undergarments and nightgowns, replacing the creams and golds of my former palette with moodier colorways. Kane won't be disappointed if I ever get naked for him again.

I watch my husband's fingertips find my nipples and tug them gently, sending an echoing pull between my legs. His lips are on my throat now, his breath humid against my skin.

Is this how Darius started banging his assistant? Did she sashay into his office one day and send all the fuck-me-now signals? How quickly and easily did he decide to pull up her skirt and bend her over his desk? Did it start with a blowjob, or did he slide right into deep cunt drilling?

And why wouldn't she want him? I thought bitterly. He's tall, dark and gorgeous with a great smile. When his voice husks with lust and his honed body heats with desire, he is irresistible. My ring on his finger probably makes him more so.

In the mirror before us, I see a fantastically complementary couple. My stylist's approximation of Lily's shade of hair is darker than his, cooler, while his is warm. His golden skin emphasizes the blue eyes that are an Armand trait. His shoulders are broad enough to frame mine and make me feel delicate. In the depths of my closet, surrounded by endless shades of beige and white, he dominates and makes my blood thrum in my veins.

'Can you FaceTime your mother and see what she's wearing?' My breath catches as his fingertips glide down my stomach.

'Who cares?' he retorts, his hand flexing painfully on my hip in rebuke.

'She does! She's always making fucked-up comments about how I look and act, what I eat and drink, where I go and who my friends are!'

He shushes me. 'Amy . . . I'll be the first to admit she's overbearing and opinionated. But family means everything to her.'

My teeth grit together. They are all fucking blind, every single one of her children. Kane is the only one who knows what she's actually capable of because she ditched him when her second husband didn't want to deal with her brat from another man. 'She doesn't see me as family.'

'Of course she does. You're my wife.'

Rolling my shoulders back, I try to shake him off. 'You'll never see her the way she really is.'

'Oh, I see her.' One hand tightens around my breast, holding me captive. His gaze meets mine in the mirror as his other hand slips into my panties and parts the lips of my sex. 'I see how she wants all of her children working together, living our lives together. She wants us all tied in a neat little knot so she can just tug a thread, and we'll all be bundled up tight.'

My back stiffens as his fingertips find my clitoris and begin to circle. Anger sizzles in my blood. 'Fuck her. And fuck you if you think I'm going to live like that.'

His teeth sink into the tender skin between my neck and shoulder. 'You *are* going to fuck me, or at least be fucked *by* me, right fucking now.'

'Darius —'

Two long fingers push inside me, finding me wet from the expert manipulation of my nipples and the dark note of threat in his voice. He knows all my buttons, knows how to push them. I hate him for that. I imagine tossing my head back, breaking his nose and feeling the hot blood spurt on my skin.

'You think Kane's the only one who can rescind the agreement and give you back control of your precious company?' he hisses in my ear, even as his fingers begin to thrust. 'My mother acts like we're all a big, happy family, but it's killing her to have Kane at the head of Baharan. She's making moves, babe, secret shit she's trying to spin as being helpful but is really about taking over.'

I go slack in his arms; my knees relax to give those talented fingers easier access. His palm presses and rubs against my clitoris with every push and retreat, driving me closer and closer to orgasm.

'I'm documenting everything,' he says tightly. 'Her electronic signature is on every step. All roads lead back to her.'

A low moan of surrender leaves me. He has aroused me with his hands and excited me with his words. His fingers aren't enough anymore.

'Take your underwear off and bend over,' he orders, his hands leaving me bereft.

I shimmy out of my panties, watching as he unfastens his belt and unzips the fly of his pale gray dress slacks. I reach for the island in the center of my closet. The cool marble chills my palms as I arch my back to present myself to him.

Darius growls as he fists his penis and rubs the head against the slickness of my sex. Then he leans in, entering me in a torturously slow glide. My eyes close on a gasped breath, my mind filling with heated memories of a different sexual encounter with a different man. Kane hadn't been gentle or slow. He'd flipped me over, yanked me to the end of the bed and driven himself into me hard and fast.

My husband winds his fingers in my hair and tugs my head up. 'Watch me fuck you,' he demands hoarsely as if he knows where my traitorous thoughts have wandered.

I stare at him, see the way he looks standing behind me – blue tie expertly knotted, white shirt crisply ironed. If pictured from the chest up, he'd look like a businessman at work. Instead, he's a man thrusting his engorged cock into a lusty woman eager to climax. I am outside my body, watching. The sight is so erotic I shiver with desire.

'When the time is right, I'll use everything against her for leverage to pull what's left of Social Creamery out of Baharan,' he bites out, punctuating his words with rhythmic lunges. 'Then I'll make sure Kane finds out what she's been up to. Once she's out of the way, I can plan what's next.'

My mouth falls open as I struggle to breathe. The relentless pull on my scalp as he uses my hair to hold me still for his pleasure is driving me mad. His plunge and retreat inside me is luscious. Everything in me is tightening and clenching, hungry for gratification. More, always more. Harder. Rougher.

I try to move, to quicken the pace, but he holds me motionless, using me to relieve the excitement of his jealous ambition.

I am turned on by being used, just as thinking of tearing down Kane and his mother has Darius harder than steel.

Aroused by his fantasies of destroying his brother, my husband fucks me to a quivering orgasm.

16

Lily

The penthouse carries the weighted suspense of a held breath as I drift through its mirrored hallways. After seemingly endless days of physical therapy, nestling in this seductive refuge is heavenly. A perfect square, it sprawls over eight thousand square feet, with the arteries – elevator, garbage chute, stairwell and ducts – running through the center. The rooms cling to the exterior walls, each with a breathtaking view.

As I move through the deathly quiet, the scent of lilies twines around me, curling from where my bare feet touch the heated floors and rising to whisper around my throat like a jealous paramour. Beneath that fragrance is you, the bracing notes reminiscent of an ocean breeze and toasted wood. I breathe in and sigh with pleasure. My pulse quickens with an exhilarating surge that most resembles fear.

Half a dozen people are in the library with you, but the penthouse is as quiet as a tomb. Nothing echoes or carries. Only the sounds of the penthouse itself are evident – a soft moan in the buffeting breeze, a groaning creak as the tower sways like a dancer in the wind. Although I can detect no movement, the building tells me of its struggles. It's a slender reed battered by the forces of nature, yet I am cradled and safe from that turbulence.

For the moment, the threats I face are within the walls, not without.

Is it because the penthouse resonates with sounds resembling a boat on a stormy sea that you chose this for your home? Lily went down with her ship. Have you lain in bed at night staring at her picture and listening to the tower, imagining you are sailing *la Tempête* together, and when the ocean claims the vessel, she claims you, too?

It's a morbidly romantic notion suggesting a fathomless love, yet you avoid me.

I'm simply unable to reconcile this new reality; the penthouse is so outside the framework within which I saw you. Was it that you needed this vantage to believe in yourself, to prove yourself? The design of the building prevents you from looking down at the ground, a sleight of hand meant to prevent billionaires' wings made of wax and feathers from failing, not from rising too high but from the grind and grime of hard living below.

Not to say I don't love what lies within the walls that enclose us. It's a gilded cage so darkly beautiful that I want to lock the door from the inside, so no grasping hand can seize and take me away. Or push me out to plummet to the ground.

It's surreal, as are you. I often hear my voice in my head, younger and softer, telling me this is all just a lucid dream. I wave my hand, willing the obsidian floor to mutate into clear glass with inky waters flowing beneath. I touch the wall, telling it to change color. Nothing I do or think or say can alter my surroundings, but it seems impossible to find myself here, in a home that looks like my deepest desire but isn't, with a husband who looks like my love but isn't.

Be careful what you wish for.

Isn't this everything I ever wanted? You've resumed control of your birthright, Baharan. I wear your ring and bear your name. We live in this dazzling penthouse. It's a devil's bargain to live this life with you, and where will that lead? You have

Baharan, but the family who abandoned you came with it. We're married, but we're strangers. And we have a dazzling aerie above the clouds, yet it's devoid of love and laughter. I dreamed of this heaven. Instead, I find myself in hell.

The view opens as I enter the main living area, showcasing New York City at her finest. I pause a moment, absorbing the feel of the space. I'm reminded of a forest at night with the full moon glistening off lush moss and a tranquil, private pond. It's opulently mysterious and unabashedly sensual.

I turn the corner from the formal dining room with its live edge table and green leather chairs and step into the kitchen, which feels like a space out of time.

The island is a repurposed antique. Dark wood, a multitude of drawers, brass pulls – possibly from an old apothecary or library. The nicks and dents give it character, while the gold-veined black granite top gives it panache. The stove is massive and modern in its features, with a black finish and aesthetic resembling vintage cast iron. The upper cabinets are stained wood, matching the finish of the island, while the lowers are painted a glossy black. Open shelving displays herbs and spices in uniform glass jars with chalkboard labels.

I reach a closed door and turn the knob. I know from the masculine scent that the room is Witte's. I close it without entering. The handsome majordomo with the sharp, assessing gaze isn't who interests me at the moment. However, the decision you've both made to house him within the penthouse rather than the staff floors farther down is intriguing.

The next room is a guestroom. With a palette of deep green and gold, it connects to the view of Central Park outside the windows. The next guestroom boasts shades of amethyst and lavender, and it's only by seeing them in rapid succession that the nebulous thoughts at the back of my mind take shape. Both are astonishingly similar to Lily's

73

Connecticut beach house guestrooms and her West Village condominium. The inspiration is impossible to miss. Is your memory so vivid? Or is it that my dreams are?

Where are *you* in this lavish home? I don't see any trace of you.

When I catch your tall figure walking the halls, it's as if the walls themselves shy away from you, uneasy with the restless energy that churns in your wake. Has my mind erased you? Is it only my obsession that imagines the briefest glimpses I catch of you, a thick column of smoke that swiftly disperses?

Is it the love burrowed like a thorned root into my very soul that conjures you into this fantastical existence I'm exploring?

Opening the next door divulges a room choked with the smells of paint. From the threshold, I note the tarps and ladders, the buckets and rollers. The blindingly white walls will be a deep sapphire when finished. Its incomplete state confuses me. Why would I create an unfinished space if this is a flight of fancy? What do I intend to do with it?

I pass the home gym without pausing but feel like I've finally found you when I enter your office. There is color here and living things. The desk's charred finish brings in the darkness from the rest of the penthouse, but that is the only piece that might blend in elsewhere. The side chairs are upholstered in warm cognac leather, while russet velvet covers a sofa with slender brass feet. I smile when I see the miniature basketball hoop hanging over the wastebasket.

Rounding your desk, I note that the lacquered knobs feature lilies. On the corner sits a framed photo of her. It's a close-up shot of the wind whipping her hair across her face, her eyes laughing, her mouth curved in a wide smile. Even here, she haunts you.

I feel the chill of her breath against my nape, but I don't dare turn around.

Perhaps I'm not the only one in the cage.

Perhaps the cage is hers, and you're the one trapped inside it. With me.

17

Aliyah

Over the rim of my martini glass, I surreptitiously study my middle son and his wife.

There's a familiarity there that disturbs me. Darius and Amy usually sit close together but maintain an icy reserve. Today, he's perched on the armrest beside her, his hip against her shoulder.

His arms are crossed, his handsome features expressing boredom. She looks somewhat sober, although she, too, has a martini. She's wearing a sleeveless navy sheath dress of a respectable length made interesting by artfully, deliberately twisted shoulder straps. The darker color suits her better than the neutral palette she's copied from me. Her long hair is loosely waved and draped over one shoulder.

Most would think she has class, but I know better. A sewer rat in Louboutin heels is still a sewer rat.

Ramin sits at the other end of the sofa, scrolling through his phone. His hair is too long, but not unattractively so, the dark waves falling into his eyes so that he repeatedly pushes them back. Unlike Darius, who sports a nicely tailored light gray suit, Ramin has shown up in dark jeans and a camouflage Henley.

My youngest, Rosana, wears a strapless romper that shows off her graceful arms and curvy legs. It's one of the new capsule pieces we've designed in collaboration with the world's biggest e-tailer. Nude-toned and sparkly, it sold out in minutes. She's paired it with athletic shoes that haven't yet been released to the public. The photos of her out and about in them today will drive pre-orders.

I taught her not to squander opportunities. Influence waxes then wanes. With collaborations such as ECRA+ – which she's also presently wearing – and fashion, I hope to set her up to maintain her lifestyle moving forward. She'll never be forced into reliance on any man for anything.

'Where the fuck is he?' Ramin asks. 'I don't have all day to sit here.'

'You don't have to remind us that you'd rather be doing shit-all somewhere else. We know.' Darius stands and holds his hand out for Amy's now-empty glass in a silent offer to refill it. He's an enabler, my son, hoping to keep his wife codependent to save their marriage.

'Fuck you, brother.'

I'm as impatient as Ramin. There is something different about the penthouse now. While it looks exactly the same, the glass walls restrain frenetic energy, an expectancy on the verge of crescendo. We all feel it skittering up our spines, and the tension is maddening. Is it Kane's dynamism, trapped here by his own choice to remain home? Is it *hers*?

Lily. A troubling presence, even unseen.

I've only talked to my eldest in video conferences over the past month. My fear that anything – or anyone – could be more valuable to my son than Baharan appears unfounded. He hasn't missed a step at work. His wife's precarious health hasn't affected his ambition. Still, his withdrawal to the penthouse is concerning. The staff perform better when feeding off his energy.

Ice is rattling in the shaker when Kane enters the library dressed in a graphite-gray suit, white shirt and silver tie. His posture is perfect, his stride commanding. He takes over the room instantly, and those dark eyes – Paul's – are impenetrable.

77

Kane is a hard man, emotionless and detached. His handsome face blends all of my and his father's best features with none of our flaws. That combination of stunning physicality and reserve has always served us well. If I feel a pang of regret that I contributed to his brutal indifference, it's only momentary. Baharan wouldn't be what it's on the verge of becoming without his heartless calculation.

Witte joins us on my son's heels like a shadow.

The majordomo is tall and well-built beneath his uniform of white shirtsleeves, black vest and black trousers. His pure-white hair is thick and expertly razored into a high fade undercut, allowing for a voluminous backward sweep that emphasizes his height. His beard is more pepper than salt, and it's exquisitely kept. There are teasing hints of flexing muscle as he moves, enticing a woman to imagine the fitness of the body beneath the provocatively proper clothes. He's extremely attractive and very sexy.

But he's come into the room without a beverage cart and makes no effort to serve anyone, so Kane has asked him to stand by solely for support. The notion of needing a servant's reinforcement against his own family infuriates me.

'Sorry to keep you waiting,' Kane says without a hint of remorse, sinking into a studded leather wingback chair and facing the rest of us with studious ease.

'No, you're not,' Ramin drawls, not even deigning to look up from his screen. 'But now that you're here let's get on with it. What's the big family emergency?'

'There's no emergency. We now have a firm grasp on my wife's situation, and it's simpler to explain once, for everyone, rather than speaking to you all individually.'

'Basically, it's more convenient for you. Who cares what the rest of us had planned?' Ramin puts his phone away and leans forward, resting his elbows on his knees, suddenly focused and all business.

He might complain about the effort involved, but when it comes to family, Ramin is the first person to show up with a shovel to bury the bodies. That loyalty is a real credit to the way I reared him.

'You know we're all here for you,' Amy says vacuously.

'What a lovely reminder, Amy,' I tell her, my tone soft and sweet. 'Even if it's entirely unnecessary.' My smile widens when she shoots me a murderous glance.

'Are we going to meet our new sister-in-law or not?' Ramin asks. 'Or is it *former* sister-in-law? Was she declared dead? Or divorced in absentia?'

'She's finishing up with a visitor, but she'll be joining us shortly,' Kane replies. 'And no, she's not new, not dead and not divorced. I've been married over six years.'

'Who's visiting?' I press sharply.

The traffic camera footage of Lily's hit-and-run was covered on local news channels in the week following the accident, with police asking for tips to identify the driver and vehicle, which had license plates registered to a different make and model car. Mercifully, Lily's name wasn't disclosed. It's of utmost importance that we keep her under wraps until we know enough to defuse any possible explosive revelations. I've tried to discuss the need for discretion with Kane, but reaching him privately has been a struggle, and when I have, he's been curt.

He waves off my alarm with an irritated flick of his wrist. 'Someone to run out for things she needs.'

'Why can't Witte do that?'

'Why don't you leave the running of my household to me?' he retorts.

My pulse races. His defensive protectiveness doesn't bode

well for making him see reason. If he's convinced she's more important than Baharan and his family, I'll have to deprogram him. 'Can I ask where Lily's been this whole time?'

Darius returns to his former position by Amy, forming a united front with his wife.

Kane shrugs negligently as if it's no great matter either way. 'We don't know.'

'What do you mean, you don't know?' I demand. 'She won't tell you?'

'She's been diagnosed with dissociative amnesia.'

'What does "dissociative" mean?' Rosana pulls her legs onto the couch and hugs them to her chest.

Kane plays with his wedding band, spinning it around his finger. It's not like him to fidget. Long ago, yes, but not since we reconnected.

'While she was gone, it's believed she had no memory of her life before. Now she knows who she is and has regained most of her memories, but she's been living as someone else and has no memory of that time.'

Ramin straightens. 'So, she's brain-damaged.'

Kane eviscerates his brother with a piercing sidelong glare. 'Eloquent, as usual, Ramin. We're discussing a psychological condition that affects a person's autobiographical memory, usually brought on by trauma.'

'Well, that explanation came straight out of a doctor's mouth,' Ramin drawls. 'So, her brain is fine; she's just crazy. Got it.'

'Ramin.' There is warning in my tone.

'What?'

Rosana frowns. 'I'm not sure I understand. Something happened to Lily that was so terrible her mind made her forget you and your life together . . . ? Why did you think she was dead without a body?'

Kane's expression turns savage.

'Sorry,' she says swiftly. 'I didn't mean it to come out like that.'

He takes a moment to rein in his temper before addressing his sister. 'It's fine, Rosie. Lily took her sailboat out and didn't return. The day started out beautiful but was forecast to turn squally in the afternoon, and it did. The Coast Guard launched an exhaustive search that lasted for days, and eventually, they found debris, but that's all. After a lengthy review, they officially declared her lost at sea.'

'Wow. Being stranded out in the ocean during a storm . . .' Rosana shudders. 'Terrifying. Does she remember it?'

'Her most recent memory, before regaining consciousness a couple of weeks ago, happened several days before she went missing.' He pauses. 'While we were still dating.'

Amy leans forward. 'She doesn't remember *marrying* you? She doesn't know she's your wife?'

'She does now, but she doesn't remember the particulars.'

'Wow,' Rosana repeats. 'How crazy is all this?'

'It's insane.' Ramin throws himself back into the black leather sofa and crosses one leg atop the opposite knee. 'One of the craziest things I've ever heard.'

I mentally sort out the timeline he's given us. 'She disappeared days after you were married?'

'Yes.' With every word he's spoken, he's grown harder and more unreachable.

'Why weren't you with her?' Amy asks.

'I had classes all day, then practice. It wasn't unusual for her to take the boat out by herself. She sailed often.'

'Oh, that breaks my heart!' Rosana cries. 'You'd just married. You must have been so happy, and then she was gone. It's all so sad, Kane. I'm sorry you went through that! Sorry you both went through that.'

'Thank you,' he says quietly. 'I'm sorry, too.'

I'm speechless, shocked that we should have something so bizarre happen to both of us – a missing spouse.

He continues. 'It's possible therapy can help with accessing her memories, or they might naturally resurface with time . . . but limiting any stress or strain will be paramount to her healing. I'm asking you to please minimize any friction while she recovers.'

'That's why you called us all here?' Darius blinks, incredulous. 'You're worried about protecting *her*? What about protecting your family? Or at the very least Baharan?'

'My thoughts exactly,' Ramin says with a brisk nod. 'Do you have a prenup? If not, we need to discuss a postnup.'

'Stop. All of you.' I'm vibrating with nerves, and the penthouse's ambiance feeds them. 'You said Lily sailed a lot . . . Did she own the boat?'

His gaze is laser-focused on my face. 'Yes, it was hers.'

'Not that one has anything to do with the other, but . . . was she wealthy?'

Silence descends so completely the library becomes a tomb. The building creaks as it shifts in the wind, a sound I've learned to ignore, but somehow, it's painfully jarring today.

His answer is brusque. 'Extremely. Haven't any of you wondered how Baharan became what it is today?'

Aside from Kane, every person in the room has stiffened into stone. Amy recovers first, tipping her glass up to gulp the last of her drink.

'Oh, wow!' Rosana breathes.

'We have investors,' I argue as if anything I could say would change the facts. '*I* invested. Ryan said you'd been cultivating business contacts all through college . . .'

But I never asked. I didn't care where he got the money. I just wanted Baharan back. I wanted as much of what Paul took from me as I could get. I sold my soul for it.

Kane gives a curt shake of his head. 'Lily is the foundation for Baharan, period.'

And Kane owns fifty-one percent of the shares, which means Lily, as his wife, has her hands firmly around the company's throat.

The room tilts. I grasp the arms of my chair. No one else has sacrificed what I have for the company, and no one ever will. They don't have it in them. They don't deserve it.

'This just gets better and better,' Ramin mutters.

Kane turns to him. 'To answer your questions, Ramin: no, there are no agreements between Lily and me, and there will never be. She added me as a manager of her LLC, which held her assets, and that LLC holds the shares for Baharan. The company exists because of her; she's entitled to a stake in it.'

Ramin laughs. 'After all this time, does she even *want* to be married to you? Maybe she just wants her money back and not you?'

Rosana shakes her head violently. 'You're seriously a dick sometimes, you know that?'

'Yes, actually, I do.'

I'm so sick to my stomach that I fear the burning gin and vermouth are likely to come up. Lily has reached up from a watery grave to seize both my son and my life's work. I can't have it. I won't.

'*Sorry I'm late.*'

We're all taken aback by the sound of an unfamiliar and startlingly high voice. It's breathy, unmistakably sexy and unnervingly girlish.

Kane is instantly on his feet. Darius and Ramin follow suit, delayed by surprise. Witte, already standing, merely turns his head.

My eldest stares at his wife with such violent lust I fear for him. And for all of us. She has him spellbound. His siblings are all arrested with astonishment. Amy licks the inside of her glass.

My gaze returns to the lithe figure striding into the room, rising from the bloodred toenails up to the sleek cap of glossy black hair. Her arms and shoulders are bare, the skin like flawless marble. Not a freckle or wrinkle mars that perfect flesh.

Her long, slim body is encased in black velvet, silk and lace. And she blooms like her namesake under the heat of my son's ferocious regard.

All the tensity in the penthouse compresses into the library. I reach for my throat, massaging it with my fingers to ease the constriction.

Lily isn't what I expected, especially considering how often I've studied her photo. Especially knowing my son as I do. He's different now, but he was once so like his father. And like Paul, Kane would've been drawn to a woman of warmth and tenderness. I'm not that woman any longer.

Neither is Lily.

18

Lily

The man I once met on the beach in Greenwich and the man you are now are not the same. That was apparent the moment I woke in the hospital. You've become very different. Powerful. You radiate authority. You answer to no one. Your home soars above the rest of the planet's population, crowning a tower that is the tallest residential building on earth.

You are the nexus of your world.

I enter the room casually as if I haven't been eavesdropping since shortly after you began this family meeting.

The library is flanked by black built-ins filled with colorful volumes and massive windows at either end, one with a view of Central Park and the other with the spire of the Empire State Building. As I walk to you, I take in the fireplace edged in Calacatta marble and crowned with a large photo of a woman's pale, slender back. An extraordinary tattoo begins at her hip and rises to her shoulder, a phoenix rising from flames. There are Blacklist lilies here, too, and they pair beautifully with the glossy bookcases.

It's astonishing what you've accomplished in so little time, not that I didn't expect it from you. You had a burning ambition, an unyielding drive for *more*. I've always known you were capable of forging empires. You exceed even that vision by building a mansion in the sky.

It seems we were both meant to rise from Lily's ashes.

You stand unmoving and eerily beautiful, like a statue

carved by an infatuated artist. A frisson of awareness moves through me. You are one of those men who exudes sex and ferocity from every pore. Your animal attraction is dark, hungry and too virile ever to be tamed. Your gaze is molten. It slides over me, touching me everywhere.

The lust between us snaps into stinging awareness like the flick of a whip.

I hate living as we have been, speaking to each other through Witte. You're a stranger who avoids me, and without you, I'm unmoored.

Your family is silent as I close the distance between us. Standing apart from the others, you bring to mind a lion in a gladiator's ring, facing off against united challengers. Witte serves as the referee and Rosana the spectator. Now I've come to stand at your side.

Who manufactured the myth of family being those who will love and protect you at any cost? Why are we told to forgive toxic behavior only because of genetics? Regardless, you don't have to fight this, or any, battle alone anymore.

And in myriad ways, I'm more dangerous than you are.

I don't know how or why you've ended up back in the nest with these vipers, but they'll have to get through me to sink their fangs into you.

Placing my palm over your heart, I tip my head up and offer my lips.

Your left hand catches me possessively by the hip; your right cups my jaw with your fingertips at my nape. You exert gentle pressure to tilt my head to where you want it, then pause, your gaze sliding provocatively over my face. I'm breathless. The cherished dream of being in your arms with you looking at me just this way is coming true.

'As always,' you murmur, your smoky voice pitched low, 'you're worth the wait.'

86

Your scent goes to my head, as do your words, stirring my blood and breaking my heart anew. Your thumb caresses my jaw, and then you lower your mouth without haste as if you savor every kiss after so long apart.

It's a superior performance, striking all the right notes. Familiarity. Affection. Passion. Our audience will think we're so lucky and happy to be reunited. You're such an accomplished actor; I must remind myself it's all fake.

Your lips brush against mine. The chasteness contrasts sharply with the erotic demand pulsing off your big body, battering my senses like storm surge against the shore. You begin to pull back, and fury flares within me because it's not enough. My craving hollows me. And the role you're playing for your family's benefit makes me want you all the more.

Desperate for a taste of you, I flick my tongue across your full bottom lip. Your heart skips beneath my palm. It's the engine that drives the honed machine of your body, and I can make it race. I'm not opposed to taking what I can get. Isn't that why I'm here?

I'm unsteady when I turn to face the room. Inflamed.

You drape your arm across my shoulders, your hand settling above my collarbone. Your fingers curl lightly around my throat, and your thumb strokes up and down my nape. The caress dissolves my pretense of composure. I feel naked and vulnerable. My pulse flutters beneath your fingertips, betraying me.

I'll have to grow stronger if I'm to maintain this charade over time. Then again, maybe you're just waiting for me to recover, and then we'll be finished.

Only seconds have passed since I entered, and we embraced, but I am profoundly changed.

'Hello, everyone. I'm Lily.'

Witte, so somber and watchful, moves to pull out a chair for me.

'I won't be staying, Witte.' I soften the refusal with a quick smile.

I like him. His model good looks are deceiving; there's clearly a great deal of depth to him. He has cop's eyes, sharp and vigilant. And it says a great deal that a man like him would choose to build his life around yours.

You make quick work of the introductions, affording me time to study all the key players. Rosana is curled into herself on one end of a black leather sofa, studying me with wide blue eyes. She is lovely and curious about me in the guileless way of one who's experienced too little heartache. Amy sits on the opposite couch, her crossed leg swinging in an agitated rhythm. My attention lingers on her for a moment. She can't hold my gaze and shifts uncomfortably under my regard. She looks to her husband and then to Aliyah. Her gaze skitters over you, but I see her mind in that brief second; she hungers for you as I do.

Your brothers are on their feet, so alike one another and so unlike you. Darius, in his gray suit, is sullen – almost defiant. Ramin smirks and projects cockiness. They are both darkly handsome, yet they fade next to you, diminished by your presence.

Rosana greets me with a tentative hug. Her smile, however, is welcoming. Darius and Amy give me assessing perusals when offering dry, firm handshakes. I pull Amy to me, wrapping her into a warm embrace. I stroke her back soothingly, our linked hands trapped between us. I know her torment and sympathize. She's stiff at the outset, and then she hugs me back with the fierceness of a creature desperate for comfort and affection.

Before I release her, I whisper in her ear, 'Frank says you came to visit me often. I'd love for us to make that a habit.'

Her face is flushed pink when I turn to Ramin. His handshake is a seduction, his thumb stroking the back of my hand, his fingertips caressing my palm as I pull away. He's clearly the scamp, constantly testing boundaries to see how firm they are. The youngest son who can't find his place, overwhelmed by his elder siblings and neglected in favor of his sister, the baby.

'Lily.' Your mother finally stands, so I turn my attention to her. She wears cream-colored slacks and a sweater in a matching hue, one shoulder exposed by its slouchy fit. Her hair is the color of wheat, but her brows and irises are dark, the gaze calculating. 'You've been through quite an ordeal. Please sit.'

There's no chance I'll stay. Lingering would be far less effective than leaving an impression.

With a soft hum of denial, I shake my head. She heard me decline a seat earlier yet couldn't resist attempting a power play in which she invites me to settle into my own home as if she is mistress here instead of your wife. The Lily who hangs on your wall would be charming and gracious. She would have had light refreshments at the ready, music playing softly and unobtrusively in the background, and small gifts for everyone.

But I'm not your first wife, and this dream life shimmers on the verge of a nightmare.

'It's never a good idea to intrude when people are talking about you,' I tell her, holding her gaze. 'Doing so leads to the most awkward conversations.'

'You've already intruded,' she says pleasantly.

'I've interceded,' I correct with a wide smile. Words are weapons; it's always essential to use precisely the right one. 'And now that I've met everyone, I'll make my excuses and go lie down for a bit before dinner.'

Your grip on my throat tightens, and tiny, chilled shivers ripple throughout my body. My nipples harden, and your gaze drops along with an octave in your voice. 'Has the stylist left?'

'Yes, but she'll be back with armloads of bags in a few

hours.' Looking up at you, I linger a moment, willing you to kiss me again.

'Stylist?' Aliyah asks sharply.

My smile returns as I note her narrowed gaze. She's worried about me spending your money; she can't help herself. 'Kane kept all my things. Everything. Not in storage but hung in the closet and tucked into drawers. It's so romantic and heart-breaking at the same time. Still, I needed a few things.'

You capture my chin in your fingers and turn my head back to you, your lips claiming mine before I realize your intent. Whether it's for our spectators or me, I don't care. This time there's pressure, heat and the soft caress of your tongue along the seam of my lips. My soul sighs with pleasure at being united with its mate.

'You're welcome to join me,' I whisper as we separate.

Your eyes are stormy when I wipe my lipstick from your bottom lip with my thumb; I glance at your mother as I do so because she's the one to watch.

She's watching me, too.

She, and the other members of your family, are eclipsed by your shadow. Things that crawl around in the shadows can never be trusted.

'Let's plan for dinner,' I say to the room at large. 'I look forward to getting to know all of you.'

Your expression is unreadable.

I'm starved for you. The sensation of having you so close feels almost desperate. Or maybe I'm nervy after meeting your family, new participants in this treacherous game. Perhaps it's a little of both.

I feel your steady gaze on my back as I walk away and hear a weighted silence in my absence.

19

Amy

I crisscross my arms and legs to occupy as little space as possible, wedged as I am between Ramin and Darius on the back seat of a hired town car. Both men spread their legs wide, taking up all the legroom. Each is silent, head turned toward their respective window.

Had I really thought I could overshadow Lily simply by changing my hair color and wearing darker clothes? The very idea is laughable now, although the lump in my throat and burning eyes make me feel like I'm about to cry.

I can still feel her nails pressing firmly into my neck as she held me trapped against her. She is slim and delicate in appearance, but that hand was like a claw, and menace laced her high, girlish voice. Fear twisted my guts. I can still smell her perfume – *her*. I hugged her back in submission. And when she pulled away, I resisted the urge to press my lips to hers as Kane had done, to see if they were as pillowy soft as they looked.

An anxious laugh gets trapped in my throat. Kane's ability to intimidate me is nothing next to hers.

'Kane will have his hands full with that one,' Ramin says cheerfully. 'She's a smoke show.'

'Too thin,' Darius mutters, and I shoot him a grateful glance.

'Model-thin,' Ramin corrects. 'I guarantee she photographs like a dream. We need to get her on board with ECRA+.

Create an ad campaign around her and use her on some of the packaging.'

Darius glances at his brother with the same incredulity I feel. 'You can't be serious.'

'She's got us by the balls. Might as well put her to work and get her invested in the company's success.'

My hands fist, my nails digging into my palms. Kane's bitch makes a ten-minute appearance, and Ramin wants to plaster her face on the venture expected to take Baharan to new heights? Using my company, my hard fucking work, to make her the envy and inspiration of women everywhere?

No way. *No. Fucking. Way.*

'Not the smartest move,' I say tightly. 'She's not right in the head.'

'No shit,' my husband agrees.

'I'm talking about using her picture,' Ramin drawls, 'not sending her on an international speaking tour.'

'We don't even know what the state of their relationship is,' I argue.

'Yeah, we do.' He leers. 'You saw them together. You saw *her*. She's the mold every other woman has had to fill. Guaranteed, he's already nailed her against every flat surface in the penthouse. Multiple times.'

I squeeze my eyes shut against the flood of unwelcome mental images, but that only makes them worse. I stare straight ahead instead, watching the crazed weaving of cars and cabs in the lanes in front of us. The ice in my stomach has melted, replaced by boiling fury. I imagine throwing acid into Lily's face and watching it melt in slabs of smoking flesh and rivulets of blood and crimson lipstick.

I want to picture her screaming and crying, horrified by the loss of that face Kane worships, but the imagined Lily in my mind just stares at me, her eyes a malevolent green in the deep sockets devoid of eyelids. Then she lunges at me with super-human speed . . .

I jolt upright in the back seat, my heart pounding.

'He's been trying to scratch that itch for a long time,' Darius says, patting my knee absently as if that will soothe me. 'You remember how he was in his teens, Ramin, always finessing his way into some girl's panties, then moving on to the next. This one happened to have money he wanted to get his hands on, but he doesn't need her for that anymore. Soon enough, he'll get bored with her pussy and switch hers out for someone else's. It's about the conquest for him.'

'Brother, we don't want him to get bored. Her, either. How'd he put it? She's the foundation of Baharan. We need those two to stay together. Kane will make it work with her if she's making him and the company look good. If she's making him money, he'll definitely keep her around.' Ramin squeezes the bare skin of my knee. 'You got that flask on you? I could use a drink.'

I drop my purse in his lap.

'Thanks, babe.' He starts rifling.

I want to ask him why he's never suggested me for ECRA+. And I hate my husband for not thinking of it. I dig deep for the courage to suggest myself as a model, but the possibility of being laughed at is unbearable.

Pulling down the hem of my dress, I think about Lily's outfit. I felt so confident when I entered the library, so sure I'd picked just the right balance between Aliyah and Lily. When I saw my mother-in-law, I'd felt even better about my choice, knowing I looked younger and classier. Then Lily walked in wearing black silk slacks and a black corset top with lace on the boning and black velvet bra cups. Overtly sexy. Casually elegant. Completely confident. The chic bob, smoky eyes and bright red mouth were sassy bows on the total package.

Kane had locked in on her, the way he does with any woman who looks like her, but there'd been something else in his eyes. A spark instead of the usual lifelessness. Something dark and hot. It was either lust so fierce he's a slave to it, or rage.

Our driver slams on the brakes, jerking us forward. He tosses a quick apology even as he lays on the horn, cursing under his breath. The traffic is a total snarl, with cars changing lanes without signaling, hoping to find a way through faster than everyone else.

Years of Lily's life have been lost to her, yet there's no timid hesitation, no loss of purpose or control, no wariness. Since I crossed paths with Kane, I haven't fared so well. I somehow wandered into a funhouse, and the life reflected at me is exactly what I'd always dreamed of but distorted. I'm married to a gorgeous, successful sex machine with a close-knit family. My business is changing lives. I have an epic home, and I can buy anything my heart desires. But it's all wrong. I haven't blossomed like Lily; I've shriveled into nothing. I'm not bold. I have no power. Even my body isn't my own.

How did Lily come out of a void with everything while I live a dream and have nothing?

Ramin tosses his head back to take a drink. When he lowers his arm, I grab the flask and take a big swallow. I offer it to Darius.

'It's the middle of the damn day!' he snaps.

Shrugging, I take another drink.

I feel like chopping off my hair. Darkening my eye shadow. Ripping the slit at my hem to expose more thigh. I once used to sail through life the way Lily does, feeling beautiful and sexy and in command. She walked right up to Kane, put her hands on him and faced him head-on when he put his hands on her. No fear, no hesitation.

I don't know what I'd expected to see. Abstractly, I must have assumed he'd been different with Lily. Open instead of closed off. Tender and kind. Playful. But maybe that's what love looks like on Kane. Intense and searing and terrifying.

'You two won't even consider that maybe they actually love each other.' My voice is hoarse, my chest tight. Kane has never been mine, and I don't even like him, yet the thought of him in love with someone else is excruciating.

Ramin shrugs. 'Wouldn't make a difference either way.'

No. Kane can't have everything. The beautiful wife, the penthouse, the high-valuation company on the verge of explosive growth.

The town car rocks gently as the taxi behind us taps the bumper. Our driver flips the bird through the gap in the two front seats.

How is Lily so fucking fierce? How could she approach Kane like she hadn't a care in the world while he looked at her like he wanted to rip into her jugular with his teeth? And the way he pulled her to him, the dominance and possession . . . She wasn't cowed by that at all, while the rest of the women Kane screwed and screwed over were all left reeling. First blissful, then hopeful, then confused, then diminished.

Is that what he's looked for all this time, above and beyond the physical resemblance? That taunting sexuality? The dauntless confidence? Had he seen those qualities in me when we met?

I remember Erika in that sleek red dress, her shoulders back and her chin high. She'd known how desirable she was when she'd headed right toward him.

She's tried to call me since, but I always send her to voicemail. It's not me she wants to talk to; it's Kane, who never gives out his personal number – the only private way to reach him. Everything else goes through his admin at work or Witte.

I've been in Erika's shoes. I know she's not so confident now and will never be to the same extent again.

'Lily will have her hands full, too,' I think aloud. 'Your brother's not a college kid scraping by with athletic scholarships and bartending anymore. Kane was manageable when she was rich, and he was poor.'

'Still, she's settled right in.' Ramin catches my eye and winks as if we share some secret. 'She jumped straight into spending money, filling her closet, ordering Witte around and putting Mother in her place.'

The pleasure of watching those two women sharpen their claws fades now. Aliyah has already left scars on me after years of swipes and barbed pleasantries. Lily handled her deftly and looked like she wouldn't think twice about escalating into all-out war.

'Happy wife, happy life.' Darius reaches for my hand as if our marriage somehow meets that criterion. I squeeze as hard as I can, just for a moment, but it feels good to hurt him a little.

I remember the way Kane watched Lily when she entered. That glowing stare, like a molten blade straight out of the forge. Six years as a widower fucking anyone he wanted to, blowing through money any way he pleased. Now he's got a high-maintenance and high-handed wife to keep happy. It'll keep him busy for a while, at least, while I get my shit together.

Now I know what's been missing from my plans – *me*. It's time to turn those carnival mirrors around to face the Armand family. Then they'll see what I see when I look at them.

Maybe then they'll know why I have to destroy them all.

20

Witte

With gloved hands, I set the warming stone with the supper plate atop it on the place mat I've arranged on Mr Black's desk. A note from Lily on monogrammed stationery is lying on the leather blotter. His name is written in her bold, feminine handwriting, the letters slanting to the left. Her signature is an upright oversized *L*, curled at the top and bottom, with the other letters leaning into it. There is no message, just the imprint of her lips in her signature dramatic red lipstick. The silver-framed photo of her lies facedown beside it.

My employer once again takes his meal alone in his office. His wife attempted to refuse dinner, but I was able to coax her to eat a quickly made soup she helped prepare.

I've noticed Lily is a competent woman regarding many things, both great and small. She reminds me of my daughter in numerous ways – the beauty and poise, the self-command. And the toughness and proficiency that come from being raised by a mother who is more child than parent. I don't know if that is the case with Lily because I don't know how much of her life she's spent orphaned. Perhaps she's simply had to parent herself.

She remains a mystery to me, as she does to the man she married. She's a woman who prefers to listen than to speak, especially about herself, so the details she shared with him long ago were scant, and he – worried about reopening old wounds – questioned little.

'How is she?' Mr Black stands silhouetted against the sparkling Manhattan skyline, his gaze fixed outward through the window, staring sightlessly. The city lights below illuminate the night sky to an ashen grey. He is utterly still, yet it *feels* like he's tearing the room apart. His inner turmoil never shows, but I hear phantom sounds of glass shattering and wood splintering. Howls of rage and self-inflicted agony.

Like lightning, his wife has charged the penthouse and jolted Mr Black out of his ennui. In so short a time, she's become vital to the household. I cannot imagine returning to our lives as they were before, just as I can't imagine the removal of her portrait from my employer's bedroom. It's a fixture, something that has simply always been. Her presence in the penthouse feels the same; she is corporeal now, but she has always been here.

'She seems unruffled by the questioning,' I answer casually, although I'm concerned. The detectives dropped by unannounced to speak with her further, despite having already interviewed her while she underwent physical therapy in hospital. On both occasions, she waved off the suggestion of legal counsel, saying it was unnecessary. 'I overheard laughter among them, and when the detectives left, they appeared to be in a good mood.'

'She got to them,' he says, sounding weary. 'She charmed and dazzled them. It's what she does, and she's very, very good at it. You've seen her in action.'

'I beg your pardon?'

Looking over his shoulder, my employer laughs softly. 'She's taken a different tack with you, Witte, but you're just as bowled over as they are.'

I don't know whether I should be offended. 'Sir?'

'One moment she's a stranger, the next you love her.' He turns his back to me again. 'There are people who can light up a room. Her gift is to take all the light with her when she leaves.'

Abruptly, I comprehend how insightful his statement is. It isn't simply Mrs Black's charisma that's remarkable. It's how reluctant one is to separate from her and how acutely one misses her when she's absent.

He walks over to the brass cocktail trolley. Lifting the cut-crystal decanter, he pulls out the stopper and pours two fingers of Macallan Fine and Rare. He holds the whiskey up in silent offer.

'No, thank you, sir.' I wait a beat, then, 'I've taken the liberty of giving Mrs Black one of the tablets so she can amuse and edify herself.'

Neither one of them has discussed providing her with a mobile. Perhaps Mr Black just hasn't thought of it. Why his wife hasn't expressed a desire to connect with old friends is more curious.

'That's fine,' he tells me. 'She knows to behave.'

I frown at his back, having no idea what he means. It's not my place to question him, though. To advise, yes, but never to pry.

He collects his glass and moves to the desk, sinking into the chair with practised grace. We'd worked on that poise for months when I saw how he dropped into seats like a bag of rocks. To sit elegantly is second nature to him now.

While Mr Black is drinking deeply, his gaze sees something I cannot.

By chance, I spied him in their shared sitting room last night, his palms and forehead pressed against the door leading through Lily's wardrobe into her bedroom. I understand his captivation. His wife is beguiling and lovely, a rival for the young Elizabeth Taylor, Vivien Leigh or Hedy Lamarr – classic, timeless beauties with sultry sensuality and girlish smiles.

I suspect he watches her sleep some nights; a chair in the corner of her room has been repositioned to face the bed. The altered placement has become apparent only since she awakened. He was reluctant to enter her room while she was comatose, as if he feared being present when consciousness returned to her. After her reaction to seeing him on the street, his caution was thoughtful.

His longing is truly a horrible thing. Or is it guilt? The woman whose memory has haunted him waits, yet he denies them both. She is not the woman we found crossing the street, a woman who ran from him with terror whitening her face. The Lily who shares the master suite would welcome him with open arms. She tells him so with her eyes, the searing green almost unworldly. She goads him with her tantalizing smiles and provocative messages. Sexual tension seethes when they are in proximity to each other, evident to all. I've scolded the maids for whispering about it, and Mr Black's family was put on notice by its strength.

I clear my throat to ease the tightness. Love heals some; for others, it's an agony. 'You could be a comfort to each other,' I suggest, 'if you went to her.'

'Lily was never a comfort, Witte. Joy, yes. Ecstasy. Every moment with her was euphoric, but under the rush, I know she's an addiction that's eating me alive. I'll always need another fix, and I'll accept any conditions to get it.'

I'm cognizant that a man in the grip of obsession – especially with a woman – is capable of anything. My employer is a man who was denied love his entire life until he met Lily. He was cursed with a father who abandoned him to poverty, a mother who abandoned him to pacify her second husband, and siblings twisted by jealousy. Lily's love is the rarest, most precious of treasures to him. But she ran when she saw him. Why? I can't stop asking myself that question.

The truth lies within the seven days before she disappeared, a week in which they married, and Mr Black became entitled to her fortune upon her passing.

He sips from his glass, his gaze on her lip print.

It's a quiet dismissal, but my feet won't move. His inaction suspends us like insects in amber. It can't go on indefinitely. 'You should know she's eating less with every meal. It was an effort to convince her to have a bowl of soup before retiring.'

His gaze sharpens with alarm and finds me. 'She won't heal if she doesn't eat.'

'She might try if you'd join her.'

'No.'

His obstinacy goads me to ask, 'Are you punishing her or yourself?'

'Damn it. She was running when I found her! I won't force myself on her. If she wants me, she knows where I am.'

My breath catches sharply. Mr Black has never mentioned her reaction when she saw him, either to her doctors or to me – until now.

Taken aback and worried, I stare at him. I'm aware that anger is one of the stages of grief and that sometimes the anger is directed at the deceased for leaving their loved ones in such pain. But distorting the manner of her disappearance into a personal rejection is unhealthy. 'You mustn't blame her.'

'Why not?' His eyes are cold and distant.

'It would be unfair.'

'Fair? Was it fair for her to shape me into a man capable of building this life for us, then leave me to live it alone? If you don't think I'm being fair to her, that I should absolve her from responsibility for her choices, well . . . I can't.'

He so rarely speaks of his wife. There is so much I don't know. About her and the young man my employer once was when he was with her.

'I met her at the beach house in Greenwich,' he says, unprovoked, his tone strangely casual, as if he's divorced himself from the sentiment of the memory. 'She was throwing a party and invited me because she was dating Ryan. Did I ever tell you that? That she was his before she was mine?'

I nod. 'Yes, you mentioned it.'

'I didn't want to travel that far, but since I was a business major with a concentration in consulting, Ryan convinced me it was a good opportunity to meet people who might come in handy in the future. I'll never forget hopping out of the rideshare I'd taken from the train station and seeing half a dozen valets scrambling to park millions of dollars' worth of luxury cars. I never thought I'd meet anyone who lived like that, who had friends who could afford cars like that. It was like something out of a movie.'

There can be no secrets if I'm to perform my job effectively, no skeletons. I cannot manage the household if there is any member of it who surprises me. Thus far, everything about Lily Black has been a revelation, the most shocking of which is that she is the source of Mr Black's fortune.

He stands again, restless, and resumes his place in front of the window. 'The weather was turning. I still remember the sky. Black as pitch. I found her dancing on the beach, her long hair whipping in the wind. She looked like a pagan goddess summoning the storm. Before I even saw her face, I knew I had to have her.'

I lost her where I found her.

'She was so far out of my league, Witte, and she was Ryan's girlfriend. I knew the right thing to do was stay away from her, but she singled me out. Within minutes of meeting her, we were walking arm and arm down the windy beach, and she was filling my head with wild thoughts. It was like a fever dream. The sexiest, most gorgeous woman I'd ever seen somehow knew everything about me – my family situation, that my father had left and destroyed Baharan. With just a few words, she flipped my world on its head. By the time she finished, she had me thinking of Baharan as my birthright. I left her house that day possessed by an entirely new ambition. I wanted that beach house and those luxury cars. I wanted Baharan. Most of all, I wanted *her*. More than I'd ever wanted anything.'

Mr Black shoves a hand in his pocket and takes another slow sip. He rolls the alcohol in his mouth, then swallows hard. 'In the days that followed, she called me. Met with me. She not only had the vision, but she also had the plan. She was my Svengali, my Pygmalion. A sorceress who waved her hand and transformed my entire existence.'

'She recognized your potential,' I say, although that's such a practical word for my employer's incendiary magnetism. I had initially met with him out of politeness to reject his offer of employment in person because his request had been so earnest, but I left him having accepted the position. He has a gift for getting what he wants and making others feel gratified to give in to him.

'She's a muse, Witte, a kingmaker – although the uninspired would call her an angel investor. Whatever you choose to call it, she has an uncanny ability to peer into strangers and find the ones she can sculpt into titans. I selfishly wanted to be the only one, but there were others. It's simply who she is and what she does.'

He falls silent, but the sensation of turbulence and destruction in the room rises to a fevered pitch. The tower creaks at just that moment, and it seems as if the forces it fights against come from within, not without.

'You doubt she loves you?' I ask quietly.

'Love?' He glances over his shoulder at me, then turns to

face me with a shrug. 'We're talking about fairness, Witte, not love.'

'I don't see how you'll attain what you want without speaking to her.'

'*She* doesn't have an explanation or answers!' he bites out. 'I don't know how to treat her, how even to *approach* her. She's not herself, let alone the woman I married.'

'And you aren't the man she married,' I argue. 'You'll have to rediscover each other, perhaps fall in love all over again as different people. With love, the trust will follow, and through trust, you'll get the answers.'

His eyes are wild. 'You assume she wants me and not Baharan or the money.'

The suggestion startles me. There seems to be no logic to his torment.

'I told you, her knowledge of Baharan was bizarre. And it went deep. She knew things I didn't. She knew my mother held the rights to chemical patents and even the damned logo. Trust me, Witte. Baharan was in Lily's sights from the beginning.'

'What would she want with a pharmaceutical company, especially one with an unfortunate history?'

'That's the least pressing question I have. Our wedding was a total surprise to me. I came home as usual, and she had a justice of the peace, neighbours as witnesses and a tuxedo waiting. She hid the papers adding me to her LLC and bank accounts among the marriage documents, so I signed them unknowingly. Then she sailed into a forecast storm days later. Think about all of that, Witte. Think about what that suggests. I haven't been able to stop thinking about it for six years.'

'I . . .' I'm speechless.

'Exactly,' he says stonily. 'She owes me answers, but I can't and won't badger her for them and cause her any further stress. She knows me better than anyone. She knows what I need and where I am. I can only wait.'

There is so much fear and pain entwined with their love. Whether they acknowledge it or are conscious of it, their instincts are aware of the danger.

What was it doing, or would it do, to Lily?

'I could kill her for making me need her this way,' he whispers, staring into his glass as if he'll find something there.

His confession chills me.

Is greed a factor, that ravenous monster? Or is her incredible beauty feeding jealousy and the all-consuming desire to possess? Perhaps it's a little of both. Maybe her money was consolation for everything he couldn't have from her.

It tears at me to have these doubts.

Mr Black finishes his drink and glances at the cocktail trolley. Silently, I hold out my hand for his glass. He sets it in my outstretched palm with his brow arched mockingly. I'm relieved to have deterred him from drinking more. He is already too volatile and his wife too vulnerable.

'You should eat,' I tell him.

Turning his back to me, my employer returns to the window. 'Enjoy your evening, Witte. I won't be needing you any further tonight.'

As I leave the room, my watch signals an incoming text.

I pull out my mobile as I walk towards the kitchen.

ID confirmed Midtown West. Continuing canvass.

Pausing on the living room threshold, I debate returning to my employer's office and sharing the update.

The address on Mrs Black's counterfeit identification was discovered to be a bodega in Gramercy. Days were spent canvassing the area while the facial recognition search was narrowed to cameras on and around the Crossfire Building where Baharan is headquartered, and she was discovered. It's been learned that Lily Black had been passing the building regularly, and once she was identified, it was possible to follow her route.

Clandestine inquiries have now led to someone who recognized her in a photo. Eventually, we'll know where and how she's been living, hopefully opening new avenues of investigation. The going is slow because discretion is paramount. It is always an exercise in patience when a search for buried secrets requires the search itself also to be a secret.

I wonder if answers gleaned through investigation will finally bring peace to Mr Black. I fear only Lily's confessions will soothe him.

Making sense of the confounding nature of her return is difficult and now complicated by questions regarding how – and perhaps why – she left in the first place. The fear I witnessed on her face, the shocked recognition and her uttering of his name are still unexplained. There's no question the sight of him filled her with terror and caused her to flee, heedless of the danger. Why then would she prowl the environs of the Crossfire with regularity, chancing discovery on a near-daily basis?

Ultimately, I slide my mobile back into my pocket and carry on. Tomorrow will be soon enough to discuss the latest with my employer. He has enough demons to wrestle tonight.

21

Lily

There's a discreet knock at my bedroom door, which I leave ajar as an invitation that has yet to be accepted. The cadence of the rapping knuckles tells me it still isn't you.

Night has fallen on the other side of my enormous bedroom windows, turning Manhattan's concrete forest into a blanket of stars. I've lost track of the days since I was released from the hospital, but separation from you makes it feel like an eternity has passed.

'Yes, Witte?' I exit the cavernous closet. I've spent a small fortune on clothes and accessories, yet even with all of Lily's garments, handbags and shoes – it's a painful convenience that you've held on to everything – there are racks upon racks and shelves upon shelves that are empty.

Witte waits in the doorway, the very definition of debonair. His remarkable sophistication has rubbed off on you over the years of his employment, helping to create a man who can move in all social circles. Still, your rough edges haven't been completely polished away. You're still a dangerous man; you are simply dangerous in different ways than before.

'You have an outing tomorrow morning, leaving at ten to meet with your doctors. Mr. Black will be accompanying you.'

'Calling a trip to the doctor an "outing" makes it sound so much more charming. A savvy word choice, Witte.'

His mustache twitches with a suppressed smile. 'Thank you.'

I have to make small talk and keep it light, or I'll cry. It's agonizing that we can't pass such everyday information to one another directly, as if you can't tolerate even a second in my presence.

Still, I am elated to hear we'll spend time together tomorrow. We've lived together for weeks now, circling each other within the penthouse and managing to never be in the same space at the same time – except when you visit me in the dead of night, slipping into my bedroom to watch me feign sleep. As if you could ever be near me without my body awakening with tingling awareness.

I've suffered, wracked with need, the tips of my breasts hard and aching, the cleft between my legs wet and throbbing. It's an instinctive reaction I can't control. My body is sharply aware when you're near, and it readies itself to be mounted and ridden, ravished and pleasured. Your stealthy presence is the most devious torture I've ever been subjected to, and I crave it. Compelled to lie there motionless, I can only regulate my breathing while your gaze covets my body.

'Will you be taking supper in the sitting room this evening?' Witte asks, returning me to the moment.

My arms cross. The penthouse is perfectly temperate, but I'm suddenly chilled. 'Is Kane having dinner in his office again?'

Witte nods. 'Mr. Black sends his regrets, but he has a great deal of work to accomplish.'

'Of course he does.' I smile thinly. 'Have you eaten?'

'Not yet. Once I've arranged your meal, I'll enjoy mine.'

'How about we enjoy ours together? In the kitchen, unless you prefer somewhere else.'

If he has any adverse reaction to my suggestion, it's not apparent. 'That would be a pleasure. In ten minutes?'

'Perfect.' I watch as he pivots neatly and disappears, leaving me an unhindered view of my reflection in the mirrored hall-way where he once stood. But it isn't me I see. The hair is too long, a sleek curtain of ink that falls below the waist. The face is subtly different. The jaw more angular, the cheekbones more sculpted, the eyes not so deeply set. She smiles.

I blink, and she's gone. There is only me.

Touching my hair, I regret its chin-grazing length. The bob is stylish, but it ages me. Of course, the actual passing of time has helped with that, too.

I head back into the closet for something to pull on over the tiered black maxi dress I'm wearing. My gaze roams over the drawers filled with undergarments, lingerie and pajamas. I don't know if you saved Lily's intimates somewhere else. Everything I've worn and have yet to wear is new, freshly laundered and monogrammed with *LRB*. The assortment is luxurious and decadent, less about modesty and more about provocation. You've amassed the collection over time, and the embroidered initials prove they were purchased for Lily. The monogram also serves as a brand, your possessive mark. I'm reminded that when you think of Lily, you think of the bedroom. Your bed. Bare skin. *Sex*.

I am also reminded of *myself* at a time when I've stepped into the shoes of a ghost, a woman whose memory, style and tastes have spread malignantly through your life, completely subsuming the man you once were.

You don't trust me, and you don't trust yourself *with* me. Does your remoteness betray desire? Are you as ravenous for me as I am for you? Or is it that I can't compete with your first wife, the woman who still obsesses you six years beyond her passing?

Why are you avoiding me?

Pulling on a crushed velvet dinner jacket in deep sapphire, I make my way down the hallway to the kitchen.

'It smells amazing,' I tell Witte as I settle onto the barstool he pulls out for me.

I'm suddenly hungry for something other than you.

'Only half the equation.' He arranges a black napkin on my lap. 'Let's see how it tastes.'

He pulls plated salads out of the industrial refrigerator. Through the glass double doors, I spy precisely organized shelves.

Witte drizzles dressing in a zigzag pattern with quick, practiced artistry. He's already poured glasses of red wine and sparkling water, and I wonder how he accomplished such robust place settings at a moment's notice.

As he sets the plate with its hand-painted lily on my black linen place mat, I touch his wrist, and he stills. 'Thank you for looking after Kane.'

He holds my gaze for a moment as if weighing his reply. 'It's my job.'

'It's *also* your job,' I amend, picking up my salad fork as he takes the barstool on the corner to my right. 'It's clearly more than that.'

I hum with delight at the juicy, tart flavor of the lemon vinaigrette.

Noting my pleasure, Witte snaps his napkin open and lifts his utensil. 'You're correct, astutely so. Just as you were the other day in the library.' He pauses. 'Mrs. Armand prefers it when she's correct.'

I laugh. 'That is the politest way I've ever been told someone hates being wrong.'

He lifts a powerful shoulder in a careless shrug that's so at odds with the formality of his bearing and appearance I can't help but love it.

'I appreciate the diplomatic warning,' I tell him. 'But it's unnecessary. I see what kind of woman his mother is. How often has she propositioned or otherwise sexually harassed you?'

Clearly startled, he recovers swiftly. 'You're very observant.'

'Is Kane aware?'

'I'm perfectly capable of handling such matters myself.'

I set my fork down. 'So, you've never told him, and he's making the mistake of not watching his family carefully enough. I'm guessing he hasn't noticed.'

Witte pats his mustache with his napkin. 'I would say you're a woman who deduces, not guesses.'

My grin is wide and delighted. I love it when just the right word is used. It really does make all the difference. And to have Witte play along . . . It's both fun and necessary. Your welfare is his purpose, and I need him to believe we're aligned in that goal.

I resume eating. The salad is extraordinary, with chunks of ruby red grapefruit, oranges, candied pecans and blue cheese. 'My compliments, Witte. This is the best salad I've ever had.'

'Thank you.' Picking up his glass of red wine, he savors his sip before swallowing. 'Mr. Black expended tremendous effort to refine himself. I see why.'

'Because I like salad? Or because I'm astute and observant?'

'Because those qualities – among others – make you formidable.'

'Ah . . . Well, now I'm also flattered.'

I slide my fork between my lips before putting it down, relishing the last drop of dressing. My gaze slides around the kitchen, noting the informal eat-in table to my right and the reflection of the city lights at my back in the glass insets of the cupboards.

'I expect it's damn near impossible to gain unauthorized access to the penthouse,' I say casually, 'but there are two armed guards outside the front door.'

Holding his glass aloft, he studies me over it, showing no surprise that I've explored beyond the penthouse. 'There are.'

'There were guards at the hospital, too.'

Witte nods nonchalantly as if I've asked a question, but fine expectation has replaced his earlier ease.

'Is Kane protected when he's outside the tower?'

'We mitigate risks.'

'Such as?'

He aerates his wine with a practiced swirl of his wrist, but while his movements are insouciant his gaze is intense and watchful. 'Why this line of questioning, Mrs. Black?'

'It would appear he's in danger.'

'Are you?' His clipped pivot signals we've moved past pleasantries.

We study each other. The obliging majordomo is gone. The man sitting across from me is someone else entirely. Abruptly, he's intimidating in every way. His physicality has shifted from fit to formidable. His gaze has gone from observant to unnervingly probing. The fact that he can diminish himself at will to fade into the background and go unnoticed when his true self is so clearly dangerous sets my mind at ease.

I smile; his demeanor has addressed my underlying concern. 'How could I be? I'm under guard, too.'

'It's always best to be cautious.'

'Well . . . It's a relief to know he's safe.' I shoot him a telling glance over the lip of my water glass. 'And that you're prepared.'

'For what?'

'Anything.' I shrug, resuming my former appearance of unconcern. 'Anything at all.'

Setting his glass down, he removes his napkin from his lap and folds it neatly on the island. He doesn't take his gaze off me. 'Mr. Black is concerned for your safety.'

'Is that what the fuss is about? I suppose I could've been involved in any number of dubious situations over the past six years.' My voice is studiously light and amused, but my pulse has accelerated. He's shrewd and will take my carefully chosen words as the warning they are and become even more cautious. 'Here I was, hoping he just didn't want me to leave.'

'I don't believe he could bear it.'

'He can,' I counter briskly. 'He already has. If he could just stop thinking of me as his finish line, his prize for all his accomplishments, he'd enjoy his success simply because he's earned it. At least I like to imagine him that way.'

'There is truth in that.' With his fingers around the stem of his glass, Witte spins it slowly, round and round. He's not a man who fidgets, so the motion is intentional, designed to put me at ease. 'I was told you transferred into Columbia's Psychology Honors program during your junior year.'

I nod. 'Southwest to the northeast – what an acclimatization that was!'

'I understand that fewer than ten percent of transfers are admitted due to the high retention rate. You were one of the chosen few.'

'Who doesn't want an Ivy League degree?' I say blithely, not wanting to get into a discussion about Lily's life. I set my hand over his again. 'There are only two things you need to know about me, Witte: I want the best for him, and I've dedicated myself to becoming the wife he deserves.'

He studies me for long moments. Then his face clears and resumes its usual kind mien. He pats the back of my hand, stands and collects our plates, placing them in the sink. Pulling mitts on, Witte opens the oven. The scent that floats on the heated air is delectable.

I watch as he plates individual Beef Wellington servings,

potatoes au gratin and green beans almondine. 'How is it that you're single if you don't mind my asking?'

'I never said I was,' he returns with a smile.

'Well . . .' There is a look of devilish mischief in his eyes. 'Do tell.'

'You remind me of her, actually. As beautiful and tempting as a serpent, and just as dangerous.'

'Oh, Witte.' I laugh, pleased that we understand each other now. 'That's the nicest thing anyone's ever said to me.'

I take another sip of my water but note the faint mist of condensation on the wine glasses which tells me the Syrah is perfectly chilled. He would know that, of course; red wine served at room temperature is a travesty. But to chill it so that the temperature is *just right* precisely when it needs to be . . . well, that's an art.

'*Witte.*'

My pulse leaps at the sound of your low, resonant voice. You round the corner from the dining room, carrying your glass and your empty plate with your silverware balanced on top. You stop short when you see me.

'What are you doing?' you ask, frowning.

'What does it look like I'm doing?' I rejoin, shooting you a long glance over my shoulder. I play it cool, but your sudden appearance has me reeling.

Your nostrils flare. I arch a brow, knowing that challenging you always gets your blood hot in the best way. I let you see how fiercely and urgently I need you; I *want* you to know.

Inwardly, I'm far less steady. You're breathtakingly handsome. Your skin is naturally a sun-drenched hue, which plays so well with the dark luster of your hair and the brooding somberness of your velvety brown eyes. Your brows have tapered into a frown, but the lines of time only season you in the most flattering way. A five o'clock shadow contours your tightly clenched jaw. Square and sculpted, it anchors a strong chin and balances the sensuality of firm, full lips.

You are truly a masterpiece.

'Let me take those,' Witte says.

'I've got it, Witte.' You jerk your hands out of his reach, taking the plate and glass with you but leaving the silverware suspended in midair.

Thrusting my arm out, I catch the knife's blade between pinched fingers. Simultaneously, Witte has caught the fork, moving with the speed of a cobra strike. For a heartbeat, we contemplate each other's dexterousness. Then, I set the knife and my glass down and wipe my fingers on my napkin.

'What the hell were you thinking?' you snap, dumping your plate and glass in the sink with far less care than the delicate items require. 'You could've hurt yourself!'

'It was instinct,' I deflect simply. 'Anyone would've done it.'

You take my hand and examine it minutely, massaging my palm and fingers to see if blood wells anywhere.

The innocent touch has a profound effect on me. Awareness sizzles up my arm. 'I'm fine.' The catch in my voice betrays my response to you. 'It was a lucky catch.'

I caress your jaw with my free hand. You become motionless, staring at me fiercely. I brush the thick silk of your hair from your forehead, then trace your brow with my fingertips. It's a joy to touch you and devastating when you lean into my palm, nuzzling for far too brief a time.

You pull back abruptly. The glare you send me could melt asphalt.

'Would you care to join us for dessert?' Witte asks you, placing your silverware in the sink. 'I've made Indian Pudding.' His voice is smooth and unruffled as he pulls a fresh wine glass out of a cupboard and sets it at the place next to me. Like all the other crystal glasses, it's etched with lilies.

Your back tenses at the blatant assumption that you will reply in the affirmative. Your jaw is so tight it's a wonder your teeth don't crack under the strain. But in the end, you pull out the barstool beside me. You sit and push your newly supplied glass aside. Your gaze is locked with mine, focused and hot with temper, as you take my wine instead.

One of Witte's salt-and-pepper brows lifts with silent reproach. You're looking at me when you tell him, 'Lily doesn't drink, Witte.'

'I can still toast,' I qualify. 'Do you remember how it goes?' Raising my arm, I offer cheers to you both with a smile. 'Here's to you.'

A quick inhalation, then you join in. 'Here's to me.'

'May we never disagree.'

'But if we do' – your voice deepens and turns rough – 'I'd bleed for you.'

'Here's to me,' I finish, tapping my glass to yours and Witte's.

The fine crystal chimes and resonates into the subsequent silence.

22

Aliyah

'Fuck, babe, are you close?' he pants, sweat from his face dripping on my thighs. The scent of his cologne, something musky and warm, fills the air between us.

I grit my teeth. 'Don't stop!'

Growling, Rogelio starts thrusting harder and faster. I'll have to find my orgasm despite his efforts, not because of them, but that's nothing new. I've always had to provide my own foreplay if I want to climax with him. Young enough to be my son, the Baharan security chief has energy to spare but lacks finesse.

Holding on to the edge of the desk with one hand, I reach between my legs to rub my clitoris as his erection drives into me. The pleasure from my circling fingers radiates outward, and my sex tightens. Rogelio growls.

'Not yet,' I gasp, feeling the pressure build. I massage myself frantically, my lower body tensing in expectation.

'God, you're squeezing me like a fist,' he groans. 'I'm going to cum.'

'Wait . . . !'

His head falls back, and he moans, his grip on my hips tightening. Then his rhythm shifts as he lets go, the speed slowing into one, two, three deep grinding humps as he empties himself.

The bestial sound of his release stimulates me enough to follow him, a soft gasp escaping me as the coiling strain releases in a rush of endorphins.

I'm still panting as he staggers back a few steps and drops into his desk chair, his penis covered in glistening latex and still semi-hard. Behind him, Midtown is a sprawl of twinkling lights in semi-darkness.

'Damn, you're a hot lay, Aliyah,' he says, leering at my vagina as he swipes sweat from his forehead.

Hiding my distaste for his crudeness, I close my legs and slide off the desk, planting my palm on the top for balance as my legs adjust to being closed after nearly thirty minutes of being spread wide.

'Made you weak in the knees?' he teases, rolling his chair forward and dropping the condom in the trash can.

'Don't flatter yourself, Rogelio. It's not attractive.'

'Good thing my dick is,' he rejoins, not the least offended.

The truth is his penis is average. It's the rest of him that's appealing. He keeps his dark hair cut high and tight, which might not be the most flattering style but doesn't detract from his boyish good looks – dark brows and irises, a firm chin, a taut jaw and a mouth that's full and always smiling. His body is meticulously maintained, muscles thick and prominent without being bulky.

But really, it was his eyes that made me want to fuck him. The way they look at me is slightly disdainful and overtly sexual. I find his gaze to be impertinent and lascivious. Putting him in his place as stud service is worth the effort.

He stands and stretches, perfectly comfortable and confident in his nudity. 'I'm going to wash up,' he says, rounding the desk and leaving his office to cross the eerily silent and dark sea of cubicles to my private bathroom.

Is anything quite as disconcerting as a huge space devoid of life and energy?

Rogelio used to try to cajole me into fucking on my desk – as if I'd ever give him that power – saying it was more convenient with the bathroom right there. He'll need to erase the CCTV footage of his trek back and forth, but that's nothing for him. For all his flaws, he's sharply intelligent and a natural predator. He not only manages the security personnel and the system that protects Baharan from espionage, he also helped build the system and maintains its cutting edge. Like Amy, he once owned his company. Now he works for Baharan, although I suspect he does some outside work just for the hell of it. He certainly doesn't need the money with what we pay him.

I wait until the door shuts behind him, then I pull out the writing-board drawer of his desk to find his login code. He changes it so often he can't remember it anymore and writes it down on a Post-it. I copy the code onto my thigh with a pen, then dress hurriedly. I'm wet between my legs, but I can live with it.

Darius has been working long hours with Kane out of the office. He's not picking up slack because Kane isn't leaving any. My eldest is steering the ship from home, taking all his meetings virtually or in person in his home office when necessary. So, Darius is up to something else, and I need to know about it. Since every keystroke and phone call made on Baharan equipment is recorded, I just need Rogelio's password to see what my middle son has been doing over the past few weeks. I could use my own login, but then there would be a trail. Can't have that.

When Rogelio returns, he's still damp all over and gloriously naked. I eye him, tempted, and he stirs under my perusal.

'The wife's waiting,' he says. 'We'd have to make it quick.'

Although the thought of a wife cooling her heels while I enjoy her husband arouses me, the mention of haste takes that small pleasure away. Plus, his password on my thigh would be impossible to explain.

'Another time,' I say, patting his cheek like I would a small child. 'I have to get home, too.'

I'll have more fun going through the security logs. A shower, glass of wine, my personal laptop . . . An evening well spent.

I head to my office to retrieve my purse and leave Rogelio to erase any evidence of our tryst.

23

Lily

Knowing you always shower when you wake and before you sleep, I sneak into your bedroom once I hear the water turn on. I take my time approaching your bed, my gaze roaming and cataloging. Even in your private space, there is none of your personal style. I sigh.

Your room couldn't be more sterile. Only Lily's photo adds color.

I stare at the massive canvas. It's so large it must have been stretched onto the frame on-site.

Do you resent me for stepping in between you and her, the idealized Lily you've worshipped for years longer than you were together? Why did you choose this image? I think I know. The angle of her wrist presents the scorpion tattoo at her pulse to the camera. Does the sight of it, your astrological sign, offer you some comfort or deepen your torment?

I glance through the open bathroom door and note the lack of steam. I can see the entire length of your magnificent body through the glass shower surround. A warm rush of desire heats my blood. The powerful muscles of your shoulders and arms flex as you scrub your fingers through your hair. Trails of suds slither along the sculpted lines of your back, gliding over the firm swells of your buttocks before running down strong thighs and calves to circle the drain at your feet.

I hungrily catalog the differences between you and the younger version of you whose body I coveted so fiercely. You were devastating even then. I wonder if I can withstand your increased power and elegance or if I'd simply burn into ashes in your arms.

You make a noise I recognize as audible chill from the cold water.

And here I am, on fire for you. You're torturing us both.

Witte's already turned down your bed, and I slip naked into it. Rolling and twisting, I rub the scents of my lotion and perfume all over your sheets and pillow. You've come to my room every evening, but I can't take the chance that you'll resist tonight. I also hope to hurry you along. It's nearly midnight. After the past few weeks, you'd think a handful of hours longer wouldn't make a difference, but after you reacted to my touch with such longing, I can wait no more.

I leave the way I came, through your closet, and into the sitting room. I think it's possibly my favorite space in the house. It's a hidden jewel box, accessible only from your closet and mine, nestled between the two with its own lovely view of the city. There is a fireplace opposite the window, set flush within a wall covered in foxed mirror tiles. Above the firebox hangs a framed mirror that is actually a television. The result is an entire wall adorned only by an antiqued reflection of New York that appears perpetually stormy.

The seating area is dominated by an oversized U-shaped sectional in a luxurious sapphire velvet. Not only is it beautiful, it's also remarkably comfortable, suitable for curling up with a book, stretching out for a nap or a quickie, or sprawling while watching a film. A tufted square ottoman of the same material sits in the center, with a large, mirrored tray atop it filled with recent periodicals, notepads featuring our monograms, a cut-crystal pen holder and spheres of quartz sitting atop brass bases. If I turned it on, a sputnik chandelier would throw shards of light onto the ceiling and walls.

On either side of your closet door and mine, mirrored console tables squat heavily, adorned with table lamps that are counterparts to the chandelier. Framed mirrors matching the television hang from sapphire ribbons and bows. I pause before the one nearest your closet, examining my reflection.

In the forgiving glow of moonlight, I can pass for the woman you desire. Too thin, yes, along with a sharpening of the lines around my lips. The smoky eye shadow hides the deeper set of the eyes, but nothing can diminish the world-liness of my gaze. Long strands of dark hair curl along the underside of my breasts.

I turn away, collecting the sheer black peignoir I left draped on the arm of the sofa. Slipping it on, I tie the sash and adjust the weight of the ostrich feathers that froth from my knees to the hem. Then I arrange my hair, draping it around my shoulders and fluffing the length that falls to my hips.

My heart hammers steadily against my rib cage. What will I do if you reject me? How will I bear it?

Settling onto the sofa's edge, I fidget with the sash of my robe. Perhaps I'm playing my only hand too soon. In a matter of hours, we'll share a car, the walk to and from our 'outing' with my doctors and the ride home. That could be a start, an opening to conversation, a suggestion that we might enjoy lunch out in the city. If I could just open the door, I could court, charm and seduce you. At least I could try.

But it's also possible that you're just waiting for me to have a clean bill of health. Perhaps your conscience won't allow you to strain an infirm woman with discussions of separation and divorce. Maybe that's why you're accompanying me, to hear firsthand that it's safe to end this farce of a marriage. If so, these hours are all I have before you cast me adrift, and I can't squander them.

I don't know how long I wait. Time slows to a trickle. My

skin chills, and I stare at the fireplace, wanting to turn it on but reluctant to banish the darkness that shelters me.

Finally, the door to your closet is yanked ajar, and you enter the sitting room like a firestorm, enraged. Your feverishly bright gaze is locked on the opening to my closet, and your long legs eat up the distance in furious strides.

For a moment, I'm arrested. Black silk pants hang low on your hips. Your torso and feet are bare. The dark shadow of meticulously groomed chest hair sweeps across hard pectorals before narrowing into a satiny trail that dips below your drawstring. Your biceps are thick and hard, tensed by the fisting of your hands at your sides. Your abs are laced tight in deeply defined rows that taper into the deep grooves of the Adonis belt and highlight the narrowness of your waist.

You are nearly abreast of me when I manage to stand in an anxious rush, my breath held with cowardice. Your head whips toward me as you draw to a startled halt. Your chest lifts and falls in an elevated rhythm.

Raising my chin, I settle my weight back onto my rear heel, the practiced movement adjusting my posture into a sinuous invitation. Your jaw tenses in response.

Your gaze bores into me, sharp with indictment. 'Who are you?'

Your words are singed and smoky. Like an inferno, you've whipped heat into the room. I was chilled before, but now I'm uncomfortably warm.

'Does it matter?' My voice, too, is lower and huskier. My mouth is dry, my throat tight. 'I'll be anyone you want.'

Your incisive gaze pins me for long moments. Your hands clench and release, the restless movement flexing muscles all along your torso. You are an erotic work of art, simmering with passion.

Cursing under your breath, you start moving again, slower,

more methodical. A predator's honed, focused approach. You round the corner of the sofa, and an instinctual prey reflex urges me to turn and maintain sight of you. Instead, as you slip beyond my peripheral vision, I keep my back to you, feigning courage and control. I untie my sash and shrug so that the peignoir falls and hangs on the crooks of my elbows. Your breath hisses, sharply indrawn.

My pulse races. My lips part as I gasp. Expectation and fear skitter up and down my spine. I can feel you behind me. Hear you. Smell you – crisp and briskly clean, powerfully male. It's the worst torture not to see you.

'There's only one woman I want,' you say hoarsely as you lift a dark curl of hair from my shoulder and rub the natural strands between your fingertips. I feel you lift that lock to your nose and hear you inhale. Your hand falls away. 'Take the wig off.'

Your tone is clipped and cold. The heat that was building against my skin abruptly dissipates.

My throat closes, blocking the air I need so badly. Am I not enough, even when I look like her? Are you offended by the attempt or disappointed by my failure?

'Take it off, *Setareh*,' you say, softer yet inflexible.

I make a sound, a soft cry of pained hope. Fate. Destiny. The meaning of the name you use as an endearment. My eyes burn, and I shut them, trying to manage the overwhelming surfeit of emotion. *Yes, my love. I am your fate.* The universe has cursed you with me.

'It's not that simple,' I say. It would take time to loosen the adhesive and more time to restore my hair to the glossy bob.

With a sweep of one hand, you brush the heavy mass over my shoulder, exposing my back. Your fingertips trace the outline of the phoenix's wings tattooed across my shoulder blades. I shiver in response, every muscle straining with anticipation and alarm. Your lips press firmly to my bared shoulder. The heat of your kiss radiates throughout my yearning body.

Then the warmth, the scent, the energy of you moves away. My head turns, and I watch, horrified and incredulous, as you walk back toward your room.

'Kane . . . ?'

You stop midstride, your hands again in fists, your breaths fast and shallow like mine. You keep your back to me when you speak. 'If you want me, come to me with the truth and leave your lies somewhere else. I've had enough of them.'

The door to your closet shuts. The click of the latch echoes like a gunshot.

24

Lily

I stand on the corner of 5th and 47th, drenched in shadow, the warmth and light of the morning sun devoured by the crowded towers of Midtown Manhattan, a forest of glass, stone and steel. Goosebumps spread across my bare arms and legs. The chill originates inside me, then radiates outward. It isn't far from here that I think I once spotted you. A glimpse, and then nothing, as if you vanished into thin air while I stood dizzy and petrified on the street. A nightmare I can't forget or ignore.

Whenever I leave my apartment, I'm aware you can find me. In a borough whose population swells to nearly four million during business days, there remains the risk that facial recognition will betray my whereabouts.

Then again, am I even an afterthought? You discard people so easily but are enraged when others choose to distance themselves first. You've either discarded me altogether or are hyper-focused on finding me, with blindness to all else. You've never liked leaving anything to chance, and you covet wealth with a deadly hunger. Did you ever really love me? Maybe as much as you were able. Maybe insofar as I belonged to you. I was an accomplishment, after all.

Before me, grungy yellow taxis and black SUVs clog the city's arteries. Behind me, New Yorkers converge into an impatient huddle on the sidewalk, waiting for the moment we can all scurry across the steaming asphalt like roaches. The traffic noise blares from all sides, but my heart is pounding louder. In just a few moments, I'll walk right past the building entrance that lures me against all sense of self-preservation.

I could avoid that gleaming sapphire tower. Take the next street over.

Leave the city, state, country. But the perversion of obsession drives me to risk. It's simply irresistible. I've been hiding for years but am slowly becoming more careless. Fleeing hasn't afforded me a new life. I'm dead in all the ways that matter, except for breathing.

Maybe I'm done waiting for that final farewell.

The light changes. I move without thought, my ridiculous heels finding every rut and dent in the street, keeping me literally on my toes. The other women around me are more sensible, wearing ballet flats or block-heeled mules. The odors of car exhausts and sidewalk food carts turn my stomach. No one makes eye contact. No smiles are exchanged. In a city so alive its pulse beats against our senses like a battering ram, we are all automatons.

My name explodes into the air like the crack of rifle fire. Shock floods me. I can't breathe, can't think.

Defiance has a price — discovery.

25

Lily

I'm awake before dawn, roused from a dreamless sleep. I reach for the tablet lying on the bed beside me, in the space I'd hoped would be filled by you, and I cancel its alarm. I don't remember sinking into unconsciousness. I only remember weeping until my chest ached from it, wrecked by the swift withdrawal of your touch and desire. I took a gamble and lost, yet the possibility that you might have wanted me had I approached you as myself is a tantalizing hope. Now it's morning, and I've weaponized my longing; it's what pushes me out of bed.

In moments, I stand beneath the punishing shower spray, surrounded by massive slabs of marble covering the walls and floor. The black veining looks like spectral tree branches choked in spider's webbing, and I couldn't love it more.

Your bathroom mirrors mine, and I wonder at your choice to create a master suite that is split in half, a separation that belies your need to lie and rise beneath a photo of Lily. I can't fathom why you chose to live on the opposite side of the penthouse when everything within it serves as a memorial to her.

With quick efficiency, I ready myself for the day. You've made that haste possible. You have cataloged so many minute things about Lily's preferences, from the feminine care products she preferred to the flavor of her toothpaste. The natural-bristle cosmetic brushes are luxurious, and the well-worn handles betray them as favorites of their previous mistress. The makeup is the sole anomaly, all from ECRA+, with the colors I wear most often having names clearly inspired by Lily.

I feel perfectly at home here, as if I've always lived in the space. It's astonishing and delightful and eerie at once.

Some women might not be able to handle an all-encompassing obsession like yours, but I'm not normal. The totality of your love is everything I want and need.

I've dressed and am contemplating my meager selection of jewelry when I hear Witte's brisk knock at my bedroom door, a quick double rap. 'I'm in here, Witte.'

I look up when he fills the doorway from my bedroom with his slim, muscular frame. 'Breakfast will be ready when you are.'

The closet has the width of the massive bedroom since it acts as a pass-through between the sitting room and my room, so a sizable distance remains between us.

He takes a few steps toward me. Looking at my clothes, he touches one of the tags hanging from the neck of a hanger.

'Thank you for ordering them,' I tell him.

'A unique organizational method,' he murmurs, studying the postcard-sized lined cardstock.

There are two versions: a graphic of a sun or moon denotes day or evening. On the front, I write down which tops or bottoms pair well with that item. On the back, I note which jewelry, shoes, belts and purses would best accessorize. I'd discovered Lily's cards stored neatly in a drawer – a stroke of luck – I just had to pair them with the right items. For the recent additions, I asked Witte to reach out to the printer whose logo appeared on the accompanying box.

There are now apps for organizing closets, but this method is in place, and it's been invaluable.

'My mother used this system in her closet,' I offer. 'She believed throwing an outfit together at the last minute was thoughtless. "Being well-dressed and properly groomed is armor for a woman," she used to say.'

'Armor,' he repeats quietly as he examines my handwritten notes.

'She told me it isn't in human nature to be kind to beautiful things; we want to possess or destroy them. She raised me to be vigilant and use layers of defenses. Clothing is one.'

'Sadly apt. Tell me about her, if you don't mind.'

For a moment, I close my eyes, picturing her. The long, lithe body. The curtain of thick black hair. The cat eyes, keenly intelligent and brilliantly green. The wide, mobile mouth painted a lush red. I can't even imagine what my father must have looked like since I can see nothing but my mother when I look in the mirror. When I was young, I believed she alone was responsible for creating me, and I didn't care that I didn't have a father like other children. I didn't need one. I had her.

'To me, she was the most beautiful woman in the world,' I murmur, opening my eyes to stare down at my hands and the brilliant stone you gave me. I decide it's all I need in the way of jewelry. Nothing else I own would suit in any case.

I wish I could dazzle you, my love, and fill you with the same pride I feel for you. Maybe I'll get the chance someday. I can only hope.

'It seemed effortless for her to be that stunning,' I continue, resigned to my appearance in more ways than one, 'but she worked hard on herself. She was self-educated. She was considered brilliant by those who knew her, and they were right.'

He moves on to the next card. 'She sounds as formidable as her daughter.'

'She was definitely that. She told me beauty opens doors. That I would have a certain privilege just by virtue of being pretty, and I should use it.' I twist my wedding band with restless fingers.

Witte faces me. 'I'm very sorry for your loss.'

'Thank you.'

His gaze assesses my attire, from the sleeveless forest green pussy-bow blouse and leather skirt of the same hue to the nude patent leather Valentino Rockstud pumps. 'Were you contemplating accessories?'

'Yes, but I'll need to work on my collection.' Pushing the velvet-lined drawer in, I shrug off the feeling that I'm naked without earrings.

'If I may, I have something to show you.' Witte extends his arm toward the sitting room.

I hesitate only a moment, reluctant to face the scene of last night's mortification and failure. But since I can't explain to Witte, I take a deep breath and lead the way.

Once I cross the threshold, I slow so he can pass me. He heads to the console table nearest my closet and stands before the mirror, pressing his thumb lightly on a heretofore unnoticed fingerprint recognition pad embedded in the frame. The mirror slides upward silently, revealing both that the hanging ribbons are an illusion and that the mirror conceals a safe. Another thumbprint later, he's pulling out hinged black velvet trays. The top tray swings upward and tilts down, revealing rows of jeweled earrings. The middle drawer showcases tennis bracelets in a rainbow of colors. The lower drawer tilts downward and displays necklaces that range from delicate to statement.

I exhale in a rush. Millions of dollars in gems glitter in front of me. 'That's . . . quite a collection.'

My voice is breathy; I can't help it. The collection you've amassed could be called nothing but monumental.

'For every success Mr. Black has achieved, he's purchased

a piece of jewelry to celebrate.' Witte's gaze reveals the depth of his affection for you. He feels pain on your behalf. 'They were selected for you.'

'He's had a considerable number of successes.' I intended to sound nonchalant but failed in that, too. I don't move; I can't. I can only clutch my aching throat and fight off more tears. Could there be more definitive proof of your commitment to Lily's memory?

I cannot compete with your first wife. She will forever and always be unattainable for both of us.

'*Wear the emeralds.*'

Since I'm already vibrating with emotion too big to contain, the sound of your voice rattles me violently. I turn and watch you cross the room, striding toward me with the same singular, predatory grace you displayed when we were drenched in moonlight. You rake me with a searingly slow glance that is tactile and . . . possessive. I feel as naked now as I was then.

Deep and low within my body, I quicken for you. Nervousness and hope flutter in my soul like moths' wings. You're wearing black dress slacks, gray dress shirt, and suspenders and tie the same hue as the shirt. You have left your jacket elsewhere. The perfectly proper attire, expertly tamed hair and cleanly cut jaw only emphasize the rawness of your sexuality.

It's all a pretty cage, but there's a beast in there, dangerous and untamed.

The room's decor has the iciness of a diamond, and your clothing palette is cool, but you bring the fire. The temperature in the room increases. I've seen how your dynamic sensuality affects those around you. Women are drawn helplessly into your orbit, lured by that potent virility. The universe expended a great deal of energy to make you perfect, then ensured you'd be irresistible so you could propagate those gifts into the future.

You come to me as Witte leaves us. The physical recognition is immediate and profound. My body responds helplessly, warming and softening. I can't take my eyes off your face, adoring the devastating handsomeness you wield so casually.

'These are almost as beautiful as your eyes.' You reach for a pair of large rectangular emerald drops on diamond-studded leverback hooks.

The compliment makes me dizzy with relief. I don't care if it's said for Witte's benefit. After last night, any sign of warmth from you is life-giving.

You take one of the stunningly beautiful earrings, tuck my hair behind my ear and slide it into place, securing the back. I'm burning with desire; the feel of your knuckles brushing my jaw and neck is as intimate as if your hand were between my legs. You're so close you fill my entire field of vision. There is no one else in the world. Only you.

You repeat the process on the other side, your breath softly stirring the hair at my crown. The smell of you goes to my head. I feel languid with intoxication.

It's strange, the sensation of borrowing another woman's jewelry. Another woman's home. Another woman's husband. Strange, yet I'm intimately familiar with all of it, with *you*. I suppose it's more dreamlike than anything. A place where everything is new, but I accept ownership after only a brief hesitation.

'And the bracelet,' you tell me, separating it from the peg it hangs on.

'Oh, why not?' Somehow, I manage to achieve the nonchalance I didn't before.

You fasten it on my wrist, your touch spreading warmth throughout my body. Your thumb strokes over the scorpion tattoo guarding my pulse, and I tremble. I watch, breathless, as you lift my hand and lower your head to press a kiss to the crisply inked arachnid, your tongue flickering wickedly, tauntingly, over the eternal symbol and reminder of you.

I feel that tongue lashing everywhere all at once. My nipples harden visibly, unrestrained by the soft silk of my bra.

'Kane . . .' I want you to cup my face in your hands and kiss me. Embrace me. 'Thank you. I love them.'

I love you.

You hold my gaze for a long moment. It's a questing look, penetrating and somber. 'You give them life, *Setareh*.'

Then you leave me, returning to the other side of the room, through your closet, and on to your bedroom beyond.

26

Amy

I stand beside the opening of my front door as a mass of loose chocolate-hued curls rushes by me like a whirlwind.

'Oh, wow!' Short and slender, Lily's stylist has a bright smile and way too much giddy energy. There's a garment bag slung over one shoulder, a Chanel bucket bag draped cross-body against the opposite hip, and she's carrying a bag from Bergdorf's. 'I can totally tell you and Lily are sisters! You're both gorgeous.'

I lick coffee and Baileys Irish Cream from my lips. 'We're sisters-*in-law*,' I correct wryly.

'Really?! You're not actual sisters? You look so much alike!'

It kills me that I have to take that as a compliment because Lily is the kind of drop-dead gorgeous you just don't see in real life. In filtered pictures on Instagram? Sure. On photo-shopped magazine covers and advertisements? Absolutely. But in-your-face, right in front of you? Nope.

I'll be damned if her face will be slapped all over ECRA+ advertisements.

'Tovah,' she introduces herself, thrusting out a hand. 'Your apartment is beautiful!'

'Thank you.' I accept the greeting. 'I'm Amy. Would you like some coffee? Water? A shot?'

It's early to start drinking, even for me, but when I saw the Google search alert in my inbox, everything stopped: my heart, my breath, time. I don't know how long I sat there in the dark, staring at that subject line: 'Google Alert – vincent searle.' Some days my mind just comes awake in the middle of the night, and falling back to sleep is impossible. I should've read a book instead of checking my email. One of Suzanne's boink fests might have bored me into nodding off again.

How many goddamn people have the same name as my father? Enough to fuck up my day with an alert about an unrelated Vincent Searle in Daytona who had something to say about the library system in a pissant local newspaper. Not my father and not an obituary. Which doesn't mean my dad's not dead, just that there's no one in his life to write something good about him. My parents are always either fucking or fighting, with rare bouts of peace and quiet in between, making them unfit company for friends and family.

I've always figured my mother will be the one to kill my father, whether by denting his skull with a cast-iron pan or by giving him a heart attack while screwing him beyond his limits. On any given day, she can go either way, depending on how manic she is and how drunk my father is. In any case, I expect they'll leave this world with the same violence in which they lived.

I deserve a fucking drink after starting my day with that bullshit alert.

'Oh my God, I wish I could take you up on that shot,' Tovah answers with a laugh, her dark eyes bright. 'I've got another client after you, though, so I can't. And I've got water in my bag, so I'm good. I started carrying around one of those aluminum bottles, trying to drink more water and be kinder to the planet. Can I put this down here, or should we head to your closet?' She folds the garment bag over her forearm.

'My room is this way.' I gesture for her to walk ahead of me so I can gauge how she really feels about my condo decor. 'Last door on the right.'

As I follow her, I sip my coffee and study her clothes. Cropped jeans, strappy heels, knotted white dress shirt and Chanel blazer in bright pastel colors. Her head turns from left to right, looking at the art on each wall, simple abstracts of gold paint on stretched white canvas. I'd wanted to style the house like the penthouse, the dark, textured sensuality of bohemian gothic. Darius wouldn't hear of it. He wouldn't allow for much in the way of color at all. Most of our condo is rendered in white, cream and gold shades. When I objected, he told me all the white shows off my beauty. How the hell was I supposed to argue with that?

Now I'm stuck living in a home that reminds me of Aliyah. I was able to add some of what I wanted via jute rugs, fur throw blankets and macramé pillows – as long as they followed Darius's vanilla-ice-cream palette. It's like he *had* to be as opposite from Kane as possible (while fucking the exact same type of woman). I heave out a frustrated sigh.

Some days I feel like I'm trapped in a padded cell.

When Tovah enters my room, her soft exclamation of surprise fills me with satisfaction. Here, I've recently redecorated to my tastes. A charcoal-gray fur comforter covers the bed, and black leather with gleaming silver tacks upholsters the headboard. A black rug with a botanical pattern lies on the floor, and a photo of a panther against a solid black background hangs over the bed. It's a sexy room, even if the walls are taupe instead of the gray I've yet to pick out. For all his love of glaring white, Darius has come to prefer fucking me in here.

'What a closet!' she says, laying the garment bag over the island. 'This is every woman's dream! And neutrals are the foundation of every wardrobe. You just need some pops of color and a few trendy pieces that we'll swap out every season. It's not going to –'

'I like Lily's style.' I cut her off because I don't think she'll shut up otherwise. 'Like that corset get-up she had on the day you were at the penthouse. That's what I want.'

The look on Aliyah's face when Lily walked into the library . . . ? *Fucking. Priceless.* It took everything I had not to snort gin out of my nose. Hours after Darius and I left, I found my sense of humor about the whole thing and laughed so hard my stomach hurt for days afterward. Darius said I was having a psychotic break because I was howling so loud.

I almost don't care that every man in the room that day – minus Witte, with the usual stick up his ass – stood there bug-eyed, like they'd never seen a woman before in their entire moronic lives. I'm glad Lily woke up long enough to freak out Aliyah majorly. But Lily's work is done, so she can die now. They can both die, actually, and end on a high note.

'Oh, I know, right?' Tovah says, almost on a worshipful sigh. 'She was wearing that when I showed up, so I can't take any credit for it, unfortunately, but it was one of those outfits that just stops everyone in their tracks. The corset was vintage. In fact, most of her closet is vintage designer pieces that she either got from her mother – who's passed, isn't that sad? – or she collected secondhand. She certainly knows where and how to shop. She's got a great eye. She knows what looks good on her, and her closet is a fashionista's dream. And she's so gorgeous and tall and *thin*. Like a supermodel. Everything looks great on figures like hers. And yours! But her style, that kind of goth bohemia, it's not really *in*, you know?'

I press my fingers to my left eye, which is twitching with an insane muscle spasm. Holy fucking hell, does the woman not know how to shut the fuck up?! How does Lily put up with it? I don't think I can. And considering how poorly Tovah's selling her ability to replicate Lily's style, I think I won't have to.

Tovah digs around in her bag. 'There were only a couple of things she bought that I suggested. Anyway, what's hot now is Millennial Pink – Pantone calls it Rose Quartz, but it's the color of the year – and with your complexion, you could really rock it.'

'Pink?!' I query incredulously. I've touched every damn thing in Lily's closet, and there wasn't even a *speck* of pink anywhere.

She unzips the bag. 'Look at this beauty! And with the accessories I brought, it will be appropriately sexy.'

It's a pale pink blazer hung over a dark gray lace-edged silk camisole with a thin black velvet choker draped around the neck of the hanger.

'Are you *kidding* me?!' I choke out, feeling heat rise into my face. My left hand clenches into a fist while my right grips the handle of my mug so tightly I fear it might break. I want to throw my steaming-hot coffee in her face and then knock her sideways with the mug. I'm paying the chatty bitch to give me a Lily makeover, and she brings me something Kane's wife would *never* wear?

With her back to me, Tovah drops the garment bag on the floor, revealing the matching pants for the blazer. 'Right? Isn't the suit gorgeous? And chokers are all the rage now. I've also brought a clutch and heels in black velvet. They're in the bag.'

She walks over to a hook, sets the hanger on it, and steps back, admiring. 'The color is unmistakably feminine, but the cut of the suit is masculine and all business.'

I take a deep breath. The shade of pink *is* pretty. Still, I say, 'I can't imagine Lily wearing anything like that. *Ever.*'

'The color? No. Maybe not even a suit, but she's not a businesswoman like you are.' She turns and looks at me, her long curls swaying around her slim shoulders. She's so petite; she makes me feel as tall as Lily is. 'But I did add some gothic touches with the black velvet, the silk and the lace, but the most powerful message we want to send is that you're a woman in charge. When I asked Lily what she did, she said her job is to make her husband look good. Not that he needs help in that department. I saw him in passing and . . . whew. Men don't roll off the assembly line fully loaded like that very often, more's the pity. Is he your brother, by the way?'

'No. Brother-in-law.' I take a sip of my coffee to wash out the bad taste left in my mouth from calling Kane that. I don't want to be his *family*.

'Oooh, so you're married to his brother. Lucky girl. Does he have another brother?'

I snort. 'He does.'

Her brows raise with interest. 'Married?'

'Nope.'

'Ugh. Too bad I am.' She grins. Her almond-shaped eyes are tilted up at the far corners, giving her a foxlike face, which happens to be very pretty. 'Anyway, looking dramatically sexy is part of her job description. You, on the other hand, have staff and clients. You want them to see the beautiful woman you are but also to respect you and understand that you're capable, fierce and in control.'

'Lily was all of that, wearing that outfit.'

'No, no, no. Lily was all that *despite* the outfit,' she corrects. 'Confidence is the sexiest thing any woman can wear. She has that in spades. So do you. Here's my rationale . . . You work in social media. That's about setting trends and being relevant. Lily's vintage. You want *now*.'

My lips purse. Maybe Tovah actually knew her shit after all. Who'd've guessed?

Shit. If I tried to launch my business today, would I fail? Three years have gone by in what feels like three weeks, and now *pink* is the fucking color of the year, and I have no idea what's trending. I've got to hop off the pity wagon and get my ass in the office, get up to speed and get my employees to remember who they actually work for. Otherwise, when Darius pulls Social Creamery out from under the Baharan umbrella and serves it to me on a platter, I'll fuck it up. No way am I giving Aliyah that satisfaction.

Better than that, though, will be the comparisons to Lily then. I can see it now, Lily and me standing side by side at one of Kane's parties, with all the guests talking about us in hushed whispers behind our backs.

Are they sisters?

By marriage.

What's the long-haired one do?

That's Amy. She's the owner and creative director of Social Creamery; they take brands to the next level.

And the one who dresses like Morticia Addams?

That's Lily. She works on her knees or her back, inflating and deflating Kane's cock.

I snicker. My sister-in-law is a worthless bitch.

'Just try it on,' Tovah coaxes. 'If you hate it, I'll have learned something that'll hone my future suggestions for you. But I think you're going to love it and look like the sexiest badass boss anyone's ever seen. And I'll pull some gothic looks together for casual and semi-formal events.'

Tossing back the rest of my coffee, I shrug and walk over to the suit. So pink. So pretty. So really *not* Lily. But I'll give it a shot.

Lily

The elevator whistles faintly as it descends from the ninety-sixth floor. I watch as the numbers race by, but they don't distract me from noticing your withdrawal into the corner of the car, your gaze on your phone, reading your emails. You've retreated into your beautiful, lifeless shell. Do you regret your kindness and warmth to me already?

I'm hurt, but anger is rising like the tide. Are you playing mind games with me? It's hard to believe the husband who hoarded a romantic treasure trove for his beloved wife and the man who won't share a meal with me are one and the same. You apparently can't even stand next to me in an elevator.

There's a platinum band on your ring finger and inlaid lilies in your cufflinks and tie clip. You want the world to know unequivocally that you're taken, but you haven't yet connected that commitment to me. I'm starting to believe you never will. Worse, I'm coming to accept it.

When the car doors open into the subterranean parking garage, the Range Rover is waiting, attended by a liveried valet. He opens the rear door for me, but you intervene, offering your hand to help me up. It's not necessary; a step extended from the undercarriage when the door opened. You're just staging another performance, and I play my part, flashing a grateful smile at you, then the valet. The valet smiles back in the cautiously polite way afforded to lovely companions of powerful men. For his efforts, you shoot him a cool glance that has him swiftly skirting the hood to talk to Witte.

You go around the rear and slide in beside me. The center of the seat back has cup holders that fold down so that we're separated. It doesn't matter. Our proximity is enough to heighten the tension in the air. It crackles between us, arcing like invisible lightning and shocking all my senses.

We leave the garage and merge into traffic. You focus on your phone again, typing dexterously with both thumbs. I look out the window, soaking in the city. The streets are congested, as always, although this time of morning can be exceptionally challenging. Cabs and town cars dominate, playing chase and chicken with buses emblazoned with ads for television shows and clothing. Pedestrians run the gamut from joggers to businesspeople in smart suits. Cones on the sidewalk warn of open cellar doors as an aproned man carries crates from the back of a delivery truck down the stairs.

There is music out there. Laughter. Meals shared with loved ones. Stories passing from one friend to another. Lovers engaging. New York is thriving; a million memories being created every millisecond. But I'm distanced from it all. It wasn't that long ago I was dreaming of never leaving the penthouse, of being sequestered with you there forever. Now, I don't think I can bear it much longer.

I sigh heavily and look away from the energy of the city. There are magazines in the mesh seat-back pocket. I thumb through them, finding *Forbes*, *Robb Report*, *duPont Registry* and *People*. The latter is so outside the others I pull it out and note that it's the Sexiest Man Alive issue. Dwayne Johnson graces the cover in a white T-shirt and jeans. He's gorgeous, but I disagree with the magazine's choice. The sexiest man alive sits beside me and wants nothing to do with me.

As I flip through the pages, I note the wedding announcements of couples previously coupled with other people, advertisements for television shows I've never heard of, and movie sequels to unknown franchises. I'm so focused on how removed from life I've been that your photo within the pages catches me by surprise. You're seated at a conference table in one of your exceptionally tailored suits. The shot is close in on your face. Your eyes smolder, and your sensual mouth is relaxed but unsmiling.

I snap the magazine closed and shove it back in the pocket. Then I lean my head back and close my eyes.

'You always get carsick trying to read,' you note absently.

It's the first time you've tied the past to the present. I squelch the ridiculous hope that burgeons inside me. You can't have it both ways: far removed and intimate. You're going to have to make a choice.

'I didn't sleep well, and I'm tired,' I retort. 'Could've used a good workout. Something to make me sweat and wring me out.'

With my eyes closed, I catch your sharply indrawn breath. But the tone of your voice when you speak is casual. 'The doctors say you should rest.'

'That's all I've done for weeks on end now. I think I've rested enough.'

'You were in a coma, not taking a nap,' you bite out. There's a pause as you rein in that unruly temper, and your voice is deceptively pleasant when you speak again. 'And I'll remind you that we have a home gym.'

'That's not really the same thing, is it?'

Your silence is chilly.

'How about you?' I prod, opening my eyes and rolling my head against the seat back to look at you. 'Did you sleep like a baby?'

Your gaze is locked on your phone screen. 'How do babies sleep?'

'I don't know. Should we make one and find out?'

A muscle tics in your jaw. 'I slept fine.'

My mouth curves. 'Liar.'

'Sheath your claws, *Setareh*.' You're contained, with only the barest hint of anger in your voice. That level of control excites me, turning me on just as much as your incendiary rage.

In the silence that follows, I hear the muted sound of Janis Joplin urging her lover to take another piece of her heart. I reach down and raise the volume from the rear-seat controls.

For the rest of the drive, I consider my options. Time is a luxury I don't have. I've borrowed, but my limited store is running out.

I'm so focused on my inner turmoil I scarcely pay attention to arriving at the hospital or making our way to the conference room.

'It's good to see you looking so well, Lily,' Dr. Hamid says with a warm smile.

She settles into a desk chair at a black conference table with chrome legs. I mirror her on the opposite side. You won't sit at all, having refused Dr. Hamid's gracious offer with a curt shake of your head.

You're pacing instead, with the methodical stride of calculating predation. You seem even taller as you loom over us, and your restlessness charges the room.

Are you afraid of doctors, love? Of hospitals? Does the smell of disease and decay turn your stomach? Does the prick of a needle sinking into soft flesh turn your blood cold?

It's something I don't know about you, one of the incalculably infinite threads that form who you are at the core. It's those filaments, from phobias to fervors, that form the weaving of an individual.

I've come to accept that asking for reciprocation of my love is unfair. You don't even love yourself. I don't even love myself.

What a pair we are, intrinsically broken but tied to one another by desire and death.

'I apologize for running behind,' Dr. Goldstein says, entering the room with a leisurely air that belies his apology. He's the psychologist who's been testing and examining me, and he pulls out a chair one removed from Dr. Hamid.

Balding, with a scruffy reddish beard perpetually kept at the three-day-growth length, he's nondescript. His olive-gray plaid suit is a size too large and couldn't be more different from Dr. Hamid's outfit; her red shalwar kameez is vibrant beneath her white lab coat. She's been responsible for healing my body while Dr. Goldstein picks through my mind.

I don't like him, not at all. His degrees are more advanced than mine, but he's only book smart, at best. He eyes me like a bug he wants under a microscope, but he can't pick my brain. He hasn't the skill or the strength to face my demons.

'Thank you for joining us, Dr. Goldstein,' Dr. Hamid says, her smile as kind as always, but I respect the censoring glint in her eye. Beneath her caring demeanor and colorful femininity is a doctor who takes her work very seriously and expects no less from others.

As agitated as you were before, you are suddenly deeply still, standing behind me and gripping the back of my chair with both hands.

Dr. Hamid begins, speaking directly to me. 'The multitude of scans we performed yielded images that several neurological experts studied, and their conclusions align – your brain is entirely without injury.'

'Physically,' Dr. Goldstein interjects.

'Yes, of course,' Dr. Hamid concurs impatiently. 'We're

discussing the brain, not the mind. Further, the reports from the physical therapist were glowing. For a woman with your delicate appearance, he says you're surprisingly strong even after three weeks of immobility. All in all, you're a woman in remarkable health.'

'Physically,' Dr. Goldstein qualifies again.

You abruptly pull out the chair beside me and sink into it with elegant physicality. It's very sexy, the power you wield over yourself.

It's not until I hear your shaky exhale and watch your body melt into the uncomfortable seat that's too small for your tall frame that I finally comprehend: it's not our surroundings that made you so edgy. You reach for my hand and hold on too tightly.

'Ah. You were worried,' Dr. Hamid surmises, her gaze sympathetic. 'I'm sorry, I thought I was clear that the prognosis was very good. We were just being cautious, perhaps overly so.'

Your chest lifts and falls, your nostrils flaring with every deeply drawn breath. We all wait for you to say something, and then I realize you can't.

I smile brightly to fill the gap. 'All good news.'

Your fingers flex on mine. 'Does she have any physical-activity limitations?'

Remembering your reminder about the home gym and what you were responding to at the time, my smile flattens, and I try to pull my hand free. Your grip tightens to the point where I can only make a scene if I don't desist.

Dr. Hamid shakes her head. 'There are no activity restrictions.'

'To be clear,' you go on, 'I'm free to make love to my wife without concern?'

My posture stiffens. Is that what's held you back? Can it be that simple?

No. That doesn't explain why you've avoided me so thoroughly.

Her smile is kind. 'I would say resuming sexual intimacy after such a lengthy and painful separation can only be good for both of you.'

'Sexual dysfunction is one of myriad complications that can arise from dissociative amnesia.' Dr. Goldstein's fingertips drum into the tabletop. His legs are crossed, his chair tilted back. 'I cannot stress enough how vital it is that you begin therapy at once. You've been resistant. I understand that guided self-examination can be especially difficult for psychology students, who might believe they can analyze and diagnose themselves without assistance. However, disorders like yours are rare and indicative of severe emotional trauma.'

The fingers of my free hand curl into my palm. 'I'm aware of that.'

'I'm not,' you interject. 'Can you explain what you're worried about?'

'The mind isn't like a VHS tape that can be erased and re-recorded over. You do know what a VHS tape is, Mr. Black?'

'Yes, of course,' you say drily, 'I was born in '83.'

'Ah, and now I feel old,' he says with a genuine wry smile. 'Your wife's mind has compartmentalized her trauma; it hasn't erased it. Her subconscious is very aware of what she's suffered, and it will react strongly when triggered. We have no idea what her triggers might be. A storm. The sight of a boat. Something as simple as a song she may have been listening to. It will be something her subconscious associates with the trauma.'

Dr. Goldstein focuses on you, but Dr. Hamid studies me.

'Generalized amnesia is most often diagnosed in combat veterans and sexual assault survivors,' he continues, 'and we can anticipate certain triggers in those situations. In this instance, we don't know if the extreme stress of fighting for survival precipitated her memory loss or something else entirely. Perhaps she was traumatized after reaching the shore or during a rescue when she was most vulnerable. We simply don't know what happened, but we know it was an experience far beyond what her mind could accept.'

You squeeze my hand until the band of my ring feels like a blade. Your dark eyes reflect the horrors of your imagination. I don't want you to torment yourself, but maybe that's what you've been doing since you found me. Perhaps this conversation is only reinforcing your worst fears.

Dr. Goldstein's voice rises as he goes on, his eyes alight with avid curiosity. Something rare has wandered into his purview, and he's greedy to study it exhaustively.

'The past six years of her life are known as a dissociative fugue,' he says. 'Essentially, her trauma was so great her mind performed a complete reset. Returning to the life she'd lived before wasn't seen as a viable option.'

You clear your throat. 'She hasn't seemed uncomfortable in our home or with me.'

'Your wife's seeming indifference to such an extreme experience is a well-documented reaction.' His dismissal is casual; he's firm in his diagnosis. 'It's as normal a response as distress or confusion. Even without knowing the source of trauma, we can presume some approximate responses. She may have nightmares and/or flashbacks. She may develop eating and sleep disorders. She may exhibit self-destructive behavior. Depression and suicidal ideation are very real concerns, especially if she doesn't resurface the trauma in the safety of a clinical setting.'

'None of that has been an issue thus far,' I argue.

Dr. Goldstein straightens abruptly and leans over the table. 'Have you had the sense of being detached from yourself or your emotions? Has your perception of your surroundings or the people around you seemed unreal or distorted? Do you feel your identity doesn't fit properly or is askew or blurred?'

My blood runs cold. Fear sinks into the pit of my stomach like a boulder.

'I'm six years behind, Doctor,' I say as calmly as possible. Damned if I'll show too much emotion and be called hysterical. 'The world has changed in many ways. I feel like a time traveler, but I'd venture to say that's not unexpected or unreasonable.'

'How is something like this treated?' you query.

'We'll attempt to retrieve her memories through hypnosis. Administering drugs can also facilitate the process. Then we work together to unpack the trauma and address it.'

I laugh silently. Mental health care is still medieval in so many ways. To say nothing of how he addresses you as if I'm not here or am incapable of understanding his advice. Joseph Goldstein isn't going to dig around in my brain for his edification.

You glance at me, and I turn my head toward you. I let you read my thoughts through the window of my gaze. Your white-knuckled grip on me loosens, then you give me a reassuring squeeze as the blood rushes back into my fingers in a prickling wave.

'Thank you for the explanation, Doctor,' you say. 'And thank you for your exceptional care of my wife, Dr. Hamid. I'm in your debt.'

'Yes,' I concur. 'Thank you so much.'

She smiles. 'Every once in a while, we experience miracles. That you suffered no broken bones or internal injuries is certainly one of them. It's been my pleasure to do what I could, Lily, and to see you looking so well.'

'When would you like to schedule an appointment?' Dr. Goldstein presses. 'I can clear some space this afternoon. We really should waste no time.'

You stand with easy grace, and then offer your hand to assist me. I need the help. My legs are weak, my thoughts tumbling. Nothing said here was a surprise. I was avoiding the consequences and can no longer.

'We're leaving the city for a while,' you tell him. 'We'll call your office when we return.'

Goldstein's mouth purses. 'I repeat that I don't recommend that you and your wife try and cope without the support of therapy. Individuals with your wife's condition have tremendous difficulty maintaining relationships. Resuming intercourse may impede emotional reconnection in your marriage, rather than strengthen it.'

'Duly noted.' You thank the doctors again, shake their hands and lead me out of the conference room.

You don't say anything as we wait for the elevator, even though we're alone, but you keep me tucked firmly into your side as you type out a quick text on your phone with one hand. Once we're inside the car and descending, you step behind me and wrap your arms around me. 'He's aggressive,' you murmur, 'and made you uncomfortable. I'm sorry he was the one to administer the battery of tests you've been subjected to. You should've said something.'

I tense, my breathing turning shallow. Your closeness now versus your distance when we left the penthouse leaves me reeling. 'It's not a subject I felt like discussing with Witte.'

The warmth of you burns into the chill within me. Your richly masculine scent envelops me, shielding me from the hostile odors of powerful disinfectant and illness cloaked in dread.

Your chest expands against my back as you grip me more securely. 'I've handled everything poorly, haven't I? I've been overly cautious.'

'That's one word for it,' I retort. I try to ease out of your embrace, but you don't allow it.

'I couldn't risk pushing you too far too fast, especially when every medical professional is warning me to limit your stress. Nothing I feel for you is delicate.'

'Or maybe it's that you feel nothing.'

'*Setareh*.' You press your lips ardently to my temple, clutching me tightly. 'I want you too much. I always have. I'm sorry.'

Not knowing if you're being honest is an insidious form of torture. 'You didn't have to lie about going out of town. I *wanted* to tell him he didn't have a shot in hell at accessing my mind with drugs, hypnotism or anything else. He wants a case study to publish and lecture on. I'm not letting someone harvest my memories for personal gain.'

'I didn't lie to him. And I agree, he's a pompous ass.' A smile enters your voice. 'Although his arrogance worked in our favor when the detectives questioned him. He'll argue the validity of his diagnosis to his grave.'

I bite my lower lip. Was Dr. Goldstein the best choice for me or the most advantageous in the circumstances? It's impossible to know the truth, even if I ask and you deign to answer.

'Was his explanation correct?' you ask.

I don't ask which part because it was all accurate and because, now, I'm overwhelmed by curiosity. And hope. Where are we going? How long is *a while*? 'Yes.'

'Would you be willing to see someone else?' Your deep, measured tone of voice calms me. You've mesmerized me with that tenor before. 'I'm going to need you to try.'

'Why? Are we going to try and save our marriage? Or are you hoping a little psychoanalysis will trigger me into forgetting about you and disappearing again? After all, you haven't shown any sign that you want me around.'

The silence that descends is blistering.

'You've lost *years*,' you hiss in my ear. 'Don't you want to know what happened during them?'

The elevator stops smoothly and opens on the ground floor. You take my hand, and we walk toward the front entrance. You moderate your stride so that we stroll through the lobby in tandem. Heads turn, and gazes follow. How could they not? You're so tall and devastatingly handsome, and my heels raise me to just over six feet in height.

You exude confidence and the warmth of the fire that fuels you. In so many ways and for so many reasons, it is a tormenting joy to walk beside you.

You draw me aside when we exit the hospital into an outdoor alcove out of the way of foot traffic flowing through the automatic sliding doors.

'I asked you a question, *Setareh*. Give me an answer.'

'What does it matter what I remember? There doesn't seem to be much to save in our marriage. What do you want from me beyond modeling your jewelry collection?'

That sculpted jaw of yours tightens.

Discouraged and bitter, I go on. 'You don't want my company. You don't want to fuck me. You don't even want to share a bedroom with me. Are you planning on fucking other women? How have you managed that, by the way, with that giant photo of me watching? Or is that the point? Do you like me to watch? Doesn't that creep them out? I guess not. You're so gorgeous, sexy and *rich* they'd probably let you nail them in Times Square.'

There is a moment of furious silence, then, 'Are you done?'

'Do I get the same sexual freedom?'

Now the fire rises into your eyes. Still, you rein it in and hold your tongue.

The fact that I can't even get you angry about me sleeping with other men tells me all I need to know. Except for one thing . . . 'Why don't you just ask for a divorce? You can have the fucking money, Baharan, everything. All I want is peace.'

I move to step around you, then gasp in surprised pain as you yank me back into position between you and the alcove wall as if I'm a recalcitrant child in need of discipline. Then you pull me into a tight hug. Your big, powerful body radiates ferocity and violence. And I realize with stunned delight that you have an unmistakable – and impressive – erection.

Your lips, so firm and sensual, are a breath away from my forehead as you speak in a low, vehement whisper. 'Is that really *all* you want?'

Hot, sexual demand emanates from you. So, too, does edgy, anxious energy.

It hits me that my answer matters to you deeply, that waiting for it has you strung tight. As if I might possibly not desire you more than my next breath.

'I don't know what peace is, Kane, to even have a hope of wanting it. *You*'re all I need. You always have been.'

'*Setareh*.' You crush me close and press your lips to my forehead. It's such a simple gesture, yet I feel relief drain the tension from your body. 'That's what I've needed – for you to tell me you still want me.'

'You've seemed so angry with me.'

Pulling back, you bare your teeth before you bite off your answer. 'You made a decision that took you from me for *six years*! You're damn right I'm mad at you.'

The chill in my blood finally warms. I'll bear the marks of your fingers for days, but I don't care. I relax in your grip, and in return, your grip relaxes.

Your voice softens, too. 'I slept like shit, just like every other night I've spent without you. If you want a baby, we'll get pregnant. If you don't want to go to therapy, we won't. We have separate bedrooms because I couldn't let your things go, but I couldn't function seeing them, smelling them, touching them every day.'

Cupping my face in your hands, you rest your forehead against mine. 'We vowed to forsake all others, and we will. *You* will. *I* absolutely fucking will. There's never been another woman in my bedroom. And divorce is not now, nor will it ever be, an option. Did I miss anything?'

Your thumb is now stroking my arm, back and forth, soothing and stimulating. It's an involuntary caress, an instinctual movement.

'What if it's better not to know what I was doing the past six years?' I ask. 'What if I did terrible things?'

'I don't care. It won't change anything.'

'What if I was a prostitute?' It stabs deep to feel you flinch. 'What if I sold illegal weapons or drugs? Robbed? Killed? Who the fuck knows.'

'Who the fuck cares,' you rejoin with a renewed flare of temper. 'I told you, it doesn't matter to me. You were someone else then. You were Ivy York.'

'But Ivy York is in me. She's not an abstract. She existed. She exists. If I have to be perfect for you to love me, we're finished already.' I look away to see the Range Rover pull to the curb. 'Is that what you want? To end this and be free?'

'You don't have to be perfect, and I don't want to be free.' You grip my chin to turn my gaze back to you. 'That you'd think for even a moment that I don't want you proves I've seriously screwed this up.'

Taking my hand, you set us on a path to the car.

Witte waits with the door open, his gaze watchful, searching up and down the street with expert vigilance. His jacket's cut is so precise only a trained eye would notice the firearm in a shoulder holster.

The sky is intensely blue. The climbing sun reflects blindingly off miles of vertical glass walls encasing iron skeleton towers. The day is too beautiful, too perfect, to last.

My heart is fluttering, my breath quick and shallow. You were *you* for a moment. I saw you. Heard you. Felt you touch me.

It's not sex I want, although I don't *not* want it. It's your tenderness I need. Your affection. I'll do anything to bring you to me. Even this.

'If we find someone I can trust, I'll go,' I offer, unable to fight the hope for more. There may be nothing left for you to give me but your lust and the trappings of your success. Bereavement is a hammer, shattering the self to remake one anew. No one is ever the same once grief has transformed them. Does Lily hold your heart so tightly it can never belong to me? Perhaps I will always be a source of pain, and she the remembered source of joy.

Can I live with having everything but your love? Do I have a choice? I'm unanchored without you.

You face me when we reach the car. 'Thank you.'

'Would you like to return to the penthouse first?' Witte asks you.

'That's not necessary. We'll have everything we need when we arrive.'

I want to ask what you have in mind, where we're going, but you'll tell me if you want me to know. The thought of residential treatment scurries through my mind, but I refuse to entertain it. You couldn't do that to me. You wouldn't. Would you?

You watch me with a faint smile as I slide onto the back seat. 'Before we go . . . would you like to see Baharan's head-quarters?'

If I've learned anything in my life, it's to seize the brief flashes of happiness when they find you. 'I'd love to see what you've built.'

'What *we*'ve built,' you correct, the tinted windows dimming the sunlight when you close the door.

28

Amy

As I approach the entrance of the Crossfire Building, I catch my reflection in the mirrored sapphire glass and smile. I'm about to spin through the copper-framed revolving doors and take charge of my company and my life.

I'm humming 'Into You' by Ariana Grande. It's already been one of the best days of my life. I woke up face down on my bed, with Darius's cock stroking inside me. Two orgasms later, he was back in his room taking a shower, and I was nursing my first cup of coffee. Then, Tovah stopped by. Now, it's time to start making those moves Darius discussed. I need to do my share and support him. And get his goddamn assistant fired.

My ice-pick-thin stilettos click a commanding rhythm across the gold-veined marble floor. I'm getting a ton of second glances. My chin lifts. Why don't I come to work more often? I feel like a goddess. A goddamn queen. All the drones milling around the lobby have no idea what it's like to actually move the needle in this world, while Social Creamery is the reason Baharan is the profitable company it is today, helping fat people get skinny and old guys get a hard-on.

Through me, Social Creamery crafted a caring, forward-thinking, accessible public image for Baharan that no other pharmaceutical company had. Big Pharma tended to lean into their research for marketing, promoting the idea that they were hard at work developing cures. People don't want to hear about what *might* come to market years from now. They want help today, and they want to believe someone gives a shit about them.

Although a relatively recent addition to the Manhattan skyscape, the sapphire spire that is the Crossfire is already a landmark favored by films and television series that shoot in the city. To headquarter your business here means something, and it's the one thing I can be grudgingly grateful to Aliyah for.

I give the black-suited guards a wave as I pass the security desk. One of them stands with a slight frown as if he doesn't recognize me.

Well, I don't recognize that idiot either. It's his *job* to know who I am. I don't have to give him the time of day. Which just happens to be close to lunch, hence the number of bodies in the lobby.

Swiping through the turnstiles with my badge, I strut toward the bank of elevators. I hit the button for the tenth floor, tapping my foot as I wait. The doors to the car on my left open, and – wouldn't you know it – Gideon and Eva Cross step out, his hand at the small of her back as they exit an otherwise empty elevator. One of the many perks of owning the building is making the elevators go from top to bottom without stopping to pick up lesser mortals.

I shimmy my shoulders to shrug on my Lily guise and flash them a smile. 'Hi! Off to lunch?'

'Amy,' Gideon says by way of greeting. He stands, as he always does, just behind his wife, in a way that has him looking over her shoulder. An easy thing for him to do because he's so much taller than her. They're always a united front, one unit instead of two separate people. Textbook codependency if you ask me.

Eva's glossy nude lips curve in a cat-with-cream smile

because she's banging that fine-ass man like a war drum. Lucky bitch. 'Yes, we're starved. You look fabulous, by the way! I love your suit.'

'Thank you.'

I preen a little because I do look epic. She looks damn good, too, as always. Today her outfit is a belted black, white and gold Versace shirt dress with the unmistakable Medusa logo. He's wearing a black three-piece suit, white shirt and a white tie with thin gold striping. They always coordinate like that. It's disgusting. The Lord and Lady of New York with their gag-inducing portmanteau, GidEva, and their cute little dog.

There's a horde of paparazzi out front just waiting for them to appear. By the time I walk past the Baharan reception desk a few minutes from now, the newest pictures of Mr. and Mrs. Cross will be everywhere. Style gurus will gush over Eva's dress and accessories. YouTubers will replicate her high, long ponytail, even if they can't quite capture that perfect shade of blond. The maker of her three-inch gold hoop earrings will bombard me with ads on social platforms using her image. For all I know, Social Creamery may be responsible for the jewelry designer's account.

Gideon, whose suits are bespoke and too expensive for ninety-nine percent of the world's population, isn't so easy to monetize, but they worship him all the same. His black hair is a lustrous mane that brushes his collar, a style that is screaming-orgasm sexy and would look ridiculous on any man except Hugh Jackman or Keith Urban, who've rocked similar lengths. His eyes are the most incredible color, a cerulean more striking than the Armands' pale blue, and the only time they invite you into the window of his brilliant business mind is when he's looking at his wife.

I find it fucking impossible to imagine their entire life isn't totally fake. No one is born with tits and ass like hers. No one looks absolutely picture-perfect every damned time they walk their dog, even in the misery that is New York during a winter storm. No normal couple lives in homes so luxurious they're featured in architectural magazines or vacations on superyachts with names like *Angel* and *Ace*. And no married couple is in constant physical contact like they are. Maybe in the honeymoon stage, but they've been married four years now. The charm should've worn off.

Whatever. I take a step toward the open doors of the elevator car in front of me and glance at their backs as they walk away. Gideon's hand has slid down to the curve of Eva's hip, which sways as she walks.

He's got to have a dick the size of my pinky, and her breast implants probably slosh like a waterbed when he rams his tiny cock into her.

I smile, picturing it.

Yep, I feel better already.

I feel even better when I exit the elevator into Baharan's reception vestibule. Four elevator shafts exit onto the floor, one next to the car I took and two more across the way. To my right, a solid pane of glass affords views of the city with its soaring towers, billowing steam and streams of yellow cabs. To the left is the reception desk, a stainless-steel station with modern curves and room for three receptionists who are all fielding calls. The Baharan logo hangs from the ceiling with delicate-looking posts, the calligraphic font feminine and flowing, with only the word 'pharmaceutical' written out in no-nonsense block letters.

Pausing, I take it all in. A frosted-glass partition behind reception offers a bit of privacy for the many cubicles beyond. The entire floor is ours, but one day, Darius and I will own a building even better than the Crossfire. Companies will fight to base their headquarters there. Movies and television shows will use shots of it to establish the Los Angeles setting. No one will care about GidEva anymore.

What will they call us? DarAmy? AmDar? I laugh, and the receptionists, three brunettes – two women and one man – look at me. I just smile back. They work for me, after all.

I stroll past the desk and head toward my office. I'd argued for a corner, but Aliyah shot me down. She told me the corner offices were for her and her three sons, but Kane sits in a cubicle, so that should've left a corner for me. I'm family, too.

'Of course you are,' she'd cooed. 'But we can't put a social media manager into a corner office.'

As if what I brought to Baharan wasn't a game-changer for them. Entering a space dominated by pharmaceutical giants that have been in business for centuries wasn't easy. More than a few startups turned to direct-to-consumer marketing, driving traffic to company websites where a stable of medical professionals consult online and prescribe, allowing for distribution through direct mail.

Knowing who to target, how best to target them, and fine-tuning the messaging and advertising creative took both skill and preexisting structure. I brought that to Baharan. I was the one who got them seen, trusted and respected. Before me, they'd had a handful of products they struggled to sell effectively.

One of these days, Aliyah will admit to my face that she'd be nothing without me. I've imagined how that moment will go in a million different ways. Any of them will work. I don't really care. But she's going to grovel. She'll beg me to keep her relevant. And I'm going to laugh in her face.

I head to my office, which is adjacent to Darius's. As I walk by, some of the bent heads in the cubicles lift. A few employees offer distracted smiles. A couple of the girls wave – we've been out for drinks before and are due to hit the town again soon. Maybe tonight. Why not? I'm ready to celebrate; as Eva said, I look fabulous. Others look away quickly when I catch them staring. Stare away, peons. I know I look *good*.

Stopping by Darius's office, I peek through the open door but don't see him. His assistant isn't at her desk either. Fury spreads through me like a hot flash, misting my skin with sweat. I glance around, turning in a complete circle, looking for them. I think to ask my account manager, Clarice, but she's not in her cubicle. Instead, an employee I've never seen before is on her phone.

I decide to call Darius from my office and see where he's at. I pivot to the closed door and push it open, taking a couple of steps through when I catch a guy sitting at my desk, rifling through my drawers.

'What the fuck?!' I snap. 'What are you doing in my office?'

'Excuse me?'

'You fucking heard me. Get the hell out of my drawers!' I look around. 'What have you done with my art? Where are my plants?'

He stands. He's a short man, his pale brown hair already showing signs of male pattern baldness. He's got a belly that hangs over his belt and a crooked tie with an ugly pattern. I see a name plaque on the desk: STEPHEN HORNSWORTH, VICE-PRESIDENT OF R&D.

The room tilts to one side, and I brace myself.

'I'm sorry,' he sputters. 'Who are you?'

'This is my office!'

'Uh . . .' He licks his lips. 'Did you maybe exit the elevator on the wrong floor?'

'Are you fucking *kidding* me?!' I scream. 'Do I look like an idiot to you?'

'*Amy!*'

I snap to attention at the sound of Aliyah's voice. Spinning, I face her. She strides quickly past the cubicles on her way toward me. She's wearing a shimmery gold sweater dress with a chunky gold necklace that matches her earrings and bracelet. Her blond hair is in an artfully messy bun, and her eyes are rimmed heavily in kohl.

'Sweetheart.' Her voice is filled with concern. 'What are you doing?'

She really missed her calling in life. She's an Oscar-worthy actress, her face creased with worry and her eyes reflecting a love I know she doesn't feel. Everyone is looking at us. Phones are ringing, but no one is talking.

My hands clench into fists. 'What is *Stephen* doing in my office?'

She reaches me and shoots an apologetic look at Stephen, who's running his finger along the collar of his shirt. 'You gave up your office last year, Amy.'

'The fuck I did!' I fight the hot sting of tears.

'It was over a year ago, actually,' she says cautiously as if I'm being unreasonable. 'We discussed it, and you told me – and I quote – "What do I need an office for when I don't have a company to run?" So, we gave it to Stephen.'

'I'm not letting you gaslight me, Aliyah. Not this time. It hasn't been over a year since I came in. How long have you been here?' I demand, speaking to Stephen. A heavy weight is on my chest, and panic sizzles on the edges of my consciousness, noxious and terrifying.

His gaze darts between the two of us. 'I was just hired a few months ago. I've had the office since then.'

I shoot a triumphant gaze at Aliyah. 'What's your story now, *Mom*?'

There's a flash of the real Aliyah, then she's hidden again behind the fake one. 'Stephen's predecessor had the office.'

'I call bullshit,' I bite out, my teeth creaking from the pressure. 'Where's Darius?'

She looks away for a minute with exaggerated awkwardness, then faces me again. 'He's working on something with his assistant.'

My molar cracks under the strain, the sound like a gunshot that visibly jolts our captive audience. Fiery pain explodes through my cheek and up into my brain. Hot, coppery blood pours over my tongue and fills my mouth.

I scream in agony, spitting crimson into Aliyah's smug face.

29

Aliyah

'Stop yelling at me, Darius!' The need for a shower is nearly overwhelming. I can smell the blood on me, mixed heavily with alcohol. I stink like a bar fight, and it's close to making me nauseous. 'Hasn't our family made enough of a spectacle for one day? Do you realize how fortunate we are to have a policy prohibiting cellphones in the office?'

My son paces behind me while I use a wet towel in my personal washroom to wipe what blood I can see out of my hair. Thankfully, I have every product and shade in the ECRA+ beauty line in my drawers and was able to repair my makeup. I'd hoped to leave for home, where I could wash Amy off me, but Darius returned before I could make my escape.

'It seems like it would've been pretty straightforward to point out that her new office is on the other side of mine,' he snaps. 'It's smaller, yes, but the view is better. She'd love it.'

I stave off the urge to roll my eyes. What a monumental waste of space. And he spent days decorating it for her, using her existing belongings and adding more. 'Of course I told her. I even tried to show her. She wouldn't listen.'

'Mother.'

My gaze narrows in the mirror. 'Don't use that tone with me. You'll embarrass us further by asking anyone out there' – I gesture to the sea of cubicles outside my office – 'what happened, but feel free if you don't believe me. They all saw the whole debacle.'

Darius curses under his breath and shoves a hand through his hair. Worry and anger are stamped all over his handsome face. 'Where did Ramin take her?'

'I have no idea. I was a bit preoccupied with having *blood* all over me! I'm just grateful he was in the office today to get her out of here. You're lucky you weren't around to witness it. She was frothing at the mouth with blood and spit. It was disgusting.'

'I appreciate your concern for my wife,' he says coldly, pulling his phone out.

'I would appreciate some concern for *me*! Look at my clothes! You have no idea how traumatic it is to have blood spat on you.'

'I should've been here,' he mutters, jabbing at his phone. 'Why the fuck did you send Alice and me up to Cross? They'd already left for lunch.'

'We want to look like we're pulling our weight, right? We worked hard on those ad creatives. Since your wife's company is handling social media advertising for ECRA+, I thought you should be the one to deliver them personally.'

His wife is the problem here; I thought he'd see that. When Amy swiped through the turnstiles, it seemed like a golden opportunity. I sent Darius and his assistant up to Cross Industries and hoped for the best.

I throw the towel into the sink and face him. 'Amy showed up here so drunk she could barely walk straight, then had a meltdown. A psychotic break, actually. She was a crazy person! You're doing her zero favors by ignoring the problem in front of you. She should be committed for observation, then admitted to a treatment center that will sober her up.'

His face is like stone. 'You're not telling me everything. I live with her, for fuck's sake. I know her better than anyone.'

'Fine. Keep deluding yourself until she stumbles into traffic one day, like Kane's girl, and gets herself killed.'

'*Hello.*'

My entire back stiffens painfully at the sound of that girlish voice. Turning my head, I find my eldest son and his wife standing in the doorway to my office. They make a stunning couple: Kane in a black suit with a gray shirt and matching tie, and Lily in emerald, which brings even more attention to those snakelike eyes. His height somehow makes her look even more willowy. One of his hands is curved possessively around her slender hip, while the other carries a black leather satchel. Precious jewels glitter on her ears and encircle her wrist. She looks like royalty.

How is it possible that this day keeps getting worse?

Kane's face is as remote as his brother's. 'My assistant caught us up.'

Lily walks in as if she owns the place, heading to Darius. 'Is there anything I can do?'

'I don't know. What *can* you do?' he retorts, bristling. But his shoulders slump when she simply stands there patiently, her face beautiful and eyes kind. 'I don't know where my wife is,' he mutters. 'I need to call Ramin.'

'Let me handle that.' She holds her arm out behind her, and Kane walks to her, setting his phone in her hand. She taps in the code to unlock it as she steps away.

Is there no privacy between them? No secrets? There must be something, or I will never be able to break them apart.

Kane and Darius exchange a glance, and then both turn their faces toward me. My eldest's face remains inscrutable, as always, but Darius has a look in his eye I haven't seen before and don't like at all.

'Why are you both looking at me like that?' I consciously work on dialing back my frustration.

Lily speaks quietly in the corner of the room. Somehow, within a minute, she's become the hero and I the villain when

I'm the one holding this family and company together. Where the hell has *she* been?

I lift my chin, resenting them all.

'Ramin took her to an emergency dentist on Madison,' Lily says as she rejoins them. 'He's texting you the address.'

'Thank you.' His face softens with gratitude. He leaves without saying a word to me.

Lily turns her gaze on me. 'Is there anything I can do for you? Anything I can get you? Water or coffee, perhaps?'

'Thank you, Lily,' I tell her stiffly, offended by being treated like a fucking visitor. 'I'm fine for now.'

What did I do to deserve *two* daughters-in-law like Amy and Lily? If Ramin even looks twice at a lanky brunette with green eyes, I'll blind him.

'I'll wait out there,' she tells Kane, but when she takes a step, he catches her hand and stops her long enough to kiss her. Like the kiss he gave her in the library when I met her, it's a chaste melding of their mouths, suitable for my viewing. But it lingers a heartbeat longer than a peck, and sexual tension heats the air around them. As they part, their gazes exchange promises that confirm my fears – getting rid of her will be troublesome.

She shuts the door behind her, and Kane stares after her as if he can't bear to have her out of sight.

He faces me with a hard look, as if braced for an unpleasant task. 'I'm sorry you went through that while all three of us were out of the office.'

I press a hand to my forehead, fighting off a headache that feels like a knife shoved through my temple. 'I'm just so upset with Amy. And upset *for* her, of course. Your brother doesn't understand how badly she needs help. Maybe you could speak to him? He looks up to you. If you suggested a rehab program for Amy, he'd listen to you.'

'In no way do I feel comfortable commenting on his personal life.'

'He's your brother!'

One of his darkly arched brows wings up as if to refute that.

I move over to my diffuser and wave the azalea-laden mist toward my face. I take a deep, calming breath. Arguing about Kane's relationship with his siblings is a battle I'm not up to waging today. 'Fine. Please, just think about it. Maybe Lily can discuss it directly with Amy?'

'I'll mention it. Is there anything you need right now? I can take over something on your schedule so you can go home and get cleaned up?'

The bitterness clogging the back of my throat eases. I appreciate that he understands how greatly I contribute to Baharan. It's infuriating having to stress the obvious all the time. 'No, I can manage from home.' I take a calming breath. 'Lily seems to be doing well. Are you returning to the office?'

'Not yet. We just happened to be close by, and I wanted her to see what we have here.'

Despair and excitement war inside me. 'Any idea exactly when you'll be coming back?'

'I'm shooting for the Monday after next, but that's subject to change.'

'You've been gone for nearly two months as it is.'

'I'm aware of how long I've been working from home. I'm going to show her around now.' He's already walking toward the door as if he's done his duty and is eager to go. 'I hope you feel better soon.'

'Yes. Of course I will.'

The moment the door shuts, I press both hands against my mouth, physically holding back the argument boiling inside me. I stumble to the sofa and drop like a stone. I want a drink so badly my mouth is watering. Oh no . . . I'm becoming Amy.

The thought is almost enough to spur hysteria.

Not again. I shake my head violently. I'm not losing control again. This is an opportunity, and I won't squander it. I will continue building the company Kane can't even envision yet. Then he'll see. They'll all see.

Although just having had someone else's bodily fluids spat all over me is sickening, I accept the discomfort and move to my desk. It's not as if the feeling is unfamiliar. I pull up the security cameras on the main floor and settle in to wait. Eventually, my utter stillness causes the motion sensor-activated overhead lights to turn off, just as they would have done if I'd left for the day. Anyone walking by would assume I'd gone. All the office doors are set within walls of frosted glass, an aesthetic choice to match the cubicles but also a way to ensure the natural light from the exterior windows brightens the entire floor.

I don't know how long I sit there, watching Kane take Lily around to all the executive offices. It becomes a repeating cycle: awe at her beauty, followed by the universally shocked expression that he would suddenly have his wife back, and finishing with being wholly charmed by whatever interaction they had with her. Kane has so easily stepped into the role of accessory, allowing her to shine. His gaze never leaves her, and he wears a warm smile of pride and male appreciation.

Any idea I'd entertained of my eldest being impartial is shot to hell.

They pause at Kane's cubicle. Kane, the CEO and Chairman of the Board, has no office. He commands from a workspace among and alongside staff. It's infuriating. If we had equal offices, it would make the right statement. Instead, his egalitarian leadership approach seems effortless, making me look like I'm trying too hard.

I square my shoulders. I'm not *trying* to look powerful. I *am* powerful. My sons' unfortunate choices of wives won't interfere with that.

Kane cleans out his desk, shoving files and other items into his satchel. Lily smiles at the employee on the other side of the glass partition. They begin to chat. Kane steps out and urges his wife into his space with a hand at her elbow. In short order, she's sitting on the edge of his desk with her long legs crossed, and everyone has gathered around. She appears to be telling a story, her arms and expression animated. There is amusement on the faces of everyone, and not a single fucking employee is doing their damn job except for reception, which one person is apparently managing because two of them are listening to Lily.

'I see you,' I hiss at her, my eyes narrowed. There is nothing sweet or disarming about her. She's a woman who understands the power of her appearance. She's observant. She compliments women on their jewelry and leverages personal items on desks and cubicle walls to establish rapport. She smiles and reaches for Kane often, touching his sleeve every few moments. It's an act I recognize, a performance any attractive woman with a brain would see right through.

Eventually, my son and his wife leave, and my attention turns to his admin, Julian. I'll have wasted my time if Julian doesn't take off for lunch. As the minutes tick by, I think that's exactly what I've done. But then he stands, stretches, pulls on his jacket, and heads toward the front.

I send my schedule for the next two weeks to the printer, then leave my office to collect it from the copy room. I pass the break room on the way and am relieved that Julian isn't there. If he's left the building, I'll have an even larger window of time. I grab the papers from the tray, shove them into a folder, then walk with purpose toward Kane's desk.

This would be so much easier if he had a damned office!

His cubicle is wide open to the floor, leaving me no way to be discreet. All I can do is act as if I have every right to log into his terminal, which I do. We're talking about my company. I'm the Chief Operations Officer, after all.

Most of the floor is empty, although a handful of employees eat at their desks. I sit at Kane's station, dropping the folder on the desktop as an excuse to be there. Pulling out his keyboard tray, I wake the system and log in with his password, which is stored in the database that logs every keystroke and phone call made on every Baharan terminal. The pharmaceutical industry is cutthroat, and we must be ever vigilant against corporate espionage and cyber theft.

Once I'm in, I look at his calendar, running through his appointments. Every meeting is set for either a video conference or a phone call. A doctor's visit was scheduled for this morning, which explains why he's not actively working from home at the moment.

I open his browser and then his private mailbox. I've never been able to get into it before and may never be able to again. Today is a rare perfect storm when he's been in the office, then left without me, and his admin is out to lunch. In the future, if he goes through the security logs, will he remember if he checked his email from his desk before leaving for nearly two weeks? Will he remember what time he left? I don't think so.

A steady stream of adrenaline pumps through my veins, dampening my palms. My feet tap to purge the restless energy. I scroll swiftly, my eyes darting back and forth as I power-read every subject line and sender. Near the bottom is an unread email that catches my attention and holds it. The sender is Rampart Protection & Investigative Services, and the subject reads, Final Report and Case Termination.

My heart pounds so hard it begins to hurt. My fingers tremble as they hover over the keys.

Is he on to me?

He's smart enough. Why else would he use an outside firm instead of Baharan's in-house team? Doesn't he trust our people? *Could* he trust them to investigate me, considering my position within the company? I can't imagine he knows I've occasionally encouraged the head of our security to fuck me on his desk. Rogelio is too thorough to get caught. Then again, Kane has repeatedly shown that he's aware of more than he should be and ruthless when necessary.

Except when it comes to his wife.

I hate the nervousness that crawls around and between my vital organs, like a million ants have invaded my body. Darius is more vulnerable to accusations of treachery than me; I ensured that. Still, I could better protect us both if I had advance warning.

'Identify the problem,' I coach myself as I open the email. 'Then dissect it.'

I recognize the guilt that mists my skin with sweat and leads me to wild conclusions without basis. I've been too careful, and Kane's been too oblivious.

Dear Mr. Black,

Please find attached the final case report of our investigation for your records. It provides a summary overview and analysis of the findings you and I discussed previously. The case is now closed, as per your request.

We appreciate your business and hope we'll have the pleasure of working with you again in the future.

All best,

Giles Prescott

Owner / Lead Investigator
Rampart Protection & Investigative Services

The sharp points of my nails dig into the soft flesh of my palm. The pain centers me and reminds me that I can survive anything. I've already survived the worst that can happen to a woman. Anything else is an annoyance, nothing more.

I open the attachment, scroll past the cover sheet, and my stomach drops. I hardly breathe, arrested and unmoving.

Lily.

Kane has been investigating his wife. And not just recently. Rampart's report begins by detailing the initial scope of the investigation and the date it began, which was shortly after she was declared dead. Six years. My mind struggles to accept the extent of the scrutiny. What could possibly take six years to dig up?

I force myself to relax muscles that have gone stiff with strain. My mouth curves into a broad smile. It's not Amy I need to focus on; it's Lily. The flight instinct transitions fluidly to fight.

I'm no longer the prey; I am the hunter.

I send the file to the printer, close the email and mark it as unread. I make a mental note: I may need to arrange a meeting with Rogelio to erase those telltale keystrokes. If our security chief were a more attentive lover, I wouldn't put it off.

I backtrack out, closing everything I opened before turning the terminal off.

Standing, I take a deep breath and touch a hand to my hair. It feels like I've run a marathon, the waning adrenaline spike leaving me shaky and breathless. I push the chair beneath the desk, ensuring nothing is out of place. Then I head back to the copy room.

Is it all an act, Kane's affection for Lily? Perhaps she's not the only one playing a role. There is something about her he questions deeply enough to investigate. Considering her stake in Baharan, I have a right to know what he suspects and how damaging it might be to the company.

The printer is still spitting out pages when I get there. By the time the job finishes, the stack is an inch thick. I straighten them, put them into a manila envelope and head back to my office for my purse. Then I leave for the day.

I have a lot of homework to do.

30

Lily

Long before we reach I-287, I know we're headed to Connecticut. The happy fluttering in my belly settles in for the ride. My anticipation and excitement are alive within the confines of the Range Rover. You are at the wheel; I am in the passenger seat beside you. Witte was picked up at the Crossfire by another driver.

Before we left the city, you relayed quick orders, which I hardly paid attention to because you were undressing on the sidewalk in front of the Crossfire.

You removed your jacket first, highlighting the leanness of your waist. The well-defined muscles of your back flexed as you hung the garment from an OEM hanger attached to the driver's seat headrest. Your tie was next; the tie clip and your cufflinks slipped neatly into your coat pockets. Then, you unbuttoned your collar and rolled up your sleeves, your biceps briefly straining the luxe material of your shirt.

You were quick and efficient, your actions commonplace, but your body moves with such power and vital sensuality. You are devastatingly handsome and urbane. It amused me how completely oblivious you were to the number of covetous glances you'd provoked in bystanders by the time you said farewell to Witte.

Then you assisted me into the front seat and revealed you were aware of my admiration all along. 'We won't make it out of the city if you keep looking at me like that.'

'If you keep looking that hot, it's your fault.'

It's a veneer, of course, a professional polishing. You must have applied yourself obsessively to have made such a perfect facade for Kane Black. But you were always eager to learn, to rise. You just needed the opportunity – and the money – to make the transformation possible.

Now, I'm free to study you to my heart's content. The city traffic is far behind us, and trees line the highway. Stevie Nicks sings about waters closing around her. The driver's seat is slid back to its farthest point to accommodate your long legs. You control the steering wheel with your left hand, leaving your right hand to rest lightly on your thigh. You are relaxed and completely in control of the powerful vehicle.

You wear no watch. There is only golden skin from your elbows to the tips of your fingers, bare but for a sprinkling of dark hair and the wedding band that proclaims you as mine. Such an innocent thing, the baring of your forearms and the minimalist adornment, but I find everything about your appearance profoundly erotic. I always have.

We talk about some of the people I met at your headquarters. It's clear you take a personal interest in your employees from the amusing anecdotes you share. That they feel free to laugh with you and share private stories reveals a great deal about your leadership style.

'Why did you bring your family into Baharan?' I ask.

'You know I didn't have a choice with my mother since she originated and owned the Baharan trademark. She agreed to assign it to the company in return for a stake, and she invested to gain an even larger share, using royalties from licensing my father's chemical patents until they expired. And honestly, the company needed someone else who wanted it as badly as I did.'

You look at me. 'I was barely functioning after I lost you.

And the company was little more than a logo that needed refreshing and a handful of staff nearly as lifeless as I was.'

With a deep sigh, I share your grief, although it's not for the girl I once was, it's for the boy you once were. Your mother's emotional immaturity damaged your self-esteem. You've always struggled with feelings of inadequacy. Working with her is the worst possible outcome. How will you ever recover when new wounds are inflicted so often?

'Why bring your brothers and sister into it?'

Your shoulder lifts in a shrug. 'They're employees, not shareholders. My mother suggested that having family in key positions would make it easier for me to do what I want, and she was right. Darius has his moments, but he falls in line. Ramin comes off as a slacker, but it's an act. He's CLO, and hates being wrong, which is an advantageous flaw when you're an attorney.'

Older trees line the interstate, their broken and vine-covered branches occasionally revealing pockets of homes that have lost the optimism with which they were built. Paint peels from warped siding, windows sit cockeyed in their frames. Power and phone cables stretch across sagging roofs, lifelines attempting to keep the American dream of home-ownership alive. Thousands of eyes pass over these houses every day, yet they might as well be invisible.

The landscape begins to blur, and my eyes close. I think I know where we're going, but I'm afraid to hope.

On the radio, Kansas begins to sing to a wayward son, and I sing along softly at first, then you join in. A smile bursts across my face before I can stop it. Creedence Clearwater follow with their ode to Suzy Q, and our voices rise in unison. I lower the window to feel the breeze, tilting my chin so air flows over my face.

Your laugh is deep and genuine. You reach for my hand,

linking our fingers before lifting them to your mouth. You kiss my knuckles. 'I missed you, *Setareh*. So much.'

I don't know what's altered to make you so easy and affectionate. I don't know how long your mood will last. You are like the sun, warm and enlivening when you shine on me but transient. I have been hopeful and hopeless too many times over the past several weeks. And the simple truth is that you couldn't stay away from Lily, couldn't stop yourself from loving her, but it's been all too easy to keep your distance from me. I thought I could don her skin and slip into her place in your life — a place you left unfilled. But that skin doesn't fit, and I am only my inadequate self.

The view outside has changed. The towns are bigger, the houses no longer ramshackle and sad. Soon, they are farther apart, less visible, larger and set farther back from the side roads. I search for the unfamiliar and strange, landmarks that are recent enough to be new to me.

'Are we there yet?' I ask.

'Less than fifteen minutes.'

I wait a beat, then tease, 'Are we there yet?'

You shoot me a droll glance, and the warmth in your amusement thrills me.

By the time we exit the interstate, my spirits are buoyed. With every turn, I grow more excited. Soon, you're pulling into the driveway of a two-story cottage covered in cedar shingles that have weathered to gray. The white trim is crisp and bright. The yard is beautifully landscaped, with massive hydrangeas and thickly planted perennials in every hue and height boarding the flagstone paths. The home blends with its neighbors yet could never be similar. I feel the pull of it, have been feeling that pull the whole drive.

The quarter-arch windows on the second floor stare down

at us like eyes. There is the unmistakable sense that the beach house waits impatiently for our return.

'Kane,' I breathe, 'have you been leasing this place the whole time . . . ?'

'It's ours now.' You put the car in park and turn off the engine. 'When your estate lawyer told me it was a rental, I couldn't believe it. And I couldn't let it go. It took me nearly two years to convince the owner to sell, but they came around.'

When your beloved face blurs, I realize I'm crying.

Unbuckling your seatbelt, then mine, you tell me, 'We met here. We were married here. If we have children, I want them to spend their summers here. I couldn't walk away from it.'

I'm made speechless by a throat that aches like a throbbing wound. I meet the house's watchful gaze again, and that unblinking stare arrests me, so much so that I jump with surprise when you open the passenger door to offer me your hand.

With your arm around my waist, you lead me up the steps from the driveway and unlock the front door with a numerical keypad. You step back as if to let me enter first, then scoop me up like a bride and carry me across the threshold.

Snuggling into your embrace, I note how much bigger you are now, how your strength cradles me easily and makes me feel safe.

The curtains in the living room are thrown wide and light floods the ground floor. Everything is just as before, like a time capsule. Every surface shines. There isn't a single dust mote in the air, yet there is a sense of hollowed emptiness, of pervasive abandonment.

'When were you here last?' I ask.

'I left at dawn the morning after the Coast Guard called off the search.' Your voice is even and untroubled, but your dark eyes reveal darker emotion. 'I haven't been back.'

You set me down by the sofa and embrace me from behind. The walls are painted a matte black with a semigloss trim in the same shade. There is a cluster of green velvet sofas in front of the fireplace and a dining table made from richly stained wood with an extravagant grain.

Throw blankets and pillows of charcoal fur and green crochet cover the couches. Potted plants and crystals of various sizes and shapes are everywhere, displayed on gray-washed rattan end tables and shelving units.

The rear of the house is entirely open to the veranda, with a folding glass wall that can be slid open to its outermost points. A framed print on one side cautions against letting anyone steal your magic. A matching print on the other side says Lily was one hundred percent *that* witch.

Outside, hills of sand grass part in the middle to form a pathway to the public beach.

Lacing my fingers over yours, I lean into you. My gaze roams. Unlike the penthouse, personal photos are everywhere here, framed on every shelf and table. Above the mantel is the only change I note. A single large image replaces the random-sized art pieces previously displayed there, dominating the space.

It's a watercolor over pencil, the image of a siren seated on a rocky shoreline, her back to the artist, her face hidden. Flowing black hair falls to her hips and flutters in the breeze. Her tail begins as pale pink at her waist, the hue deepening into progressively darker shades of red until the fins at the end are as inky as her hair. With her left hand, she beckons a three-masted schooner with black sails and hull; she calls forth a storm to wreck it with her right.

Such a fanciful image. I'm curious as to why it speaks to you, although I agree it's striking and perfect for the space.

Your lips touch my temple. 'I need to prepare for a meeting I have in a few minutes. Will you be all right?'

'Of course.' I steel myself to be alone for however short a time. It's worse because I have begun to hope we've turned a corner.

I straighten, digging for inner strength, and you step back. Then you round me, coming into my field of vision, staring at me with firestorm eyes. I watch, apprehensive and expectant, as time slows. Your eyelids grow heavy as your dark head lowers and tilts to find my mouth. I clutch your waist.

There is no one to see us. This is not a performance.

This moment is for me. For us.

Your lips brush mine. The caress is light and so very gentle. A silent sob of longing escapes me, and your hand at my hip flexes fitfully, tightening and releasing.

Your tongue strokes the seam of my lips, and I open to you, my fingers twisting into the fine weave of your shirt. The deep lick you reward me with makes me shiver.

Pleasure floods me in a searing, drugging rush. Strength melts into languor.

You tighten your grip, pulling me fully against the hard column of your muscled body.

Oh . . . you taste like honeyed whiskey. The flavor of your kiss is extraordinary and intoxicating. I'm already addicted, desperate for more. My lips circle your tongue, and I suckle softly, seeking your smoky-sweet essence. We're aligned from chest to thighs. Your deep groan vibrates against my breasts.

With one hand curled around your nape and the other holding the back of your head, I won't let you retreat, although you're not trying to. I drink from you, devouring, my tongue following yours into the heated depths of your mouth. Your embrace tightens, your body begins to quiver . . . or perhaps I'm the one trembling. Soft, desperate cries flow from me, my hunger so great I can't stop them.

You drench my senses. Your skin has warmed with lust. As your scent deepens, I breathe deeply and surge onto my toes, responding instinctively and fiercely to your silent demands.

Your hand at my hip dips to the lower curve of my buttock, and you tug me into your straining erection. Your penis is hard and thick against my lower belly. My tongue plunges into your mouth as I need your body to plunge into mine. Your honeyed flavor grows deeper, stronger. Your returning kiss is feverish, your tongue a velvet lash. It strokes into my mouth with furious licks, your hunger ravenous. We're fucking each other's mouths, our tongues frantic and tangling.

You break contact first. We're both breathing hard. My fingers weave into the heavy silk of your hair as your forehead touches mine. Your rough gasps betray the limits of your control.

'Kane . . .'

'You shatter me, *Setareh*.' There is erotic heat in your words. 'I'm in pieces.'

Covering my hands with yours, you pry my fingers open with tempered strength so you can pull away. You press soft, lingering kisses to my knuckles. Then you let go.

I watch as you walk backward a few steps before turning to take the hallway to the only downstairs bedroom. Restless, anxious, filled with vibrating energy, I take in my surroundings and debate what to do. I'm aflame, bright and burning. I feel like running, dancing, screaming, spinning, fucking you until I can't move, can't think, can't torture myself anymore.

Kicking off my shoes, I untie the bow of my blouse and pad on bare feet to the patio doors. I unlock them and push each side open. The house feels like it takes a big deep breath, the stagnant air inside dispelled by the salt-laden breeze.

Here, in this house, we are a couple. In the penthouse, there is only me without you.

Moving to the bookshelf, I study each of the photos in turn. I pick up the large silver frame that holds wedding photos. Lily wore floor-length red lace with a high-neck halter secured by three pearl buttons at the nape. The back of the dress was open and plunging, falling into a short train. Her hair was worn up with sprigs of baby's breath tucked within the black strands and elaborate pearl earrings dangling from her ears. The bouquet was Blacklist lilies and red roses.

And you, my love. No man has ever been as gorgeous in a tuxedo. Even in a photograph, you take my breath away.

So young, so radiantly in love. No hint of the secrets behind the smiles.

I return the frame to its place and move on, studying them all. I hear laughter echoing through the house, snippets of conversations, sensual cries entwined with pleasured groans. I know that's why you haven't returned. You hear the ghosts, too.

When I reach the stairs, I ascend. Two guestrooms are at the front of the house with their window eyes. The master bedroom at the back overlooks Long Island Sound and smells like you. Your colorful kantha quilt is folded over the foot of the bed.

Lily's clothes still hang in her closet, and when I move to yours, I see all your clothes are there. Not the bespoke garments of the Kane Black I woke up to but the thrifted clothes of the man I first met.

I change, stripping to my underwear sans bra and then dropping a red slip dress over my head. It's slightly too big, which randomly reminds me that lunchtime has passed, and you haven't eaten.

In the kitchen, I search the cupboards, pantry and fridge, finding them well stocked, which I'd expected, considering Witte. I weigh the options and decide to put together a charcuterie plate for you: various salumi, crackers, olives and peppers, and sliced cheese. I drizzle a bit of honey over the cheese and add a splash of chili garlic-infused olive oil over the meat. I arrange a cocktail fork atop a linen napkin so you can keep your hands clean and finish it all off with a glass of sparkling water.

I carry everything to you on a wicker tray, stopping in the doorway of the former bedroom to take in the space. For several moments, I just absorb *you*. You're leaning back in a navy-blue leather office chair, talking into a headset while spinning a basketball on the tip of your finger. You're confident and relaxed, speaking with assurance and occasionally listening. I smile.

Your desk is a mid-century antique, with signs of both age and frequent use. The rug is also vintage, with bare spots, and the battered leather sofa in an avocado hue looks like it weighs a ton. Even the accessories and wall art are clearly second-hand. You have racks of dumbbells and medicine balls in one corner, kettlebells, a jump rope, resistance bands, and a TRX strap anchored in the wall.

It's so *you*; I'm instantly in love with the room.

The space is far removed from your home office in the penthouse, which – while certainly the most cheerful and colorful room in that residence – is unmistakably upscale and lavish. The only similarities between that office and this one are the pale walls and the small basketball hoops affixed above the trash cans.

You glance toward me and immediately straighten, a tension in your frame that wasn't there before as if I've caught you doing something you shouldn't. You set the ball on a clear acrylic base on the corner of your desk and wave me in, even as you continue speaking. I come around to your side, setting the tray down. There is a framed snapshot of Lily by your monitor, this one of her laughing, her eyes meeting the camera lens through splayed fingers as if she'd just covered her face to hide her amusement at being photographed.

I squeak in surprise when you catch me by the wrist and tug me into your lap, tapping a button on your headset mid-sentence before giving me a quick, hard kiss.

'Thank you,' you tell me, lifting me off you and sending me away with a swat of your hand to my rear. You tap the button again and pick up your discussion right where you left off.

I look at you over my shoulder, so startled I trip over my feet and stumble. You felt like a stranger just then. I feel suddenly chilly and apprehensive, my hands rubbing goosebumps on my arms.

A smaller version of the siren portrait is hanging on the wall beside the closet. The room is yours in every way. It's only you who inexplicably seems strange and vaguely sinister as if the sea breeze banished an enchantment, revealing something dark and previously veiled.

Dr. Goldstein is fucking with your head.

I leave the room abruptly, shivering.

I'd hoped the change of location would free us of Lily's seductive, all-consuming hold on you. Instead, we've moved into a home with something worse.

It's not Lily's ghost who fills this house with savage, unchecked rage.

It's yours.

Lily

I turn on the living room fireplace using the remote on the coffee table, then settle back into the deep-seated sofa and pull one of the faux-fur throw blankets over my legs. It takes me a minute to figure out that the siren painting is like the mirrored television in the sitting room of the penthouse; with the push of a button, the image fades into a screen.

'Hey.'

Your voice turns my head toward the hallway. Leaning your shoulder against the wall, you're relaxed and breathtakingly handsome. For a heartbeat, I see the younger man I once knew overlaying the man you are now. His lanky body is narrower than yours, his hair longer, his smile open and cocky. His eyes gleam with humor, mischief and love. Then I blink, and he's gone.

'Hey,' I rejoin.

'What are you up to?' Your gaze is dark and watchful.

I release my grieving for the young man I once knew and focus on you now. 'Well, it looks like I've missed a new *Jack Ryan* film, two James Bond flicks, and one *Mission Impossible*. I figured I'd start catching up.'

Your mouth curves in an indulgent smile. 'Mind if I join you?'

'It would make my night if you did.'

'Oh, I bet I could up the ante.' You straighten. 'What are your thoughts on pizza?'

'When are my thoughts *not* on pizza?'

'When I'm inside you.' Your smile widens at my startled reaction to your naughty playfulness. It wells from a place of long-standing intimacy, and I must accept that. 'I'll make the call. Give me ten.'

You leave, and I feel the weight of night settle around me as you turn the lights off on your way out. Focusing on the television, I scroll until I find *Jack Ryan: Shadow Recruit*. I start, then pause the film, catching the distant sound of your voice as you place our order.

In the first few weeks after you found me, I just wanted you to accept me with open arms. We've moved beyond our former impasse, and now it seems I can have my desire. But nervousness makes me shift restlessly. I'm a woman who reads people well, but you're a mystery now, so different from the bereaved widower I've been living with.

There's only one woman I want, you said. Is it me? Or *her*?

This cycle of ecstasy and misery, desire and dread, began long before we met. Women damaged by the men in their lives raised us, unfit mothers who were incapable of providing consistent kindness and attention. Because of them, we expect and crave unrequited love. Neither of us is emotionally mature. If we were, we would've known to stay far away from each other. We'd crave security instead of this mad game we're playing with our hearts and minds.

I know falling in love shouldn't feel like falling off a cliff, but you and I have never stood on solid ground at any point in our lives. Would we still want each other if we established safe boundaries, or would we miss the full-tilt spin of our dizzying obsession?

You come down the stairs and move into the kitchen. 'I'm grabbing a brew. You want something? Water, maybe? A soda?'

189

'I'm good, thanks.'

I hear you move around in the heart of the home, but I don't watch. We're strangers in more ways than one. I can't shake my apprehension. We are very much alone here. The beach house cocoons us together, away from the world.

Rounding the sofa, you fold gracefully into the deep cushions with a bottle of beer in hand. You've changed into striped pajama pants and a black T-shirt. Your feet are bare, and your wedding band is your only adornment. My body tenses pleasurably. The faint scent of your cologne arouses me, and the radiating power of your body stirs my inborn feminine awareness of your virile masculinity. You tilt your head back as you drink, your throat working on a swallow, casual and relaxed, while I sit inches from you, suffering the ache of wanting you.

You've shaved for the second time today. Of all the things my mind is struggling to piece together and accept, that revealing courtesy is the hardest at the moment. It signals how you expect our night to end and the thoughtful avoidance of chafing my skin in delicate places. My breath quickens.

You set the bottle down on a coaster, clearly absorbed in thought. There is a weighted concentration about you.

'What's on your mind?' I ask.

'You. Always.'

Your elbows are on your knees, and you've clasped your hands. You face the television. It's devastating how beautiful you are in profile, burnished by firelight, the shadows hugging the hollows beneath your cheekbones and outlining the defined strength of your biceps.

Shifting, you position yourself to face me, bending one knee onto the cushions and draping your arm over the back of the sofa. 'You're the reason I breathe. Nothing anyone could say or do – even you – can change how I feel about you.'

For a long moment, there is only silence. Then a soft sob escapes me. I close my eyes, feeling dizzy from the sudden rush of anguished joy.

You take my hand, your fingers playing with the ring on my finger. 'I haven't left your side since I found you. I've been nearby, waiting for you.'

Could it have been that easy? To just find you in the penthouse and say something? Anything?

No. You want answers, not conversation. Revelations that will change everything between us. But isn't that what I secretly want? To be loved as I am and not as she was.

I exhale in a rush. Is there anything more difficult than facing a truth you can't bear? Your eyes meet mine in silence.

'How could you stay away from me, though?' I ask fervently. 'For this long?'

'You answer first,' you retort. 'The same applies to you.'

Surprise arrests me. I was so focused on my misery. It never occurred to me that you might be mirroring my turmoil. 'I tried.'

Your brow arches. 'To fuck me. Not talk to me.'

'You're not being fair,' I argue, then the fight drains from me. I don't want us to be at odds, and I must admit my many failings. My eyes burn, then my vision blurs. 'I didn't know what to do, how to narrow the gap between us. You've ... changed. My feelings haven't, but you have.'

You brush the tears from my cheeks with cool fingertips. 'Watching you get hit by that car ... I felt the impact. I started breaking into pieces right there on the street, holding you in my arms while hundreds of people pressed in all around us. I thought my punishment must be to lose you over and over again.'

'Oh, Kane.'

'I've been so focused on the past, on who you've been, on

everything I don't know or understand ... You owe me answers – you'll concede that – and I have a ton of reasons for being cautious about prying them out of you. But expecting you to provide those answers without first making you feel safe was idiotic. You can understand, can't you? You didn't come back to me willingly. I found –'

'– me. You found me, and we're together now. Does anything else matter?' Can I convince you to leave the past behind, or does it imprison you?

You caress my bare shoulder with reverent fingertips. 'The need for those other answers is urgent, *Setareh*, but I already know the most important thing – I'm dead without you. I've been dead without you.'

'No.' *No, no, no.* How can anything hurt this much and be survived? It seems impossible.

You clutch me so tightly I can hardly breathe, but I don't care. 'Let's start over. Just promise me I'm safe with you, and we'll go from there.'

For several slow, wrenching heartbeats, I let your words sink in. All that you've said and all that you didn't. I pull back to meet your gaze and see hope, love and sadness.

I take both your hands and hold them tightly. 'You're safe,' I vow quietly, knowing full well what the covenant will cost me. 'And I'm going to make you happy.'

As you study me, your features soften, and my fear eases.

'I'm sorry, Kane. Sorry for everything. Sorry I made you –'

'Stop.' Leaning forward, you kiss my forehead and speak against my skin. 'I don't want apologies. I just want you.'

My head bows. I play with your wedding band. Beneath it, I spy skin so pale I know it hasn't seen a moment of sun in years. 'You never let go.'

'I never will.' You grip my hands. 'I can't.'

Tilting your head, you press your lips to mine. It's sweet at first; brief, gentle presses. Then you taste me. Need bursts to life so swiftly I gasp with the force of it. Your tongue delves through the opening I've given you, tangling with mine and stroking. Your spiced honey flavor fills my mouth.

I sway toward you, my hands still trapped in yours. 'Let me touch you.'

'Not yet.'

I want to run my fingers through your hair and feel the warmth of your skin.

'Kane. I need –' I jolt at the sound of the doorbell.

Your mouth smiles against mine. 'Pizza?'

Disengaging, you stand. I watch as you disappear down the hallway to the front door. My lips throb. My nipples are tight and hard, my skin too hot. The promise of more is between us now, and I can't think of anything else.

I hear your voice and a reply, then the door is shut and the deadbolt locked. You come back with pizza, handing me the box with paper plates and napkins balanced on top before you head to the patio doors. You check the lock, then pull the heavy drapes, sealing us in the dark belly of the house. Then you type in a code on the security panel and fully shut out the world.

When you turn back to me, I'm still holding the box in the same position as before.

You scrutinize me, your body growing taut. 'If you're giving me the choice,' you say quietly, 'I'm happy to eat cold pizza. In fact, I'd prefer it that way. Hours cold.'

Expectation sizzles between us.

You're going to make love to me.

Accepting that as inevitable after weeks of believing it impossible makes me tremble. I'll finally feel you everywhere. All over me. Inside me. I task a corner of my mind with memorizing the coming hours in graphic detail. Every caught breath, every shiver of pleasure, every hard thrust of your gracefully muscled body must be remembered in XXX-rated specificity to savor again in the future. It may be all I'll ever have.

'If you don't kiss me again right now,' I say thickly, swallowing past a suddenly dry throat, 'I'm going to die.'

'No.' You come to me with that dangerous stride. 'Next time, I go first.'

I toss the pizza box on the coffee table. The plates and napkins slide off and hang precariously on the edge, but neither of us cares. You sink onto the sofa beside me, pulling me close. My head drops back in supplication, I grip your lean waist and my mouth lifts to yours.

The moment your lips seal over mine, my hands clutch the soft material of your T-shirt. The slow, deep glide of your tongue sets me on fire.

'*Setareh*,' you breathe, pressing your lips to the corner of my mouth, 'our love can survive anything, even death. Tell me you know that.'

I kiss you.

You hold my jaw in both hands, your thumbs pressing gently to keep my mouth open. Your tongue thrusts in smooth, quick dips. I tug at the blanket that is now twisted around my hips, too hot to wear. I push onto my knees and scramble into your lap, my legs straddling yours without breaking the kiss. I'm not good or bad in your arms, right or wrong. It's such a reprieve not to fight that battle, if only for a few hours.

I take over as your hands drop to my hips and savor you with lush licks. You groan, your hands flexing into my flesh. I pull at the hem of your shirt, sliding my hands beneath to touch you.

You gasp, arching into my palms. 'Yes . . . Touch me everywhere.'

My fingertips trace the rigid lacing of your abs, then slide around to the small of your back. Your hands caress my thighs, your thumbs dipping into the grooves on either side of my sex.

'Take this off,' I order, tugging at your T-shirt.

Reaching over your shoulder, you grab the back of the collar and yank it over your head. You toss the T-shirt aside and seize me again.

'Kane . . .' I run my hands across your broad shoulders. 'You're so beautiful.'

You laugh, the sound deep and delighted. You're no longer waging an inner battle either. That's the magic of love, isn't it? The permission to be ourselves, knowing the other is blind to our faults.

I touch you everywhere, learning your extraordinary body's sensual, powerful lines. My mouth follows my hands, my lips pressing to your throat before moving downward.

'Your turn,' you say hoarsely, bunching the hem of my dress around my waist.

But I can't stop touching you. Your arms tangle with mine as you try to undress me. To make it easier, I reach for the ceiling, then press against you as you fling the dress in the general direction of your T-shirt. A shuddering sigh leaves me. Your skin is so warm against my breasts, the hair on your chest soft and springy. Your splayed hands rub up and down my back, arching me gently so that we're tightly together.

'Hold on,' you warn.

The room spins as you cradle and lower me to lie beneath you. I'm still wearing the emeralds, and they sway, reminding me they're there. You bought them for someone else, but now they're mine. *You're* mine. You crouch between my legs. The sculpted lines of your gorgeous face and your full, sexy mouth are taut with lust. Hot male awareness smolders in your eyes and reminds me how well you can hide that predatory gleam and easily mask your animal nature when you want to.

You curl your hands beneath the waistband of my underwear, and I lift my hips, then stretch my legs toward the ceiling.

'I fantasize about these long legs.' You press your lips to my knee, then you tongue the hollow behind it, making me shiver. 'And this freckle, right here.'

'I fantasize about every part of you.'

You pull my panties up the length of my legs, then toss them over the back of the couch with the rest of our clothes.

'My heart is beating so fast,' you tell me, your eyes gleaming with reflected flames from the fireplace.

'Mine, too.'

You caress me from the sides of my breasts to the outer curve of my hips. I shiver and giggle, tickled by that fleeting touch.

A smile curves your mouth. Such a simple expression of delight, but the sight of it breaks my heart.

'You're safe with me, too,' you murmur, lowering your head to my breast.

Fresh tears flood my eyes.

You scorch my tender nipple with the wet heat of your mouth. My back bows, a harsh gasp escaping me at the lash of your tongue. The tip, already peaked from the press of your body against mine, tightens further. Your low growl vibrates against and through me, stimulating the aching cleft between my legs. As your tongue flickers like flame, I feel its phantom echo in my sex. My fingers tangle in the hot silk of your hair.

You shift, moving your attention to my other breast, engulfing the taut point with the hungry suction of your lips and the rapid stroking of your tongue. When your hand delves between my legs, the calloused pads of your fingertips find me slick and swollen. I moan your name, shameless.

Two long, strong fingers enter me as your mouth tugs

rhythmically on my nipple. You begin to stroke deep, leisurely and skillfully. Your thumb rubs over my clitoris with every plunge and retreat. You deftly target a hypersensitive spot inside me, rubbing back and forth over that tender place with merciless finesse.

I pant with delirious pleasure. From the first, I knew your sexual experience was considerable and triumphant. It's evident in everything about you. The predacious sinuousness of your movements. The explicit promises your eyes make. The assured arrogance of your seductions. You know what your body can do to women, and it shows.

It's the reverence I'm unprepared for, the tender veneration that takes us beyond sex into a splendidly physical act of love. Or is it gratitude? What a gift it is to be perfect in someone else's view.

The feel of your pectoral, biceps and shoulder contracting and releasing as you thrust your fingers into my slick core is incredibly erotic.

The orgasm builds, straining my body.

It's entirely physical and entirely not because my soul is trembling, and my heart is aching.

You watch me unravel. 'There's more, *Setareh*. Give me this, and I'll give you the rest.'

The dark promise goads my desire. My hips lift and fall, fucking my greedy sex onto your pumping fingers. There is pressure as you rub into my thrusts, stroking over and over until I'm mindless for release.

'Kane —'

You cover my mouth with yours. Pressing your thumb and fingers together, you apply pressure to my clitoris from within and without. My body locks at the abrupt brutality of the surging pleasure, then I writhe, moaning, my sex tightening and clutching at your fingers. The orgasm is violent and stunning. I hear the rumble of your voice, low and soft, comforting, but the roaring in my ears drowns the words.

Breathless and dazed, I sag boneless into the fur throw beneath me. You blanket my body with your own, your skin so hot it nearly scorches. Your weight soothes and shelters me. I cling to you, running my hands everywhere, kissing you anyplace I can reach.

Your mouth slants across mine for a heart-stopping minute, then you push up onto one forearm and shove the waistband of your pants down just enough to free yourself. You take your penis in hand, stroking it from root to tip in a tight fist. Your erection swells further, lengthening and thickening. I swallow a moan. Everything about you is oversized as if the universe was so captivated by your promise that it gave you more than your share.

With fast, strong tugs, you prime your body for mine, your gaze hotly feral on my face as if challenging me to take you at your most extreme. It's deeply sexual watching you touch yourself, pleasure yourself. You're rougher than I would be, your knuckles white with strain, your biceps bunching as you stroke.

Your jaw is tight with determination as you use the broad head of your erection to part the lips of my sex. You are so aroused you're slick with pre-ejaculate, providing lubricant that blends with mine. You notch the broad crest into my opening, and your eyelids lower heavily as if the contact has drugged you. The pressure of your entry is daunting. It's also delicious.

'You'll take me,' you assure me, with a soft slurring of your words. 'We were made for each other.'

I adjust the angle of my hips and am rewarded as a few inches fill me. My back arches and my body strains into the sensation.

'Oh . . .' I moan. 'You feel so good.'

Your low, deep groan vibrates through me.

Sliding one hand beneath my hips, you lift me, using short, hunched lunges to drive deeper in small increments. The snug fit causes the thick crown of your penis to drag decadently back and forth over urgently sensitive folds, creating friction that's an intense delight. Your biceps bunch and release as you circle my hips into your slow, easy thrusts, teasing my sex with the promise of ecstasy. My core tightens, trembling with renewed arousal, and you growl, the sound so raw and animalistic I, too, go wild.

Erotic demand is thrumming through my veins, thick and hot. I want to shift, mold my curves to your rigid planes, signal to your rutting instincts that I am in desperate heat, but you are a monument of a man, and I haven't the strength to move you.

My only solace is the sounds you're making, the deep groans and stuttered breaths. Your pleasure arouses me to a fevered pitch. Erasing your pain with vivid, mindless pleasure is a goal that consumes me.

You withdraw completely until the wide head of your penis heats my labia, then thrust hard, finally sinking to the root with an exultant roar. The pressure is sublime, and I hold my breath, absorbing that secret sensation of your pulse beating so deep inside me. You pull out, then plunge again, the deep penetration fluid now and luscious. Pleasure is coiled tighter, ratcheted to the limit, poised and impatient. My sex trembles around you, stimulated merely by your size and the staggering elation of being joined with you wholly.

Your teeth catch your lower lip as my core pulsates rhythmically around your hardness. With a low moan of tormented pleasure, you rotate your hips. My orgasm breaks with such force that I scream. You growl with triumph and begin to fuck.

My hips thrust frantically upward, chasing your withdrawals because I can't bear to let you go. Your hips buck hard into the V of my thighs, your body a powerfully sexual machine committed solely to pleasure. You're lost in the moment, voracious and relentless. You grow rigid, breath caught, then shout hoarsely and ride my climaxing sex with unbridled lust. Your orgasm is long and wrenching, your big body wracked with violent tremors aligned with the pulse of each thick ejaculation.

Gasping, dripping sweat, you kiss me as if you're a moment away from death and my mouth alone can save you. We share the very air we breathe. Your lungs draw in my frantic exhalations, and you pant your breath into mine.

Holding you against me, I stroke your heaving back, gentling you as your body quivers in the aftermath. I'm taking the full force of your weight, and it's everything I've ever wanted. I'm achingly aware of your delicious fullness inside me, your heated length dominating me in the most primal way.

Long moments pass. What are you thinking? If someone occupies your thoughts, is it me? I run my big toe up and down your calf, telling myself it doesn't matter.

Eventually, you murmur, 'I was right.' Then you nuzzle your sweat into my skin.

'About what?'

'You didn't have a single thought about pizza.'

I laugh, relieved, and hug you tightly, feeling your lips curve in a smile against my shoulder.

'Let's renew our vows,' you murmur, kissing my neck.

My body responds to your proposal, tightening around your penis with possessive delight. You hum your approval.

'Only if we honeymoon for months,' I barter. 'I don't care where as long as there's no one else around.'

Your head lifts. 'Deal.'

Your face is flushed, and there is sweat on your brow. I register how incredibly handsome you are, then you swivel your hips, and I register how hard you are. If I didn't know better, I'd think you were unsatisfied.

'Impressive,' I say with a laugh.

'Ridiculous,' you counter. 'I'm a man in my thirties now, not a randy kid in college. I shouldn't lose it two minutes after I start fucking my wife. And I should need some damn recovery time.'

You kiss me deeply, thoroughly. When you lift your head again, your eyes are dark with hunger. 'I can't feel my legs, but my cock is ready for Round Two.'

Pushing up onto your forearm, you reach between us until you touch where I'm stretched to hold you. I'm soaked with your semen, and you massage it into my skin, rubbing my clitoris in an unhurried circle. Your waistband gently abrades my inner thighs, reminding me that you were so desperate to be inside me you barely got your pants down.

You bite your lower lip when my inner muscles clench. Your stroking thumb is tireless, the pressure featherlight. My sex tightens until you growl with the pleasure of it.

'You keep milking me like that, *Setareh*, and this won't last long.'

'Oh!' I start writhing beneath you, desperate to ride your erection, but your weight holds me down.

You rub and squeeze, relentlessly stimulating, then quickening the pace. I'm trembling. Your kiss takes me over, the stroke of your tongue too much to bear. The climax breaks in a rush of sparkling sensation, shimmering through me until even my toes and fingertips tingle.

Panting, I blink up at you through a sensuous haze.

'You're so beautiful,' you tell me, brushing your lips back and forth over mine. 'The most gorgeous thing I've ever seen.'

'You must not look in the mirror, then.'

Your grin is brazen as you straighten away from me. I whimper as you leave me, my sex clinging in protest. The firelight halos you as you stand and shove your pajama pants to the floor.

Oh, but you're magnificent.

You arrange me to your satisfaction: straddling one of my legs on your knees with my other calf propped against your shoulder. You take yourself in hand.

'Kane, you can't be serious.'

'Six years,' you say grimly, finding me again and pushing inside with a rough purr. 'I've craved you that long, and I'm not satisfied yet.'

I gasp. My sex accepts you more easily now, slick as I am with your semen, but your proportions still border over-whelming. The position you've placed me in allows you to press impossibly deeper. Restless, I moan and shift, packed deliciously full.

A roll of your hips stirs your penis inside me. I'm swollen and hypersensitive, so the subtle move has an unsubtle impact. You fluidly withdraw, hovering with just the tip inside me. Gripping the arm of the sofa above my head with both hands, your next sleek thrust through my scissored legs hits the end of me. It's ecstasy, and I moan, suddenly greedy for more.

You stare down at me, your features taut with lust. 'I'm still in love with you.'

My eyes squeeze shut against your pain and mine.

'Don't shut me out,' you order gruffly. 'Keep your eyes open.'

Watching you make love to me is as erotic as feeling it. The visual of your powerful muscles flexing with exertion, your virile body devoted to arousing and satiating mine as often as I can bear it is a singular provocation, and you know it. You ruthlessly exploit your physical perfection as another weapon in your extensive sexual arsenal.

You withdraw and thrust quickly, grinding against me for a long moment before another rapid withdrawal and thrust. The irregular tempo of swift retreat and entry paired with lingering penetration kindles a white-hot need.

The way you've positioned me – one leg balanced against your shoulder, the other bracketed by yours – ensures there's no way for me to reach you. I can only lie still and take the skillfully timed thrusts of your extravagant erection. The wide, flared head of your penis massages the delicate channel of my sex. The sensation of being overly full and then emptied in rapid succession is maddening. My body rocks back and forth into that deliberate, wickedly knowledgeable stroking, the fur beneath me a further stimulation.

I'm overcome. The pleasure becomes unbearable. I'm mewling and can't stop; you feel too wonderful. It's too much. Then you shift me slightly, and the next drive glides over the spot inside me that threatens my sanity.

'Kane.' My hands fist in the fur beneath me as if holding on will make the approaching climax endurable. 'I ... I'm going to come.'

'I know.' The full fiery intensity of your focus is on me, your eyes pools of deep black, your cheekbones flagged with high color. Your tongue glides over your full lower lip in a blatantly erotic gesture. Your hips are tireless, your abdomen lacing tightly as you fuck with ruthless, concentrated strokes. Your first orgasm grabbed you by the tail and yanked the beast from its cage. This time, you're chasing satisfaction with furious deliberation. 'I'll be right behind you.'

It only takes two more precision thrusts to hurl me into orgasm. I breathe your name as my body shivers violently, my legs shaking with the surfeit of delight. I hear you groan, then your head bows like a supplicant between your straining biceps, your damp forehead resting on mine. Your breath hisses as your climax grips you, your body shuddering, your hips surging rhythmically.

Moments later, you slump against me, breathing hard.

'Jesus,' you wheeze, struggling for breath. Your tone is both awestruck and chagrined, and it makes me laugh.

'Stop that,' you order gruffly. 'You'll make me hard again, which will definitely kill me.'

Sliding from me in a wet, heavy glide, you shift between my hip and the sofa back, then flip us both to drape me over you.

'Even you can't go again.' I lift my head to look down at you because I'm not absolutely sure that's true.

Your brow arches. 'If you'd asked me this morning if I thought I could screw us both to death, I would've said those days are behind me. Now I understand my cock isn't a team player. It doesn't care if it kills me. And while dying making love to you is exactly the way I'd choose to go out, I have a lot of bucket-list items to check off with you before then.'

I rest my chin atop my crossed arms. 'Like what?'

'Like catching up on all those spy-movie franchises you love and eating cold pizza.'

'You haven't been keeping up?'

'Without you?' Shadows flicker in your fire-lit eyes. 'It would have shredded me even to try.'

My palm presses flat over your heart. I study your face. Release has softened your features, and there's the liquid shine of love in your eyes. I want to touch you all over, claim every inch of rough-silk skin.

'A kiss, my queen,' you murmur, licking your lower lip. 'My kingdom for a kiss.'

Nuzzling the tip of my nose against yours, I whisper, 'What if it's just the king I want?'

'He's already yours. He always has been.'

I take your mouth, my skin hot and sensitive as if I'm sun-burned. I've danced with fire in your arms and feel the effects.

I've died for this, for you.

Now, I'll have to kill for it.

32

Amy

A hot, wet, horrible-smelling tongue drags across my face. My arms flail, pushing at a heavy, muscular body covered in hair. 'What the fuck?'

God, my jaw aches like I've got an ice pick rammed into the bone.

The tongue licks my upper arm, and my eyes pop open. I squint against the sun's bright light. 'Damn it. Get the fuck away from me.'

Pushing onto my elbows, I find myself on a low-slung, wide-seated cream sectional sofa. It takes me a moment to survey the space and figure out I'm in Suzanne's living room. Landscape tapestries and carved wooden masks hang on cheerful yellow walls, intensifying the sunlight already burning my eyes. A high-pitched whine turns my attention to the black Labrador sitting impatiently and expectantly beside me.

'Oh, fuck. I'm sorry, Ollie.' I rub his head in apology. 'I'm not a morning person. Also, your breath is horrendous. But I still love you madly.'

'It's not morning,' Suzanne says drily as she enters from the kitchen. A colorful head wrap restrains her dark curls, her face is devoid of makeup and a stunning silk kaftan drapes her voluptuous figure. 'It's nearly three in the afternoon. And I'm giving Oliver the probiotics the vet recommended for his breath. It's definitely better.'

'Ugh. If that's better, it must've been like decomposition

before.' I sit up and rub sleep from my eyes. 'What the hell am I doing on your sofa? And where is my purse? I need my pills.'

She grabs my Gucci Dionysus bag off the mirrored console table by her apartment door and brings it to me. 'What are you taking? And why?'

'I had an emergency root canal a few days ago. They gave me Norco and some megadose ibuprofen.' I throw the blanket off and sit up. I'm dressed in the pajamas I'd put on the morning before, the wide-legged pants being the closest I could find to what Lily wore at the family meeting in Kane's library. My lingerie set has a matching top with a corseted back that shows off my stomach. Really, my ensemble is sexier and more comfortable than what Kane's bitch was wearing.

Standing, I walk over to Suzanne's brass and glass bar cart and pour myself a gin and tonic. Keeping my head down, I hide my horrified expression. I'm sore between my legs and sticky. There's no mistaking that I've had sex, but I don't remember it.

Please, God, let it have been my husband.

'You shouldn't drink and take painkillers,' she tells me.

Turning, I look her in the eye as I wash down my pills. Room-temperature gin and tonic should be disgusting, but it tastes like ambrosia to me. 'Darius threw out all the alcohol in our apartment.' At least what he could find . . . 'I need a damn drink.'

'You need to eat something, too. Those pills on an empty stomach will make you vomit for hours.'

I shoot her a look, but she's already turned her back to me and returned to the kitchen. With a quick, practiced toss of my wrist, I polish off my first cocktail, then fix a second one, drinking that one down to the same point in my glass as the previous one so Suzanne won't know.

Dropping the half-filled glass onto the trunk that serves as her coffee table, I go into the bathroom and take stock of my body. My breath quakes out of me. There is a copious amount of semen in my underwear and faint traces of blood mixed in it. The smell makes me gag. I sniff myself, but I don't reek like a whore. I must've showered at some point, and what I'm drenched in now has leaked from me since. Revulsion crawls over my skin in waves.

My eyes burn from dryness so severe it hurts to blink. I sit on the toilet, and when I've finished relieving myself, the water is pink.

'It's not unusual for Darius to be rough,' I whisper. He's a passionate and dominant lover. I've been sore after sex with him many times before.

I use Suzanne's flushable wet wipes to clean myself and shove the underwear – one of my new, beautiful lace boy shorts – to the bottom of her trash can, piling the tissues and other waste on top of it.

Washing my hands, I look at my reflection. There are deep grooves framing my mouth. Lines are starting to deepen their tracks across my forehead. I'm overdue for my Botox injections, but I haven't made the time to go. Still, it's my eyes that hit me hardest. Rimmed with shadows, the green of my irises has darkened until they look like solid black holes, and through them, I see a soul-deep horror that chills my blood.

I yank the towel off the rack, press it to my mouth and scream into the terry cloth until black spots dot my vision.

When I exit the bathroom a few minutes later, I've rolled my shoulders back and lifted my head high. I grab my drink and take another big gulp, trying to dull the throbbing of my jaw, which is worse after my mini-breakdown. I can't avoid it anymore; it's time to set up hidden cameras around my apartment. I have a dozen buried beneath clothes in one of my

208

closet drawers, where they've been for over a year. I had the nerve to buy them but not to actually use them. I've been afraid of what I'll see.

Now, I'm more afraid of what I'm *not* seeing.

Suzanne has set a croissant on the dining table. 'Come and put something in your stomach.'

I join her, studying her over the rim of my glass. Her skin is flawless. Unlike my own, there's no wrinkle or line to be found. Her dark eyes tilt up at the far corners, and a worried frown presently caps them.

'What time did I get here?' I ask.

'A little after five this morning.'

'That's damn early. I'm sorry.'

'It's okay. Darius called around seven, looking for you.' Her lips purse. 'I told him you'd been here the whole time.'

I release a relieved sigh. 'Thank you.'

'He's on his way. Is everything okay with you two?'

'Sure.' When she just continues to study me with those thickly lashed eyes, I elaborate. 'Since Kane's been out of the office, he's been working overtime. Kane is on a trip with his wifey now, so Darius is really putting the hours in.'

Otherwise known as taking care of business he doesn't want Kane – or his hag of a mother – to know about. *And* probably fucking his assistant every day of the week, instead of just Friday. He comes home so late there is no way it's all work and no play.

'Really?' She perks up. 'Where'd they go?'

'No one knows for sure, but Lily called to see how I'm doing, and the number had a Connecticut area code. I looked it up, but it's unlisted.' I rip off a piece of the croissant and shove it in my mouth. 'I'm sure Witte knows exactly where they are,' I go on while chewing, 'but he's gone, too.'

'With them?'

'Maybe. Maybe they're ménage à trois-ing it right now.'

'You can't be serious.'

'Can't I?' I take a big bite of the croissant. It's buttery and delicious, and I realize I'm ravenously hungry. 'Witte's crawled so far up Kane's ass he's probably another appendage.'

'Oh, good Lord, girl.' She huffs a laugh, leaning back in her chair. Her kaftan has a beautiful copper and turquoise floral pattern that plays flatteringly off her milk-chocolate-hued skin. There's something regal about her that I detest with everything in me. It's a quietly fierce nobility that seems effortless.

'Is Lily gorgeous?' she asks.

'It's stupid how beautiful she is.' I wipe my mouth. 'Like she doesn't seem real when you're standing in front of her. She's like an android or something.'

'Does the family like her?'

I laugh and catch a hint of hysteria in the sound. I remember the feel of Lily's arms around me, the whisper of her voice in my ear. She almost made me cry, and I can't figure out why. I hate her for it, though.

'She's won Ramin over,' I reply while chewing. 'He won't stop talking about using her as a model for the new makeup line. I don't really know how Darius feels. He doesn't trust her, but then he doesn't trust most people. Rosana thinks Lily is the heroine of a tragic love story. I'm pretty sure Aliyah just wants her to die again. She can't stand her boys having women in their lives they like better than her.'

'Your mother-in-law sounds like a nightmare.'

'She's the antichrist. Goddamn hell on earth.'

'How do you feel about Lily?'

I stare out of Suzanne's plantation shutter-covered windows. The buildings across the street are shorter, so I can look right over them at the clear blue sky. Somewhere out there, Lily has spent *days* with Kane all to herself. Knowing Kane, I imagine she's as swollen and tender as I am right now. I had trouble walking for days after he fucked me.

The mental box containing the need to scream unhinges at the thought of sex. My throat hurts from strangled tears as I swallow the croissant that now tastes like cardboard and sawdust. 'She's all right. I don't really know her. She drives Aliyah crazy, so there's that.'

'Where were you last night,' Suzanne queries, 'between when Darius last saw you and when you showed up here?'

'I just needed to get out of the house. And I needed a drink. I went to a bar, then I hooked up with a girls' trip group of tourists and went back with them to their hotel to smoke weed.' The lies roll easily off my tongue, and the minute they hit the air, they become the truth. I've rewritten the night's events, the unknown deleted forever from my narrative. 'I guess that, plus the booze, plus the pain meds did a number on me.'

'You drink too much, Amy,' she says softly, with judgment in her gaze. 'I say that as your friend.'

'Well, as my friend, mind your own business. I had fun. The girls were great. From Minnesota, I think they said. Or Michigan? Somewhere like that.' I dig my phone out of my purse. There are dozens of missed calls and unread texts from Darius.

The doorbell rings. I wait until Suzanne walks away before I gain my feet and run to the bathroom again. I splash water on my face, then pinch my cheeks to give them some color. Suzanne thoughtfully keeps travel-size hygiene products in a wicker bowl for her guests, including mouthwash, which I struggle to open and rinse with before Darius smells alcohol on my breath.

When I step out of the bathroom, Darius is waiting in the short hallway for me, taking up too much space with his tall, fit physique. I'm instantly claustrophobic. My breath shortens and grows labored.

'Do you know how fucking worried I've been?' he barks, grabbing me by the upper arms and yanking me closer. He's livid but keeps his voice low enough so Suzanne won't overhear. 'What the hell are you upset about now? Whatever it is, fucking off and ignoring my calls is bullshit.'

'I'm sorry.' I regret the apology the moment I voice it. Why can't I do what I want? But then I see that look in his eyes, the grim desire, and my stomach roils. Anytime Darius feels like I'm not where he wants me, he fucks me into compliance with his talented dick. Considering the state of my vagina, I think I'd literally lose my mind if he took that tack with me now. 'It's not you. You're working all the time, and I just felt like I needed to talk to another adult, you know? I'm on my period. My fucking mouth hurts. Low iron and pain pills . . . I fell asleep on Suzanne's couch. That's all.'

He stares at me with narrowed, suspicious eyes. The scream I'm holding back in that shakily closed box inside me begins to spill out again. My eyes water from the effort of not howling directly into his handsome, angry face, and I use my tears to my advantage.

'Baby.' He sighs and pulls me into a hug.

His smell is so welcome and comforting that I can't hold back the flood of tears any longer. They escape in rivulets, then emotion bursts from my chest in wracking sobs.

His embrace tightens. 'Why don't you talk to me about stuff like this? You know I'm working on our future, but I can always make time for you.'

I cry into his hard, muscular chest until I'm so exhausted I can barely keep my eyes open.

We say goodbye to Suzanne and Oliver. When I hug

Suzanne, it's as tight as Lily's hug, and I can tell she's surprised. She's been a good friend to me, even though I despise her.

Darius and I leave, heading down the hallway to the elevator. I overlook the sand in my mules until the grains start chafing my feet raw.

33

Aliyah

The second floor of a five-story brick building in Tribeca houses the Rampart Protection & Investigative Services office. I spot a boutique hotel, a café, a hair salon and a branding agency farther along the street. I suspect the latter is responsible for the proliferation of too-similar business logos rendered in an earthy color palette with flourishes of leaves and flowers for scant distinction. The neighborhood appears to be collectively targeting consumers who place a premium on eco-friendliness and natural ingredients. I don't grasp how private investigation fits in, but then I don't really care.

The pedestrians are dressed and groomed according to the latest trends. A blend of musical styles wafts in the air, and the overall feel is of youth, vitality and creativity. The staidness of established New York is figuratively far from this community of startups.

I enter through the heavy double iron doors painted orange-red and find myself in a tiny vestibule, with an unmarked door on the left and a staircase and elevator on the right. I unwrap the scarf draped around my hair and shove it into my clutch. A fierce-looking black man with wide shoulders and a cool glance half sits on a stool backed into the corner of the elevator car with a baseball bat near at hand. He takes stock of me with zero expression and waits.

It doesn't seem like the neighborhood would require such

an intimidating elevator operator, but so many things in this world change their face when it's dark.

'Second floor, please.'

He tugs easily on a pull chain that simultaneously lowers a gate from the top and raises its twin from the bottom, like a mouth snapping closed. He pushes the button, and we start our ascent.

I exit into another vestibule more aptly described as a landing and enter through the metal door distinguished by a placard denoting that Rampart is on the other side.

A pretty redhead wearing statement eyeglass frames in a bright blue greets me. 'Hi! Can I help you?'

Her station is a vintage-looking metal piece reminiscent of a teacher's desk. It's squeezed in by the door, but beyond her is wide open space, with windows on every brick wall except the one at my back and columns holding the upper stories aloft. There are four rows of desks, two lining the outer walls and two down the middle comprised of desks placed side by side and face to face.

Unlike Baharan, Rampart affords no one the relative privacy of a cubicle. Instead, it's a shared space, the desks boasting wood-veneer tops that can morph into standing workstations by levered brackets. At the opposite end, a glass wall and door provide delineation for a conference room. The windows are all open, allowing the scents and sounds of the city free rein.

'I have an appointment with Giles Prescott,' I reply.

She checks her monitor. 'Ms. Armand?'

'Yes. Tris, isn't it?'

She beams at me, inordinately pleased that I remember the name she gave me over the phone. 'Yes.'

Hopping to her feet with excess energy, she rounds the desk and leads the way. 'I'll show you to the conference room and let Giles know you're here. How are you doing today?'

'As well as can be expected.' I can't imagine anyone coming to Rampart would have a pleasant reason for doing so.

'I love your dress, by the way.'

'Thank you.' Vaguely Grecian in style, the one-shoulder ruched dress in fire-engine red is one of the few pieces of clothing in my closet that isn't neutral. It hugs my waist and emphasizes my curves. With gold hoop earrings and nude kitten-heel slingbacks, it strikes just the right note of casually, effortlessly sexy.

I'll change before heading to work, but the dress is perfect for my initial meeting with Mr. Prescott. I want sex to flavor his first impression of me; it'll make him more manageable. Young men the same age or younger than my sons fill the room, but their eyes spark when I enter, and their heads turn to follow me.

'Can I get you something to drink?' she asks. 'Coffee, water, soda? I can also bring you a menu for the smoothie place across the street.'

'Do you have sparkling water?'

'Yes. Perrier okay?'

'Perfect.' Going against my nature, I sit in one of the chairs on the side, closest to the head of the table. He'll have to either sit directly beside or across from me. It's essential to assume the position of power in any interaction, so I typically would take one end of the table but adopting a more vulnerable persona is the goal in this case.

Giles Prescott is a retired police officer. He's hardwired for heroism. A damsel in distress should trigger that innate protective instinct. If I can also trigger his mating instinct, even better. The red dress has a one hundred percent success rate so far.

I scroll through my emails while waiting, but it's not long.

'Ms. Armand.' The deep voice snags my attention. 'Here's

your water. I'm Giles Prescott. I'm sorry to keep you. I had an offsite meeting earlier, and it took me longer to return to the office than anticipated.'

A strong hand sets a bottle of Perrier in front of me, along with a glass and napkin. The wrist is thick and adorned with a gold Rolex. Rolled-up shirtsleeves display powerful forearms, the muscles flexing under café au lait-hued skin. I note the broadness of the shoulders before finally allowing myself to study his face and meet his eyes. I expected I'd have to feign feminine interest, but my admiration is genuine. Giles Prescott is an attractive man.

'Thank you. And the wait was no bother. I appreciate your time.'

His smile is boyish, which softens the bluntness of his masculinity. He's a mix of races, the result compelling if not classically handsome. A gifted barber crops his curls and precisely shapes his beard. His shoes are respectable, his dress slacks off-the-rack but tailored. He eschews jacket and tie and leaves the collar of his dress shirt unbuttoned. He wears a wedding band, but that doesn't mean he's unavailable . . .

I wait until he assumes his position beside me, at the head of the table. 'Mr. Prescott, I'm Kane Black's mother.'

He nods. 'I know. I looked you up this morning. It helps me prepare. Did he refer you?'

'In a way. I want a better understanding of the investigation into his wife – if they're even legally married, considering she's operating under an assumed name. I've read your final report, but it doesn't seem complete. She used the earliest alias you recovered in her late teens. What about before then?'

'Before then, she was the responsibility of a parent or guardian. She –'

'A mother.'

'*If* she was telling the truth about that,' he qualifies, and with that, he alters, the easy charm hardening into the flat gaze of a cop. 'She's been honest too rarely to believe her about anything. For all we know, she could have two parents who are alive and well. We have to assume that any information provided by her is a fabrication.'

'She's been diagnosed with dissociative amnesia and has been living under yet another alias. Is it possible her identities are symptoms of that mental illness? Bluntly, can we determine if she's a victim or a criminal?'

'A shrink would be better able to sort through *why* she is who she is. I can only tell you *how*.'

'That's fair.' My fingers drum on the tabletop. 'Kane ended your investigation. Did you reach a dead-end, or did he act prematurely? Could you have possibly unearthed more?'

He studies me. 'Didn't he tell you?'

'Honestly, Mr. Prescott, I can't believe anything he tells me when it comes to her. He's been obsessed with her for years, to an unhealthy degree.'

He nods as if that's no surprise. 'I think we could have dug up more. She's unforgettable and hard to mistake for anyone else. Once we narrow in on a location, people have remarkably detailed memories of her.'

'Yes, I've seen her in action. She's incredibly charming, which helps make her a terrible blind spot for Kane. A possibly dangerous one, from what I gather. Your report suggested underworld ties . . . ?'

'She doesn't live modestly. Thorough background checks are required to lease the sort of multimillion-dollar properties she prefers. As you saw, copies were always made of her identification, but that alone wouldn't be enough. A deep dive into her history would be routine, and she would have to hold up to scrutiny. Someone – and it could be her – is skilled enough to insert false information into government databases, then delete those entries later when that identity is no longer needed.'

His reports were detailed, so I knew all this. Ivy, Lily, Daisy . . . she liked her botanical names, didn't she? And didn't their very similarity suggest premeditation? Or perhaps the opposite is true. Either way, it was doubly concerning to have it laid out verbally.

'I don't understand how Kane could know all this and let it go.'

'He didn't let it go,' he corrects, leaning back in his chair. 'He let *me* go. We believe he's retained the services of a different firm.'

'He hired someone else? Why would he do that? Did you fuck up?'

Prescott's smile is wry. 'No. I run a tight ship here at Rampart. My staff is comprised of retired law enforcement officers from police departments, branches of service and federal agencies. I have a slew of lawyers on staff and paid student interns from a cross-section of disciplines. We don't make mistakes, Ms. Armand.'

'Aliyah, please.' The siren of an emergency vehicle abruptly pierces the air. The alarming sound, mechanical chirps and beeps designed to be impossible to ignore, pours in through the open windows, chafing my nerves and setting me further on edge. The frenetic sound grows louder by the second as the vehicle draws closer.

His eyes crinkle in the corners as his smile widens and he raises his voice. 'We work directly here. We knock on doors, ask questions and dig. I document things minutely, and we act within the scope of the law. While some of the professionals on my team are familiar with undercover work, we aren't covert intelligence specialists.'

I reach for my water and attempt to unscrew the metal cap,

but my hands aren't quite steady. Prescott reaches over and gently takes the bottle from me, opening it and pouring the contents into the glass.

'Why would Kane need to act covertly?'

'There are two ways to come into money: honestly and dishonestly. For a woman as young as your daughter-in-law to come into her fortune honestly would mean she either inherited it – and there would be a paper trail for that – or she earned it. That amount of money isn't earned without a lot of people knowing about it, including the IRS. We haven't found anything that would legitimize her or her fortune.'

The room spins, and I take a deep, slow breath. Gideon Cross would never do business with a criminal, especially someone who'd stolen or embezzled money. He overlooks Paul's misdeeds because he sympathizes with Kane, having also suffered the sins of a father. But Lily? A woman who owns a majority share of the company alongside Kane . . . ? We would lose all of the investment into ECRA+ if Cross pulled out. It would be a near-fatal blow to Baharan.

'Your son used her assets to build his company,' he goes on. 'If a crime ties to those assets, they'll be reclaimed. Whenever an inquiry is made into her background, someone becomes aware that she's being sought. You make a lot of inquiries; a lot of people know. She's been changing her identity for years. You don't do that unless you're hiding, so taking a more covert approach – perhaps stepping outside the lines of the law, which we don't do here at Rampart – would help minimize the risk of turning over the wrong rock and having something really dangerous crawl out.'

Oh no . . . Bile rises into my throat, burning acid that devastates soft tissue. I swallow hard, pressing a hand to my stomach in a vain effort to stop its roiling.

It's not just Cross's partnership we stand to lose. It's Baharan itself. It's everything.

'This is a nightmare.'

'There are a lot of pieces in play, but your son is still searching for answers. He's just taken the search underground. He's following the money, tracing it back to its source. If he knows where it came from, he has something or someone – maybe multiple someones – to keep an eye out for.'

'What if I paid you to keep looking?'

'Why would you take that risk?'

My brow arches. 'He's my son. I know him. And I know he's incapable of being objective when it comes to this woman.'

Anger bubbles up at the understanding that everything I own is in jeopardy, every member of my family. Fury boils over.

I push back from the table, my chair legs scraping like nails on a chalkboard. The siren passes just below the window and deafens.

Is Kane working to save the company? Is his focus still on Baharan? Have I misjudged him? I certainly haven't misjudged how he looks at her unless it's all an act. Gaining her trust would be the smartest and most expeditious way to resolve this. Is that why he took her away? Is he building a rapport to gain the information he needs?

His choice is between Baharan and whatever-her-name-is. Which will he choose? Or is he working to keep them both?

I move to the window and look down at the narrow street below. The traffic prevents the ambulance from moving any faster than a crawl. Someone is waiting for help somewhere in the city, and it will be some time before it arrives. Perhaps it will come too late.

Baharan cannot wait until it's too late.

221

I start thinking about how I can raise the money to pay Lily back and send her away with her troubles. I haven't a clue how to pull off a buyout of this magnitude, but if I can manage it, Kane won't have the majority any longer. I just have to make sure that no other single board member steps in and takes it over. I'll confide in Ryan. Kane is his friend; he'll never do anything to hurt him, and he'll make sure we handle this in a way that's best for my family.

My growing hatred for Kane settles my nerves and gives me strength. He should be the one coming up with the money. He could simply sign over the penthouse to his pseudo-wife, and that would probably be enough. He could even institutionalize her – for her own good, of course. Having researched Dr. Goldstein, including watching his video lectures on YouTube, I'm sure he would zealously argue the benefits of committing her. Lily and Amy could be locked up together and keep each other company.

Instead, we'll have to rely on the loyalty of friends to hold on to Baharan. I need to get everything in place, then sit down with Lily and get rid of her.

Prescott reaches around me and pulls down the window sash, marginally lessening the din.

I glance at him. I'm vibrating with vicious energy that needs an outlet. 'There's a hotel up the street.'

His brows raise. I see the moment he understands the invitation. 'I'm married.'

'Congratulations. The offer stands.'

'It's a flattering offer, but I love my husband, and I don't cheat.'

'Ah.' I move around him to retrieve my clutch. 'A pity.'

'Should I assume you've decided against continuing the investigation?'

I pause, considering.

He crosses his arms. 'Ms. Armand, you're clearly a form-idable woman used to getting what she wants, but I urge you to let your son manage this. The woman you know as Lily has been ably protecting herself for years in ways that imply a high threat level. Whatever you think you can leverage is unlikely to exceed what she's deftly avoided so far. You're quite frankly not in her league.'

'I appreciate your candor, Mr. Prescott. Can you tell me the full value of the LLC's assets when my son inherited them?'

'She leased the properties she resided in and her cars. As for bank accounts, I can't access prior statements, only the assets in their accounts now.'

'I guess I'll just have to ask her.' I turn toward the glass door, and he nimbly outsteps me and opens it. 'It really is a pity,' I tell him again.

I hurry through the row of desks to the exit, anxious to get a failsafe in place.

34

Lily

I stand on the beach in Greenwich, drenched in sunlight, the warmth and light of the morning sun glittering off the undulating waves of Long Island Sound. Goosebumps spread across my bare arms and legs. The chill originates inside me, then radiates outward.

Of all the mistakes I've made in my life, exchanging marriage vows has revealed itself to be the worst. How could I have failed to see the monster inside you?

That's a lie. I knew it was there. I took comfort from it, knowing it slept nearby, protective and fierce. My failure was believing that your love would prevent that beast from turning on me.

I wasn't taught to believe in fairy tales. I was raised to understand that Prince Charming is the costume worn by the beast. There are no castles on high, no knights in shining armor. Planting roots is for the uninspired. Relationships are for those too weak to stand alone. But here I am, wearing a thin gold band on my finger. And now someone must die.

I'm not blind anymore. I know what I must do.

Brine licks at my toes, as soothing and stimulating as a lover's caress. Something deep within me surfaces in response — something that seeks to escape.

A shiver wracks my body. Our argument circles in my mind in an infinite loop. Your sibilant voice, the fire in your eyes. Your temper, always quick to flare, raging out of control.

Your verbal blows were shocking. If you'd struck me with your fists, it wouldn't have hurt as much as your scathing words and violent disgust.

The avarice wasn't a surprise. Haven't you always wanted more, to rise above your station in life, to seize power and control, to make something of yourself? You never hid your ambition. And haven't I always admired it? But realizing your tenderness was contrived fractures my soul. There's no love lost here. How could I have ever convinced myself otherwise?

I can't believe I ever thought you didn't care about the money. I was so confident you loved me. Or was I? In retrospect, I can admit I was lying to myself.

You threw your head back with a rich, dark laugh. 'Not care about the money? I've embarrassed myself in secondhand clothes, worked all hours, fucked just to have an excuse to raid someone else's fridge, groveled trying to make contacts, and debased myself in countless other ways. Money means I'll never have to suffer through any of that again. Money is power. If you don't appreciate having it, well . . . I will.'

There was a bright, unnatural light in your eyes, and it pierced my gut like a lethal blade. All the charm, the head-turning attractiveness, the easy affection was gone as if it'd never existed. At that moment, I saw you. The real you. Wrong and strange. Mad. Capable of anything.

It's been only days since I said vows meant to last a lifetime, not knowing the sands of time began slipping in an unchecked stream the moment I said I do.

I hear my name and turn away from the water. The beach house waits, its windows and doors framing a deep blackness as if entering it will be akin to stepping into nothingness. Each step toward it grows heavier, my feet getting sucked deeper and deeper into the sand. The surf pools around my feet. The Sound roars like a storm-tossed ocean at my back, and a wide shadow rears behind me. I can't move my feet as the danger looms, a tsunami that won't let me leave the water's edge.

I reach my hand toward the house, screaming, and hear that dark, rich laugh as the sea claims me.

35

Lily

The beloved sound of your voice reawakens me. You woke me earlier with heated kisses and greedy hands until I was left quivering with exhaustion and drugged with orgasmic delight.

'You'd tempt the devil himself,' you murmur, nuzzling your nose against my temple as you pull the blankets off me.

Blinking, I roll onto my back as you return to the bed and straddle me. The sun's light coming through the window tells me it's still early morning.

My sleepy gaze rakes your naked body. You are a dazzling vision of sleek lines and rippling muscle. Your hair is still damp from a recent shower, and humidity is thick in the air. 'You're one to talk.'

Your grin is a throwback, a flash of cocky amusement from your younger self. You've been growing younger by the hour, your face softening and your shoulders' rigidness relaxing. Sexual excess suits you. You become more energetic by the day as if you don't need sleep at all, just orgasms.

Your skin is cool, as mine is becoming without the duvet's insulation, and your face is smooth and soft. You've adopted the ritual of rising before me to shave, then returning to the bed and the slick depths of my sex. Making love is now penciled in before your first shower, a scheduled daily activity as obligatory as hygiene. How would you write it out, my love, if you were to? *Keep wife cooperative?* Or perhaps, *Impregnate wife?* You're certainly doing your absolute best to ensure I'm never not soaked with your semen.

I'm not complaining, not only because I'm well-pleasured but because your animalistic nature is a match for my own. When you grow up struggling for a place in this world, bereft of the safety net of parental support, you don't have the luxury of civility. I know your soul recognizes its mate in me and revels in the knowledge that you can be as feral as you want, and I'll relish it.

'Tell me the truth,' I say, looking up at your devastatingly gorgeous face and body, 'you're an incubus.'

Your deep, husky laugh reaches inside me and caresses that dark, quiet place I hadn't known existed before you. More than anything you do or say, it's the feeling of being touched in the deepest part of my being that enflames me.

I smile. 'That's why you're growing younger and stronger, and I'm left weak in the knees.'

'That's the way I like you.' You bend to kiss me with such heat my toes curl.

I'm still trying to process that we've had a handful of such days. We've wallowed in each other to the point that the ravening need has eased into luxuriant insatiability. You are warm and playful, the very picture of a hopelessly infatuated man.

But I'm not deceived by that guise to any degree. My mother didn't suffer fools.

Beneath your charming, relaxed facade is calculating predation. I catch those incisive looks you throw my way when you think I'm not paying attention. I understand that while you're innately a highly sexual man, the frequency of our love-making is very much about control, something you've suffered without since the day we met. You're cataloging my response to every caress and position. Each new encounter hones your technique. You were already a consummate lover, but now you're focused on mastering me in particular.

Even as my mind comprehends your intent, my body has become your slave. When you joined me in the kitchen yesterday, looking over my shoulder at the sandwiches I was putting together, it seemed like innocent curiosity. Then your lips touched my shoulder, your hand slid between my legs, and in less than five minutes, I was quivering in orgasm, my body held upright solely by your hand at my breast and your fingers inside me. Then, as quickly as you'd appeared, you strolled back to your office. I was left sagging against the cool countertop, trying to gather my wits enough to finish making lunch.

It's a siege. I've been pondering to what end you're strategizing. I expect it's a blend of pride and punishment. You can't stop trying to prove your worth to Lily, even as you seek to punish her for leaving you. You're certainly trying to constrain your obsession within the lens of sexual desire. Between work and sex, you've hardly the time to examine what it is that really ties you to me and how utterly terrifying it is.

Now, you look down at me with such love I can't breathe. Joy suffuses my heart the way sunlight brightens the room. I am cherished, adored and desired by an incredible man.

This perfection can't last. We exist in a bubble we've created, but reality spreads around the periphery in a thin, oily film whose iridescence hides a mounting horror. The whisper of parting is forever between us, the foreboding that we're stealing moments.

'You're perfect,' you praise me, a distorted reflection of my thoughts. Your hands stroke my torso, and I stretch sinuously into your warm palms. 'I don't think I'll ever get over how lucky I am to have you.'

Lowering your head, you seal your mouth over mine.

The sweet stroking of your velvet tongue makes me sigh with pleasure. I melt into the luscious delight of your thorough kissing. Your lips are so firm but soft. Your deep, slow licks savor me. There's a low hum of pleasure in your throat, like the purr of a big cat. You cradle my head in your hands and take my mouth as if the taste of me is all you need now and forever.

I convey my gratitude for your love with worship, running my adoring hands over every bit of your tremendous body I can reach. You arch into my touch and catch my lower lip between your teeth, tugging.

Stretching over me, you hold on as you turn onto your back, taking me with you. Your chest pillows my cheek. Your fingers tangle in my hair. 'If I don't get up and start working, I'll end up staying in bed with you all day.'

'Not yet.' I reach over to grab your phone off the night-stand. Settling into the crook of your shoulder, I open the camera and hold the phone high in the air.

You huff out a laugh. 'I'm surprised I have any storage left with the number of pictures you've taken.'

I snap a picture while kissing your cheek. Then look up and smile wide, not just for posterity but because you've got the sexy, satisfied look of a man who's just had great sex, then you've capped it off with a smile so bright with happiness it makes my heart sing. I take a burst of pictures, which makes us both laugh.

'I'm going to get dressed,' you tell me, 'and you're going to review the ECRA+ advertising creative and give me your opinion over lunch.'

It's not a question. Over the past few days, when you've been sated enough to keep your body idle, you've caught me up on events both big and small. It's been a flood of inform-ation as if I'm cramming for a quiz you don't want me to fail.

'I said I would,' I concede, 'but I'm still waiting on your reasoning for wanting my opinion. You have employees who handle your marketing; you've trusted their instincts before. And this is your sister's project. I'm sure she's done a wonderful job. I'm sure your mother guaranteed she did.'

Your chest lifts and falls heavily beneath my cheek. 'I want you involved with Baharan. It's yours as much as it's mine.'

'I don't want it.'

'You don't get to say that,' you retort, with a playful tug of my hair.

'Why not?'

'This was your plan, the reason you groomed me. You –'

'"Grooming" isn't the right word,' I say wryly.

You shoot me a look. 'I never even thought of Baharan before you came along. You brought it up and suggested I revive it.'

'I *asked* if you'd ever considered reviving it.'

'Semantics.'

'Elucidation.'

'That's fucking annoying!'

I smile. 'You know how I am about using the right word.' Crossing my arms on your chest, I set my chin on my forearms. 'Sell your stake if you don't want it.'

'*Our* stake. And I never said I don't want it. I want you involved in it.'

'And I said no, and you said I don't get to say that.'

Your hand thrusts into my hair to grip my neck. 'Why wouldn't you want to work with me? You're so good at seeing into people, seeing their potential and capabilities. Why wouldn't you share that gift with me?'

'I'll share whatever I can with you, Kane. What's mine is yours, the good and the bad. I'm sorry about the bad. It's just –'

'Don't joke.' Your face is hard, the face of the man I woke up to weeks ago. 'And get to the point.'

'You don't need my approval. I'm proud of you for a million reasons that have nothing to do with your job or bank account. You're doing brilliantly without me.'

'I don't want to do anything without you, brilliant or not. And are you seriously psychoanalyzing me?' you snap. 'I ask you to work with me, and you try to shrink my head. Okay.'

You slide away and move to get out of bed. I fall onto my back and stare at the ceiling.

Marching toward the closet, you pause midway. I lift my head to study you. You're still for a moment, your hands clenched at your sides. I know you're irritated, but your backside is so glorious I can't help but admire it.

Cursing under your breath, you return and sit on the edge of the bed. Your face is austerely beautiful as you ask, 'Why me?'

It's a question I know is one of the most important, and it's the first you've asked me. That you would even wonder why someone would see your potential and invest in your dreams breaks my heart. It also puts me in the terrible position of glorifying Lily.

'You're a hard worker,' I begin. 'You knew to live within your means. You weren't sloppy with anything – how you lived, cared for your body or handled the women you dated. You weren't intimidated or diminished by successful men like Ryan Landon, his friends or me, for that matter. You always have good ideas. People seek and value your opinions. I could go on, but you get the idea.'

Your gaze has narrowed into a look of menacing calm. 'You shouldn't know anything about how I handled women I slept with because I never slept with anyone after I first laid eyes on you. I didn't want anyone else.'

Pursing my lips, I gaze back at the ceiling. 'You know what I mean.'

'No, I don't.' You lean over into my field of vision. 'How long before I knew you existed did you decide you wanted me for yourself?'

I'm as still as you are, wary now. You're too clever. You grasp a far-reaching but correct conclusion with a tiny slip on my part. Now you're wearing the keen look of a sniper who's locked in on his target. 'Does it matter?' I answer cautiously. 'That's not the point.'

'Oh, lover,' you croon dangerously, 'you couldn't be more wrong about that. Every minute we could have been together matters. Those are all moments you owe me. That's time you've stolen, and I'm keeping track of every second, so I get my due.'

I shift to pull the duvet over me, feeling too exposed. It's much easier to hide wearing makeup and clothes. 'I'm a boots-on-the-ground investor, so to speak. There's only so much you can learn from reading. If I find someone interesting, I like to do a little in-person reconnoitering to see how they behave when they're not trying to impress anyone.'

Your brows lift. 'You stalked me?'

'I wouldn't say that.'

You continue giving me that dubious look. 'Well, come on then. Give me your preferred word for following me around on the sly.'

'Scouting.'

'Yeah . . . okay. Where did you scout me?'

'On shift at McSorley's. At games. Stuff like that.'

'Stuff like that . . .' Your eyes are so dark as you examine me. 'What did you see?'

'All your conquests and groupies.' I laugh when you wince. 'Don't you have to get to work?'

232

'How long did you follow me?'

'Not long. A few weeks before we met here at the party.' I sigh. 'I knew I was in trouble the first time I saw you. You were flirting with a girl. You laughed at something she said, and you were just . . . wow. How you looked – relaxed, sexy, confident – knocked the wind out of me. I knew I wanted you to look at me that way, every day, for the rest of my life.'

Rolling away, I move to slide off the bed. You lunge for me, yanking me back under you.

The look on your face breaks my heart. '*Setareh* . . . What am I going to do with you?' You sigh heavily. 'If you'd caught my attention, I'd've started looking at you like that right then and there.'

'I was afraid. You scared the shit out of me.' I brush a wave of your hair back from your forehead. 'In a perfect world, I would've put myself in front of you and let Fate weave her magic. You wouldn't have Baharan. We would've packed up and left the country. You would probably be a father now, all things considered. Maybe we'd live on the coast somewhere, and you'd work remotely since your sexual appetite doesn't leave you room to do much else.'

I tease you to lighten the mood, and it appears effective.

Your features soften, and your eyes warm with tenderness. 'What would you be doing?'

'Oh, you know, fending off your amorous advances because I'm busy chasing little replicas of you.'

You rest your forehead against mine. 'You would go insane. Your ambitions are too powerful.'

'So are yours.'

'No. I've never wanted the world. I want answers, and I want you, that's it. I'm a much simpler man than you give me credit for.'

I disagree with you, but don't say so. You are the child of

a narcissist, and that's made you an overachiever. You will always strive to be successful and perfect, to earn the validation of a mother who can show pride one day and vitriolic disappointment the next. A complicated, unstable infatuation with a chimera has entangled you for years. Obsession, rooted in insecurity, has consumed you. But once our destiny is determined, you'll seek other challenges. You'll need them.

'I wish we'd had all that time together,' you murmur.

'Haven't you ever wished that we hadn't met at all?'

'Never. And I know you wouldn't change that either.' You study me intently. 'You said I wouldn't have Baharan. Were you serious? You wouldn't care if I sold our shares?'

'Not if it made you happy. That's all I want. If rebuilding Baharan hasn't made you happy, get rid of it.'

You kiss me hard. Then let me go. 'If I don't resist you now, I'll miss all my morning meetings. Maybe even the afternoon ones, too.'

I shake my head, amused. 'Go. Conquer the world. I'll take care of coffee.'

You hop out of bed with boundless energy and head toward your closet with your long, easy stride. 'The creative is on the tablet,' you toss over your shoulder, 'in the file-sharing app. You'll find it. Be sure to look at both the marketing and social folders.'

I push up onto my elbows. 'Why are they separate? Shouldn't social fall under marketing and use the same creative for cohesion?'

You stop at the threshold to the closet and face me, leaning into the jamb. You're unabashedly naked. And why not? You have the most perfect masculine form. You're a dream realized.

'Two different divisions,' you reply. 'Marketing is in-house. Social is, too, kinda. It was Amy's company, and we merged it into Baharan after she married my brother. We haven't fully integrated yet, as far as I know, so they're separate for now.'

My brows arch. 'As far as you know?'

One of your powerful shoulders lifts in a careless shrug. 'My mother oversees that end of things. As you know, she came up with the Baharan name and logo, so branding is just something I've left to her.'

I remember the frosty looks the two women exchanged in the library and Aliyah's reaction to Amy's emergency at work. I remember some other things, too. 'She has feelings for you.'

An emotionless mask drops instantly over your features, hiding your thoughts. 'My mother? That's debatable.'

'You know I'm not talking about your mother,' I chide.

You scrub a hand over your face.

I wait for you to either say more or turn away. I won't push you. I don't need to – I saw how Amy responds to you.

'For a fraction of a second,' you say gruffly, 'she reminded me of you.'

I knew it but am still unprepared for the blow of hearing it. I drop onto my back and return my gaze to the coffered ceiling, where my chaotic thoughts latch on to the perfect symmetry. 'You don't owe me an explanation, Kane.'

'I caught her in the periphery of my vision on a rough day,' you go on. 'One of those days when you were the only thing on my mind. It was one night. Less than a night. She ended up meeting Darius because of it.'

My disappointment is fierce. But not for the reason you might suppose.

'You've every right to be upset,' you tell me.

'No, I don't.'

'I'm murderous at the thought of you with anyone else.' The words drip with molten fury.

We're both quiet for a long time. Ages, it feels like, as my thoughts dance with my demons.

'Can you forgive me, *Setareh*?' you ask softly.

'Kane . . .' I shake my head. 'You're asking the wrong woman. You should be apologizing to her.'

You exhale in an audible rush. 'That's fair.'

'I can't offer you absolution, but your wife was dead, and you were lonely. Give yourself grace – you're human. That said, try not to forget you're like catnip for women. Tread with care.'

'I hear you.'

I nod. 'I find it miraculous that you aren't married with children.'

'I would never have married again or built a family.'

'You don't know that.'

Your arms cross. 'The hell I don't. I would never settle for less. I would never raise a child with less.'

I wince. It's not jealousy in its usual guise that plagues us. We don't fear alienation of affection; our affinity is too deep. We envy the giving and taking of pleasure because our relationship is defined by pain.

My lips attempt to curve into a smile. 'You could be with another woman, but I'm here instead. I'm happy about that. That's all that matters.'

'I would never bring another woman here or anywhere. There was never anyone special. Who could ever compete with you?'

I look away quickly, hiding my tears.

'The longing for you was crippling. I learned to live with it, but some days were nightmares.' You stop, held for a moment within the memory of agony. 'Some days, I couldn't stop myself from looking for you, searching for you, in every woman I saw. If someone managed to make me look twice, to *hope* for even a second, I'd go a little insane. The disappointment was infuriating.' You pause. 'So, I'd fuck them.'

I inhale sharply and cover my face with my hands. When I met you, you weren't capable of such callousness. No, that's not true. We're all capable of it; you were simply too kind to indulge in cruelty. Heartbreak has twisted and refashioned you.

'Rage sex is cathartic,' you continue, your words singed with temper. 'Then I'd hate myself for being weak. I'd hate you for making me weak. For making me settle for women who didn't smell, taste or feel like you. Women who would never see in me what you do. So, I'd fuck them again because it made me sick to do it, and I deserved to feel my skin crawl for being so pathetic. Then I couldn't stand to see them again.'

I twist away from you, my legs curling into my chest. A moment later, I feel the duvet lift and the mattress dip. Your cool skin presses against mine as you spoon me, curling your body to match my fetal position. Your heavy arm drapes over me, pulling me into you, and your lips press contritely to my shoulder. You wanted to hurt me as you've been hurt, to punish me as you've felt punished. That's the craziest thing about love: it's hate turned inside out.

You weren't a man capable of such honest cruelty when we met. Love for Lily has warped you, and I accept responsibility for that; I can do no less. I catch your hand in my own and link our fingers together.

We don't say anything. The embrace alone is comforting for both of us. We lie that way for a long time. The position of the sun's rays on the walls and ceiling shifts.

'Are you okay?' you ask finally.

I nod. 'Are you?'

'I feel like scum. Other than that, I'll be okay if we are.'

'We'll be okay.'

You start to move. 'I'll call Julian and take the day off.'

I look at you over my shoulder. 'Don't do that.'

Your gaze narrows. 'Why not?'

'Because I'm okay,' I insist. 'We're okay. Really. And you need to clear the decks so we can take that honeymoon you promised me.'

Your eyes dart over my face, searching. You're apparently satisfied because you press a quick, hard kiss to my lips. 'I love you.'

I take a deep breath, then sigh. 'I know.'

It's a mad, suffocating, vicious kind of love. You once sought softer, gentler sentiments, but you've adapted. I grieve for the tender young man you once were, but I'm madly, breathlessly, viciously in love with the man you've become.

'Nothing's beautiful from every point of view.'

– Horace

36

Lily

I hear the hangers sliding as you rifle through your closet, searching and considering options. I leave the bed, leaning a hand heavily into the mattress when I realize my legs are weak. You do that to me for reasons physical and far more profound than flesh.

Slipping on a red silk kimono, I belt it around my waist and start toward the stairs. I'm halfway down when the doorbell rings and gives me a start.

'I'll get it,' I call up to you. 'Take your time.'

Instantly vigilant, I descend in a rush, dipping my head around the corner for a split second to peek through the door's inset glass. Surprise visitors have an entirely different connotation for us than for anyone else. And if someone poses a threat, they'll have to get through me to get to you.

Paused on the final step, I scrutinize the mental picture I took with a glance. An imposing man stands on the porch with an enormous bouquet of red roses in his large, scarred hands. He is not as tall as you, but he's over six feet. Possessing the shoulders of a linebacker, he's tamed his sandy-blond hair into a military cut and keeps his eyes hidden behind mirrored aviator sunglasses. His jaw is sharply square. His attire of a black T-shirt with black dress slacks makes it hard to mistake him for anything other than a bodyguard. If it's meant for the bouquet to serve as a false front, it's terribly deficient.

I curse the fact that I'm inadequately dressed. I'm also growing increasingly wet between the thighs as the evidence of your pleasure yields to gravity. All around, the situation is less than ideal. I'm not prepared for fight or flight, although I know the man must be yours. Any genuine threat would be cunning enough to catch us unawares.

Padding to the foyer on bare feet, I smile through the glass. 'What a nice surprise!' I say cheerfully, noting the florist delivery van as it pulls away from the curb. 'Could you just set those down on the porch, please?'

He does as I ask, then straightens. The sunglasses shield his eyes, making them fully unreadable. 'Is Mr. Black available?'

'Do you work for us?' I ask the question despite knowing the answer. Sadly, sometimes it's more advantageous for a woman to hide her intelligence, and I've learned to excel at dissembling.

'Yes, ma'am.'

'I'll let my husband know you're waiting. I'd invite you to wait inside, but I'm not dressed for it, as you can see.'

'No problem.'

I watch as he leaves the front porch, his steps silent despite his size and the thick soles of his combat boots. A second, similarly conspicuously dressed fellow appears on the stoop of our guesthouse across the street.

So, we're under guard here, too. Interestingly, you haven't mentioned it. Are you keeping people away or just keeping me?

Tightening the tie at my waist, I focus on the delivery. I open the door and softly exclaim my delight. The arrangement is extravagant. The scent of the roses, lavish and sensual, engulfs me. I feel a flutter of joy that you would send me flowers. They're a lovely, sweet symbol of courtship.

The bouquet is so huge and heavy it takes both of my

hands to lift and steady it. Kicking the door shut behind me, I carry the cut-crystal vase to the kitchen island. I take a moment to admire each rose's perfection; there are at least three dozen. Their color is a deep, luscious crimson, the petals softer than silk. I tug the card free of its stake and open the envelope to pull out the folded paper. The message is printed in a scripted font.

You're always in my thoughts.

The smile that curves my lips is so wide it's nearly painful. I set the card aside and reach with both hands to cup the silky petals in my palms. The bell sleeve of my kimono catches the paper and sends it fluttering to the floor. The card separates from its envelope, and as I squat to collect them both, I see the intended recipient's name. I freeze, arrested by disbelief.

The flowers aren't from you, and they're not for me.

I choke back a wrenching sob. I pick up the envelope with shaking fingers, then reach for the card. I fall back to sit on the floor as I reread the message, my legs too weak to support me. It's cold in the house, like the breath of a ghost, and abruptly dark. The sunny beach outside is another world, a make-believe place of warmth and light.

I don't know how long I stay there on the cool kitchen tiles. I might have remained there all day, my thoughts racing, if I hadn't heard you descending the stairs. I don't want you to find me weak and shaken.

The island acts as an anchor for me to grip as I crawl to my knees, then I grab the lip of the counter to pull myself to my feet.

When I turn away from the bouquet, I nearly run into you.

You loom over me. You've dressed in a dark gray T-shirt and faded black jeans. Your closet here is several years old, bought by the man you once were, so the shirt strains around your biceps and the breadth of your chest. I've become used to seeing you this way over the past week, but seeing your thirty-two-year-old body in the clothes of your twenty-something self is eerie. I suddenly feel as if I've been unchanged all these years, my life uninterrupted, and you are a doppelgänger of the man I love, out of sync with time and me.

'Let me see that.' You take the card and envelope from my nerveless fingers.

I watch your features harden as you read the message first. Your gaze narrows with fury when you see Ivy York's name. The note is crumpled into a tiny ball in your fist that you drop onto the countertop with disgust.

'Are you okay?' you ask, pulling me into a tight hug.

I sink into your warmth and strength. 'I'm fine.'

In hindsight, the red roses are a calling card easily identifiable despite the sender's chosen anonymity. The knowledge of Ivy York's name is chilling, but beyond that is the hidden message of the delivery: you're a target.

You press a kiss to the crown of my head. 'I love you. You're safe with me.'

That you would repeat that sentiment now shakes me to the core. This time, you're referring to my physical safety, and a tight knot of alertness I've long lived with loosens a fraction. Ensuring my safety has always been my responsibility. I've learned to protect and defend myself and manage both quite well, but knowing you have my back . . . well, that's a gift as precious as the jewels in your safe.

You pull back, stroke my cheek and deliver another blow. 'I wasn't what you needed before. I am now.'

You press your lips to mine, then back away, your jaw tight and your eyes burning with fury. Snatching your keys off the foyer console, you leave by the front door. Through the kitchen's picture window, I see the security specialist waiting for you on the walkway. You cross the street together and disappear inside the guesthouse.

The sanctuary of your zealous love has transformed my existence. It's my greatest failure not to have given you the same security.

My past has caught up with me. More, it's found me in my safe place and endangers you. I turn my gaze to the back of the house, to the patio doors that lead out to the beach. I could go now. Disappear.

The painful prick of a thorn draws my attention to my hands. I don't remember pulling a bowl out of the cupboard, but one sits beside the vase in front of me, half-filled with petals. Blood wells from a hole in the pad of my thumb and falls onto the lush pile, looking like a drop of morning dew. I have been beheading the roses and placing their wickedly sharp stems aside in a neat pile. The fragrance is hauntingly beautiful, a joyously sensual promise that taunts me with a fantasy not aligned with my reality.

What am I doing? How much time has passed?

I need to shower. Dress. Prepare.

Prepare for what?

The roar of the Range Rover's powerful engine brings me back to the moment. I watch as you back out of the driveway, then take off down the street. Leaving the roses, I race up the stairs. I'm restless and, for the first time, feeling trapped. I start to untie the sash at my waist. There's a weekender in the closet. It won't take me long to pack what I need.

A flash of movement in the periphery of my vision draws my eye to the full-length mirror hanging on the wall . . . I pause.

My face is bloodless, my eyes bruised black holes. I stare at that reflected haunted woman, then spy the bed behind her. I change the sheets every morning, and you've folded the duvet into a neat accordion at the foot and removed the pillowcases. The job of stripping the bed was likely interrupted by your security team's notification of the delivery. Still, it's how we work together, meeting halfway. What we are is matchless and precious. We see the best in one another and subsequently strive to better ourselves, to become more than we thought possible even while embracing the parts best hidden from others.

My knees weaken again, and I move to the bed, sinking onto it. My hands fist in the sheets. Your scent is in the air. And our scent.

Everything I want is right here. While my proximity threatens you, it also affords me the best chance of protecting you. And there are promises between us that may not survive being broken. The most crucial question: will *you* survive if I stay?

Six years have gone, and you are alive and flourishing. Isn't that a compelling enough argument for my departure?

A heavy sigh deflates my shoulders. You weren't flourishing, you were successful, and those aren't the same. The fire inside you had been slowly suffocating, that raging flame unable to breathe as you turned into stone. Another year or two, and it would've burned out entirely. That's why it took so long for us to bridge the gap between us. You were locked away inside yourself, alive without living. I couldn't reach you.

I can't do that to you – to *us* – for any reason, but primarily because I don't think it would make a difference. I'm with you. Your importance to me is inarguable now.

I shower and pull on a sleek floor-length column of black satin. It hangs from my shoulders by thin straps and dips so low in the back I can't wear anything beneath it. I can put my makeup on with my eyes closed. Since I wear it every day, it takes mere moments to complete. It's another layer of armor and another habit instilled in me by my mother.

Once I feel ready to face whatever comes our way, I remake the bed and toss the sheets in the wash. I'm anxious. I feel the need to act, but what can I do?

As I step outside, the slate pavers on the patio feel too hot against my bare feet, but gently warmed sand soon engulfs my toes. The glistening water straight ahead beckons, and I can't resist the call. The salt breeze caresses my bare back like a phantom lover, and ghostly fingers comb through my hair. I reach the shoreline, the sand turning damp and firm. Waves lap over my feet, coaxing me closer and deeper. Behind me, I feel the pull of the beach house urging my return.

Troubled, I turn and walk to clear my head. You're safe with your security team, and I've never been the one in danger. The air is crisp, the breeze holding aloft seagulls whose raucous cries seem to originate inside me. In the distance, a large ship powers out to a sea spread with glistening points, like millions of dagger tips bobbing in the sapphire waters.

I stop in front of the prettiest house on the shore, which is painted the softest of pinks with a pale gray trim. The upper and lower floors have a balcony and deck the same width and length, creating a covered porch upon which sit two rocking chairs and a wrought iron table with seating for four. A man is sitting at the table, a familiar and beloved figure.

I wave. Ben stands slowly and with difficulty. It pains me to witness his decline, more noticeable because of the yawning gap of time since I last saw him. I run to him.

'Hey, Ben.' I ascend the steps and embrace him. 'I've missed you.'

He trembles as he hugs me back. 'Have you come to take me to heaven, angel?'

I pull back. His face is craggier than before, his eyes deeper set. He's got his flat cap on, and the gray tweed has darkened with age. He's shorter now, his back curved into a hunch.

'Now, Ben . . . I'm a married woman, and you're too suave to use a line like that.'

'Well, you're off to take me to the other place, then.' He nods sagely. 'Can't say I'm surprised. Maybe not about you ending up there either, come to think of it. We've both enjoyed a sin or two, haven't we?'

'One or two. Do you mind if I bum a smoke off you and sit awhile?'

He frowns at me. 'Angels don't smoke.'

'How do you know?'

His rheumy eyes peer dubiously at me, but he motions for me to join him at the table. I sit, and he follows suit, watching as I help myself to a cigarette and light it with his lighter. The first inhalation is deep, my eyes closing against the familiar and longed-for head rush.

'Ah, that's so good. You're a saint, Ben.'

'Am I?' he queries eagerly.

Opening my eyes, I study him. 'You know I'm not dead, right?'

Even though I say it, I'm not sure I believe it. It feels like I'm in a snow globe, trapped in a contrived moment in time.

'They say you are. Drowned in your pretty little boat. It used to worry me, you sailing off alone all the time. It broke my heart when Robby told me you weren't coming back.'

'Oh, Ben.' I set my hand over his. His knuckles are thick, the age-spotted skin nearly translucent. 'I'm sorry.'

'And your poor husband.' He shakes his head. 'He worried me, too. I don't think he slept all the days they searched for you. The night Robby told me, I sat here on the deck and cried, but Kane . . . That boy walked to the water's edge and yelled with all his might.'

Oh, my love . . . You've suffered so much because of my weakness for you.

248

Ben rubs his chin thoughtfully. 'It sounded like somethin' between a wolf's howl and a banshee scream all twisted together. It was the eeriest thing I ever saw or heard, a man standing under the moon and falling apart that way. Could you hear him up there when he did that? I think he was shouting for you.'

My hand is over my mouth. The pain in my chest feels like a heart attack, and maybe it is. Possibly my heart can't survive the picture Ben has painted in my mind.

If there's a part of you that will always hate me for what you've endured, I'll accept that. Anyone who hurts you should pay, including me.

The screen door swings outward with a creak and Ben's grandson, Robert, steps out. 'Oh, my heavens. *Lily?*'

'Can you see her, too?' Ben asks, alarm on his face.

I notch my cigarette in the ashtray and swipe at my face, knowing my makeup must be a fright from all the tears I've shed.

'Hi, Robby.' I stand and hold my arms out to him.

'How are you here?' he asks over my shoulder, hugging me tightly. 'Where have you been?'

Through Robert, I can picture Ben as he must've once been. He's about my height and lanky, his face square and earnest. Freckles dance across the bridge of his nose. He's near my age but looks much younger. Like his grandfather, Robert's a charmer, the kind of guy who never settles for one girl but is so sweet that there's never a fuss.

'It's a long story,' I tell him, resuming my seat and taking another drag on my cigarette. My fingers are trembling, but I feel like I've smoked marijuana instead of tobacco. Everything is murky and odd, distant and dreamlike.

'You're really not dead?' Ben asks, his gaze narrowed.

'I don't think so.' But they are both looking at me so strangely. 'What?'

'Are you back in the house down the beach?'

'Yes, we're back. We live in the city, but we're here for now, and we'll hopefully return often.'

Robert runs a hand through his auburn hair. 'I need a drink. Pop?'

'Yes. Me, too.'

He heads inside.

Ben leans back, shaking his head. 'If you're really alive, you should know your house is haunted.'

I pause mid-exhale, smoke trapped in my lungs. 'How do you know?'

'We've seen you there, Robby and me. It was just Robby at first; he walks the beach more than I do. He saw you through the patio doors, staring at him. I told him it was a trick of the light and grief. He's carried a torch for you a long time. But then he saw you in the upstairs window a couple of years later.'

He pauses to light a cigarette, exhaling heavily. 'I saw you last year. It was dark, and the upstairs light was on. You stood in the window with a glow around your head. Like a halo. It scared the bejesus out of Robby every time, but I felt real peaceful about it. Like everything was going to be okay.'

Robert returns with a tumbler in each hand and a bottle of water under his arm. The door slams shut behind him, and even though it's a familiar and expected sound, it makes me jump. Filled with anxious energy, I rise to help, taking the water for myself and one of the drinks for Ben, which I place on the table in front of him.

'Whew.' Robert stares at me. 'Why'd you cut your hair?'

I crush the end of my cigarette, extinguishing it. 'I don't know.'

'You still had long hair when I saw you last year,' Ben says.

'About that . . .' I focus on Robert because his mind isn't

yet clouded by age. 'Can you tell me more about what you've seen?'

He takes a long drink of whiskey, stretching back in his chair. Then he shrugs. 'I don't know what to say. I've never told anyone but Pop because it's crazy.'

'You saw a woman in the house. Why'd you think it was me?'

'She was tall, like you. Thin, like you. I was down by the water, so it wasn't like she was right in front of me, but she was a knockout, like you.' He shrugs again, clearly embarrassed.

'It was you,' Ben insists. 'I'd know you anywhere.'

Your words echo through my mind. *I haven't been back.*

'*Lily!*' The wind carries your voice to me, scattering my roiling thoughts. That you're shouting for Lily is a soul-rattling shock, as it's the first time you've called me by her name since I woke.

Shoving the chair back, I leap to my feet. I search the beach and see you running. 'Kane!'

Your head turns toward me, and you sprint with the astonishing speed and grace I once admired on the basketball court, your feet flying across the sand. Your beautiful face is pale. Your eyes are dark coins, a payment for Charon to ferry you across the River Styx to me, your hell. Guilt settles in my gut. I race to you, meeting you partway. You snatch me up, squeezing so tightly I fear a rib will crack. I welcome the pain.

Your hand thrusts into my hair, anchoring me against you. My feet hover above the sand. You're quivering violently, and I hold you as tightly as I can, keeping you together. The picture Ben painted of you on the shore wracked by grief is in the forefront of my mind. Coming back to an empty house must have revived that pain in you, and I beg forgiveness.

'I'm sorry,' I tell you, a sob in my throat. 'I should've left a note.'

'You can't just leave like that. I need to know where you are.'

'I know. I'm sorry.' I gentle you with my hands, stroking your back. 'I wasn't thinking.'

My gaze scans the beach for danger. It frightens me to have you out in the open. The flowers are a taunting revelation that our location is known, as is my recent past. We're exposed in every way possible, and you are the target.

Ben's gruff voice calls out, 'You didn't have a wake, boy. She's trapped in purgatory, held between this life and the next.'

Your chest expands in a shuddering inhale. 'I'll keep holding her tight then, Ben,' you shout back, 'so she'll stay.'

37

Witte

Shirtless and barefooted, sweat from exertion slowly drying in the afternoon air, I lean against the balcony railing and read the latest text to my mobile.

> Paid in cash. No name. No license plate. VIN obscured.
> Full video emailed as attachment. The Range Rover had
> a tracking device on the undercarriage.

I study the grainy black-and-white surveillance photo of a gentleman exiting a florist shop in Greenwich. His head and face are clean-shaven, his eyes hidden behind dark sunglasses. He is a large man, muscular – in some parlance, he would be called 'the muscle' – dressed well in a suit with the jacket loose enough to conceal a gun.

Movement through the black-framed French doors draws my gaze to Danica as she collects my discarded clothes from the white carpet of her living room. My lover of many years picks up after me, cooks for me and pampers me. All of which is unnecessary but lovely. My daughter says it's serendipitous that I found a woman willing to accommodate the demands of my career. That Danica is a dazzling beauty who charms me with her wit and easy companionship is a bonus.

I smell her on my skin, and a primal need stretches inside me.

Opening my email, I skim the written report and then watch the video. It begins on the street, the vantage courtesy of a camera on the opposite corner. He arrives in a black

Bugatti, a vehicle so distinct it's evident he doesn't care if anyone remembers him. He unfolds from behind the wheel, neatly buttoning his jacket before entering the shop. While he's far too large to be truly agile, he conveys danger and menace in the fluidity of his movements and the way he thoroughly assesses his surroundings for hazards before stepping away from his car.

I forward the email and ring Mr Black. He answers immediately, and I begin without preamble, 'I suggest returning to the penthouse. The beach house is too exposed.'

'I'll discuss with Lily.'

Danica has slipped into a sheer white kimono, her nude perfection still on full display. She moves with the sinuous grace of a cat, her platinum hair falling to her waist.

Even after years together, I am still too eager and too lustful with her. I've just taken her on the floor, which she'd demanded I do the instant we rushed laughing through the front door, hot with desire like teenagers. *Fuck me now, Nicky*, she'd ordered, pulling me down on top of her in a tangle of silken limbs. Nothing could have deterred me from responding to that command. And when I'd pulled free of her sated body in a rush to answer my phone, she evinced no pique at being abandoned so swiftly after orgasm.

'I've reviewed the surveillance footage. The man is unquestionably a professional.'

My employer exhales harshly. 'Of course he is.'

'You should have it already.'

He's quiet as he watches. 'The Bugatti should be easy to trace,' he murmurs, with the absentmindedness of split focus.

'We're working on it,' I assure him.

'He tracked my car?!' He swears viciously as he crosses that piece of information in the written report. 'How did that happen?'

'We'll check the footage of the penthouse garage, but it would have been easier to attach it while we were out in the city on any number of occasions.'

'Why toy with her like this?' There is helpless fury in his voice. 'Tracking her. Taunting her with those flowers.'

'A message. Only she knows what it means and whether it was intended for you or her.'

Danica approaches, her full breasts and slender hips swaying as she walks with seductive grace. She pushes the door open, her lips curving in a feline smile as she sets a tumbler of whiskey with a ball of ice on the patio table. *Lunch in thirty minutes*, she mouths, before slipping back inside and shutting the door. Although I've just enjoyed her thoroughly, my cock stirs at the lushness of her figure so tantalizingly displayed. I've been with her for days and have scarcely been separated from her body the entire time. As pleasurable as that has been, I cannot help but feel I'm not where I should be.

'You don't think I should trust her,' Mr Black states. 'Have you seen the way she looks at me, Witte? She's no threat.'

The assessment is too blithe. Hasn't their relationship been mostly agonizing for him? His grief was so terrible only the single-minded focus on transforming himself into a man of substance had kept him going. He would not have that great a distraction again. If Lily broke his heart this time, I don't believe he would survive it.

I catch Danica's eye as she moves through the open-plan kitchen. She is a lavishly tempting creature gliding elegantly through the space, a seductive wraith trailing a gossamer white train and lustrous silver hair that drifts like fog around slender shoulders. She gives me a come-hither smile, her gaze languid and hot.

Is anything as intoxicating as being the object of desire for a stunningly beautiful woman? Is any man capable of being rational in that circumstance? Before meeting Danica, I would've said heedless love and desire were the folly of youth. I'd believed myself past all that nonsense. Can I judge Mr Black, lecture him, when my circumstance mirrors his?

'Let me tell you about Lily,' he says tightly. 'Ryan texted me one day, inviting me to spend an evening at his place. It'd been a few weeks since we'd hung out because I was avoiding her. I couldn't stand even the possibility of seeing them together. I knew she was at least half in love with me, and it drove me insane that she stayed with him just to keep me at bay. She tried to gaslight me, to convince me I was seeing a reaction from her that wasn't there, but the love was obvious every time she looked at me. So was the fear.'

Abruptly my first sight of her on the street in the city takes on a different connotation. Does her fear stem from her feelings for him rather than fear *of* him? Is such a thing possible?

'A hard choice for a woman to make,' I murmur, my thoughts spinning. 'You are both exceptional men.'

'Not then, I wasn't. Ryan was already making moves with LanCorp, but it was only a pipe dream for me to buy what remained of Baharan.' He sighs heavily. 'I accepted his invitation because I missed his friendship, but I also wanted to see the photos of her he had at his place. That's how starved I was for the sight of her.'

I glance at Danica. I, too, turn to photos of her when being together isn't possible. At times, memories alone are not enough to appease the ache of separation.

'I showed up right on time,' he continues. 'Maybe even a little early. The doorman knew me and knew I was coming, so he just waved me by. I took the elevator up. Ryan's front door was propped open by the deadbolt. I walked in and was about to call out when I heard sounds coming from the bedroom.'

The pain in his voice is a deep throb that affects me acutely.

'I should've walked out,' he goes on, his voice rough and raw. 'I walked to the bedroom instead. I couldn't stop myself. She was there, under him. They'd barely undressed. She'd lifted her dress, he'd dropped his pants, and he was in her, moaning like he was losing his mind.'

He pauses for a long moment before continuing. 'She was looking straight at me when I reached the doorway, and there was zero surprise on her face. She had her hand on the back of his head, holding it against her shoulder and turned toward the far wall so he wouldn't see me.'

'Mr Black, I don't –'

'She planned it, Witte. All of it.'

I don't want to hear any more. It's my job to put myself in his shoes, and with Danica in front of me, that's far too easy. She and I are of an age and beyond classifying our relationship. I'm monogamous; I've never asked if she affords me the same courtesy. She is a sensual woman, and I'm not often available. I never visit her unannounced, but it's possible that if I did, I would witness a scene like my employer described. The thought alone torments me.

'She'd used his phone,' he bites out, still furious. 'Set the time. Called the desk downstairs. Propped the door open. And stared at me with dead eyes while he fucked her in front of me.'

I shift on my feet, repulsed. I see the picture he's painting with his words. The Lily he speaks of is a woman I don't know. She cannot be the one who looks at him with such fervent longing and love.

But she could be the woman to whom a professional killer sent flowers and romantic sentiments.

'Her goal was to end us before we began. Because even though we hadn't seen each other in weeks, our intense attraction was still growing. It was only a matter of time. Ryan had been telling me he felt like she was easing him into the friend zone. She was declining sex with him and limiting their time together. It made it so much worse that I'd been building up hope of her coming to me soon.'

I hear his desk chair squeak as he shifts and find myself mentally noting the need for lubricant to address it, an instinctive grasp for withdrawal from the conversation. It's both too personal and too painful.

'Up until that point, I'd thought *I* was the issue. That I wasn't good enough, that my prospects as a life partner were too limited for her. At that moment, I realized the reverse was true in her mind. For whatever reason, she believed I was better off without her, and she was willing to degrade us both to protect me from her.'

It takes me several seconds to frame a tactful reply. 'Not many men would come to that conclusion in those circumstances.'

'Somehow, I knew – even at that moment – that she loved me. She staged a scene that had to be for my benefit, Witte. There was nothing in it for her but suffering. She didn't understand that I'd only stop wanting her if she stopped wanting me first. As long as she loved me, I had to keep going. Can you understand that?'

'Partly, yes.' I don't say that I wonder if she'd known the scene, as he calls it, would only deepen his desire for her. And put her at much greater risk – every man has his limits, and Mr Black's temper can be explosive. I certainly would have nothing further to do with Danica if she were to ambush me so cruelly and deliberately. But Lily had, perhaps, more insight into Kane Black than anyone else, in addition to her study of psychology.

'Lily didn't get it. She tried to change *my* feelings for *her* because her love was too strong to fight. And for a minute, she succeeded.' His voice sharpens into a blade that pierces me. 'I've never felt hatred like that. Not before or since. I wanted to murder Ryan – brutally – and strangle her for wounding me that way. I wanted to wrap my hands around her throat and squeeze. It took everything I had to stop myself from tearing them both apart. I remember thinking her eyes couldn't be more dead if I killed her. She wouldn't have fought me. She would have lain there, beautiful and vicious as a rose, while I choked her to death.'

I don't know this man who can so casually describe murdering the woman he loves. I also don't know the woman he's describing. His wife would never surrender to violence. I've looked into her eyes, too, and saw a woman who will always fight to the death.

'Her scheme almost worked. I figured if she were that desperate to push me away, I would give her what she wanted. I turned and left. If she'd been able to hold it together until I was gone, I would have been a danger to anyone who crossed my path because I still wanted to kill something. But she couldn't bear to see me go. She made this – I don't know – this terrible noise. This sound of – of anguish. I can still hear it in my mind.'

I am left to imagine it as he pauses.

He heaves out his breath. 'Ryan panicked, thinking he'd hurt her. I heard him begging her to tell him what was wrong as I walked out without him ever knowing I was there. She broke up with him that night and destroyed him. He'd already bought an engagement ring, hoping that would fix what was going wrong in their relationship. He ended up leaning on me in the aftermath, and it was rough. I felt like the biggest piece of shit. There I was, consoling my best friend while hiding that I was the reason he was hurting.'

'Questionable choices were made,' I offer grimly, 'but you didn't betray him.'

'The lies we tell ourselves,' he murmurs. 'Can you understand love like ours, Witte? I can survive anything except losing my wife, but she would leave me so I can survive.'

Reaching up, I rub at the tension in my neck. We cannot prepare for the unknown. 'If she wants you protected, she needs to be forthright about the danger.'

'Things are different now. *She's* different now. I'll have more information by morning.' Rage singes his words. He's been controlled for so long, but no longer. 'And we'll think about returning to the city tomorrow. I'm not letting a thug in a Bugatti run us out of here. This house is sacrosanct. I'll leave it when I'm damned good and ready.'

'I urge you to stay home and indoors until then.'

'We're not going anywhere,' he says curtly. 'We've got a lot to discuss. If someone wants her, the money, or both, I want that resolved *now*. I've worked too hard to build this life. I'm not giving any of it up.'

Discussing the present – and what the future might hold – is somewhat of a relief. I can't fix the past, but I can make plans for the present and the future. 'We don't know how she's carried on the past six years or before you met. Abandoning some lifestyles can't be done by choice. In certain situations, the only way out is to kill or be killed.'

'I'm aware of that.' There is no hesitation in his voice, no regret. He is resolved and resolute. 'You understand, though, there is only one viable option for me.'

38

Lily

'It smells amazing in here.' I enter the kitchen and pause by the island. You've thrown out the roses, and the sea breeze, assisted by whatever you're cooking, has fully eradicated their cloying scent.

You're at the stove, wearing old jeans that are both comfortably loose and molded to the shape of your body. Your feet and chest are bare, your back muscles rippling as you stir whatever is in the big pot on the burner. Your phone lies on the counter by the spoon rest, steam rises from the vents of a rice cooker and Billy Joel sings 'She's Always a Woman' through the surround sound speakers – a song you once said reminds you of me.

'It's gumbo,' you say over your shoulder, your attention on cooking.

'I love gumbo.' I rest my hand against the doorjamb with practiced nonchalance. I want to be seductive. Confident. I feign both. 'But you should be wearing an apron.'

This easy, settled domesticity is very you, down to your soul. All you ever wanted was Lily as your wife and the creature comforts of a proper home.

'And miss an opportunity to entice you with my body?' You adjust your position to keep me in your sights and wink. You've already shaved again.

You seem relaxed and serene at the moment, and your smile lights up the room. It's like you've completely wiped the flower delivery from your mind. Erasing the day isn't so easy for me. I know I'm the source of your deepest stress and worry. It's a cruel trick of the universe that I'm also your comfort and haven.

'I'm enticed.' You've trained my body to associate yours with pleasure, and addiction to that dopamine rush stirs an immediate physical reaction. On every level, I'm aware of what you can do to me and how well. My nipples strain against the black satin of my dress, visibly aroused. They're tender from your frequent suckling, as is my mouth and sex. Previously underused muscles are sore. I'm never unaware of how your hedonistic pursuit of erotic gluttony is tailoring my body to your specific needs.

You grow very still as you register my obvious response to you, your glorious physique tense and breathless. Every muscle is defined by its tautness, turning you into a sensual work of art. Your body readies to provide the stud servicing you've conditioned me to crave.

'I thought you might want to return to the penthouse tonight,' I say quietly.

Setting down the long-handled spoon, you face me. 'Are you afraid?'

'No.'

'Good.' You lean back against the edge of the counter and fold your arms, showing off the beauty of your thick biceps and hard pectorals. Your jeans barely restrain a prominent erection. The top button is undone, allowing the denim to ride low on your hips. You're noticeably wearing nothing underneath.

You are, quite simply, the sexiest man I've ever seen. Erotic and boldly virile. I'm so grateful you're mine, and I get to have you whenever I need you. The raking glance you give me is a caress of its own – hot, appreciative and possessive. You always look at me that way, as if I'm both priceless art and titillating pornography.

Do you see me clearly, or does the fog of old sentiment blur your vision? Which would benefit me more: acceptance as I am or the forgiveness of nostalgia?

I shift my stance, frustrated and restless. My hunger for you is sharp and urgent. I want so much more from you. I want it all. And that ungratified greed drives me to take you any way I can get you, as often as possible.

You straighten, turn off the burner and cover the pot with a lid. 'If we leave now, our last memory here will be that damned flower delivery. I'm not letting anyone or anything change what this place means to us. We don't have to run. I'm fully capable of protecting you.'

As always, your passionate heart moves me. Who would have thought a woman raised to be contemptuous of love would fall so deeply for a romantic?

You make me want to be a better person so fiercely I can't imagine not transforming. Larva to butterfly. Sinner to saint.

You prowl toward me, a sleek panther, big and fluidly graceful. I find myself taking an involuntary step back as adrenaline surges through me.

'I'll catch you,' you warn softly.

My pulse races, and my chin lifts. 'I'm not running.'

Your hands encircle my upper arms as if, despite my assurance, you expect me to bolt. Your grip flexes, tightening then releasing. Desire smolders in your eyes, but it's fury that burns brightest.

'Do you do it on purpose?' you murmur, your gaze on my mouth. 'Everything about you makes me want to fuck. The look of you, the way you smell. Just the thought of you makes me hard. You're a compulsion, *Setareh*.'

Your thumb lifts to my lower lip, rubbing it. I lick the pad, then suck your thumb into my mouth. The suction is firm as my tongue strokes the calloused pad. You growl, pressing against me, your erection growing with every circle of my tongue.

I release you, and your arm falls to your side. 'You're angry,' I say, and it's not a question.

'I'm way beyond angry.' You rest your forehead against mine. 'Six *years*, *Setareh*. Six years of being so desperate for you that I thought I'd go insane. And now someone's threatened you when I've just gotten you back. Even rage doesn't begin to touch what I feel.'

Your love never lessened. I think of the canvas on your wall; you've tortured yourself to keep Lily close.

Leaning forward, I press a kiss over your heart. Somehow, I will take that hurt away and replace it with love. Your last memory of us in this house will be of joy, even if it's a recollection made hazy by mind-numbing pleasure. It's the least I can do, considering all the pain I'll be causing you in the future.

You groan as I move my mouth to the flat brown disk of your nipple and kiss it, too. While my tongue flickers over the tight point, I release the steel buttons of your fly one by one.

Your jeans slide to the floor. You step out of them and kick them aside, brazenly naked. I take your penis in my hands, my lips curving when a hard tremor wracks your big body. There is undeniable power in taking control of an authoritative man like you. It's exhilarating having you in my palms – satin-smooth, thick and feverishly hot.

It's been strange and wonderful to touch you intimately, yet I can't shake the odd sense of interloping. It's maddening, unsettling and dreadful. I want to believe that what we ignore will simply disappear, but I know only honesty can set us free.

And separate us.

I begin a gliding tug from root to tip. I've got both hands

wrapped around you, one atop the other, but the head of your penis extends past my grasp. I give you a two-fisted stroke, knowing the pressure you like. Your serrated moan rewards me. I brush my lips across your chest to find your other nipple.

Sliding my right hand between your legs, I cup the heavy weight of your sac, freeing my left hand to move faster over your thickly veined length.

'I've never been this hard,' you bite out, jaw clenching.

'Not even our first time?'

'I want you more now.' Your hips begin to rock into my grip.

'Kiss me,' I order, touched by your confession that I affect you as no other ever has. When you lower your head to mine, I capture your lips in a breathless melding, indulging in your honeyed flavor. My hold on you tightens, just enough to increase the friction. You weren't lying – you're hard as steel, engorged with need. It's heady. You're a man who could have anyone but who wants only me, and while I'm always yours for the taking, even total surrender fails to assuage your craving.

As my tongue traces your parted lips, your moan pours upward from somewhere deep and dark inside you. Your extreme reaction makes me slick between the thighs, but this moment is yours, just as you are mine.

I want to take my time with you and savor this rare opportunity to focus minutely on your pleasure, but you grip my wrists and force me to release you. Before I can protest, you spin us around and propel me into the cool glass of the refrigerator door.

Your body radiates the primal heat of a healthy male at his apex. At night, you warm our bed. When we make love, you nearly singe my skin. You've trapped me between hot and cold, pinned. The only part of my body I can move is my arms, and I reach down to your muscular buttocks, pulling you closer and squeezing.

Our open-mouthed kiss is frenzied. It's wet and covetous. Your hands shove into my hair, gripping my scalp to hold me still as you take command with a deep, harsh growl. A frisson of fear slides through me, even as my toes curl. Your greedy lust is delicious and edged with roughness.

'Please . . .' My hunger for you overwhelms me.

The groan that escapes you rewards my desire, while the masterful stroking of your tongue against mine reminds me of how well you pleasure my sex with it.

You grab fistfuls of my dress, pulling it up to my waist. Then you drop to your haunches and lick through the seam of my cleft. I shiver violently, the direct stimulation just what I need. You hold my dress up with one hand while the other catches my leg behind the knee and drapes it over your shoulder, opening me to your tongue's delicate flickering over my clitoris. I'm swollen and tender, and you're gentle and attentive, using the flat of your tongue to soothe in long licks and the stiffened tip to work my clit. My core clenches in protest at its emptiness, needing you inside me.

'Kane . . .'

All of your tight, determined focus is on the center of my pleasure, and your consummate skill unravels me thread by thread. You're all I see or hear or feel; the heat of your palm splayed flat against my buttock to angle my sex to your talented mouth, the soft suction, your undeniable pleasure . . .

Your tongue pushes into my channel, and heat blooms across my skin. I'm panting, my legs trembling. The teasing thrusts are destructive. They're not enough yet too much. I never knew this need was inside me, how voracious it is or that only you can satisfy it.

My sex tightens around your thrusting tongue, and you make a purely animal sound. I gasp in protest as you pull away, steadying me on my feet before straightening to tower over me. Your dark eyes are bright and hot as you lick the taste of me from your lips.

'I'll feel you come around my cock,' you say darkly, bending to grip the backs of my thighs and lifting me so that I sit in your arms. You are a solid column of strength, and I cling to you, so grateful to hold you.

Raising me higher, you take my nipple into your mouth, your tongue teasing through the satin.

The intense pleasure borders on pain. Sensation radiates from that sensitive tip. The rhythmic pull tugs at places lower in my body. My fingers tangle in your hair. Your scent and your barely controlled desire inflame me.

'Don't make me wait,' I gasp, near frantic as you lower me to take my mouth in a profoundly erotic kiss.

A slight shift of my hips aligns my clitoris with your length. I begin to massage that bundle of nerves by undulating against you, rubbing up and down. I'm slippery with arousal. Anguished sounds begin to rumble from your chest, your control slipping. You hold me with unshakeable strength, allowing me to use you. I am in control of the pace, the pressure.

'You're killing me.' You pull on my lower lip with your teeth. 'You're fucking killing me.'

Tightening my legs, I lift enough to position my sex against the wide, heavy crest of your penis. You're so stiff, and I'm so wet you slip effortlessly inside me. I shiver at the delicious pressure of your shaft stretching my sheath. Your fingers grip my thighs hard enough to bruise.

Your hips begin to churn, moving in short, hunched thrusts that provide friction while driving you deeper. Your biceps bunch and release as you bear my weight and circle my hips into your sleek, deep thrusts. You snarl with savage pleasure when I take you to the root, the sound so animalistic and erotic that my core clenches with arousal.

The sight of you unravels me. Muscles ripple and flex beneath perspiration-sheened golden skin. A rivulet of sweat courses down your chest, dipping and rising over the tight lacing of your abs. Your penis, so long and thick, so brutishly masculine, drives powerfully in and out of my sex. You hammer into me, stroking that broad, flared head over nerve-laden tissues. My body unlocks from my mind, serving only you.

My climax builds with frightening intensity. Your hips roll with every pump and withdrawal in that practiced, powerful way that speaks of your prowess. Your rage is a firestorm, like a whip crack driving you, every hard and fast plunge a declaration of possession. Your rhythmic stroking spurs violent quivering. My entire body is tight and steaming. Blood roars in my ears.

Nothing else exists. There is only you, only me, only our ravening need.

'I can't,' I tell you urgently, wild with desire and afraid my emotions are too fraught. The approaching climax seems too vast, a heated wave that will take me under. 'I can't . . . Please.'

'You can. You will.'

You shift me, lowering me further so that my shoulder blades bear my weight and my thighs open to their widest point. Nothing impedes your furious fucking, your penis withdrawing to the tip and sinking to the hilt with every rapid-fire thrust. I watch, arrested by your body's vigor and power harnessed solely for mindless carnality.

I cry out when the orgasm takes me, moaning your name in an agony of release that seems never-ending. You don't stop, prolonging my pleasure until my core seizes again, clenching around you.

'God, yes . . . You're squeezing me so hard . . .' Your dark head falls back, the cords of your neck stretched tautly. Tension hardens your body, and your muscles strain. Your teeth grind on a ragged groan, and then I feel the spurting of your seed. You grind your hips against mine, filling me at my deepest point. The sounds you release are tormented ecstasy.

When you finally sag heavily against me, I don't mind. Not at all.

I press my mouth to the hammering pulse in your neck.

'You okay?' you ask in a voice so hoarse it's foreign to me.

'Not sure how we ended up this way,' I answer breathlessly, 'but I'm glad we did.'

Your husky laugh is the most beautiful sound I've ever heard. 'I know I'm crushing you, but my knees are weak, and I don't want to drop you. Gimme a minute.'

I wrap my arms around your shoulders and hold on tightly. 'There's no rush.'

Eventually, you regain the strength to straighten and pull me away from the refrigerator. You're still hard inside me, and I know from experience you are indefatigable. But the edge has smoothed a little, and your dark eyes reveal heartbreaking affection. We're so often distracted by the sizzling chemistry between us, that irresistible gravitational pull keeping us orbiting one another. Only in these brief moments of satiation do we acknowledge what's growing between us, the connectedness stemming from acceptance and esteem.

My fingers comb through your sweat-slicked hair. 'I love you. The words don't change, but my feelings do. I love you more each minute. I love you more now than I did this morning or yesterday.'

Your throat works on a hard swallow, and your eyes sheen

wetly. The silence stretches, and I think you won't speak, which is fine. I don't need words, only you. Then you find your voice.

'You just love me for my body,' you tease, your emotions thickening your speech.

'Well . . . you do dispense orgasms like a vending machine on the fritz.'

Your smile is wicked. 'Hold on tight.'

You turn to the stairs and then take them as if I don't weigh anything. We spiral upward in shadow, the briskness of your stride bouncing me on you. I don't know how you manage to keep us connected. It should be awkward or uncomfortable, but you're so strong I'm secure. Still, when we reach the bedroom, I'm laughing so hard I can barely hold on.

You walk to the bed and lower me to my back. You're not even short of breath, which flatters me, considering how winded you were from your climax.

Brushing my hair back from my face, you surprise me by saying, 'I don't want you to worry. We're safe. Cameras are surveilling the house and perimeter, and we monitor motion detectors 24/7. Guards and drones canvass the property line at regular intervals. No one's getting close without us knowing about it.'

'Oh, Kane.' I sigh and press my hand over your heart. We can hide but ignoring reality won't be so easy. The world would come between us if we let it. We must choose each other above everything, always.

'We can defend a location,' I agree, 'but you won't always be homebound. You'll need to move around at some point, and you're vulnerable at multiple points in your workday. A needle prick on the sidewalk in front of the Crossfire. Poison slipped into your drink at a business lunch. Even a long-range rifle shot, right here on the beach. You can't live like a prisoner.'

'I could – as long as I'm imprisoned with you.' Your gaze is as somber as your voice. 'But you're going to explain why you reacted to the flowers the way you did, so I have the information I need to deal with it.'

I lie beneath you, rigid with surprise. I recover instantly, forcing my body to relax. 'You say that as if I know.'

Such an obvious tell reveals my thoughts, but my guard is down with you. You ensured it would be by keeping me perpetually in a woman's most vulnerable state. Even now, your thick penis is shoved deep inside me.

Has that been your intent all along? I'm beyond impressed if you can command physical arousal with such calculation and frequency.

Your dark eyes harden into black diamonds. 'I'm crazy about you, but I'm not an idiot.'

'I never thought you were.'

'You think I've forgotten walking in on you and Ryan? That I'll ever forget? You were already afraid of someone before we got together, and you think being with me puts me in danger, so you've done your damnedest to keep us apart.' The curve of your mouth takes on a cruel edge. 'It's time for you to tell me why.'

39

Lily

'Why were you afraid for me,' you persist, 'and not for Ryan?'

Ryan. Navigating my past will always be treacherous. 'I didn't love him,' I tell you, breathless.

Your brow arches. 'Obviously. Later, you'll tell me why that relates. Right now, I want to know where the man who sent you flowers fits into our timeline? Before I met you or since you've been Ivy?'

I study you while my thoughts spin. You're menacing at the moment. There is nothing soft or comfortable or infatuated about you. The danger perversely excites me.

I gather myself for the moment I've dreaded. 'Did you ever look for your father?'

You scowl, displeased by what you perceive to be a change in topic. 'It's your turn to answer questions.'

'What happened to your father pertains.'

You withdraw from me to turn onto your back, your erection gleaming wetly as it curves proudly toward your navel. I push the hem of my dress down and roll to my side, facing you. Nothing cools amorousness like thinking of your parents.

You speak up at the ceiling. 'We found his name and passport information on a flight manifest to South America around the time he disappeared.'

I prop my head in my hand to look down at you. The sun is setting. The gloaming has swathed the room in a lush blend of warm color and cool darkness. Your gorgeous face is half lit and half bathed in shadow. I embrace the dusk and the cover it affords me.

'Cartagena, wasn't it?' I ask. 'You didn't send someone down to Colombia to look for him?'

As I did moments ago, you stiffen abruptly, and your head whips toward me. A heat I can feel begins to radiate from your skin. 'How do you know where he went?'

I leave the bed and move to the window. The Sound has a dark sheen, like a lake of oil. I'm cold now, separated from your body heat and intimately wet. The darkening sky silhouettes me, and that will affect you, which might give me an advantage. I'm well aware that despite how recently we've made love, we haven't been this emotionally distant from each other since we arrived at the beach house.

I raise my voice, so you'll have no trouble hearing, but keep the tone purposely casual. The information is dreadful enough on its own without dramatizing it. 'I was there when my mother met with a man to remove her name from a flight manifest to Colombia. She'd been designated a no-show but wanted her name deleted, and her traveling companion changed from a no-show to a passenger who'd boarded. I remember thinking Cartagena is such an interesting sounding word, that combination of hard and soft. You know how I love words. And Paul Tierney – that name stuck. I don't even remember what alias my mother used at the time, but your father's name never left me.'

You've since abandoned your father and stepfather's surnames and adopted one of your choosing: Black. Then you gave it to me. You're creating a legacy with no taint from the past, but the past follows. We can never really be free of it.

There is the sound of the mattress shifting behind me. 'Our parents knew each other?'

The house is still and expectant, holding the evening and our love intertwined like a captured breath.

'She paid the man in cash,' I press on. 'It was a huge stack of bills. I couldn't stop staring at it, sitting like a green brick on the table between us. We'd been poor for so long. It was shocking that she'd have that much cash, let alone give it away. I remember her hand shaking when she set the money down, but that was her only tell.'

I pause, digging in my mind for more of the memory, but it's like a projection against roiling fog. There are only fragments of images and impressions. I can't even be sure I haven't embellished the recollection to fill in gaps. It was so long ago, and I was a child more devoted to my mother than to anyone else.

You're quiet. Savvy enough to know you can't pull the past from me and are unable to doubt me. It's a terrible gift to be seen so completely, to know that you're aware of the darkness that shrouds me like a lover. Perhaps you even embrace it. Maybe that's the only way we work – if I'm the tarnished side of Lily's gilded coin. Similar enough to preserve the fantasy but different enough to keep her memory inviolate.

Although she wasn't so lily-white after all, was she?

You rise from the bed. There's enough light emanating from the skylight in the bathroom to outline your tall, powerful frame in the window's reflection. We're two shadows, appearing as if we're standing beside one another while, in actuality, the entire room and a lifetime of secrets separate us.

'She'd packed her bags the week before.' The pad of my thumb worries the band of my ring. 'Since she didn't pack mine or tell me to do it, I knew she was going without me. It wasn't unusual for her to leave me alone. When I was old enough to turn the television on and use the microwave, she'd sometimes be gone all night. When I started middle school, she started staying away longer. She'd give me some money, leave food in the refrigerator and tell me to go to school every

274

day so the attendance office wouldn't call about me when she wasn't there to answer. Thinking about it now, I don't know if she meant to return from the trip to Colombia. You know how much your father embezzled. She might have thought her ship had finally come in. Certainly, your dad had to know he couldn't come home without facing jail time.'

Movement on the beach draws my gaze downward. I find my neighbor, Ben's grandson Robert, staring up at me from the shoreline. I don't move, knowing I'm just a dark shape in the shadows. I remember his assertion that he's seen me here over the past six years. An overwhelming sense of déjà vu swamps me, and I sway with sudden dizziness.

I sense your move toward me more than hear it and thrust out my hand to stay you. 'No, I'm fine. Let me finish.'

I couldn't stand it if you touched me now. I'm trapped in the space between the child I was and the woman I am now, not quite one or the other, which leaves me unbearably and frighteningly vulnerable.

'You think they were lovers.' You've moved closer.

'Love had nothing to do with it, at least not for my mother. She was incapable of loving anyone. I think she saw your father as a bank balance, and your father saw an irresistible woman. Men stumbled over themselves for her, Kane. She could drive a man beyond his limits with so little effort.'

'I believe it.'

I watch as Robert turns away and continues down the beach. 'You can't imagine what she was like.'

You embrace me from behind, nuzzling your temple against mine. 'Can't I?'

'I'm a pale imitation.'

'You're radiant when I touch you. Your eyes glow when you look at me.'

You said I was safe with you. Your patience in waiting for

275

the answer to your question is irrefutable proof. Outlining how our lives began to intersect feels like peeling off layers of my flesh. I feel a phantom kiss of air across my skin, which is nearly enough stimulus to drive me mad.

Your words are a whisper of warmth. 'If she was incapable of love, she could never be as beautiful as you are.'

Your acceptance is the emotional security I was taught not to believe in. In a distant corner of my mind, I can hear my mother mocking my hopeless sentimentality, my unquench-able yearning for you. Her laughter's musicality echoes through me. In my mind's eye, I see that heartless glint in irises as brightly green as my own, the look that says every-thing is unfolding the way she'd predicted it would. She foresaw everything and had her hand in everything. No one escaped her. Nothing surprised her, especially me.

Despite her merciless tutelage, love caught me unawares. It bears your face and speaks with your voice. I feel it as your skin brushing against mine. You've undone me. Another lesson learned. And every life lesson I've survived has only brought me closer to becoming the very epitome of my mother.

'There are a million answers I want from you.' You lean your head against mine. 'What happened to my father wasn't one of them.'

The feel of your bare chest against my exposed back thaws the chill that has sunk into my bones. Every word burns my throat like acid as I speak it. 'Your father had a weakness, but my mother may have been the only woman able to exploit it. And it's possible your father had a change of heart. Maybe he realized on the way to the airport that he didn't want to leave you and the life he'd built, but my mother was too close to getting her hands on his money to let him back out. Some-thing went wrong, Kane, and neither of them boarded that plane. She came home with the money, and no one's seen your father since.'

The band of your arms tightens. 'Are you trying to make me feel better because maybe he didn't have the option of coming back? That doesn't change the choices he made to leave his wife and child in the first place, to destroy his life's work, to rob and bankrupt his business partner, and ruin the livelihoods of his employees . . . All for a woman incapable of loving him but capable of killing him?'

Everything about you – your posture, tone and words – betrays a festering resentment and fury. Your disgust burns like a blaze inside you, heating your body even more.

I settle against you, my spine curving to meld with the hardness of your chest, my arms wrapping over yours. I turn my cheek toward your heart, offering what comfort I can. 'That doesn't mean he deserved to die.'

'I'm not saying that.' You rest your chin on the crown of my head. 'I know how it feels to need a woman more than air, but he'll never have my sympathy, and I'll never forgive him. I'm at your mercy because you love me. If you didn't, it wouldn't matter how much I loved you, I wouldn't ruin my life or anyone else's for you.'

'I'm sorry, Kane.'

'Don't apologize for him.'

'I'm apologizing for not telling you sooner. You should've known that I believe my mother killed your father. I had no right to keep my suspicions from you, and I did it because I'm selfish. Because I was afraid that history might destroy our future.'

Your chest expands on a deep breath. 'That history is why you tracked me down and "scouted" me.'

'You call me your fate. Your destiny. But it didn't start with us – it started with them.'

'My father's actions brought you to me, *Setareh*. How could I wish things had happened differently when our marriage is the result?'

'It's okay if you do.'

'I don't.' You urge me around to face you. 'I won't.'

Tilting my head back, I look up at your breathtakingly handsome face. The two halves of myself — the woman my mother raised me to be and the woman who loves you to death — war with each other. 'I'm not going to make excuses for my mother, but you must know a little of who she was to understand the rest.

'She despised men. She believed you're all inherently weak, easily led by your dicks and unreliable. She'd say all that with a laugh like she wasn't deathly serious, but I realized later how severely damaged she was. I don't think killing your father was premeditated, but I think she enjoyed it enough to develop a taste for wet work. He was the first, but he was by no means the last.'

My confession hangs in the air between us, heavy and chilling. Your pupils expand, and your tanned skin blanches. Your entire body grows taut, like the string of a bow. Your fingers flex in the flesh of my hip.

I hold you as tightly; my fingers splayed over the hardness of your back as if I'm keeping you close, which of course I can't. 'One of her marks ran a business that was a front for organized crime, so the money she took from him actually belonged to a gangster named Val Laska. It was probably all too easy for Val to track the money to my mother. People who meet her tend to remember her well. But once he did, he fell for her, just like every other man, and she found her king. Val complemented her, made her even more deadly.'

I picture them together in my mind. They had respect for each other, recognition of their true selves, and fear.

The combination was a deadly aphrodisiac blended just for them.

And if we're being honest, are we any different?

'Her marks were always good family men before Val,' I go on. 'That was part of her game, seeing if a guy who had it all could still be greedy and selfish enough to want more. If they resisted her, she let them live. If they didn't, they died. But Val didn't need to be lured into hell – he ruled it. Human trafficking. Underage prostitution. Murder for hire. Torture was a pastime.'

'He sounds like a catch.' Wrath laces your sarcasm. 'How did it affect you?'

'It didn't really. My mother moved in with him, left me where I was, and life for me went on as it always had, just with less of her in it. She gave me money, clothes, food and kept paying the rent on the apartment. I took care of myself, which I'd always done anyway. It wasn't until I got older and started looking like her that she took an interest in me.'

I think I'm speaking and comporting myself with detachment, but something gives me away. Your eyes have softened with pity. I don't know why I kept talking. I could've shrugged the question off and told you I'd obviously turned out fine. I only meant to bring you full circle to an explanation of the flower delivery. But I didn't shut up, and if I taper off now, you'll imagine things you shouldn't.

Maybe I secretly wanted to tell you more.

Lifting my chin, I finish what I started. 'Around the time I hit puberty, she stopped viewing me as a separate individual. It was like she thought of me as her clone, a new and improved model who would live her perfect life without the mistakes.'

My eyes sting with tears. 'I loved her, Kane. I will always love her, despite what she did to you, your family, and so many others. At first, I loved her as any child loves their mother, even though she wasn't fit to care for anything, let alone a small human being. Later, as an adult, I realized how valuable her lessons were, and I was grateful to her for teaching them. She made me strong. She taught me about people, about men. I've never been naïve or gullible. I've never been in vulnerable situations with predators.'

'You don't have to be ashamed for how you feel about your mother,' you tell me.

'She told me I could have anything I wanted in this world, so I never set limits on what I could accomplish. *Live as you please*, she told me. *Don't let the world stop you*. I still hear her voice whenever I'm faced with a decision, telling me what I should do, and her direction – whatever it is – is always empowering.'

You hold my gaze in the deepening darkness. 'You're not like her, Lily.'

'The best parts of me are. So are the worst.'

'Well, I love every bit of you.' Your hand strokes down the curve of my spine, soothing, when it's you who should be comforted. 'I'll say it as often as you need to hear it: nothing can change how I feel about you. You empower people, too. It's your gift.'

I take a deep breath, then let it go. My pliant body sinks into your embrace.

'So,' you begin, 'our friend Val . . . Big guy, tall, bald and has a thing for flashy cars?'

Apprehension grips me. 'Yes, that's Val.'

'He sent the flowers – personally.' You tuck a loose strand of hair behind my ear. 'Does he want you? The money? Both?'

'No. He wants *you* – dead.'

Your entire body stiffens.

'You have to understand the way they think, Kane. On the surface, I appeared to achieve everything my mother wanted

280

for me. I was independent, men were entertainment, and I was accountable to no one. Then I fell in love with you, and everything changed. You were the catalyst, so you have to go. And while my mother didn't have the first clue about love, she knew that killing you would be the final stage of my development. I would be truly ruthless then.' Closing my eyes, I let my forehead rest against your chest. 'If something ever happened to you, I would become the thing she always hoped I would be – *her*.'

Your lips press hard to the crown of my head. 'Nothing's going to happen to me.'

'Val will follow my mother's wishes. That's the message of the flowers: he's gunning for you. Because if he lets me have you, he fails her, and he won't fail.'

Shifting a little, I gauge whether you'll let me pull away. Your grip tightens, holding me in place.

'Don't regret falling in love with me, *Setareh*. I'd rather have five minutes with you than fifty years with someone else.'

Furious, I push you away. 'Damn it, Kane. You have to put yourself first! You have to love yourself first. Don't just *accept* this. You should be furious that my selfishness has put you in mortal danger.'

You look at me with an arched brow. 'Cut the shit. I'm not in the mood.'

My temper flares. 'I'm just a moving target, something you're perpetually trying to earn because you don't think you deserve love. Thanks to your parents, you don't believe it's possible for someone to love you, not really. Who are you if you're not the man trying to deserve Lily?'

You throw up one hand and turn away. 'Don't start with the fucking psychobabble.'

But I can't stop. You're not reacting the way I need you to. Where's the disgust? The anger? The fear? Where's the *rage*?

'We're codependent. Everything about us reinforces negative behaviors in the other, don't you see?'

'Is this when you give me a summary of one of your psych classes?'

'You think earning my love will complete you, but it's become an obsession that undermines you.'

'Okay, fine. You want to fight?' You pivot to face me. 'You're on. I'm pissed enough about those fucking flowers.' You grab me by the arms and give me a firm shake. 'Every person on this planet is a little nuts. You've never been happier than when you're with me. I would never have become the man I am without you. Who gives a shit if your disorder does something with my disorder and reinforces whatever-the-fuck? It's not crazy if it works.'

Night has descended like a shroud. The house is still and quiet, a dark sentinel protecting us from the world outside. You're a shadow, your eyes glittering stars.

'Stop,' you say gruffly, releasing my arms to cup my face in both hands. 'Stop that now.'

I don't realize I'm crying until you brush the tears away with your thumbs. You press soft, gentle kisses all over my face, murmuring loving words and words of understanding I don't deserve or even want. I hold you by the wrists, soaking up your torrential love like scorched earth because you're right; we work. We make each other happy. But this isn't what I wanted for you. In that perfect world we fantasized about days ago, we'd never hurt anyone, especially not each other.

In the deceptively coaxing murmur of a lover, you ask, 'How much of what you've told me is the truth? A rough percentage will suffice.'

I push at your chest, but it's like pushing a brick wall. 'How can you ask me that?'

Wry amusement curves your lips. 'You lie like you breathe –
without thinking twice.'

That's not true; I think about it a great deal. Piqued, I taunt
you. 'Maybe everything I've told you is a lie.'

'Oh, I'm sure there's truth in there somewhere.' Your
thumb strokes over my cheekbone. Your gaze is on my mouth,
the part of me that voices deceit. But the look in your eyes is
still hotly sexual.

We must have been irredeemable people in our past lives.
There must be some reason karma should see fit to lock us
together in a boundless love that comes at a dreadful cost to
so many.

'How can you love me if you don't trust me?' I challenge.

Your smile turns indulgent. 'I trust you implicitly. That
doesn't mean I don't know you've rarely told me the truth.
What was your mother's last alias?'

'Stephanie. Steph Laska. And before you ask – no, I don't
know if Val is a nickname or a diminutive.'

'And your name? Is it Lily? Ivy? Violet? Rose? None of the
above?'

I blink. My ability to think has come to a screeching halt.
The silence becomes deafening. Whose skeletons have you
managed to unearth?

Ah, my love, I've corrupted you. Have you become my
match? Should I grieve or rejoice?

'It doesn't matter,' you assure me, holding your lips to my
forehead for a long moment, your hands rubbing up and
down my bare arms to warm them.

Wild, joyous hope riots inside me. You're still looking at
me with such furious love. Somehow, for some reason, you
love *me* – the far from perfect woman I genuinely am.

'How did your mother die?' Your voice is pitched to soothe
and lull. 'Did Val kill her?'

Would it matter if I lied? Who would it harm if I did?

'*Setareh* . . . Tell me how your mother died.'

'It wasn't Val.' I sigh. 'It was me. I killed her.'

40

Amy

I almost gag as I step out of the town car, fighting the sickening panic that makes me want to hit a bar or crawl back into bed and pull the covers over my head. I hate that the mere sight of the Crossfire building can traumatize me all over again. Aliyah has taken everything that once gave me joy or pride and made them into things that make me instinctively recoil.

Straightening my skirt, I pause on the sidewalk and give myself a pep talk. Today's outfit is decidedly more Lily. Tovah paired a long, flowing black skirt with peep-toe booties, a snug white dress shirt and a tiny fitted black leather vest. The shirt's collar is open to the deep V of my cleavage, which Tovah said was appropriate, considering the rest of my body is completely covered, and I'm small-breasted. Layers of gold chains fill the gap in between, down to a gold pendant hanging over the vest. Gold hoops in my ears and 'Blood Lily' lipstick finish it all off.

I'd agonized over what to wear all evening and into the morning. Going back to Baharan after my last visit is so hard. I want some fucking sympathy after what Aliyah put me through, but I also want to look like I can deal with her bullshit and run my damn company. Finding something that blends soft and hard requires more style than I apparently have. It would have been a hell of a lot easier to pull on a sheath dress and earrings. Whether I've succeeded in striking the right tone or not, the soundtrack in my head isn't Ariana Grande this time; it's Creedence Clearwater Revival. That's thanks to Lily, who sent their greatest hits as a gift while I was recuperating from my dental nightmare.

Since she's also recuperating, and I'm not going to be the asshole who's less thoughtful, I sent her a gift, too – a signed copy of one of Suzanne's potboiler books. I wanted to send a bottle of wine with it, but when I asked Witte if she preferred white or red, he told me she doesn't drink – ever.

'Does she have an allergy or something?' I'd asked.

'I believe it's a personal preference of long-standing,' he replied, in that clipped, haughty tone. He wouldn't even give me the address where Kane's holed up with her. He had a courier pick the book up and deliver it. He hates me, but the feeling is mutual.

I'm turning to enter the Crossfire when I spot Ryan Landon heading toward me. I pause. He cuts his way quickly through the cluster of people on the corner waiting for the light to change. With a cup of takeout coffee in one hand and a black leather briefcase in the other, he's wearing a pinstripe suit of deep blue and an atypical frown. Since he's the mellowest man I've ever met, that furrow between his dark brows is peculiar.

I wait for him. He glances my way, his thoughts elsewhere, but then he locks on me with startling focus. A long moment later, his handsome face smooths out, and he smiles. We meet in the middle, and I return his thorough once-over. Yeah, he lacks Darius's dramatic coloring and the ferocious intensity Kane radiates, but he's still hot. Tall and fit, with a sexy smile and easy confidence.

'Amy.' He comes to a halt in front of me. 'For a moment, you reminded me of someone I used to know. You look great. How are you?'

'I'm awesome, thanks.' Better now because I know it was

Lily he saw in me for a second, which makes me giddy. The hair color, the clothes, the lipstick . . . It's all coming together. Thrilled by the thought, I shoot for the same self-assured sexuality Lily wields so expertly. 'You look very fine yourself. Are you stopping by the offices?'

He nods. 'Aliyah wants to run something by me.'

'Better you than me. Can you keep her tied up all day? All week, maybe? The rest of my life?'

He laughs, and the sound is warm and rich. Yep, he's definitely spicy.

'I might be able to make a dent in her morning, but I'm meeting Angela for lunch. Shall we go up?' He walks beside me, and we thank a gentleman who holds a door for us. 'What's on your agenda today?'

'I'm running through the ECRA+ creative, making sure it's comprehensive. Then I'm going to see if we can refresh Baharan's social. We've used the same imagery, fonts and colors for years. It's time to switch things up, especially before a big launch.'

It feels good to talk about work, even if I am completely clueless at the moment. I rub my damp palms against my skirt. The supplement purported to help with liver detoxification doesn't feel like it's doing anything. At least I have a few painkillers left.

'Cross has Baharan doing all the heavy lifting,' he says tightly, stopping at the desk to check in with security.

I eye the guard with an arched brow, daring him to ask me to sign in. He scowls back but wisely holds his tongue. Holding up a handheld device, he takes a quick photo of Ryan, prints a visitor's pass and slips it into a clip-on sleeve. 'Drop this off on your way out, please.'

I roll my eyes. 'He's not an idiot. He's been here before, or his name wouldn't be on the list.'

'It's fine, Amy.' Ryan smiles at the guard. 'Thanks.'

We clear the turnstiles and wait for an elevator.

'With the Cross partnership,' I begin, knowing I'm speaking too fast but unable to slow down, 'you know that's an Aliyah thing, right? She has to be in control.'

'That may be, but Cross doesn't give up control of anything unless it suits him. Aliyah can't go toe-to-toe with him. Few can.'

'Can you?'

'I try. Sometimes I win.' He flashes a smile with sharp edges, and I feel a little flutter of attraction. I know LanCorp wouldn't be successful if he were always easygoing and affable, but I don't think I ever realized before that he had it in him to be truly dangerous.

We move to wait in front of the elevator arriving earliest. After the car empties, others enter with us, and we end up stuck in a back corner. I become aware of just how fit he is. His arm against mine is hard, and the definition is noticeable even through his jacket sleeve.

'This is our stop,' he says when we reach the tenth floor, and a path clears for us to exit.

We part ways as we pass Aliyah's office. I can't help looking at Kane's cubicle. The vacancy at his desk seems like a black hole. The energy that usually thrums in the air is absent. All of the Armands combined can't replace Kane. He's the heart of the company, its lifeblood. Kane's fire lights the employees, and no one else sparks the same drive when he's not here.

I debate saying hi to Darius, then decide against it. I didn't even tell him I was coming into work today. I just kissed him goodbye and watched him leave before rushing to get ready. I don't know why I didn't say anything to him. I suppose I didn't want him to talk me out of it or start a discussion about how to deal with his mother.

That's the thing with Darius; the only time he wants me dealing with friction is when his cock is inside me. I think I'm supposed to feel coddled, but I'm aimless. Aimless Amy. I huff out a rueful laugh as I open the door to my office and pause on the threshold.

The truth I'm beginning to face is that I've been reduced to providing the services of a blow-up sex doll. Half the time Darius makes love to me, I don't even realize I'm being fucked until the orgasm snaps me into consciousness. I've been telling myself for years that I'm damn lucky to have a hot hubby with a high sex drive, but lately . . . I don't know. Something has changed. I'm restless. Angry. I feel like I'm wearing skin that's become too tight, and I want to rip out of it. I have to because I'm suffocating.

The overhead lights winked on when I opened the door, and I acquaint myself with what I have to work with. This office is even smaller than the one I had before. You could fit a compact car in the corner suites; it'd be a miracle to fit a bicycle in this one. That said, the view is more open than the one Hornsworth stole from me. Darius maximized the space by installing open glass shelving in place of the bookshelves I'd had before, leaving room for a small sofa and a table in the corner. My desk has been downsized to a small, mirrored piece with a single drawer and delicate legs. Two gray leather visitor chairs face it. There is also a petite silver bar cart with crystal decanters of liquor and cut-crystal tumblers. My mouth waters.

Photos of Darius and me in silver frames decorate the shelves, and my degree hangs above the bar cart. The walls are an icy blue, like the velvet desk chair and sofa. I sigh. The whole effect is pretty and feminine and more Darius's color palette than mine. I make a note to buy some natural crystals for the shelves. Getting rid of the bar cart and the degree only

I care about will open up space for a tall, slender piece of fierce artwork.

My gaze lingers on the decanters filled with jeweled liquid oblivion.

'Hey, how are you feeling?'

I turn at the sound of the familiar voice and feel a rush of relief. 'Oh, thank God you're still here, Clarice.'

The petite blonde smiles. 'You look fabulous. I love your outfit! I wish I could wear long skirts.'

At just under five feet in height, Clarice is child-sized but has the energy of three men. She was my first hire at Social Creamery, and I feel like an asshole for not considering her.

'We've missed you,' she says.

I've missed myself, too . . .

I find myself going to her and hugging her. Touching people isn't my thing, but then I remember Lily grabbing me and holding tight with surprising strength in those delicate-looking arms. The scent of her perfume, which I'm wearing now, is noticeably different when exuded from her skin. In any case, when Clarice clutches me tightly, I think maybe I should use hugging as a tactic more often. It's intimate but also aggressive.

'Well, I'm back,' I say as briskly as possible with tightness in my throat. I drop my purse on the desktop since there's no purse-sized drawer. As thoughtful as Darius was about putting the office together for me, he has no idea what needs a woman has that a man doesn't. 'First thing: I'll need logins for the file-sharing. I tried my old passwords, but nothing worked.'

She nods. 'I'll get them.'

I settle onto the sofa and gesture for her to join me. 'Who's been managing the creative direction?'

Clarice shuts the door. She's wearing slim gray trousers, a navy polka dot blouse and ballet flats. Her earrings are where she has a little fun; they're bright red Lucite hoops. 'Aliyah. If you call keeping everything exactly the way you left it a direction.'

'I noticed that. How about the launch of the cosmetics?'

'Passable. Safe.' She sits. 'We've got Eva Cross and Rosana Armand, so it doesn't need much to get noticed.'

'Along the same vein as what you're already posting in the lead-up?'

'Yes.'

'I don't mean to be critical, but it's a little . . . medicinal.' I rub my palms against my skirt again, noticing they've begun to shake a little.

She rolls her eyes. 'That's because Aliyah *really* wants to stress Baharan's contribution to the formulas. The Cross brand is luxury, self-indulgence and hedonism, so the packaging is upscale and beautiful. Aliyah's worried that it will slap you in the face as a Cross Industries product and Baharan – who's done most of the work developing the products – will become something of a silent partner.'

'I get it. Let me see what you've got so far.' I watch her stand, forcing myself not to look at the liquor.

I don't *need* a fucking drink because I don't have a drinking problem. I have a memory problem, and that's because I don't eat right, don't drink enough water, and don't exercise regularly. I just need to get through this cleanse and I'll be ready to tackle the world – and the Armands.

A week or two to reset, and my head will clear. Lily coming back has been stressful. 'How many of us are left?' I ask Clarice.

She pauses in the doorway, her hand on the knob. 'Three. With you, four.'

'Three?!' Damn it. We had twelve full-time employees when Baharan absorbed us. 'What happened?'

Clarice shrugs. 'Aliyah cut us in half pretty quick, and she wasn't wrong to do that. We're only working on Baharan now, so –'

'Wait. What?'

'Yeah.' She sighs heavily and brushes her bangs back from her forehead. She wears her hair shorter than before, chin-length with flipped ends. It suits her. 'That's why we lost half of the people Aliyah kept on – they missed the challenge of taking on new clients. We don't even have a separate website now, Amy.'

My office tilts on its axis. Everything goes dark for a moment. My blood roars through my ears. My God. Why didn't Darius say anything? Why tell me he'd get my company back when it doesn't even exist anymore? Social Creamery managed the accounts of pop stars and athletes, celebrities and corporations. Our specialty was growth, and we could replicate authentic results with Every. Single. Client. Every. Single. Time.

How was it allowed to shrivel into nothing?

'Hey.' She takes a few steps back toward me. 'I thought you wanted it this way. That you were focusing on the family business.'

'They're not my family! They're goddamn leeches, sucking the life out of everything.' I ram stiffened fingers into my forehead, where a headache has been building all morning. 'Shit! I let Aliyah push me around and push me out. That stupid bitch. She couldn't stand that I'd built something on my own. All she's ever done is ride the coattails of the men in her miserable fucking life.'

Clarice hurriedly shuts the door.

I stand. 'I don't care if she hears me. I don't care who hears me. It's the fucking truth.'

'You don't want another scene.'

'Don't I? I'm about to rip this place apart.' I dig my nails into my palms. 'I'm . . . Just give me a minute, okay?'

'Yeah. Okay. Sure. I'll . . . um, just get those logins for you and the rest.'

'Thanks.' I move around the desk, eyeing the bar cart. Why the fuck is that in my office anyway if I'm not wooing clients? I'm not allowed to have liquor at home, but I can drink at work . . . ?

'Hey . . . Amy?'

I look at her.

Her brown eyes are soft as velvet, but her jaw is hard. 'You did it once. You can do it again.'

'Right,' I scoff, shaking my head and turning away. I hear the door shut behind me. I settle into the desk chair and discover the cushion is hard. Apparently, actually using the chair wasn't expected.

My gaze turns to the wall separating Darius's office from mine. Fury bubbles like lava in my gut. He's misled me, neglected my life's work and failed to stand up to his mother. I'm so disgusted it makes my skin crawl thinking of how he'd touched me just hours ago. What a pathetic piece of shit.

How the hell do I fix this? I'll have to start over. Do I want to start over within Baharan? On the one hand, I've earned the right to use the resources at my disposal. On the other, repeating a mistake and expecting a different outcome is the height of stupidity. The biggest problem is that Baharan, my most recent 'client,' is a piss-poor example of how my team can manage a company's social messaging. It's stagnant, dated and – worse – boring.

But . . . I can make that work for me by completely overhauling it. Then I'd have a recent case study of massive improvement. I'll have strong examples in two completely different industries with the launch of the new cosmetics line.

I'll also help Baharan, which I don't want to do. Haven't I already given them enough? Then again, I would prove Aliyah wrong definitively.

The flip side of that is to just get the fuck out. I could say Social Creamery was so successful I sold it to Baharan and am now developing something next level. I can leverage some new features and apps. The platforms themselves are only a component. The most significant factor is understanding and delivering the desired messaging; I still know how to do that. Clarice can help me with the rest.

My purse begins buzzing on the corner of my desk, and I reach for it, digging to find my phone. The contact's face on the screen is unforgettable, even though it's been years since I saw him last. It might've been handsome once, but it's weathered a lot. The bridge of the nose leans askew from a previous break – or few – that wasn't set correctly. The brows are thick and low, made more noticeable by the baldness of the head above it. The lips are full and firm, but the dark eyes are flat and icy. The body that goes with that face is heavy with muscle in a very intimidating way.

'Amy Armand,' I answer.

'Ah . . .' There's a pause. 'I'm attempting to reach Amy Searle.' The Eastern European accent inflects a deep voice.

'That was my maiden name. I've since married. It's a pleasure to hear from you again, Mr. Laska.'

41

Amy

'How's business at the gym?' I ask my former client, attempting not to sound too eager.

'You remember me.' Valon Laska sounds pleased.

Leaning back in the chair, I wonder at the odds. It was at lunch with Laska that I first met Kane. Laska and I had been seated in view of the door, and I'd been startled into staring by Kane's unusual height as he walked in with two other business-suited gentlemen and was seated at a table nearby. He was so handsome my heart stopped for a moment before launching into a frantic rhythm. His gaze had locked with mine the moment he stepped inside, and I felt it on me throughout my meal. I'd hardly been able to concentrate on my pitch to Mr. Laska.

I went up to the penthouse with Kane that afternoon, and those hours with him led to this very moment: an office in Baharan Pharmaceuticals and the discovery that my business had died while I was home trying to be a perfect wife.

'Business has remained steady since you helped us,' he replies. 'My problem now is a restaurant. It could be doing better. I was hoping you could assist me as you did before.'

I don't have any illusions about Valon Laska. If he wore a sign saying his businesses were shady as fuck, it couldn't be more obvious. While he was polite to me and even charming, a lack of life in his eyes set off alarm bells. Kane, too, could look at you in a chillingly vacant way, but I always knew there was fire in him. Laska radiated the bone-chilling cold of Siberia.

Still, it had been an easy job cleaning up the social accounts for the gym. A few days of photographs and a new logo were all he needed. After that, several businesses reached out for similar facelifts. Clarice had commented on us becoming a go-to resource for the criminal underworld's legitimate endeavors. I'd been a bit wary about that and had been relieved when things with Darius got serious quickly and afforded me a way out. Now . . . Well, things were a hell of a lot different now. I could use a steady stream of new clients, regardless of whatever the owners masked behind their storefronts.

Valon Laska had put me on the road to the Armands; he could also put me on the road out.

'I would love to work with you again, Mr. Laska.'

Searching for a notepad, I pull open the single drawer of my desk, and my muscles lock so tightly that I stop breathing. The room narrows once again into a pinprick of light. I can feel my blood pounding against my eardrums. My breathing is quick and shallow.

Condoms fill the wide drawer.

That douche nozzle I'm married to has been fucking his assistant in my office! How convenient. Fix yourselves a nice drink, loosen up, then fuck like rabbits. I glare at the couch, feeling disgusted that I'd sat on it and determined to get rid of it.

'Amy?' Mr. Laska queries. 'I'm sorry, I don't remember your new name.'

'Amy is fine. And I apologize. I was digging around for a pen. I have a new office, and things aren't where I'd put them. Could you please text me the website of the restaurant? I'll check out your existing social media, then swing by and look at the location itself.'

'Bring your husband with you and enjoy a meal. I'll leave

your name with the hostess stand. On the house. You should know what you're going to help sell.'

'That's very kind. Thank you.' However, it'll be a cold day in hell before I take Darius there. Clarice has earned the meal for sticking around and putting up with Aliyah. 'I look forward to working with you again, Mr. Laska. I'll put together a proposal and submit it to you by the end of next week.'

'I'll keep an eye out for it. Goodbye.'

Placing the handset back in its cradle, I glare down at the pile of condoms and debate scooping up a handful and tossing them onto Alice's desk before punching her lights out. Or, better yet, barging into Darius's office and throwing them in his face. It's long past time I confronted him.

I just don't understand it. I spread my legs for him whenever he wants me to. Why am I not enough for him?

There's a peremptory knock at the door before it opens, and Clarice comes in.

'You're not going to believe the timing,' I tell her, 'but Valon Laska – the guy with the gym in the Bronx – just called with a new job.'

Her brows lift. 'The gangster?'

I shut the drawer just as I shut away my growing rage for the time being. It feels like something is loose inside me, rattling so violently my entire body is quaking. I stand on shaky legs and carefully approach the bar cart. 'We don't know that.'

She leans into the doorjamb and shoots me a look. 'Right. What did you tell him?'

'That we'll do it. Wanna drink?'

'Um, sure. Just a splash.'

How the hell does Lily go through life deliberately sober? There's no fucking way. Maybe she's a stoner. Of course, with Kane pumping orgasms into her with his delicious dick, perhaps she's getting all the buzz she needs.

I shakily pour myself one finger of liquor and mentally applaud my restraint, then pour the same for Clarice. The stopper clatters against the lip as I plug it.

Discovering the condoms threw me over the edge, and I need to settle down. A little splash doesn't violate the no-drinking-before-five-o'clock rule. Besides, I have something to celebrate. I'll take the worthless detox powder after my shot.

'We'll need a website,' I think aloud, 'and a new name. I'm going to work on Baharan and the relaunch separately. I need your help. Are you open to juggling two jobs? We get Social Creamery 2.0 off the ground, and then we can both leave this hellhole.'

Taking one of the visitor chairs, she sets the folder in her hand on the edge of the desk. 'I'm always open to new challenges, you know that. But I need a raise. Can you pay me for juggling?'

'Yes, I'll take care of it.' I set her glass in front of her and resume my seat behind the desk. As chief financial officer, Darius is the money man, and I'll get what I want from him. He owes me. 'We'll need outside staff. People who can work from home for the time being.'

'If they're working from home, you can spread a wide net.'

'Yes. I'll post the jobs today.' I force myself to sip instead of swallow, then sigh with relief as the familiar burn warms the chilly place inside me that's shivering so hard. It's so good, I want to drink a tumblerful. But I won't. 'We've already got our first client, so we need to pull a team together fast.'

42

Aliyah

'Ryan.' I stand as the handsome young man steps into my office, my smile genuine. It's not just his arrival that pleases me. Security also warned me that Amy has dragged herself back to the office. I have to give the girl credit for showing some spine. Now let's see if she shows her true colors after she has a few drinks and bothers to open her desk drawer. 'Thank you so much for stopping by.'

'No problem.' Ryan Landon flashes his charming smile and sets his satchel carefully on top of my console by the door. The gorgeous cognac leather has warmed and grown supple with use. Kane carries the same satchel, only in black, and gifted Ryan his after he'd expressed appreciation for Kane's. 'I needed to chat with Kane anyway. Is he in a meeting?'

I'm momentarily startled by the question. 'No . . . You haven't spoken to him lately?'

'We touched base the day before yesterday.' He adjusts his trousers and jacket for comfort before settling into one of the two visitor's chairs in front of my desk. Relaxed and unaware of any issue, he sips his takeout coffee.

Ryan's the type of male a woman enjoys perusing. Tall and dark, easy on the eyes, with a powerfully self-possessed physicality. Like Kane, he's a man whose father was careless with his family's financial security. The elder Landon invested and lost everything in Geoffrey Cross's Ponzi scheme. Having unreliable, selfish and foolhardy fathers is an experience that has bonded Kane and Ryan in an unshakeable way. They seem to trust each other to some degree, although not entirely, which is not unexpected after they both grew up with – and overcame – the disastrous consequences of someone else's failure on such a massive scale.

They've done well, though in different ways. Ryan is now married, and Kane has been a widower, limiting their opportunities to spend time together, but they'll always look out for each other. Some college friendships last lifetimes, and I believe theirs will.

'Did he tell you he was in the office?' I ask.

'When isn't he? He practically lives here.' Ryan is plainly bemused by my questions. I'm equally puzzled as to why Kane hasn't leaned on his closest friend more heavily in a time of upheaval. 'What's going on?'

I focus on my cream palazzo pants as I fluff them, trying to hide how my thoughts are scrambling. I've been preparing for this meeting for days now, planning exactly how I'd introduce the subject of Lily's past and elicit Ryan's help in dealing with the risk. Now, I'm wary of saying too much. I don't understand why Kane wouldn't mention his absence from the office. Perhaps the two men have drifted apart. If so, how much do I want to share?

'Aliyah?'

I straighten and decide to take the other visitor's chair next to Ryan. Position is everything, and for this, I want him to feel like a confidant. 'You've known Kane a long time,' I begin.

'You could say that. Columbia does seem like it was a lifetime ago.'

'Did you know Lily?'

'Lily . . .' Ryan's gaze darts away. 'Yes, I knew her.'

'Knew her well?'

He smooths an imaginary wrinkle from his slacks, then looks at me. 'She was my girlfriend when I introduced them.'

'Oh.' And yet I find I'm not that surprised. 'Would you mind telling me why you broke up?'

His gaze narrows on me in a way that is out of character for him – at least as I know him. 'Why do you ask?'

I consider how to speak truthfully without showing my hand. After all, Ryan and Kane are friends who share confidences – or so I believed – and neither feels any loyalty to me. If I don't tread carefully, I'll alienate them both. 'She has a powerful hold on him. If I just understood her better, I think I'd have a better understanding of my son.'

He sighs. 'I don't see how this helps, but . . . She's the one who broke things off.'

'To be with Kane?'

'No. I don't think so.' His jaw tightens briefly. 'I don't know, honestly. I know they weren't together immediately after the breakup because he spent all his free time with me. He practically moved in for several months afterward. I didn't handle losing her well. Spent some time drowning my sorrows and being promiscuous. I dragged Kane around for moral support.'

He takes another sip of coffee, and I note how he spins his wedding band with his thumb. Frowning, he stares straight ahead, his thoughts elsewhere. 'I knew he wanted her,' he says quietly. 'I caught him looking at her a few times, and it was obvious how he felt. Then he started refusing invitations to do things with us as a group. But every guy I knew had a little crush on her. He wasn't the only one.'

'It didn't bother you?'

'What're you gonna do? With a gorgeous, sexy woman on your arm, you have to expect other men will want her to some degree. Kane was respectful about it. I felt bad for him, actually.'

'Did you feel bad for him when he went on to marry her?' I ask bluntly. Maybe there's a rift there. It would be good to know either way.

'I didn't find out until after she was gone. I only learned they'd been together and married when he told me she'd passed.' He runs his hand through his dark-chocolate waves. 'I never saw or even *thought* of them together, so I suppose how I felt about it didn't register. Things were serious with Angela by then, so . . .'

I study him, registering his restlessness and the practiced answer as if he's thought of Lily's death often enough to have a canned reply. I don't know what to make of it or how I can use it. Baharan certainly wouldn't benefit from any tension between Kane and Ryan. Lily's causing enough trouble as it is.

'Are you saying it didn't affect you when you found out?' I prod him.

'Sure. Of course it did. Lily was important to me once. Which reminds me, I saw Amy on the way in,' he murmurs, 'and for a second, I thought she was Lily. It knocked me sideways.' He takes another sip of coffee. 'I haven't thought of Lily in a long time, and now twice in one morning . . . Anyway, I don't see how this is of interest.'

'It's fascinating.' Not many years ago, on the cusp of marrying Ryan, a wealthy and successful CEO, Lily pivoted to marry Kane instead, when he had few prospects and a mountain of student loan debt. It would suggest she genuinely loves him and possibly loves him still. Call me a cynic, but I simply can't believe it. The woman detailed in Rampart's investigation doesn't act without ulterior motive. But I can't risk making insinuations or outright accusations that might get around to the wrong person. Better to lead Ryan to his own conclusions and let him go from there. 'Kane's been working from home for the past two months.'

'Really?' He's noticeably taken aback. 'Well, he's certainly earned that much leave, although I wouldn't say working from home constitutes a break. If that's what you're worried about, I can tell you he sounded really good on the phone, like he used to back in the day. He even laughed and ribbed me a little. Said we should grab a drink soon. We haven't done that in ages.'

My jaw sets. Men are such fools. A pretty face and a sinuous body could so easily turn off their common sense and their self-protective instincts. To hear that my son seems happier now than he's been in years incites a burning in my chest. I feel nothing but revulsion for Lily.

'A steady sexual partner is usually a mood lifter,' I say snidely, unable to help myself.

Ryan's brows lift. 'Is he finally seeing someone romantically? Good for him. I was getting worried about him. I'll admit I hoped that Sexiest Man coverage would put him in the cross-hairs of a woman he couldn't resist.'

With every word he's spoken, I've felt the temperature drop until I shiver with cold. My top is cropped, with short, puffed sleeves engineered so that one shoulder is bare. My upswept hair leaves my neck with no warmth. I come to the awareness that goosebumps dot my skin. I almost expect to see my breath frost in the air.

'In thinking about it,' Ryan continues, crossing one ankle atop the opposite knee, 'I couldn't be mad at him about Lily if I wanted to. He had her for less time than I did, and he's grieved for her a hell of a lot longer.'

He's much too forgiving, in my opinion. There's no way my son simply *forgot* to mention his wife's re-emergence, especially to his closest friend.

Is Lily that devious? Has she deliberately isolated Kane from everyone who cares about him, tightening her grip until she has total control? With power over Kane, she controls the money and Baharan. She's already pulled him away from his home and Witte. And it was probably far too easy to do. Years of sleeping beneath her picture and surrounding himself with reminders of her primed him for an even deeper obsession. Like his father and me, Kane is a sexual creature, and he's essentially been alone for too long, blowing off steam far too infrequently with one-night stands.

Did she beg him? *Stay home with me. I need you.* Did she suggest they leave? *Let's go somewhere, lover. Let's be alone to reconnect.*

How could Kane say no when he's been fixated on her so completely for so long?

She already has a legal claim on at least half of his assets. If she gets pregnant, she'll be able to claw out even more.

A baby. Could there possibly be anything worse?

I know he won't take precautions; she's his wife. Wearing a condom when he fucks her won't even enter his mind, and it's been patently obvious every time I've seen them together that all he's thinking about is fucking her. *He* might've been the one to suggest they go away, leaving Witte behind, so he'd have fewer distractions from his frenzied rutting. He'll rely on her to protect against pregnancy, and why would she?

'Was there something else on your mind?' Ryan asks.

With his intimate knowledge of both Kane and Lily, Ryan may be the only one who can get through to my son. Then again, maybe Kane won't listen to Ryan at all out of jealousy. I don't know what to do, what move to make.

'Aliyah?'

'He's with her,' I blurt out. 'Lily, I mean. And as worried as I am about her, I'm more worried that Kane is hiding her from you.'

'What are you talking about?' He straightens, his hazel eyes turning a stormy green.

'Kane hasn't come into the office since she came back. He's been with her constantly –'

'Who?'

'Lily!'

'That's impossible,' he snaps, his spine painfully straight. 'I don't know what you're –'

'I know.' I speak in a rush, leaning forward. 'I could hardly believe it, either. It's such a bizarre situation, and Kane is –'

'Aliyah.' His voice cracks my name out like the lash of a whip. 'Lily is dead.'

'She's *not*. We don't know what happened. She has some sort of amnesia and –'

Ryan stands abruptly. 'Who told you this? Kane?'

'Yes, of course. He explained it to all of us.'

His head is shaking back and forth in a quick, violent negation. 'He's lying to you. I don't know why, but he's lying. I'm going to call him.'

I watch him pull out his phone and jump to my feet. 'Ryan, wait! You should know more before you talk to him. There's a reason he's been hiding her from you. We need to figure –'

'Aliyah, I know he's lying!' His face has blanched. 'There's something very wrong here. I've been growing increasingly worried about him. He shouldn't still be grieving this deeply. It's been too long. And the lilies he has on everything . . . ? It's sick. He's sick. He's been out of the office for *two months*? Have you *seen* him? *Talked* to him?'

My heart is beating too quickly, making me feel off-balance and dizzy. 'I've been to the penthouse, of course, to meet her. And they were in the offices just –'

He holds me off with an outstretched palm. 'You've met the new girlfriend?'

'Lily! Ryan, you're not listening to me. Lily is back. She's with Kane.'

305

'That's fucking impossible!' he roars, hot color flooding his bloodless face. 'Lily. Is. *Dead*. I was with Kane when he identified the body. *I* identified the body with him. She was my girlfriend, too. I'd know her anywhere.'

'*What?* No. That can't . . . Rosana asked Kane about a body. He said there wasn't one. That the Coast Guard stopped looking and declared her lost at sea.'

He sets his cup on the edge of my desk, then grips the edge in both hands, his head bowed. 'Yes, they initially declared her lost. But then her body was recovered in a fisherman's net. It was . . .' His muscular shoulders quake. 'It had been a few weeks. Her beautiful face was unrecognizable, and one of her arms was gone. She was the right height, though. And slender, even after being in the water so long.'

'You misidentified . . . whoever that was. Under the circumstances –'

'No! She had tattoos. She had a massive phoenix on her back. And it wasn't flash – the art you pick off the wall in a parlor. A friend had drawn it specifically for her. There were still parts of it identifiable on the body. There's no way to mistake her for anyone else.'

I breathe carefully through my mouth, feeling like I might vomit. I remember Lily in the library, dressed in black slacks and a corset. Her short, sleek cap of hair allowed a lot of skin to show. I remember the tattoo. One doesn't forget body art of that size. I remember looking at the photograph above the fireplace and realizing they were identical – the photo of Lily's back and the back of the woman who entered the library.

'She has the tattoo,' I get out, my voice hoarse. 'The woman with Kane.'

Ryan's head jerks up and swivels to look over his shoulder at me. 'I need to see her – face to face. There's no one like

Lily. The best plastic surgeon in the world couldn't re-create her. I'll know right away.' His teeth grind audibly. 'Whoever this woman is, she's preying on a desperate man's grief.'

I nod repeatedly. 'Yes. She's dangerous. I knew that the moment I laid eyes on her.'

'There's a reason he's kept her from me, Aliyah. He knows Lily is gone. He knows I know. If he tells me about this woman, the fantasy doesn't hold up and falls apart. It's a stage of grief: denial. The first stage. The fact that Kane hasn't progressed past that after all this time is a serious red flag. He needs help.'

Swallowing the rush of bile that has filled my mouth, I struggle to make sense of it all. I've looked at that photo of Lily hundreds of times. The woman I met in Kane's library has her face. Ryan won't be able to grasp that until he sees her himself. The resemblance is beyond uncanny, although there's clearly been a passing of time.

Who had Giles Rampart been investigating – the woman pulled from the Atlantic or the woman presently sleeping with my son?

We knock on doors, ask questions and dig. They'd shown her photograph and relied on people's memories of that unforgettable face. It would be all too easy to conflate the histories of two equally stunning women.

Maybe the woman he married six years ago was exactly who she'd said she was. Perhaps the woman he found recently is the one Rampart was actually investigating.

Whenever an inquiry is made into her background, someone becomes aware that she's being sought. You make a lot of inquiries; a lot of people know.

What if this woman found out Kane was looking for her, thinking she was his wife, and saw an opportunity? Is it

307

possible two different women's lives became tangled up together? An orphan and a con artist?

Turning, Ryan resumes his seat and leans forward with his elbows on his knees. His face is taut and solemn. 'Start from the beginning and tell me everything.'

43

Witte

As I follow Mr Black down the hallway, I'm astonished by the change in him. His suit is the same one worn the day he departed the city, but he's not the same man inside it. The gentleman who returned from Greenwich with his wife is . . . rejuvenated. His stride is light and quick, and his movements have a new fluidity. His hair is slightly too long, but he's as smartly clean-shaven as if I'd seen to the task personally.

Before he turns into his office, he glances down the hallway towards the living room. I know he's looking for Lily. She's not in view, but he can't help but check. He struggled to be in the same room with her before they left for the beach house. Now, he struggles to be without her.

The mailroom was holding several packages for her when I returned to the penthouse in anticipation of their return – boxes from Tiffany & Co., Hermès, Bergdorf's and more. She's sorting through them now.

Sitting at his desk, Mr Black gestures for me to take one of the visitor's chairs. He settles, his gaze sweeping over his desk: his sleeping computer monitor, the accumulated mail I've opened and organized on the blotter, the framed photo of Lily lying face down. His gaze lingers there, but curiously, he doesn't set it to rights.

'Will you be visiting the beach house regularly over the coming season?' I ask. 'Should I keep it open?'

He seems lost in thought for a moment, uncomprehending.

Then his gaze clears. He looks at me and nods. 'Yes, keep it ready.'

I wait for him to broach the more pressing topics we touched upon during our calls last night and this morning, although I've had less than a day to expand our search.

'Val Laska?' he queries. 'I know it's early, but do we have anything?'

'His full name is Valon Laska, and I've confirmed his identity as the man who sent the flowers. Mrs Black's characterization of him as a gangster is apt, although the breadth and depravity of his crimes beg for a stronger descriptor. He was under investigation by the Organized Crime Control Bureau for decades, and the case file remains open. He's occasionally been arrested, served brief amounts of time in prison, but seems suspiciously fortunate in evading more stringent punishment.'

He rocks back in his chair with his elbows on the armrests and his fingertips steepled together. There's a hint of a smile. 'So, she was honest to some degree.'

'It's a family operation,' I continue, 'with several cousins, nephews, brothers and the like. There's no legal documentation that Laska has ever been married, nor is he known to have any children. However, a wife is rumoured, and she's said to be more terrifying than he is.'

I pull my mobile out, unlock it and set it on the blotter with the screen face up and brightly lit.

He moves swiftly, straightening and spinning his chair to face the desk. He studies the displayed image with a narrowed gaze.

The photo is one taken by the OCCB during surveillance. Valon Laska is unmistakable simply by his sheer size. He's a bruiser of a man.

They captured his image on a wintry day. The city's snowploughs had shoved dirty ice to the edge of the pavements. The sky was a deep grey, as cold and lifeless as a corpse.

They caught Laska stepping onto the street behind a woman half-hidden by the waiting car at the kerb. She's tall, with a waterfall of sleek black hair that falls below her waist. A thick fur coat obscures her figure, and she wears a matching papakha on her head. Oversized sunglasses partially conceal a compelling face that is a familiar mystery. Her skin is pale as cream, and her lips are sensual curves enhanced by slaughterous red lipstick.

My employer says nothing, staring at the photo with wide, dark eyes that are empty of all but shock and horror.

'We'll get more with time,' I tell him. 'The Bureau disbanded a few months ago, so I didn't expect to have anything for you so quickly, but my contact was able to produce that image. It was taken several years ago, just a block from the Crossfire.'

He sets my mobile down carefully, as if it might break, then rests heavily into the seat back of his chair. His eyes close.

'No one's seen Laska in New York in years,' I go on. 'It was believed a rival may have assassinated him, or even someone within his organization who wanted to advance. His reappearance six months ago was an unwelcome shock to the NYPD. So far, there's been no sighting of the woman in the city, but my contacts say she must be nearby as the two are inseparable. They don't even suspect that she's deceased. Is Mrs Black worried about retaliation or prosecution for her mother's death?'

'No. My understanding of their family dynamic is that Steph Laska expected her daughter to follow in her footsteps and ultimately kill her. Laska apparently understood this and accepted it.' Mr Black's fingers drum restlessly on his armrests. 'You said there might be a lead at a consignment shop?'

'We've interviewed personnel. Lily was a regular for a short time, always paid in cash – small bills. She purchased entire ensembles. If she bought jeans, she also purchased shoes, shirt and accessories to pair with them, which aligns with how she maintains her wardrobe here. None of the employees recalls seeing her prior to six months ago. She was a frequent customer for a few months, but she hasn't been in recently – obviously, because she's been with you.'

I study my employer, feeling disturbed. Helpless. Angry. The vigour he'd returned with has drained from him. He's pale, his mouth tense and bracketed with lines of strain. His shoulders have risen into a defensive hunch.

My voice softens. 'You mentioned discussing your safety with Mrs Black. Were the examples you gave me her own words?'

'Yes.'

'Exactly?'

'Yes, verbatim.' His voice is clipped and hard, conveying a dangerous meld of frustration and irritation, impatience and resentment.

My thoughts tumble around what he's told me. Micro hypodermic injection, public poisoning, sniper marksmen – covert methods of assassination requiring means and specialized training, and unlikely threats coming from street criminals.

'I find it curious for her to suggest such scenarios,' I state honestly because he must be vigilant, something quite difficult to do when love demands that you lower all defences. 'I would expect suggestions less aligned with espionage and more with immediacy – knives or handguns, for instance.'

'She's into spy films,' he says with fond exasperation. He opens his eyes and looks at me, his features softening again. 'Bourne, Bond, Jack Ryan . . . that sort of thing.'

That may be true, but the woman we know as Lily isn't given to overstatement or theatre. She chooses her words carefully for the greatest impact. I wish I'd been present when she said what she did so that I could've heard her voice and read her eyes. Her subterfuge runs deep and has been maintained for the length of her adult life, if not longer. Predicting her intent is impossible, and that's what makes her especially dangerous.

Mr Black's slight smile fades. 'Why haven't we figured out where she was holed up? We didn't find her with a suitcase, so all those clothes she bought must be somewhere.'

'It's possible she discarded them after wearing them.' I know I haven't answered his question.

He stares at me.

'Perhaps someone removed her items from wherever she was staying,' I offer, 'and the unit is no longer vacant.'

'By a landlord or super,' he prompts, but with a tone of insistence.

'Conceivably.' Or a friend, an accomplice, partner or lover. He knows this; he's a shrewd man. But obsession grips him. He shut himself off from love and joy for far too long, ending each day and beginning the next with a vision of pain and sorrow hung opposite his bed. The depth of his loneliness and grief left him uniquely susceptible to just the right woman.

Such incendiary chemistry is exceedingly rare. Some couples exchange revealing looks. Others are comfortable with public displays of affection. But couples who radiate erotic chemistry simply by being near one another are few and far between. Gideon Cross and his wife, Eva, are such a pairing, as are Mr Black and Lily. My employer's consuming lust for his wife is impossible to overlook. She has at least three secret weapons: she makes him laugh and feel loved and happy. He's completely captivated – one might even say bewitched.

She obfuscates more than she reveals, and Mr Black allows it to gain what he wants most: her. She has all the answers he seeks, yet he waits for her to reveal them in her own time. It's almost a game between them, the cat and the mouse. To what end?

'She received several packages while you were away. A courier delivered one from a jeweller here in the city. The receipt notes payment by wire transfer.' I deeply regret being the bearer of a succession of pieces of bad news. 'There have been no transfers or withdrawals, from any of the accounts, to that vendor or for that amount.'

He's still for a moment, then startles me with a feral smile that's all teeth. 'She has access to other accounts.' His eyes gleam as he rocks back in his chair. 'When the estate attorney told me about the LLC and its assets, it didn't line up with what little I knew. I suspected there were separate accounts. Lily wouldn't just hand over keys to the kingdom, even to her husband.'

'I thought it might be a gift,' I posit cautiously. 'Like the flowers.'

He waves the suggestion off with a careless wave of his hand. 'She would've already been in this room telling us about it. No, there's a war chest out there, Witte, and I've finally got her feeling safe enough to reveal it.'

I don't understand his conclusion or his reaction. The fierce glee. It's almost like . . . avarice, which makes no sense. Neither does his trust that she would disclose a gift from Laska when he suspects and knows of innumerable other deceptions on her part.

I've been mindful of my role in supporting Mr Black's introduction to making decisions and assuming command. Tutoring him in all aspects of living among the moneyed elite of this great city is a primary facet of my contract.

Yet I decide at that moment to selectively throttle the flow of information regarding the situation with Lily. After all, another facet of my work is to ensure Mr Black's safety. I will do so despite him, if necessary.

Straightening in his chair, he starts sifting through the mail. 'Keep me informed, Witte.'

'Of course.' I stand, dismissed. 'By the way, Mr Landon has made multiple attempts to reach you, including visiting here. When he called me, I suggested he try your mobile, but he said he hasn't been able to reach you. He sounded quite perturbed and asked about Mrs Black.'

'He's left me a few voicemails. I knew my mother would approach him eventually, so I didn't ask her not to. She would've reached out to him earlier.' He crumples an invitation to a political fundraising dinner into a ball and tosses it neatly through the basketball hoop over the dustbin. 'What did you say?'

'Since it was apparent he hadn't learned of Mrs Black through you, I avoided confirming or denying anything about her and advised him to direct questions about your personal life to you.'

'You're the best, Witte. I don't know what I'd do without you.' He exhales harshly and nods. 'Keep telling him that for now.'

I don't know why my employer avoided communicating with his closest friend. Is it because Mr Landon once dated Lily? Is it jealousy or evasion?

'There's something else . . .'

'Damn it.' He rocks back in his chair. 'Remind me why we left the beach to return to this crap?'

With an arch of my brow, he sighs and looks chastened. I continue. 'Ms Erika Ferrari has enquired after you at the lobby desk on two occasions. I asked Julian to inform me if she attempted to contact you at work, and she has, twice.'

He scrubs a hand over his face. It isn't the first time a woman has pursued him after a night together. In the past, he showed a cruel disregard for the perceived irritations, and I've always been the one to handle the subsequent awkward interactions. His feelings for Lily have, perhaps, made him somewhat more considerate.

'I don't even know how to reach her,' he says grimly, 'or what I'd say to her if I did. No, that's not true. I need to apologize. My wife set me straight on that point.'

'Did she? Yes, that would be in character for her. She views womanhood as a battle requiring armament and vigilance.'

'Her mother raised her that way, and I've provided the perfect example of why she was right to do so. I can't stand cheaters. I wouldn't even reach out to Lily until Ryan was serious about Angela, and now I've got to tell a woman I took to bed that I was married at the time – and still am – and would appreciate it if she doesn't bother my wife or me again.'

'Your situation is novel. The truth is all you can give.'

He laughs without humour. 'I don't even have that, do I?'

'I'll let you know if she attempts further contact. And I'll instruct reception and Julian to note her contact information.'

I exit and head back to the kitchen to begin dinner preparations. I pause on the living room's threshold when I find one of the maids, Lacy, studying a framed photo. She starts guiltily when she notices me. 'Witte, you scared me.'

'My apologies. You were engrossed.' I step down into the sunken living room after noticing photos now strategically placed around the space. One graces an end table, and a few others sit among the items on the bookshelves flanking the fireplace.

'She just put these out,' she says unnecessarily.

The frames are a selection of sterling silver, shagreen and precious wood; each positioned to blend tastefully with the decor and other decorative items around their placements. I think of Mrs Black's deliveries and realize that some must have been the frames, then marvel that her memory of the penthouse was so precise.

Clasping my hands behind my back, I study the images. All are of Mr and Mrs Black together in moments of intimate joy and love. All are revelatory of a couple mutually enthralled, and – most peculiarly – all are recent. None are earlier photos relocated from the beach house, where he keeps the preponderance of their visual history.

The room has utterly changed. With these few thoughtful additions, the space is now warm, personal and inviting. It feels like a home.

I understand why Lacy is captivated. We both stand motionless, astonished by the man revealed in the photos. I've never seen my employer look so well, so alive. His stunning transformation is almost enough to make me want to be as wilfully blind as he is choosing to be.

I've wished for his happiness for so long. It tears at me that he's found it with a woman who broke his heart and has endangered his life. That I like her is even more divisive.

Still, there's one disturbing detail he hasn't yet revisited, although I can't imagine he's forgotten it: Lily recognized him when she saw him on the street.

His wife knew him, remembered him. And yet she hadn't come home.

44

Amy

The instant the chilled vodka hits the bottom of my empty tummy it's like an orgasm. My eyes close, my breath catches, my toes curl in my heels. I hear the piped music beneath the dozens of conversations. The scents of garlic and basil, oregano and thyme fade. I moan as the alcohol hits my bloodstream with tendrils of dreamy heat. For a far too brief moment, I'm in a perfectly happy place.

'That good, huh?'

Opening my eyes, I look at the bartender, who's grinning and leaning on the bar in a way that makes the barrier somewhat pointless. It's not the best vodka martini I've ever had. Too much vermouth and stingy with the olives. Still, he's cute and flirting, so I smile back. 'So good, I'll take another.'

'Rough day?' he asks as he flips the emptied shaker in the air and catches it deftly.

'The worst,' I lie with feeling because I know the rules. One martini after work is no problem; two is either a rough day or a celebration. Three martinis is the point when the bartender's smile loses its luster, and four martinis is when they stop smiling altogether and ask if you'd like them to call a cab to take you home.

I realize I may get to three tonight, considering why I'm in the restaurant.

'Coming right up,' he says with a wink. His gaze shifts to a point over my shoulder, and I watch his brows raise, and his lips circle to form a low whistle. His smile widens enough to reveal a small dimple, and the appreciative look he gave me kicks up a notch for the new arrival.

My back stiffens just before the expected hand rests lightly on my shoulder.

'Hey. Sorry, I'm late,' Lily says in her breathy, girly voice that reminds me of Jennifer Tilly. 'Traffic was nuts.'

I turn my head as she steps into my field of vision. She's wearing a black mini slip dress and a gorgeous sapphire-blue kimono with metallic floral embroidery. A single strand of pearls hangs from her neck to her hips, with a knot below her breasts.

She holds out her arms, expecting a hug, and the adrenaline of fear spurts palpably in my chest. I'm awkward sliding off the barstool, almost stumbling into her. Her embrace is strong and more prolonged than perfunctory, but she still ends up being the one to let go first. I hate her for that. I hate her for how the bartender looked at her and because she's glowing from being thoroughly reacquainted with the joys of Kane's exceptional cock. Haven't I seen that morning-after radiance on enough of his discards to recognize it?

Does Lily remember all the lurid details I told her while she was unconscious?

'You look great!' she exclaims, raking me with a friendly head-to-toe glance. 'I love your jacket.'

'Thank you.' I didn't know I'd be meeting Lily for a drink after work, so I didn't dress for the occasion. While she's in happy hour attire, I'm wearing slacks and a blazer. Luckily, my outfit is one of Tovah's picks, and Lily's not the only one who complimented the cropped green velvet blazer.

'I love your kimono,' I tell her because I grudgingly do and am expected to say something nice back.

'Oh, thank you. Me, too. It was my mother's.' She hangs her purse on the hook beneath the bar.

319

I don't have any of my mother's clothes. I don't think she even owns anything resembling an heirloom like the lustrous silk draping Lily. My dear sister-in-law has it all, everything. Yeah, she had an accident and lost a few whacky years she can laugh about at parties, but really . . . her life is fucking perfect.

'What'll it be, gorgeous?' the bartender asks her as he sets my new martini next to my first one, which I've consumed only halfway. 'You two are making my night. The genetics in your family make for a fine view.'

I wait for Lily to correct him and tell him we just look alike, but she simply thanks him and orders the same thing I'm having but better – filthy, with only a swish of vermouth and extra olives.

So . . . Witte lied about her being a teetotaler. Why? To ruin my gift idea so hers would be better?

With a tight smile, I add him to my shit list.

'You got it.' Winking at her, the bartender adds a rap of his knuckles and has no idea his tip is decreasing by the minute. Seriously, his martinis are shit.

Lily cants her body to face me. 'How'd your day go?'

I shrug and take another drink. I force myself to take a sip instead of the gulp I want. I'm getting through each workday sticking to the detox, but by five o'clock, I can't stand sobriety another damned minute. 'It was work.'

Setting her elbow on the bar, she rests her jaw on her hand, looking elegant, relaxed and engrossed in anything I might say. If she only knew what's on my mind . . .

'Would you mind telling me about it?' she goads. 'Kane mentioned you had a social media management agency you folded into Baharan?'

'It didn't fold. It got digested.' I stare at her, wondering what her angle is.

She looks to the bartender as he serves her drink, then he

sets a votive candle between us. The Italian restaurant sits on the corner opposite the Crossfire and has floor-to-ceiling glass windows on three sides. During lunch, sunlight floods the space enough to require window shades, but night is falling and votives twinkle on every table. While Lily focuses on sampling her drink for the bartender, who waits for her approval, I take the opportunity to knock back the rest of my first martini and shove the glass away.

When she looks back at me over the rim of her glass, I'm chewing on my lone olive.

'Kane showed me the creative for the launch of ECRA+,' she says. 'It's really impressive.'

'Thanks.' I try not to sound irritated. What the hell does she know? 'I think it's run-of-the-mill. I'm working on something better right now.'

'What aren't you happy with?' Lily genuinely seems interested.

'Everything. The colors, the imagery, the messaging. Packaging, science and Rosana and Eva's flawless faces aren't going to be enough to compete in a crowded celebrity beauty space, but that's what they're focusing on.' I'm relieved when the bartender clears my empty glass. It looks much better with just the one drink in front of me.

'So, how do you fix it?'

I push back my irritation with her incessant questions. I like talking about my work, even if I don't like talking with her. And as far as I'm concerned, if I answer a bunch of questions, she'll have to do the same.

'By showing the product at work, on everyone, highlighting dermatological conditions that show improvement. Vibrantly real, untouched photos and videos.' I take another sip. She'd be horrible as a brand ambassador. 'It's not reinventing the wheel, but it's telling people what they want to know: the product isn't just beautiful wrapping, and it's not just worn by influencers they admire. The product is truly a good bang for the buck.'

Her smile is luminous. 'I can't wait to see it.'

I've drunk enough courage. 'Why do you care?'

She leans into the bar. Her legs are crossed and canted to one side; with her short dress, they look a mile long. Skin that pale should be blinding, but she just looks beautiful, like she's perpetually lit by moonlight.

'I think we could help each other.'

My brows shoot up. Unless she wants me as her stunt double for Kane's mattress gymnastics, I can't imagine anything she could offer that I'd want. 'How so?'

'Has Kane ever told you what I do?'

I shake my head, which is more diplomatic than saying she's a convenient vagina to fuck.

'I meet people. If I like them and they've got a dream I can monetize, I help them get started.'

'You're an angel investor,' I drawl. Does she think I'm stupid?

'Yes. When you're smart about who you choose to invest in, it's very lucrative. Startups need help with their messaging and social advertising, as you know. I can refer those businesses to you, you'll help them hone their brand and messaging, and that'll be one less thing they have to worry about.'

My gaze narrows. 'What's in it for you?'

'A ten percent referral fee on their first-year spend.'

'Only ten percent?'

She smiles, tucking her hair behind her ear. 'Keep in mind, I'll also be rewarded on the other side of the transaction by accelerated growth and increased profits for my investments.'

Her hair has grown since I first saw her weeks ago and now brushes the top of her shoulders. She's wearing stunning chandelier earrings of sapphires and diamonds. The stones sparkle insanely, catching the light at the slightest movement.

'Don't forget the trifecta.' I take another sip, my foot tapping on the rail that circles the bar. 'Baharan would profit on those contracts, and you'd get a cut of that, too.'

Something about her smile dims, arousing my curiosity and making me happy.

'Yes,' she concedes reluctantly, 'there's that.'

I debate saying anything, but why not let the cat out of the bag? I've been struggling for days, weighing whether I want to start over from scratch. Staying within Baharan means my hard work and talent will enrich Kane and Lily. So, the decision is easy: I'm getting the hell out.

'Well,' I begin, 'you're the first to know: I'm leaving Baharan and starting a new company.'

Lily's brows lift as if she's surprised, but . . . she doesn't seem surprised. 'A new company. That's a bold move.'

'Listen, I'm not leaving Baharan in the lurch. What they've got in the pipeline is fine, it's just not great, and I'm going to fix it before I focus on new ventures.'

'Why abandon Social Creamery, though? All that work, the brand, the past clients.'

I run my finger along the lip of my glass, wondering if this is what she's been fishing for all along: getting me to say aloud what an idiot I was when I signed those papers and effectively signed over my company. 'Don't you know how acquisitions work?'

She shrugs, and the kimono slips off one shoulder in a move so perfectly seductive I wonder if she's practiced it. 'Of course, but I've read your agreement with Baharan. I don't see why you wouldn't take advantage of your exit clause. No, that's not true. I understand wanting a fresh start. I can't imagine working with Aliyah has been pleasant.'

I straighten on the stool, forcing myself to loosen my grip on my glass before I snap the stem. 'What are you talking about?'

Her smile fades, and her brow furrows. 'Which part?'

I let go of the glass entirely because I feel like throwing the contents in her face. 'The fucking exit clause part!'

The frown lifts into arched curves of surprise. 'Amy, don't you know the terms of your agreement with Baharan?' she asks, slowly and carefully, like I'm a bomb that might go off at any moment, which is exactly how I feel.

I look away. I'm unpleasantly surprised to see Hornsworth, that office-stealing asshole, having drinks with a woman too pretty for him. I look away, disgusted, and feel a jolt when I find Rogelio, Baharan's Chief of Security. He's having drinks at a table with a guy sporting the same military crew cut, possibly another Baharan employee, but I can't tell. And one of the girls from Accounting is having dinner with three friends.

I rein in my temper. God forbid Aliyah hears reports of me losing it again publicly.

Taking another drink, followed by a deep breath, I reply, 'It's been a while. And at the time, I didn't think I'd ever decide not to be part of the family business.'

Lily also takes a sip of her martini, as if there's no reason to hurry with enlightening me.

'You have the option to reclaim the Social Creamery brand twenty-four months after execution if it no longer functions as a separate entity. It's a unique clause, very interesting really, but advantageous for you. I assumed your legal team inserted it to protect you, or perhaps Darius saw to that?'

I feel the color drain from my face. The room spins like a merry-go-round. It's like I've had those four martinis and am halfway through a fifth.

'Amy.' She sets her hand on my forearm. 'Are you okay?'

With a jerk of my arm, I throw her hand off. I didn't have

a legal team; I had Darius. Why wouldn't I trust my husband? 'I'm fine!'

'Let me help you.'

'What do you get out of it?' I snap, pivoting on the seat to sit face to face with her.

'We're family,' she says simply. 'You're my sister, even if it's only through marriage. I don't have any other siblings. No cousins or aunts or grandparents. I have Kane and, hopefully, you.'

We're family. I remember Kane saying something similar. *It's good to have family*. Total bullshit. What have any of them done to welcome me? When have they put me first or had my back? Now Lily thinks we can sit down for drinks, and she can casually twist my mind into knots for entertainment?

'Family,' I repeat, my mouth twisting with distaste. 'Did Kane tell you he screwed me? For a good twelve hours straight, I'd guess. Time kinda blurs when you're locked in a non-stop orgasm. Does that make us an *incestuous* family?'

She's calm and cool, unruffled by my anger. 'He told me, yes.'

I want to grab her by the hair and slam her face into the bar.

'I'm sorry.' She looks me in the eye so that I can read her sincerity. 'And you're right to call me out for being facetious. I want to help you because you're a woman who's lost some power, and that's dangerous. I want to help you because I want to make amends. Kane hurt you because of me. He's a grown man and responsible for making his own amends, but I can still feel regret for his pain and how that pain affected you.'

'Oh, great. Just what I need. Your goddamn pity.' I take a big swallow, relishing the burn in the pit of my stomach. I gesture for another drink.

'Reject my pity,' she says. 'Accept my help. I'll revise my

offer. Instead of taking a referral commission, I'll invest directly in Social Creamery, or I can offer a loan.'

'I can get a fucking loan!'

Her eyes never stray from my face as she takes another sip.

'Did Kane put you up to this?' I force myself to dial back my temper. She's totally in control of herself and this conversation, and the madder I get, the more I look like I can't hold my own. 'Or is this all your idea? Get me out of the office so Kane doesn't see me daily? Is that why he hasn't come back to work?'

'I don't worry about Kane being around any woman. I don't say that to be cruel. It's just the truth. And you and I being at odds only helps Aliyah. I'm not your enemy, Amy, or your rival. We can help each other and come out ahead. That's all I'm proposing. If we can find our way to being friends or allies, I'd like that, too.'

A voice in my head tells me she's right, that I can use someone on my side. I could certainly use an influx of cash. I don't know what to think about Darius anymore. When I'm with him, I'm sure he loves me. But then there's all this other shit. Could he possibly be ignorant of an exit clause? Has he been stringing me along? *Why?*

Lily's posture has changed subtly. It's not something I can put my finger on, but there's the sense that she's settled into her element. She's powerful, confident, sexy. I can see why Kane's such a lunatic over her, and I understand why I'll never have him again. At least not while she's breathing . . .

'I'm sorry I've been . . . abrasive,' I say tightly, knowing it's best to wear my Lily guise. I'm powerful, confident and sexy, too. I roll my shoulders back and manage a smile when the bartender takes my empty glass and presents me with a new drink. He doesn't smile or even make eye contact. 'I've had a few rough days recently, and this is a lot of information to digest at once.'

'It's fine,' she dismisses with an artless wave of her hand. That stone Kane gave her catches the light, and I realize it's the reddish-purple color of a human heart. 'You don't have to apologize. Trust is earned, and I'm happy to earn yours.'

I imagine her heart beating in my hand, strong and sure, never anxious or afraid. Then I close my fingers, feeling the rubbery flesh give under pressure until hot blood the shade of her lipstick runs down my forearm and drips from my elbow.

As delightful as that fantasy is, my pulse is racing, and a distant part of my mind registers my panicked thoughts. I need to read the contract. I need to know what it says. I lick an icy vodka droplet from my lip. I don't even taste the vermouth anymore, thankfully.

'What time is it?' I ask.

'Almost seven.'

'Oh! I have to go,' I lie. Because I can't sit here another minute, making small talk, feeling inadequate and exposed. Feeling like a moron. I have to act and take control.

I have to be Lily.

Sliding off my stool, I grab my martini and gulp it down. 'I'm sorry to run off like this. I didn't realize the time.'

Lily's smile seems fragile around the edges. 'Maybe we could do this again sometime soon? And not talk business.'

'I'd like that.' I lean forward and press my lips to her cheek. I hold them there for a beat too long because she smells so good. I wonder if she notices that I'm wearing the same perfume. I wonder if she misses her long hair and covets mine. Her skin is soft and plush beneath my lips. When I pull back, she has a lip print on her face the same shade as the lipstick on her mouth. 'Bye!'

Digging in my purse, I toss cash on the bar and rush out like I'm in a hurry. I wave my arm at the curb, and a cab cuts recklessly across lanes to reach me. I hop in and pull out my phone, looking through my contacts for Ramin's address. As Baharan's CLO, he can find out what is in the contract if he doesn't know offhand. By the time I tell the driver where we're going, he's already rejoined traffic.

Ramin lives in the trendy Meatpacking District, in a three-story brick building that was once a warehouse. When the driver pulls over and says we've arrived, I search for the street number because I can't quite believe it. I expected something sleek and modern, like his office, all chrome and deep, dark masculine colors: rust and forest green and navy. His building is more industrial, with awning windows that most residents have open.

I pause on the sidewalk, firming my balance and twisting my hair into a lobster clip to get it off my hot neck. Traffic was horrific, as it always is at this time of night. You'd never think two and a half miles could take forever to drive. It took so long that the alcohol has well and truly kicked in, yet it also feels like my buzz will disappear at any moment. I need another drink.

As I move toward the entrance, the doorman rushes to push it open for me. 'Hey, Lily. How's it going?'

I'm startled by being called the wrong name, not to mention the coincidence of being called the one he used. I look at his badge. 'My name's *Amy*, Dev. Can you let Ramin Ar—'

'I called up already,' he interjects, looking at me strangely. 'He's expecting you.'

My dry eyes burn, and I squeeze them shut for a minute. I have to open them again quickly because I'm a little unsteady on my heels. Why the fuck can't Lily be of average height?

I start through the lobby, but it branches off to each side, with two different elevator banks. 'Um . . . which way?'

Dev frowns back at me, his big grin gone. 'To the left.'

'Okay . . .' I wave at him over my shoulder and veer to the left. I recheck my phone for the floor and condo number.

The elevator is more like a service elevator than one for residents and guests. Since the doorman's desk was also heavily industrial, I guess that's the aesthetic. Once I exit the car, I see concrete floors treated to look like stone lining the hallway. My heels click like gunshots. It takes me a minute to figure out if I should head left or right, then I'm standing in front of Ramin's with my finger arrowing toward the doorbell.

Before I can push it, the door swings open.

'Hey.' Ramin is positively commando in jeans he hasn't bothered to button; the carefully groomed dark hair at his groin is visible. 'I was getting really worried.'

'Huh?'

He steps into me while I'm still too baffled to ward him off, slinging one hard arm around my waist and tugging me into him, his lips sealing over mine. I stand frozen, shocked, disoriented as he takes my mouth as if it belongs to him, his tongue thrusting deep and circling. He groans softly, and his chest vibrates against my breasts.

'It's been almost two weeks,' he complains, resting his forehead against mine.

'Get your hands off of me.' Come to think of it, he's been weird at work, too. Stopping by my office and asking how things are going. Every. Single. Day.

He pulls me inside and shuts the door behind him. 'What did I do to piss you off? Because I don't have a fucking clue, and I'm sick of being punished.'

I step into the living room. It's a loft space, massive, with awning windows on three sides. He must've bought the apartment next door and combined them. In one sweeping glance, I can see his bed against the far wall, the dining table and kitchen, and the space he's mapped out as the living room with a rug, sectional sofa and open-cubicle entertainment center that serves as a divider.

Candles flicker on the coffee table, and two glasses wait, with a bottle of wine in an ice bucket.

I spin around, wanting to get on my way before his latest slut shows up. 'I won't keep you long.'

Ramin's gaze narrows. 'That's what you're going to say to me? You don't come over. You don't call. I'm stuck here thinking about my brother fucking you, and when you finally show up, you're already planning to leave?'

My whole face pinches tight with confusion. 'Are you on something?'

'I wish I was.' He goes into the kitchen.

I follow. He pulls a glass out of the cupboard, grabs a bottle of vodka out of the freezer and pours himself a drink. He doesn't offer me one.

'I don't know how long I can do this,' he says wearily, leaning his hip against the island with one ankle crossed over the other.

I'm not a nun. I've slept with the man before, so I know what it's like to be under him. Ramin fucks like he's making porn. I can't say I didn't find it exciting in its way. And he's attractive, I'll give him that. Cuter than Darius, nothing like Kane. He's more compact, his body thickly muscled. He wears his hair in a rakish sweep across his forehead and usually has a three-day beard shadowing his jaw.

Reaching down, he pushes his hand into the open fly of his jeans and adjusts himself with a taunting stroke. 'You just come over to stare?'

'For fuck's sake.' I turn away, taking in his condo again, even though what I want is his drink. The sounds of the city at night pour in through the open windows. There's something visceral about the noise. It makes me edgy. 'You drafted the agreement to acquire Social Creamery, right? Or was that someone else in Legal's job?'

He doesn't answer right away, so I turn back to him. He's straightened and put his drink down. The lazy challenge is gone.

He's sharply watchful. 'I wrote it up. Why?'

My hands go to my hips. I teeter a bit on my heels and step out of them, even though I know that will make it more uncomfortable to put them back on. Ramin's gaze darkens.

'Lily tells me there's an exit clause.'

His eyes slit, and he comes toward me. 'Lily read the agreement?'

'That seems obvious.' I roll my eyes. 'Is she telling the truth?'

'Kane's given her access to everything then,' he says, his barefooted stride fluid and graceful.

I wish I'd kept my shoes on because now I feel petite and vulnerable. 'You're not answering the question.'

'You already know the answer.'

'The fuck I do!'

His face flushes with anger. 'We've discussed it a dozen times! I've been telling you to get out for over a year.'

I stare at him for a long moment, chilled by the weight of a heavy fog that squeezes me from all sides. My tongue is thick and dry in my mouth. My heart is hammering against my rib cage. As Ramin comes up to me, I skirt him and head to the island. Snatching up his drink, I take a deep swallow. The iced heat slithers down my throat, and I lean heavily into the counter. I feel sick. I haven't eaten since lunch. Bile flavors the back of my throat, threatening to spread into my mouth.

When Ramin wraps himself around me from behind, I don't even twitch. His nose and mouth nuzzle my hair. 'I've missed you, baby. Whatever I did to piss you off, I'm sorry.'

It suddenly hits me: they're all gaslighting me.

It's a concerted effort. Kane, Aliyah, Darius, Ramin. Maybe

even Clarice. She's been a good little soldier for Baharan for years now. Is Lily in on it? She's the only one who's told me the truth. Or maybe it's lies.

Why? What's the point? What's their endgame?

My breath catches as another possibility enters my mind. What if Lily's a victim, too? Maybe Kane drove her crazy. What if her dissociative amnesia was brought on by him screwing with her head? Not just with his champion ability to mindfuck but maybe with some chemical formula of his dad's that he pulled out of a dusty shoebox.

Maybe I'm unknowingly participating in some clinical trial for a new drug. Something for the mind. Alzheimer's. Dementia. Schizophrenia. What if I'm just a guinea pig?

How do we get away? Lily already managed to once, but Kane found her. She wasn't dead. He knew he'd track her down eventually. That's why he kept all her clothes. And once he found her again, he had guards at the hospital and penthouse so that she couldn't get away a second time.

How did she get out tonight? They must have wanted her to. Maybe they're testing me to see if I'm trying to escape. I'll have to be careful until I know for sure.

Ramin's hands are trespassing everywhere, rubbing between my legs, kneading my breasts. He's lapsed into porn star mode. His dick is so hard. He's dying to fuck me. He needs my hot little cunt wrapped around his dick. He can't wait to blow his load inside me.

Perversely, the nipples he's tugging so well are hard little points, and a trickle of warm arousal is sliding through my pussy. I don't think about it or how good Ramin smells. How do all the Armand men smell so deliciously, seductively male? Another sinister use of Baharan R&D? Some sort of aromatic roofie? My eyelids and limbs grow heavy.

I can't let them know I'm on to them. I've got to play along until I know enough to take them all under. With that in mind, I sway in a sinuous half-circle to face Ramin and close my eyes as he kisses me with bruising force.

45

Aliyah

'Thank you,' I tell the liveried attendant as he seats me at a small grouping of upholstered chairs between two arched windows. Sheers afford privacy while heavy red drapes with gold tassels frame the views of the city beyond. It's midday, but massive chandeliers draped in strings of crystals light the enormous room. Ornate cornices and molding adorn the walls, windows, ceiling and doorways. There's a sense of age, wealth and prestige.

The private club has been an institution since the mid-1800s. Less than a thousand men can claim membership in a city of over nine million people. Likely, I will never revisit the clubhouse, and I'm astonished and horrified that Lily's fake identity doesn't bar her from such rarefied establishments. Who is the man who allowed her in as a guest?

Around the room, I recognize several people I've only ever seen on the news or in films. I attempt to sit with the same leisure and ease, but my back is up, and fury simmers in my blood. I always dress well but took special care today, knowing this meeting with Lily lay ahead. My white belted jumpsuit has wide legs and half-length sleeves. The bodice is ruched to accentuate my breasts and rests right at my collarbone while my back is exposed to the waist. Classy, elegant, sexy. I can hold my own with any woman in the room.

When the server comes by, I order a champagne service for two and check the time. Another three minutes and Lily will be late.

If I'd had a choice, I would've preferred to meet in my office. The ideal battleground is always the most familiar and has a tactical advantage. But Kane would hear of it, and I'm not prepared to fight them together. Not yet. I want to suss her out first, alone. Let her see what she's up against. My second choice would've been to meet at a neutral-ground hotel, but she gave me this address instead. I didn't know where I was going until I arrived.

The whisper of a disturbance shifts my attention to the lounge entrance as Lily walks in. The attendant is smiling and chatting with her. Though she walks with a purposeful stride, she's attentive to what he's saying.

Her red silk skirt skims from waist to shins, then flares slightly around the ankles as she walks. She's taken one of Kane's white dress shirts, wrapped the two halves across each other, and knotted the ends at the small of her back. Rubies dangle from her ears and encircle her throat and wrists, yet they somehow don't seem like too much. It's a daytime look very few women could pull off.

'Here she is,' the attendant says unnecessarily, extending his arm toward me as if presenting me.

'It's a lovely spot. Thank you.'

I'd forgotten that voice. To look at her, you'd expect her to speak like Jessica Rabbit, not Betty Boop. Yet, once she starts talking, that voice not only fits her but also manages to sound dangerously sexual. She's catnip for Kane, and he'll do anything, believe anything, to wallow in her.

The attendant smiles and offers a slight bow. 'It's good to see you again, Lily.'

'You, too, Ari.'

She settles into the chair across from me, sets a red leather envelope clutch on the table and crosses her long legs. 'Ah . . . it's good to be out in the city. I couldn't be more in love with the penthouse, but sometimes, you just need to spread your wings a little.'

'Is this the first time you've left Kane's side?'

'Yes.' She laughs. 'Although he came with me. He's having lunch here with Gideon Cross.'

Cross, of course. Although, that doesn't explain why the attendant seemed to know her well. And apparently, only I considered hiding this meeting from Kane. We could've met at Baharan. It would have been far better for me if we had.

Two servers work in tandem to bring the champagne in a standing ice bucket and two delicate flutes. Lily orders sparkling water with lemon.

'I thought we'd toast to your return,' I say mildly, hiding my irritation. She's a contrary girl, seemingly determined to do the opposite of what I wish.

Her smile is sweet enough to make my teeth hurt. 'I'm not a drinker.'

I wave the champagne away and order a flat white coffee instead.

When we're alone again, I strike quickly to reap the advantage of surprise. 'Does Kane know your real name?'

Her mouth curves in an easy smile. 'What makes a name real?'

My lips purse. She didn't even blink.

'I find it very strange,' I say, 'that it doesn't bother you to be called by another name in private moments with the man you love.'

'Have I ever told you I love him?' she queries curiously. 'You and I have barely exchanged a handful of words, as I recall, and we've never discussed Kane.'

I shift, my back automatically straightening. 'You like playing games.'

'I do.' Her leg swings to and fro. 'I'm very good at them. You might want to find a different opponent.'

Her water and my coffee arrive, and she gifts the server a beatific smile.

'What do you want?' I ask. 'How much do you want?'

Resting her forearm on her knee, she leans forward, her emerald gaze focused like a laser. Not for the first time, I notice how cool and calculating those eyes are. Kane doesn't see it because she's always careful to look at him with heat. Of course, maybe she doesn't have to fake that. Kane has the same exuberant sexuality as his father, and women can't resist it.

'What do *you* want, Aliyah?'

'To protect my son, my family and my business.'

'Your motivations aren't nearly as noble,' she dismisses. 'You could manage Kane more easily when he was half dead with grief, and there was nothing for him to live for but Baharan. You want me to go away in the hopes that he'll go back to being a workaholic, but he's been fundamentally changed by my return. You can't unring that bell.'

I reach for the delicate saucer holding my cup of coffee. 'You think you have the power to manipulate Kane? Because his heartache over another woman has made him desperate, and you've clouded his mind with sex? It won't last. You'll get tired of playing a role, and he'll get tired of you.'

Her brows arch. 'Another woman?'

'I know about your aliases. I know there's no legitimate trail for the money. I know you're not Lily because the Coast Guard recovered her body. You're running a stupendously elaborate con, but you've made mistakes.'

Her nostrils flare on a deep breath, and she flows back into the chair, settling comfortably into the plush seat back. Subtle tells, but a retreat, nonetheless. Satisfaction fills me. She's not so self-assured now.

'You want his money,' I press on because my first salvos

were so effective, 'and you're feeling confident you can get your hands on at least some of it, but you forgot Kane's friends, many of whom knew Lily very well. And Baharan's board and investors will ensure you don't affect their bottom line. And don't underestimate Gideon Cross. He has an almost neurotic concern about bad press. The longer your charade goes on, the more invested people will be in seeing it end.'

Her leg starts swinging again. 'Do you love your son?'

'Of course.'

'Tell me why he was so utterly alone when I met him in college. Why he celebrated his birthdays alone. Why none of you ever attended his games.'

My jaw tightens. I can't believe he's discussed such things with her. It's one thing if he's lust-crazed; it's another if he's truly emotionally invested. 'I don't have to explain myself to you.'

'You want me to give you answers.' She leans forward so quickly I feel physically threatened. 'Here's one: *you're* responsible for his obsession with me. You cut him loose when it was convenient for you to do so. You left him alone and rudderless, just like Paul did. Between the two of you, you left a hole in him parents are supposed to fill. So here we are. I complete him.'

'Oh, that's rich.' I laugh, but there's no humor in it. 'Kane was an adult when he left home, and I had my hands full with his brothers and Rosana. It should come as no surprise that he was always popular. He had girls panting after him in middle school, and it only got worse when his sex drive kicked into high gear. I can't tell you the number of times I caught him with a girl in his room. Why would he want to spend his birthday with bratty younger siblings when he could get his cock sucked instead? Why suffer a post-game dinner with out-of-town family when all those girls waited to celebrate underneath him?'

Frost tinges her smile. 'You don't see him as a human being with feelings at all, do you? Is it because he's a man or because you can't live with yourself otherwise? Not only is that a really terrible excuse, but it also defies your logic about my intentions. Women take numbers to hop into bed with him, but I'm just after his bank account? Has it never occurred to you that maybe I just want *him*? Because you value money more than Kane, you can't imagine I wouldn't feel the same way.'

Setting my cup carefully into its saucer, I hold her gaze as I stand. 'You're making yet another mistake, thinking I'm in the dark. You'd do better to think of a payoff amount that'll tide you over until you find someone less insulated than Kane. You've carved yourself into a beautiful woman. You won't have any trouble lining up someone else.'

'And you'd do better working with me to make Kane happy.'

I grab my handbag and round the coffee table. The hairs on my nape and arms are standing straight up. The caress of air across my bare back, usually so sensual, feels like a ghost hovering.

I stop by her chair. 'I'm planning a welcome-home party for you. I'm inviting all of Kane and Lily's friends. Also, Sage's friends, Daisy's and every other floral name you've gone by. It'll be quite an event. You might want to call that stylist back and buy a new dress. You'll get the invite soon. Thanks for the coffee.'

There's an easy smile on my face as I walk out of the lounge, but I'm trembling.

'Aliyah.'

It takes tremendous effort to move confidently when I turn back to her. I arch my brow in silent query.

Her mouth curves. It's so slight, the change in her. Visually, she looks perfectly tranquil. There's a small, secret smile on her beautiful face as if we're two close confidantes enjoying

339

a private moment of amusement. But the energy around her has changed; I feel the chill from a few feet away. Her eyes, those bright, sparkling emeralds, have lost their fire and turned soulless. She's dangerous in a different way than I previously gave her credit for.

'Don't forget to invite your contractor friends from Seattle,' she says pleasantly. 'I'm sure Kane can't wait to meet them.'

I stare at her. I don't know how long I'm frozen there, my smile solidified, my body rigid. I'm afraid. Down deep in places I avoid inspecting too closely.

Leaving, I reach the Greek cross of the main hall, with its coffered dome and dual curving staircases. My son takes a meal somewhere in this building with a powerful man. Kane's probably flushed with good health and the satisfaction of having a stunning woman at the ready to relieve all manner of stress and tension. He may already be anticipating tonight, having no idea he's curling up with a snake in his bed.

I pull a sheer white scarf from my bag and drape it over my hair and around my throat with practiced speed before exiting onto the street. I debate calling a cab, then decide I need something more potent than caffeine. I spy a restaurant and bar up the street and take a walk. The weather grows warmer by the day, the moisture in the air thickening as we push deeper into the year. The sun is high in the sky, so bright I lament not having sunglasses. I'm relieved to enter the restaurant's cool interior, and I stand a moment, letting my eyes adjust.

The hostess, a young woman in the requisite little black dress, smiles. 'Hello. Do you have a reservation?'

I glance at the barroom. 'I'm just here for a drink.'

'It's open seating at the bar,' she says, but I've already walked away. I take one of the barstools and push my scarf back. I'm more rattled than I want to admit. When I return to the office,

I'll have an emergency meeting with Darius, then call Ryan. I lied about the party because I couldn't stand walking out of the clubhouse with my tail between my legs. I will not be cowed by a woman too clever to reveal anything useful and too dangerous to take on by myself.

I order a glass of pinot noir. I should drink white wine if I'm going to indulge midday, but red feels like it has the appropriate gravitas. When I take the first sip, I sigh. There's a television behind the bar, and I watch it.

The volume is muted but unnecessary since the closed captions convey the information to anyone interested. I look away, noting the predominance of empty tables in the bar, although the dining room shows brisker business, and the entrance door chimes frequently.

'I thought that was you.'

My spine locks up tight at the sound of that voice. Sweat spurts from my palms and scalp. My heart pounds, the sudden surge of panic and fear making me woozy. I spin on the stool, praying I'm wrong and just upset and distracted.

It can't be Paul's business partner. It just can't be.

When I complete the revolution, I see the face of my nightmares. My stomach heaves.

Alex Gallagher leers in that knowing way that makes my skin crawl. 'The blond dye job threw me off, but that body . . .' His tongue slides along his lower lip. 'I know that body *real* well.'

My mouth is dry. I want to scream, but there's no spit in my mouth. He taunts me on purpose. My violent disgust arouses him. The more he hurts and debases me, the more pleasure he gets.

I take a drink, my shaking hand sloshing the wine in my glass. The cool liquid loosens my tongue. 'Get away from me.'

Paul's former partner just smiles and reaches for a lock of

my hair. With a jerk of my shoulder, I prevent the contact. 'Don't touch me.'

'Aww . . . don't be like that. We're old friends.'

He leans in, and his smell makes my body convulse with loathing. All the images I've locked inside that deep, dark place come tumbling out. Lily loosened the lid; Alex's voice, scent and scornful gaze pry it wide open.

Our hatred is mutual. It sprouted after he partnered with Paul. I was so excited in the beginning. They were a great team, both men attractive and charismatic, whip-smart and ambitious. They were going to disrupt an industry together, and our futures held so much promise. Alex's wife, Ingrid, and I handled the entertaining and spent all our free time together. She was a statuesque blonde, and her daughter was just as golden. We once imagined Kane and Astrid might end up together.

And then things began to change. Paul attracted more recognition. I thought it might be as simple as his height commanding attention, as it does with Kane, but Paul was also at ease with himself, humble and humorously self-deprecating. He was less aggressive than Alex, more easygoing and fun. He began to receive more personal invitations than his partner. People tended to look at him when they spoke during business meetings and only glanced at Alex.

A few years into the partnership, the inappropriate comments started.

I've always preferred brunettes.

I like women with curves.

You've got beautiful lips. I bet Paul loves them wrapped around his cock.

Then came the touching – the hand on the knee under the table and the not-so-casual brushes against my buttocks and breasts. I had to avoid being alone with him and always remain at Paul or Ingrid's side.

I didn't know how to explain it to Paul. It wasn't simple sexual attraction or even the weakness of coveting. It was a toxic stew of resentment and anger that Alex didn't have the balls to take out on Paul. I was merely a stand-in.

And when Paul left me, alone and defenseless with Kane, I had nothing to offer in return for the Baharan name and the chemical patents for which Paul was directly responsible. But the newly broke and divorced Alex had ways to make me pay for all the insults he felt had been inflicted on him.

I'm still paying. And I will for the rest of my life.

His hand settles on my arm, and my entire body revolts violently. My arm jerks. The wine glass in my hand tips. The bowl shatters on the bar top, and bloodred wine spills in a river.

My body moves with a will of its own, rage burning through my mind in a fiery rush. He screams, the desperate sound horrifically inhuman.

Pain sears my fingers and palm. I instinctively yank my hand away from the source.

And gape, horrified, at the sight of the jagged wine glass and stem protruding from Alex Gallagher's groin.

46

Lily

I wake before you and lie quietly in the darkness, watching you sleep.

You've thrown one arm over your head; the other drapes across your ridged abdomen. The sheet rides low on your hips and tangles around your thighs, exposing your long legs. The duvet is bunched between us. You sleep hot, radiating feverish heat. I sleep cold and need the weight of the blankets.

You are, as ever, a deeply seductive enticement.

I've photographed you like this before. How could I resist? You're sexy and powerful, even in repose. Your body is masterfully sculpted, so perfectly defined in every respect. I don't know how I survive your strength when lust holds you in its unrelenting grip.

You once said making love with me feels like dying, and perhaps that's the reality. Maybe I don't survive your love at all. Perhaps, like the phoenix, I'm simply reborn again and again.

La petite mort, my love. As you said, I hope I take my final breath in your arms.

It's going to be a big day for us. The farthest we've been apart was yesterday when you had lunch on a different floor of the same building. Today, you're going into the office to work, and I'll be without you close at hand for the first time since I woke. We've jointly and without discussion adopted that measure of time: before I woke and after. At some point, you decided to focus only on the after. But then you're holding secrets from before, aren't you?

I knew once you had lunch with Gideon Cross, you would be drawn back into the corporate world you so blithely dismissed. The hunt is in your blood; the need to chase and taste victory. Your knowledge of self is rudimentary, at best. I hope to help you discover all your facets, appreciate your inner beauty and love yourself as deeply as you love me.

Your breathing changes. The even tempo hitches on a quick, deep breath. Closing my eyes, I feign sleep as you stretch, then turn toward me. I feel your gaze on my face and hear you sigh. Some nights, you sleep restlessly, and when you slide over me, there's a frantic edge to your lovemaking. Do you dream of the years you were alone? I don't know how to take that pain from you.

You leave my bed, and I hear the soft pad of your footfalls as you head into my bathroom. You've abandoned your bedroom with its portrait of Lily and now share my room and bed. Your toiletries surround my second sink. You keep your closet as before, but there's a section in mine where you keep a few items. I like seeing our things together.

My room smells like the two of us now. I hope we'll have the opportunity to fine-tune our master suite in a way that clearly defines one room as *ours*. I hope for a lot of things. With every day that passes, I hope for more and more.

But those possibilities only exist if I succeed today.

I roll to my side of the bed and pop a mint in my mouth. I hear the rush of water in the sink. What do you think of in these moments while you prepare to make love to me? I wish I could read your mind. It's not the act of shaving that gives you an erection.

The water turns off, and my nipples bead tightly. Between my legs, my sex dampens with need. You have me well trained;

345

my circadian rhythm has become inextricably entwined with your desire. I curl back onto my side as you return fully naked and aroused. I smile as you lift the sheets and slide between them.

'Hey,' you murmur, returning my smile as you hitch an arm beneath me and move me to the center of the mattress. You blanket my body with yours, your skin cool and your flesh hot. Your jaw is damp and whisker-free.

Your lips seal over mine. I fall into the drugging arousal of your intoxicating kiss.

An hour passes before you collapse onto your back beside me, dripping sweat and breathing hard. My entire body tingles and throbs, even my toes and the tips of my fingers. The abundant wetness coating my sex illustrates the intensity of your climax. Sunlight now pours through the enormous un-adorned window in the bathroom, infusing the room with enough ambient light to see clearly.

You feel around for my hand and link our fingers. 'There's no hurry for me to go back to the office. I'm managing just fine from here.'

Turning my head, I meet your gaze. Your eyes reveal concern and so much love it steals my breath. I can hide many things from you, but *I* can't hide from you. You see me so well and read my feelings so clearly. You must've sensed my turmoil. I hate feeling so anxious about the hours looming ahead, yet I know it would be wrong to feel calm. That apprehension will keep me on my toes and separates me from my mother.

I lift our joined hands to my mouth and kiss your knuckles. 'I just want you to be careful. Be overly cautious, even if it makes you feel silly. Do it for me.'

You face me and brush the damp tendrils of hair off my cheek. Then you kiss me softly and sweetly. 'I'll do anything for you, silly or not.'

'Thank you.'

'I'm working on our Val Laska problem. I've got a lot of men on it. And the NYPD is all over him, too.'

'I know.'

The curve of your mouth is supremely confident and undeniably sexy. 'You're okay? Really?'

'I just had three orgasms, Kane,' I say drily. 'I'm more than okay. Go. Get ready. I may have a surprise for you before you head out to conquer the world.'

Your brows lift. 'Give me a hint.'

'No. Get moving if you want to find out.'

You heave an exaggerated, long-suffering sigh and rise from the bed. 'When have I ever left you in suspense?'

I laugh. 'As often as possible, and you know it!'

Considerately, you go to your shower so I can get ready in mine. I dry my hair and make up my face.

I know I should dress, but I can't muster the energy to change again, as I'll have to once you leave. So, I stay in my kimono. There's so much to do and so much risk involved in doing it. I'll have to live up to my fullest potential. I must be everything my mother ever hoped I would become.

When I see you next, it's in my vanity mirror's reflection. Witte's freshly trimmed your hair, although it's now closer in length to how you wore it in college than it was when I woke up in the hospital. You've dressed in a navy three-piece suit, the rich material boasting a slight sheen. The color is beautiful, something like midnight sapphire, and you've paired it with a pearl-gray dress shirt and tie. The lilies on your cufflinks squeeze my heart a little.

I'm so arrested by how urbanely handsome you are I forget what I was doing until you take the silver-handled brush from my nerveless fingers. You grab its twin from the vanity and take over the job, using both hands in an easy rhythm.

My eyes close as you carefully run the boar bristles through my hair. It's not the same with short hair, is it? Hardly a need to use both brushes, but you do, and you're adept at the task.

'I honestly pity every other woman in the world,' I tell you. 'They'll want you, but they'll never have you.'

'You're stalling.' Your voice is low and warm with amusement.

'Haven't you heard of delayed gratification?'

'Yes, and it doesn't suit me.'

'Clearly. Let's eat breakfast, then —'

You stop brushing. 'You try my patience, *Setareh*.'

I've never seen you quite like this, as eager and anticipatory as a child at Christmas. It's delightful.

Laughing, I decide not to torture you. It's too essential to make you happy. I rise to my feet and go to my nightstand. I find you directly behind me when I turn to give you the hinged leather box. I laugh again. 'You're terrible.'

Your smile is smug as you take the box. 'That's not what you said an hour ago.'

'I wasn't saying anything an hour ago.'

'I can translate your moans.' You open the box, and your head tilts slightly. You carefully extract the antique pocket watch and its chain.

I take the box to free your hands and watch as you open the case.

You read the inscription aloud, very softly, 'The seconds I owe you and more.'

I'd wondered if you would remember what you said to me at the beach house. When you swallow hard, I know you do. You close the cover, your thumb brushing over the etched images of the moon and a starry sky decorating the front and back of the casing. Lilies no more. Your hand closes around it.

'Thank you,' you say hoarsely. 'I'll cherish it.'

Pulling me close, you kiss me thoroughly.

At breakfast, you show the watch to Witte. He glances at me and smiles as if the gift pleases him. 'It's an impressive piece and a lovely gift.'

With your permission, he attaches the fob to the buttonhole of your vest and slips the watch into the pocket. I'm biased, of course, but I find the chain's addition very sexy.

When it's time for you to go, I walk you to the door and kiss you goodbye. It's a poignant parting for me, and that causes you to delay.

You search my face. Without heels, I'm several inches shorter than you, and you seem larger than life. 'You make it very hard to leave you, *Setareh*.'

'I'm sorry. I don't mean to.' I grip your wrists. 'I promise I'm okay. I have Witte and a million things to do. Before I know it, you'll be home.'

You continue to stare, clearly torn.

'Why don't we watch a movie after dinner?' I suggest. 'We'll see how far we can follow along before we're distracted by necking like teenagers.'

Your smile doesn't reach your eyes. 'I'm already looking forward to it.'

Rising onto my tiptoes, I kiss you. 'Go, before I don't let you. And stay alert. Keep your head on a swivel. You've got my heart in your body. Don't break it.'

'Make the same promise to me.'

I watch until the elevator seals you inside. I note the two security professionals in smart black suits flanking the entrance, meeting each of their glances with a brief nod. Then I close the front door and lean heavily against it.

Witte rounds the corner from the kitchen and stops when he sees me. He looks refreshed and vital. While we were in

Connecticut, the time to himself appears to have suited him. I can't help but wonder how much longer he'll be with us. Now that you have a wife to look after you, I'm curious if he contemplates new challenges. I hope that's not the case. I hope he stays for many years to come. He loves you so, and you should have many people in your life who do.

His features are soft when he asks, 'Would you like anything? Some tea, perhaps? Juice? More coffee?'

'No, thank you.' I straighten. It's easier for me now that you're not here. 'I'm fine.'

'I'll be heading to the Greenmarket today for some things for dinner and breakfast tomorrow. Would you care to join me? It would be helpful to know what you like.'

'You're doing everything right. I've loved everything you've made so far – Michelin should rate you.' I ask the following question as if I haven't already pinned down his schedule. Witte is a creature of habit, and I've been very observant. 'How often do you go to the farmer's market?'

'In some cases, daily. Some weeks, only once or twice.'

'The thought of a day out in the city is *very* tempting, but the stylist is coming by shortly. She has a few more things for me.' I move away from the door. 'I'd love to accompany you whenever your next outing might be.'

He smiles at my word choice. 'It's a date.'

'Could you please call the beautician who took care of me before and see if she can fit me in at some point?'

'It would be my pleasure.'

I head to my room, my gaze following my reflection in the mirrored hallway.

The maids have already stripped and remade the bed. I wonder what they think of you now. After years of widowhood broken only by the occasional one-night stand, our sheets now bear the evidence of a man who enjoys his wife multiple times a day. Perhaps it's not such a surprise, considering the forcefulness of your sex appeal. And household staff see so many intimate things. There are no secrets from them.

Witte's knock seems to come so quickly.

'Yes, Witte?'

'The beautician – her name is Salma – says a client canceled this morning, and she could head over now. Would that be acceptable, or would you prefer another day?'

I feign delight. 'This morning is perfect. A little pick-me-up before I pick up the pieces.'

He smiles and nods.

After that, the next time I see Witte, he's laden with garment bags and department store totes, walking into my room on the heels of Tovah, who startles me again with her oversized energy packaged in such a petite frame.

'Good morning, Lily! How are you? I love that kimono! So classy yet so sexy.' Her smile is brilliant. She's arranged her long, chocolate curls in an elaborate updo of braids and twists. Her sleeveless wrap dress has a giraffe print, and her heels are sky-high.

'Thank you. You're looking very classy and sexy yourself.' I smile at Witte as he heads into my closet with his burdens.

'I've been holding on to these for you since you left town,' Tovah says, dropping her purse into the chair where you used to watch me sleep. 'Please tell me you lounged around on a beach with aqua waters and drinks with little umbrellas.'

'That sounds lovely,' I agree, 'and you must be clairvoyant. We went to a beach but didn't have the rest. Does it still count?'

'Any beach counts, umbrellas or not.'

Witte steps out and pauses by the door to the hallway. 'I'll be running out now. I've notified reception about Salma's arrival, and Lacy will get the door. I've prepared three shredded chicken salads for lunch, and you'll find them in the fridge if you make a day of it. I expect I'll be back around three.'

'You think of everything, Witte. Thank you so much.'

As he's leaving, Tovah sets her hands on her hips. 'Where do I get a Witte?'

'You'll have to ask Kane about that.'

The door latch clicks, signaling privacy, and our smiles drop instantly.

She sighs heavily. 'We've all been talking about this, and we don't think it's the right time.'

'It's the right time.'

'It feels rushed.'

I move into the closet. 'It's not rushed. We've been planning this for years. We could pull this off in our sleep.'

'You were just hit by a car!' Tovah follows me. 'Under suspicious circumstances. You were in a coma, for chrissake!'

'I haven't forgotten.' I open the garment bag and eye the ensemble inside. 'This is really good.'

'Of course it is. I'm good at my job.'

Glancing at her, I find her chewing her lower lip. 'I've got this, Tovah. *We've* got this. It's normal to be nervous when you've planned something forever, and it finally comes together. I had some anxiety this morning, too.'

She throws up both hands. 'That's a sign! You should wait. Let's get our bearings. Make sure you're one hundred percent.'

'We've waited long enough. Aliyah's going to stir up problems. We need to execute before she figures out a way to fuck this up.'

There's another knock on the bedroom door, then Lacy's voice. 'Hey. He's gone.'

I return to the bedroom with Tovah.

Lacy stands inside the door. 'And Salma's here.'

Dressed in jeans and an artfully ripped band T-shirt knotted at the waist, the voluptuous brunette wheels a baby-pink trolley case into the bedroom behind her. Her face is flawlessly made up, with elaborate cat eyeliner and perfect thick brows.

'We're sure Witte's gone?' I ask.

Lacy nods. 'Left the parking garage and everything.'

Salma glares at me. 'You already did your face!'

'It needs more work,' I assure her. 'And I need help with the wig. I used too much adhesive when I did it myself. I thought I was going to rip my scalp off.'

She shakes her head and scowls.

'Hey,' I protest, 'don't look at me like that. If I didn't make up my face, Kane would've stayed home thinking something was wrong. It was an effort to convince him to go as it was.'

She curses in Spanish under her breath. 'He's a serious complication.'

'I know.'

Lacy slouches against the jamb. Dressed in a gray maid's uniform, she's restrained her red hair in a bun at her nape and pops a huge bubble of gum before telling me, 'We don't think it's the right time.'

'I've heard,' I say wryly, going back into the closet for the wig. When I return, all three women are staring at me. I pause and give them the attention they seek. 'How many chances do you think we're going to get?'

'At least one more,' Salma says with a defiant tilt of her jaw.

Tovah crosses her arms. 'Aliyah's already giving her grief.'

'Fuck her,' Lacy says. 'I never liked that bitch. When she's not trying to tackle Witte into the nearest bed, she treats Bea and me like dog shit stuck to the bottom of her shoe.'

'How is Bea?' I ask.

Lacy's nose scrunches. 'She's okay. I talked to her this

morning. I feel bad about doctoring her tea yesterday. She said she's been in the bathroom all night.'

'Her tummy trouble will feel better by dinner. And since we don't want to make her sick again in the future, we seriously need to get going. We don't have a ton of time.'

Grim-faced, we keep the plan rolling.

By eleven o'clock, the woman in the mirror has my mother's face. Contour has sculpted my cheekbones and jaw. A heavier hand with the eyeshadow deepens the sockets of my eyes. Black hair falls down the center of my back in a thick braid.

Makeup has finished the job of transforming me into her very likeness.

A tall, dark figure lures my gaze to the open hallway door behind us. 'Hey, you're early.'

Rogelio studies me as he enters the room, his face tight with concern. He's dressed in jeans and a Yankees jersey rather than the dark suits he wears at Baharan. His normally clean-shaven jaw is stubbled, his crew cut slicked back with glossy pomade, and a thick gold chain circles his neck. The flat, watchful gaze is the only thing that distinguishes him from a random guy on the street. 'I don't like this. It doesn't feel right.'

'You, too?' I ask softly. I always take him seriously. We've been together a long time.

His hand comes to settle on my shoulder. 'You're too beautiful, *querida*.'

'As if she doesn't know that,' Salma says with a roll of her eyes, carefully repacking her trolley.

'*She's* too beautiful,' I correct. 'This isn't my face.' I catch my team's worried expressions in the mirror. 'You all have to trust me.'

Rogelio reads my determination and sighs heavily. 'Fine. You're the boss.'

Turning in the vanity seat, I look up at him. 'It would save me time if you could open the jewel safe. Can you get through the fingerprint recognition?'

'Of course. My crew handled the installation.'

'I'll help him,' Tovah says. They leave through my closet.

A movement across the room catches my eye, and I see that one perfect Blacklist lily bloom has inexplicably fallen from its stem. It lies on the dresser top, beneath the abundant bouquet, facing me. The stamen has shed across the glossy surface in an explosion of bright orange that inexplicably resembles blood splatter. There's a thud at the window, and I jolt. Salma curses. A bird thrashes against the glass, clawing for purchase, flapping frenziedly until it slides out of view.

'Jesus, Mary and Joseph,' Salma mutters, crossing herself.

A shiver runs down my spine.

'Go help Lacy,' I tell her.

Her hand presses over her belly, briefly hiding the letters that spell out PANTERA. 'You're my family. If anything happens to you, I will haunt your ghost and kick your ass when I die.'

We hug tightly. She smells like strawberries and champagne. She's sniffling as she leaves the room with a quick stride.

Tovah returns with Rogelio on her heels. She carries a weighted blue sack with her and pats the side of it. 'We're all set.'

'Time to get dressed.'

She passes the bag to Rogelio and follows me.

'I can dress myself,' I tell her wryly.

'Not this time. If something fucks up, it will not be because of your wardrobe.'

When we've finished, I look at myself in the mirror. The gray slacks with the navy tuxedo striping are baggy and held on by the grace of a slim black leather belt. The long-sleeved

355

button-up top is a paler shade of grayish blue and has a patch with the image of an eagle on the breast. It, too, is oversized, even with the silicone breastplate that gives me the appearance of having huge breasts. My rear is also padded, and I wonder how I'll sit during the drive.

'There's a hat and sunglasses in the bag,' she tells me. 'Put 'em on, keep 'em on.'

'Got it.'

She grabs me by the forearms. I'm wearing flat black orthopedic shoes. With her ankle-breaker heels, Tovah barely hits my eye level. 'I expect you to call as soon as you're free and clear.'

'I will,' I promise. 'Stop worrying.'

Her mobile mouth puckers, and I know she's fighting the urge to argue more. 'Okay,' she says finally. 'Okay.'

I follow her out of the closet but pause on the threshold as she disappears into the hallway. Rogelio paces in the fluid way of a man who's trained his body to be a weapon. Leaning into the doorjamb, I cross my arms and watch him.

'You look ridiculous,' he says.

'I feel ridiculous.'

He stops and holds my gaze from across the room. Then he grabs the bag off the bed. 'You ready?'

'As I'll ever be.'

47

Lily

Lacy waits for Rogelio and me by the front door, twisting the handle of a feather duster nervously between both hands. 'I'll see you later.'

I kiss her cheek. 'Take the time to think about what you'll do next. Places you've always wanted to travel to, maybe?'

'I've got a binder.'

That makes me grin. 'Of course you do. I can't wait to see it.'

Rogelio holds the door open for me, and we step into the elevator vestibule. He looks at the two men stationed there. 'Fix the CCTV. I was never here. She never left.'

They nod, and one breaks off for the utility closet.

'Tuck your braid into your shirt,' Rogelio tells me, looking me over again. 'And put the hat on.'

I do as he says. 'Better?'

'Hardly.' He pushes the button to call the car. 'I wish you'd let me handle this.'

'No one else would make it out alive.'

He says nothing further until we've made it through the parking garage and are on our way in a rental van with switched plates. The car that hit me had switched plates, too. But that's just a coincidence. There's no way it could be anything else.

'Here's where we're at so far,' Rogelio says grimly, his eyes on the road. 'The reservation for lunch is at twelve-thirty. Laska texted Amy earlier to confirm. That message came to the clone, and I replied. I told Clarice I'd won a lunch for two at a restaurant in the general direction of the meet-up. Today's the expiration date, and I can't make it, so she's taking Amy. My tracker on Amy's phone will let me know if they deviate. If Amy's followed, they'll think she's en route for up to half an hour. It buys us some time – but not much.'

Remotely accessing Baharan files requires installing proprietary security software on the device. Rogelio managed that installation for all of the Armands, and it's been our window. Through it, we saw our chance after Val made contact.

We've hunted him for years, and in the end, he came to us.

'I already have a man in place at the meet-up,' he goes on. 'He'll grease the water glass. We hope the glass will slip and spill, but even if it doesn't, the grease has a dye and will stain. You said Laska's fastidious, so using a napkin won't be enough in either case. I'll give you the go signal, and you'll start walking. The bathrooms are individual and unisex. All the locks have been tampered with. A hard bump with your hip, and you'll be in. Then it's you and Laska, one on one.'

I nod. 'Val will have protection scattered around the restaurant. If they suspect you or your man . . .'

'I know what I'm doing. So does my team. You're the one out of her league.'

'I won't screw it up.'

I stare out the window, trying to make sense of where I am and what I'm doing. There's a queue of schoolchildren following their teacher down the street. A couple makes out against a tree. A deliveryman yells at the driver of a double-parked car. It's all so surreal. The sunlit city with its teeming life seems like a nightmare vision. A taunting promise of normality meant to contrast reality with a deeper horror.

Looking down at my wedding ring, I don't have the heart to remove it. I spin it around to hide the stone in my palm. 'We've been over this a million times.'

'Your desperation dulls your edge. If he attacks you, you're not –'

'He won't.'

Rogelio slams his palm into the steering wheel and shouts, 'You don't know that! You're blowing off the car accident as random, but none of the rest of us are. And it's been weeks since we practiced. Weeks of you recovering. All these years of waiting and planning, and you won't take the time to prepare!'

'Time for him to prepare, too,' I point out calmly. 'Do you think the timing of his return to the city is coincidental? That he hired Amy before, and again, by chance? That meeting with her in a restaurant he doesn't own wasn't deliberate? There's something bigger at play here.'

'No shit. It's still too risky.'

'It's never going to be without risk!' I sag back into the seat, pressing my palm against my forehead. 'Do you know how hard it is to have *all* of you get cold feet *today*? Why not some other day? If anything's screwing our chances now, it's you guys making me feel so nervous when I need to be sharp!'

'It's not just today.' Rogelio pulls over to the curb, parks and turns the engine off. Releasing his seatbelt, he twists to face me. His mouth is hard and tight, his eyes beseeching. 'We've been talking about this for months.'

'Behind my back?'

'You haven't exactly been available!' he snaps. 'We're not the same orphaned kids you tracked down. We're different now – because of *you*. There was a time we all needed the idea of revenge against your mother and Laska to drive us forward. But then you helped us discover our talents and provided the education to make them marketable. You gave us a new family. We have each other now. Maybe that's enough, *querida*. Maybe all of us making good is the best revenge.'

359

I study him. I let his words sink in. 'I wish you'd said something earlier. I wouldn't have made you come this far.'

'For fuck's sake!' He grabs the steering wheel in both hands and shakes it hard. 'I really want to throttle you right now. You know we'd never let you do this alone. I'm just telling you – you don't have to do this *for us*. You don't owe us anything. What your mother and Laska did to our families . . . that's not on you.'

I nod, then pull out a tube of lipstick so nude it completely erases my lips. 'We'll have to plan for a family night after this. Air all this out.'

'You're still going forward.'

'I have to save Kane,' I say simply. 'I have to try.'

'All right.' He extends his hand and squeezes firmly when I set mine in his. 'The town car will be waiting at the curb right outside.'

'Got it.'

He hands me a small box from the center console. 'Here's your earpiece. I'll tell you when to start walking. Get in the back until then. And put the damn sunglasses on!'

Rogelio reaches between the seats and grabs a Gucci ball cap, tugging it on. He checks for traffic, then opens the door and hops out. I move to the back of the van and watch him head down the street and around the corner. Then I slide the shades onto my face and pull on a pair of blue gloves.

'There's a guy on the door, outside,' he murmurs through the earpiece. 'And two undercovers across the street.'

I nod by instinct, then scoff at myself for doing so. The van is already growing hot. The silicone prosthetics intensify the heat. Sweat beads on my skin then runs in rivulets. My makeup feels greasy, and I expect it's begun to run, too.

I focus on my discomfort, on how my skin prickles. I can't think about you. I can't risk second-guessing a plan that's been years in the making. It may not work, and I accept that. But I have to try. For you. For us.

'Walk.'

The one word is hissed but sounds like a shout. I hear it even over my panting breaths and the frantic beat of my heart. I check for anyone looking and hop out, sliding the door shut quickly. I adjust the weight of the blue bag on my shoulder and trace Rogelio's steps. I walk briskly, with purpose, but roll my shoulders forward as if I've spent my life being awkward with my height. I notice people move out of my way more quickly than when I'm not wearing a mail carrier uniform. They're not friendlier, but there seems to be some awareness that the mailperson should win by default in a game of pedestrian chicken.

There are two stores before I reach the restaurant, and I stop in each one, dropping off junk mail bundled with rubber bands. A lady in the stationery store asks if there's a way to reduce the deluge of crap. I tell her to toss it in her recycling can.

When I step back outside, the sun seems blinding even with the dark, oversized sunglasses I wear. I can't spot Val's henchman or the cops. The people eating at the sidewalk tables across the street are animatedly engaged in conversation. Those who aren't talking are looking at their phones.

The restaurant's door chimes as I open it. I've already got the bundle of advertisements and coupons in my hand. I see Val's broad back disappear down a hallway straight ahead.

'Thanks,' the hostess says, taking the mail and shoving it into the podium. She's a tiny brunette, nearly as petite as Tovah but curvier.

'Mind if I use your restroom?' I ask, jutting out my lower jaw into an underbite that alters my face and deepens my voice.

'Sure. Straight back. How about ice water to go?'

I'm startled by her thoughtfulness. 'I'm good, but thanks.'

The restaurant is less deep than wide, with the kitchen along the back wall. The floor is stone that's seen more decades than I will, and the booths are notable for their ornately carved privacy screens and thoughtful hooks on the sides to hang jackets and handbags.

That's all I see as I walk back like I'm in a hurry. I don't want to look too closely at anyone or anything. I don't see Rogelio, but I don't doubt he's there. I don't know which of the servers or bussers might be his man. I reach the hallway and remove the sunglasses and hat, shoving them in the mailbag. While my hand is in there, I take inventory. I feel the weight of flawless jewels wrapped in satin.

'He's in the second water closet,' Rogelio tells me. 'Wait for the distraction.'

I pass the first bathroom. My footsteps slow as I see the second one. There is a third and then the entrance to the kitchen. I hear a crash behind me and the breaking of glass. At the collective gasp, I bump my hip into the second door, feel it give, and stagger in.

The rest passes in a blur of muscle memory. I rush forward, using the force of gravity to my advantage. For such a big man, Val moves like a ninja. He's coiled and ready to strike in the blink of an eye. Then he sees my face and seizes. There's a heartbeat of recognition and pleasure.

I don't waste energy pulling out the knife. With all the momentum of my running entry, I shove it through the bag and into his chest. The layers of his clothing give way to the wickedly sharp dagger, but the flesh and muscle resist, followed by the scraping of blade against bone.

I've practiced on enough dead pigs to know the strength required for the task. But the addition of life – a gasped breath and hot, viscous blood . . . I am not prepared for those. I'm not prepared for death.

I try to help him to the floor gracefully, but he's too heavy and nearly takes me down with him. I pull back when he's seated on the tile with his legs stretched out and lock the door. I expect Val to be dead. If my aim was good, he's got a knife in his heart. But he breathes shallowly, and there's a smile on his face.

'I can't let you kill him,' I tell him, crouching between his spread legs. I don't have time for this. I need to remove the knife and let him bleed out. He's made his living exploiting women and children – the younger, the better. He's destroyed so many lives and wants to end your life. He doesn't deserve mercy or my hesitancy. 'I didn't mean to fall in love with him, but I did.'

He chuckles, and blood runs from the corner of his mouth. It's ghastly. Like a horror movie.

'The boat,' he wheezes with a crimson bubble of spit that bursts into tiny spatter. 'Find it.'

'What? Val . . . what did you say?'

'Your mother' – he grins with bloodstained teeth – 'will . . . p–proud.'

'Tell her I said hi,' I mutter, 'when you join her in hell.'

But he chortles, and a gleam in his eyes makes my stomach drop.

My gaze searches his face anxiously, but his eyes lose focus, dimming into sightlessness. A moment later, the acrid ammonia smell of urine and the more offensive smell of feces foul the air.

I yank the knife from his chest with both hands, freeing the mailbag. Blood soaks the material of his designer dress shirt. Spreading the bag wide open on the floor, I tug the thick gloves off and drop them in. I stand and toe-off the shoes while unbuckling the belt, then unsnap the fasteners securing the faux buttocks. The shirt and breastplate follow, leaving me standing in a sweat-soaked bodysuit. The silk wrap dress in fire engine red takes no time to put on.

'If you're still alive, hurry the fuck up!' Rogelio orders in a fierce whisper. 'And grab his cellphone.'

I scrub the nude lipstick off with a paper towel and drop it into the bag. I slather on red gloss with shaking hands and loosen the braid while sliding my feet into heels. I fumble with the jewelry, panicking when I drop an earring in the sink. Thankfully Tovah selected easy: French hooks, a long necklace I can pull over my head and a bangle bracelet.

I look in the mirror. There are kinks from the braid my mother would never tolerate. My skin shines with sweat, my lipstick bleeds and there's a tear in the dress from the knife. I take a deep breath, let it out. I slide Val's phone into a clutch the same hue as my dress and leave the bag on the floor as I step out to the hallway.

A man is passing by with a broom, and I panic. Then he jerks his head toward the exit, and I know he's with Rogelio. As I walk away, I hear the bathroom door open behind me. He'll get rid of the mailbag. Val will lie there until someone discovers his corpse. It won't take long.

'Would you please get the fuck out of here!' Rogelio growls.

Rolling my shoulders back, I walk out of the restaurant like my mother would, as if I'm the most beautiful woman ever to walk the earth. Empress of the world. As if everyone around me has significance only if I deign to give them my attention.

I feel the stares of Val's men as I pass through the dining room. When I step onto the sidewalk, I feel more stares. A black town car pulls up to the curb, and the back door swings open from inside. I step down from the sidewalk and slide into the back. I don't have time to shut the door. The velocity with which the car accelerates closes it for me.

Tovah sits beside me. Her gaze is anxious on my face. 'I couldn't wait.'

'I see that.' I pull out Val's phone and power it off so no one can trace it.

'It's done?'

'Yes.'

'Oh God.' She melts into the seat, looking pale and dazed. 'Oh God. That sick bastard is finally dead.'

She reaches for my hand and holds on tightly. I know what that means. Her father's death preceded Val's entrance into my mother's life, but still, she feels some justice. As Rogelio said, we're family – bonded by an inconceivable commonality and a burning need for vengeance, if not justice.

Tovah's father didn't pass my mother's vile morality test. Val tortured and ordered the gang rape of Lacy's mother over an ex-boyfriend she hadn't seen in over a year. Salma's brother had the misfortune of catching my mother's eye. Rogelio lost his sister to Val's trafficking ring.

'I'll call the others,' Tovah says.

There are more of us outside of New York. So many families were devastated by Valon and Stephanie Laska's insatiable appetites for death and wealth.

Lacy nicknamed us The Avengers. Each team member played a part in our success today. If only this were a comic book where we could write our storylines and draw our endings. So much time, energy and sacrifice. So many lives suspended. All to kill a single soulless man.

There was nothing worth saving in Val. That I mourn him even a little is proof of my inner rot. He looked after me in his twisted way when I had no one else who would. He didn't do it out of love, and the results were not in my best interests, but it was something.

I look out of the window. Although Tovah appears comfortable, I'm freezing. I bite hard to keep my teeth from chattering, but it doesn't help. I rub my arms with my hands, trying to warm them. Resting my head against the seat back, I close my eyes. The adrenaline that gave me such strength in the bathroom has drained away, and I'm exhausted. My limbs feel heavy. My eyelids are weighted.

'Come on. Let's get you in and warm you up.'

Blinking, I find myself in my bathroom. I'm naked. Steaming water fills the deep soaking tub. Tovah holds me up on one side, Lacy on the other. My body jolts as if I've been shocked with a defibrillator, and the two shorter women cry out in alarm and struggle to keep me upright.

'Fuck it,' Rogelio says, and I hear his boots cross the veined marble. 'I tried to preserve your modesty, *querida*, but if you fall and hurt yourself, Black will lose his shit.'

I realize I've lost time along with a chunk of recent memory. The last I knew, we were racing home, but there were pre-arranged changes of vehicle and clothing in between, followed by the return to the penthouse. The plan was set. Somewhere along the way, my mind checked out.

Lacy moves out of the way. Rogelio picks me up and carries me to the tub. I hiss in discomfort as my icy feet slide into water that feels like it's boiling, but he doesn't stop pouring my limp body into it. Under the water, my skin turns bright pink. The steam carries the scent of azaleas.

Rogelio studies me, careful to keep his eyes on mine. 'You're in shock. You're going to sit in this hot water while Salma gets the wig off and all that crap off your face. Sip some strong coffee. I'd tell you to add some brandy, but I know you won't. If ever there was a time for a drink, though, this is it.'

I grab his wrist as he starts to straighten. 'Is everyone okay?'

'Everyone's good.'

I sit up, wrapping my arms around my tucked legs. Salma wheels her trolley to the tub.

'They questioned me,' he elaborates, turning his back and

walking a few feet away to give me privacy. 'Just routine. I was visible to the UCs through the window the whole time, looking at my phone, so they're probably done with me. They'll interview all the employees and look at my man in the restaurant, but everyone saw him cleaning up broken glass when the hit went down.'

I exhale my relief. The bathtub sits parallel to the window, and I rest my cheek on my knees to look at Central Park and Harlem in the distance. Millions of people are going about their day, having no idea I've just taken a man's life.

'The plan is holding so far,' he reassures. 'My NYPD source says they like your mother for the hit since the UCs watched her stroll out of the restaurant in broad daylight. We're already in Laska's cloud backup, deleting anything that could tie to you. The authorities don't know Steph Laska had a daughter, and we'll keep it that way. If someone's paying attention, the IP address is the NYPD's, which won't be a surprise.'

'You never miss a trick.'

'That's my job description. Listen . . . I'm proud of you. Thank you for what you've done for all of us. We'll talk later. Aliyah's been blowing up my phone since yesterday. It would've been better if you hadn't mentioned the contractor in Seattle – she's going to wonder how you learned that info. I've got to clean up and get to work.'

'Tilt your head back,' Salma orders, a spray bottle of glue remover in hand.

'Rogelio.' With my neck resting against the lip of the tub, my gaze is on the ceiling. The marble veining in the corner by the sink looks like a spider's web. 'I need to know if there's anything about a boat in Val's cloud. Photos, mentions . . . anything.'

'Close your eyes,' Salma instructs.

'What kind of boat? A yacht?'

'Possibly a small boat. A sailboat.' Abruptly, the hot water isn't warm enough to fight a chill, and I shiver. 'He told me to find the boat.'

'*Your* boat?' he asks sharply.

'I don't know. Maybe.'

'It's a sick joke. The only way to find a shipwreck is to sink to the bottom of the ocean.'

'He wasn't in any condition to make wisecracks.'

'Okay.' His words are clipped. 'We'll look.'

'Something else . . . I think she might be alive.'

'Who?'

'You know who,' I retort wearily. 'When Val first saw my face, I'm sure he thought I was her for a split second. He didn't look shocked.'

'You can't know that. You rushed the guy with a knife. It's all instinct at that moment, for you and him. You can't read anything into facial expressions.'

'He said she'll be proud of me. Not that she *would have* been, but that she *will* be.'

'That doesn't mean anything,' Salma dismisses, rubbing the spray into my hairline.

'He was lying on a bathroom floor with a knife in his heart,' Rogelio argues. 'That he even said anything at all tells you he had the strength of an ox. He was dying and gibbering. Not to mention you're in shock. What you're thinking and feeling, what you remember or don't . . . it's all going to be scrambled in your head. Remember, eyewitnesses are notoriously unreliable.'

'Forget what I saw,' I tell him. 'Go with what I felt. Okay?'

'There's no way she's alive, *querida*. I know you'd feel better if you'd buried her body, but she went overboard miles out to sea during a storm. The chances of her surviving are non-existent.'

'I survived.'

'You didn't have a bullet in your chest!'

'Rogelio, please.'

He exhales heavily. 'If Laska's been communicating with your mother, the evidence will be on his phone. If it's there, we'll find it.'

'She has multiple aliases. She might even be using a masculine name. She and Val may use a coded language or –'

'I know what to look for. I'll let you know if I find anything. The jewels are back in the safe.'

'Thank you.'

I listen to him leave, then hear Tovah's lighter steps approach. Salma resumes tugging on my scalp annoyingly.

When Witte returns, rolling into the kitchen with a wire cart filled with groceries, we're seated at the kitchen table, eating the salads. Lacy is working in a distant part of the condo after the security team gave us a heads-up of Witte's return. Tovah, Salma and I are reading a gossip blog on the tablet and laughing over a photo of Tom Hiddleston wearing a tank top with 'I love T. S.' – i.e., his girlfriend Taylor Swift – emblazoned across it.

'Would Kane wear something like that for you?' Tovah queries.

'Never,' I say with feeling.

We all laugh, Witte smiles, and I feel like I'm living a sitcom version of my life. Nothing feels real. The salad, which has Tovah and Salma in raptures, feels and tastes like I'm eating damp chunks of cardboard. My stomach revolts against digesting anything, but I force it to comply. I can make my body do many things it instinctively doesn't want to do.

'I was able to pick up some lovely ripe strawberries,' Witte says. 'I can serve them with fresh whipped cream if you've any room left for dessert.'

'That sounds amazing,' I tell him.

'Do you have a brother, Witte?' Tovah asks. 'Please say yes.'

'Or a son?' Salma quips.

It's all so horribly, frighteningly normal. I play my part, telling myself I've done what I must to keep this unexpected life with you.

When you come home, I'm waiting by the door. It swings open, you step inside, and I launch myself at you the way I did at Val – with all the force I possess. You rock back on your heels and drop your satchel, catching me with a laugh. My feet leave the floor.

'Well . . . I definitely like coming home to this, *Setareh*.' You give me a youthful grin followed by a deep, lush kiss. 'I missed you like crazy, too. Almost more than I could stand.'

And while I have you in my arms, I think it's all been worthwhile. I hope the worst is over. I'm also terrified it's not.

48

Witte

Manhattan shimmers like diamonds on black velvet as the city sprawls around the penthouse tower. A storm is brewing. The skyscraper where we reside creaks as it sways in ever more tempestuous winds. Light rain pelts the windows, clinging to the glass like tears. In the distance, I see lightning. The flashes of destructive beauty briefly illuminate the roiling clouds, then plunge them into stygian black.

My employer sits at his desk, looking at my mobile's screen. He's freshly showered and has changed into black silk trousers, and a matching dressing gown belted at the waist. His hair is still damp.

His hand covers his mouth in the absent way of deep thought. A frown sits heavily on his brow.

I wonder if he sees what I do. The woman who left Valon Laska's body on a blood-drenched lavatory floor carries her clutch tucked under her right arm. When previously photographed, Stephanie Laska carried items tucked under her left arm. The difference is not insignificant when one considers left- and right-handed dominance and the natural tendency to leave the dominant arm unencumbered.

Lily is left-handed.

Mr Black stands and passes my mobile back to me. 'I'll discuss his death with her tomorrow.'

I wait for him to say more, but he rounds his desk.

He pauses beside me, the two of us facing in opposing

directions. He sets his hand on my shoulder. 'She seems fragile today. I felt it this morning and debated staying home. I don't want to get upset right now because it'll upset her. So, let's pick this up in the morning, okay? That's soon enough.'

'Of course.' I haven't noted the fragility of which he speaks. There was some melancholy directly after he left, but Tovah and Salma lifted her spirits. It was fortuitous that they had time available when Lily most needed a distraction.

Why a woman known for having dozens of friends would prefer passing the time with strangers is yet another mystery.

In any case, I'll have to thank Lacy again for recommending the two women. In the few years she's been with us, Lacy has proven to be an asset beyond her duties as a member of my household staff.

My employer pauses on the hallway's threshold. 'Gideon Cross gave me a recommendation for a psychologist – a Dr Lyle Petersen. See what you can find out about him, would you?'

'Of course.'

He goes to his wife, and I make my final rounds for the evening. The interior of the penthouse is dark and silent. Outside, fierce winds whistle through the tower's blow-through floors and sheet lightning flashes below the clouds. The rain is steady now and lashing against the glass.

I collect the delivered dry cleaning from the elevator vestibule cupboard, nodding at the two guards, who are still drinking the coffee I provided earlier. I wonder if my employer will see a need for security services now. I'll have to convince him that it's best to leave things as they are for the time being. I'm still unsure whether the threat is within, but caution is the eldest child of wisdom, as Victor Hugo once wrote.

I head down the hallway with its mirrored walls to the private side of the residence Mr Black now shares with a wife we'd thought for ever lost to him. I pause on the threshold of his former bedroom, absorbing the sense of desertion. We freshen the room daily, as we do the entire penthouse, yet there's a feeling of neglect here. I suppose because it never truly held life. It was a place of stasis, of longing that consumed all hope.

Lily beckons from her place on the wall, a seductive siren luring her husband to join her in an infinite moment. Never evolving or ageing, living or dying.

I stare at her. The image arrests me, as always. She is a mystery as deep and vast as the ocean, a puzzle that remains unsolved. A flurry of questions scratches at the back of my mind, giving me no peace.

In Mr Black's wardrobe, I hang his garments, then straighten his shoes and adjust the angle of his ties. Lightning flashes with growing frequency as the storm churns in from the Atlantic. I hear voices and find myself moving to the open door of the sitting room.

The television is on, its glow reflected off the various mirrored surfaces. They lie together, Mr Black and the woman whose name we don't know. He sprawls against the corner of the sectional sofa. She reclines against his bare chest. They watch an improbable motorbike chase in which leather-clad men shoot at each other between fast-moving traffic. He embraces her, his hands stroking her arms in soothing motions. Her long, sleek legs are wrapped in a throw blanket, and his dressing gown has been tossed aside on a chaise. His trouser legs ride halfway up his calves.

Lightning flashes in an explosion of reflected illumination. A moment later, thunder cracks so loudly that I flinch. Everything vibrates.

She gasps, and he laughs, holding her tighter. When she tilts her face up to him, he stares for a long moment, a smile curving his lips. When the lightning strikes again, it illuminates two lovers in a moment of deep connection.

Didn't I once wonder what a force of nature Mr Black must have been with his wife at his side? As the tempest howls and the tower groans, I realize I was wrong. Together, they are the eye of the storm, anchored and at peace. While destruction and chaos rage around them, they've found shelter in one another.

I back away silently.

My employer is correct – tomorrow and all the days that follow will be soon enough to unearth the secrets yet buried.

Acknowledgements

Bringing *So Close* to life took a great deal of hard work, and I couldn't have done it without my editors: Maxine Hitchcock, Hilary Sares and Clare Bowron. Thanks also to my agent, Kimberly Whalen of The Whalen Agency, who gave feedback on numerous drafts.

I'm very grateful to Tom Weldon and Louise Moore for their support. It has always been a joy to be published by Michael Joseph, and I'm thankful for each team member who helps shepherd my books with great care.

I'm also thankful for my editors at Brilliance Audio, Sheryl Zajechowski and Liz Pearsons, and the wonderful teams at Heyne, J'ai Lu, Psichogios, Swiat Ksiazki, Harper Holland, Politikens and Kaewkarn.

The striking cover concept is the brainchild of Frauke Spanuth of Croco Designs. I've been so fortunate to have such a fine artist work with me on my novels for nearly two decades. I'm grateful for her perfect visual rendering of my story, which inspired the lovely UK/Commonwealth jacket.

Many things haunt the characters in *So Close*: past choices, character flaws and mental illness, to name just a few. Rebecca de Winter also casts a vast, deep shadow. Daphne du Maurier's *Rebecca* instilled in me a deeper appreciation for flawed women and the hopeful and sinister ways marriage can alter one's sense of self.

On the personal front, I couldn't have made it through the rough spots without the encouragement of my children:

Justin, Jack and Shanna. And the support of my dear friends: Karin Tabke, Christine Green and Tina Route.

And finally, I'm grateful to my readers. Thank you for following as I hop genres and experiment with new-to-me ways to tell a story. I'm a writer who loves to experiment, grow and continually challenge myself to try harder, do better and imagine greater. I'm so thankful to have an audience willing to journey with me. Your loyalty is a precious gift. Thank you so much for your support!

Lily and Kane's story continues in *Too Far*

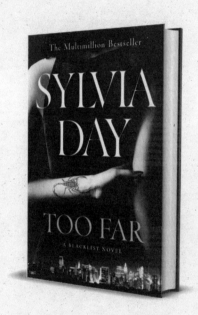

Don't miss out!

Don't miss Sylvia Day's Crossfire series

Over eighteen million copies sold worldwide

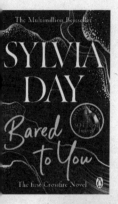
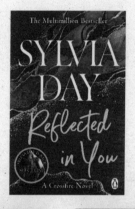
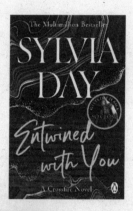

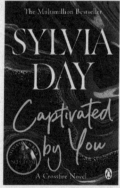

Available to buy now

WHICH BOOK WILL YOU READ NEXT?

A tale of **love** and **awakened desire**

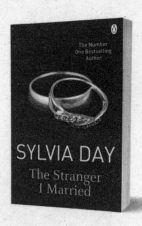

A tale of **mistaken identity, lusty liasons** and **dangerous deceptions**

NURTURING WRITERS SINCE 1935

A tale of **ambition, love** and **lust**

A tale of **adventure, resistance**
. . . and **surrender**

NURTURING WRITERS SINCE 1935

A tale of **deception, lust** and **deadly** **desire** in Georgian England

A tale of **devastating heartbreak** and a **forbidden love**

Classic sensual tales of **wicked rakes** and the **flawless aristocratic young women** whose hearts – and bodies – they melt

Her desire becomes **his pleasure**

NURTURING WRITERS SINCE 1935

He just wanted a decent book to read ...

Not too much to ask, is it? It was in 1935 when Allen Lane, Managing Director of Bodley Head Publishers, stood on a platform at Exeter railway station looking for something good to read on his journey back to London. His choice was limited to popular magazines and poor-quality paperbacks – the same choice faced every day by the vast majority of readers, few of whom could afford hardbacks. Lane's disappointment and subsequent anger at the range of books generally available led him to found a company – and change the world.

'We believed in the existence in this country of a vast reading public for intelligent books at a low price, and staked everything on it'
Sir Allen Lane, 1902–1970, founder of Penguin Books

The quality paperback had arrived – and not just in bookshops. Lane was adamant that his Penguins should appear in chain stores and tobacconists, and should cost no more than a packet of cigarettes.

Reading habits (and cigarette prices) have changed since 1935, but Penguin still believes in publishing the best books for everybody to enjoy. We still believe that good design costs no more than bad design, and we still believe that quality books published passionately and responsibly make the world a better place.

So wherever you see the little bird – whether it's on a piece of prize-winning literary fiction or a celebrity autobiography, political tour de force or historical masterpiece, a serial-killer thriller, reference book, world classic or a piece of pure escapism – you can bet that it represents the very best that the genre has to offer.

Whatever you like to read – trust Penguin.